™

THE TEMPEST

WITHDRAWN

D1209112

ILLUSTRATED BY

PAUL DUFFIELD

Amulet Books, New York

PUBLISHER'S NOTE: This is a work of fiction. Names, characters, places, and incidents are either the product of the author's imagination or are used fictitiously, and any resemblance to actual persons, living or dead, business establishments, events, or locales is entirely coincidental.

Library of Congress Cataloging-in-Publication Data

Appignanesi, Richard.
The tempest / illustrated by Paul Duffield.
p. cm. — (Manga Shakespeare)
ISBN-13: 978-0-8109-9476-8 (Harry N. Abrams)
ISBN-10: 0-8109-9476-3 (Harry N. Abrams)
1. Graphic novels. I. Shakespeare, William, 1564–1616.
Tempest. II. Title.
PN6727.L47T46 2008
741.5'973—dc22
2007028211

Originally published in the U.K. by SelfMadeHero
(www.selfmadehero.com)

Illustrator: Paul Duffield
Adaptor: Richard Appignanesi
Designer: Andy Huckle
Textual Consultant: Nick de Somogyi
Originating Publisher: Emma Hayley

Published in 2008 by Amulet Books, an imprint of Harry N. Abrams, Inc.

Printed and bound in China
10 9 8 7 6 5 4 3 2 1

HNA
harry n. abrams, inc.
a subsidiary of La Martinière Groupe

115 West 18th Street
New York, NY 10011
www.hnabooks.com

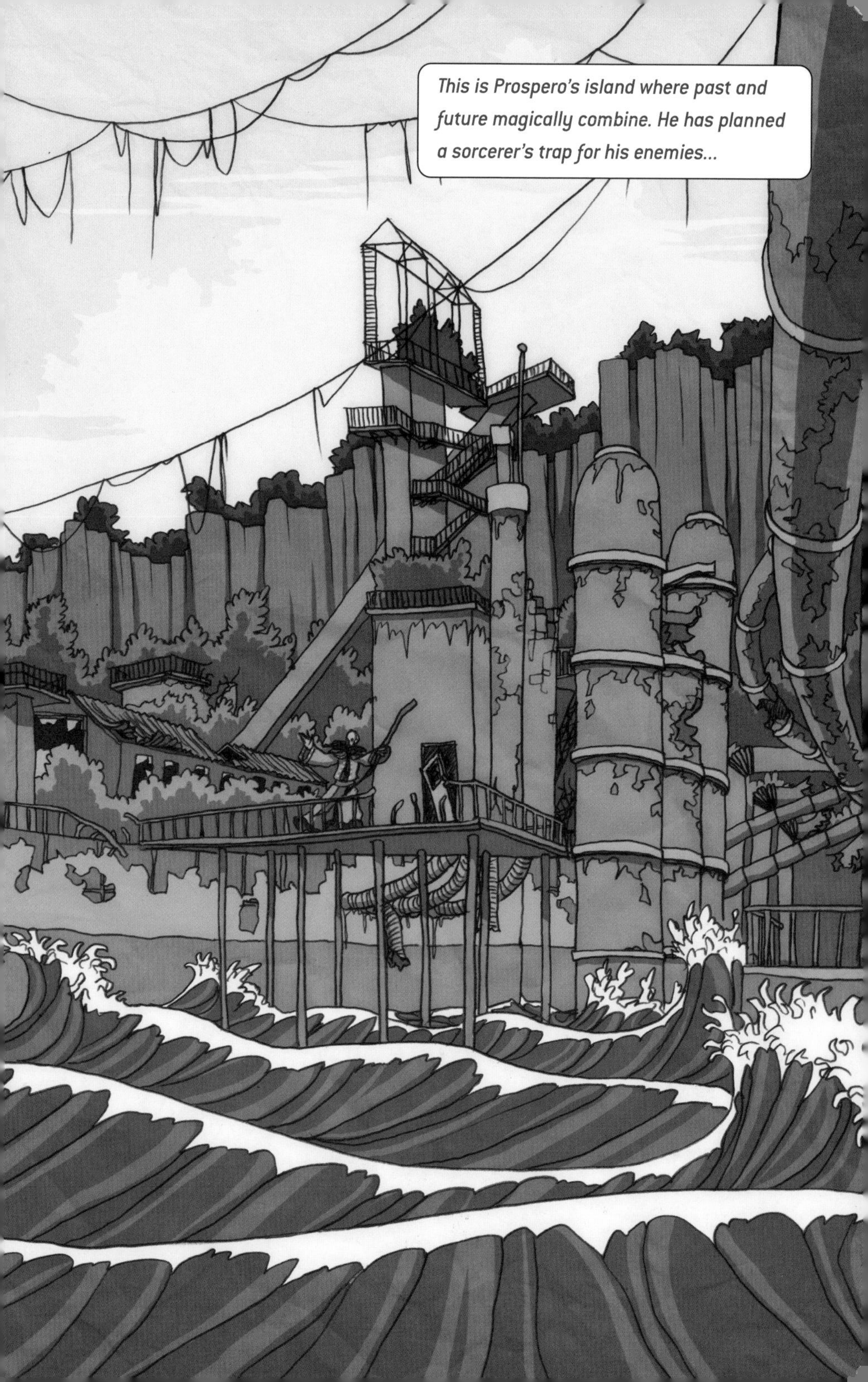
This is Prospero's island where past and future magically combine. He has planned a sorcerer's trap for his enemies...

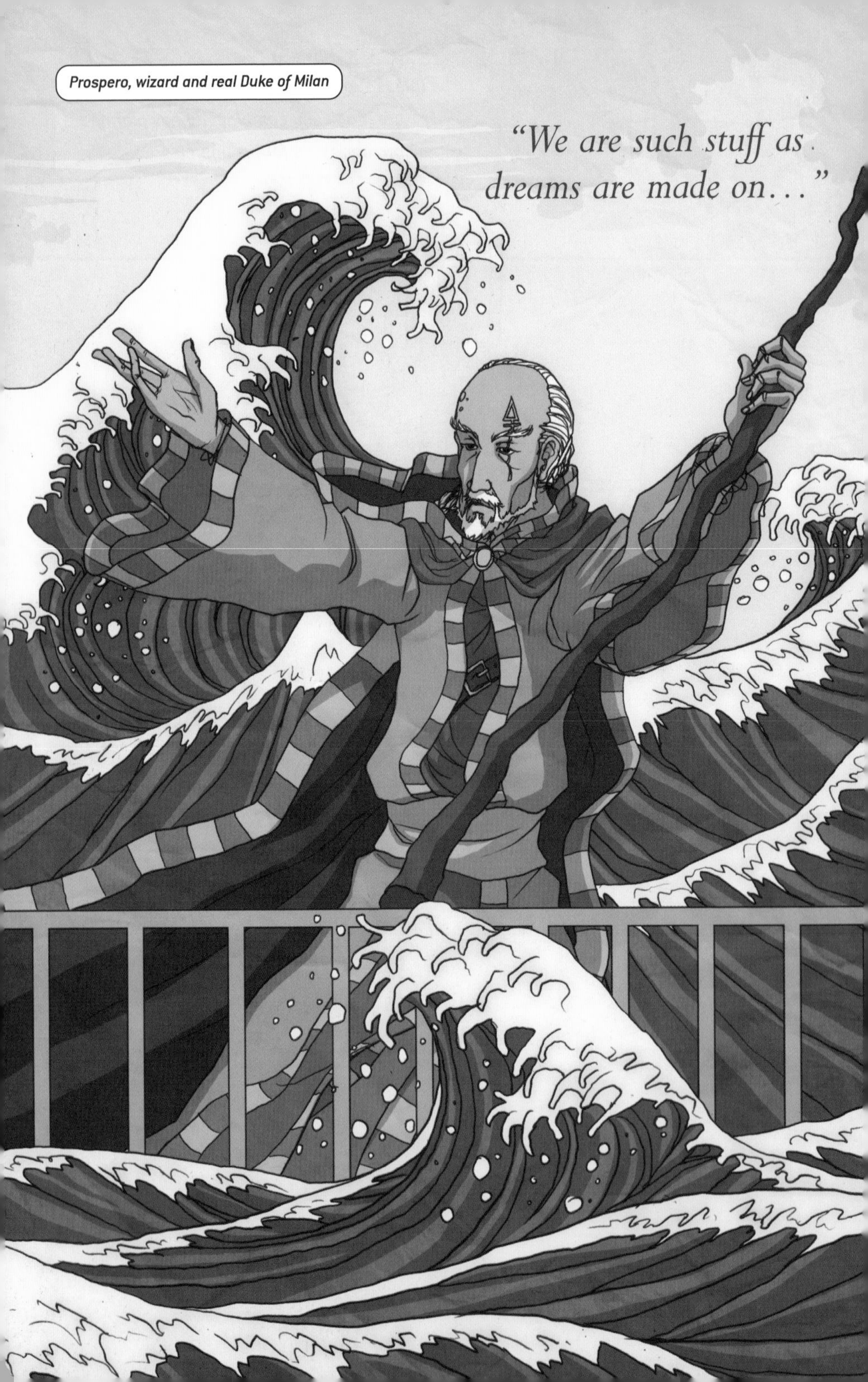
Prospero, wizard and real Duke of Milan
"We are such stuff as dreams are made on…"

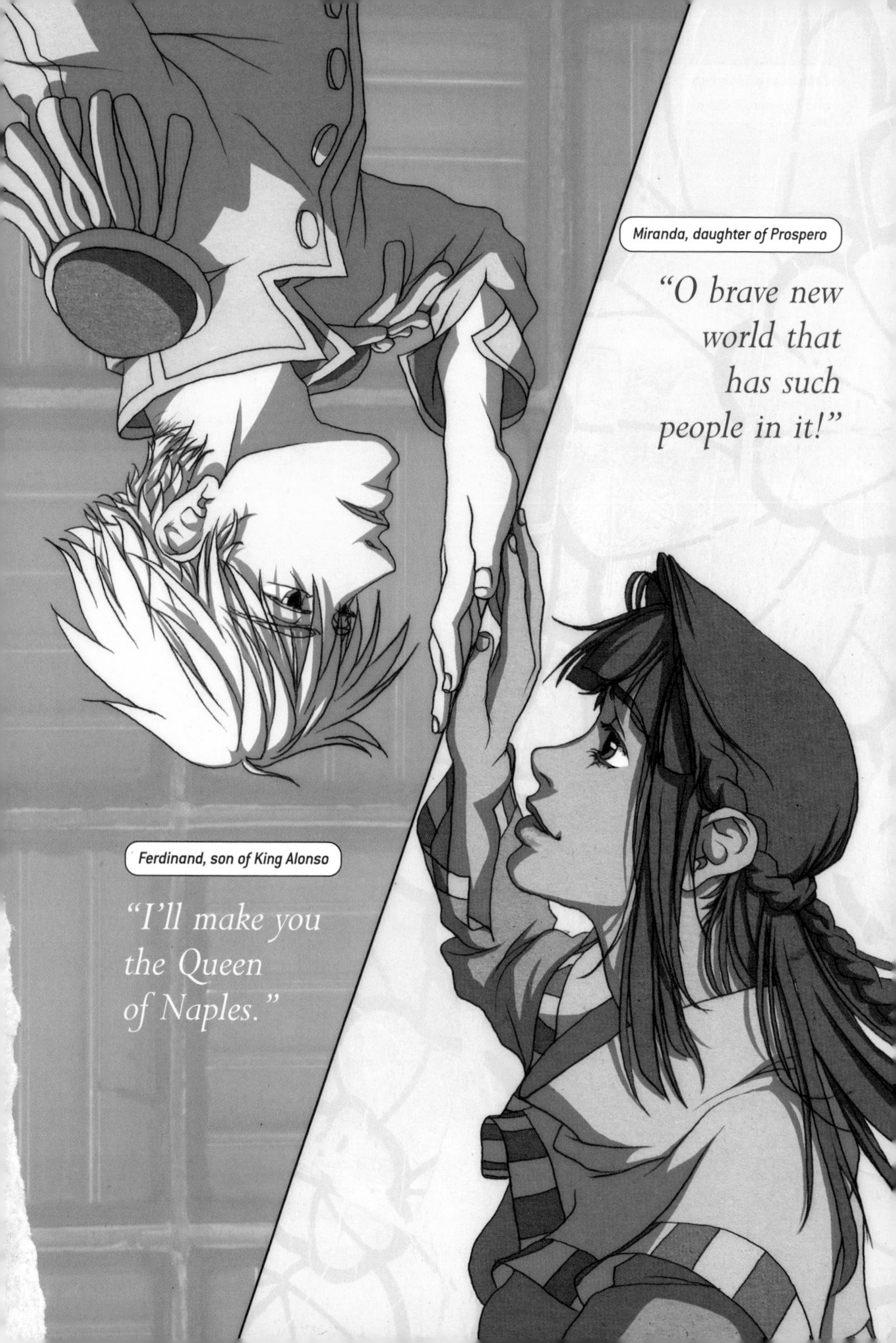
Miranda, daughter of Prospero
"O brave new world that has such people in it!"
Ferdinand, son of King Alonso
"I'll make you the Queen of Naples."

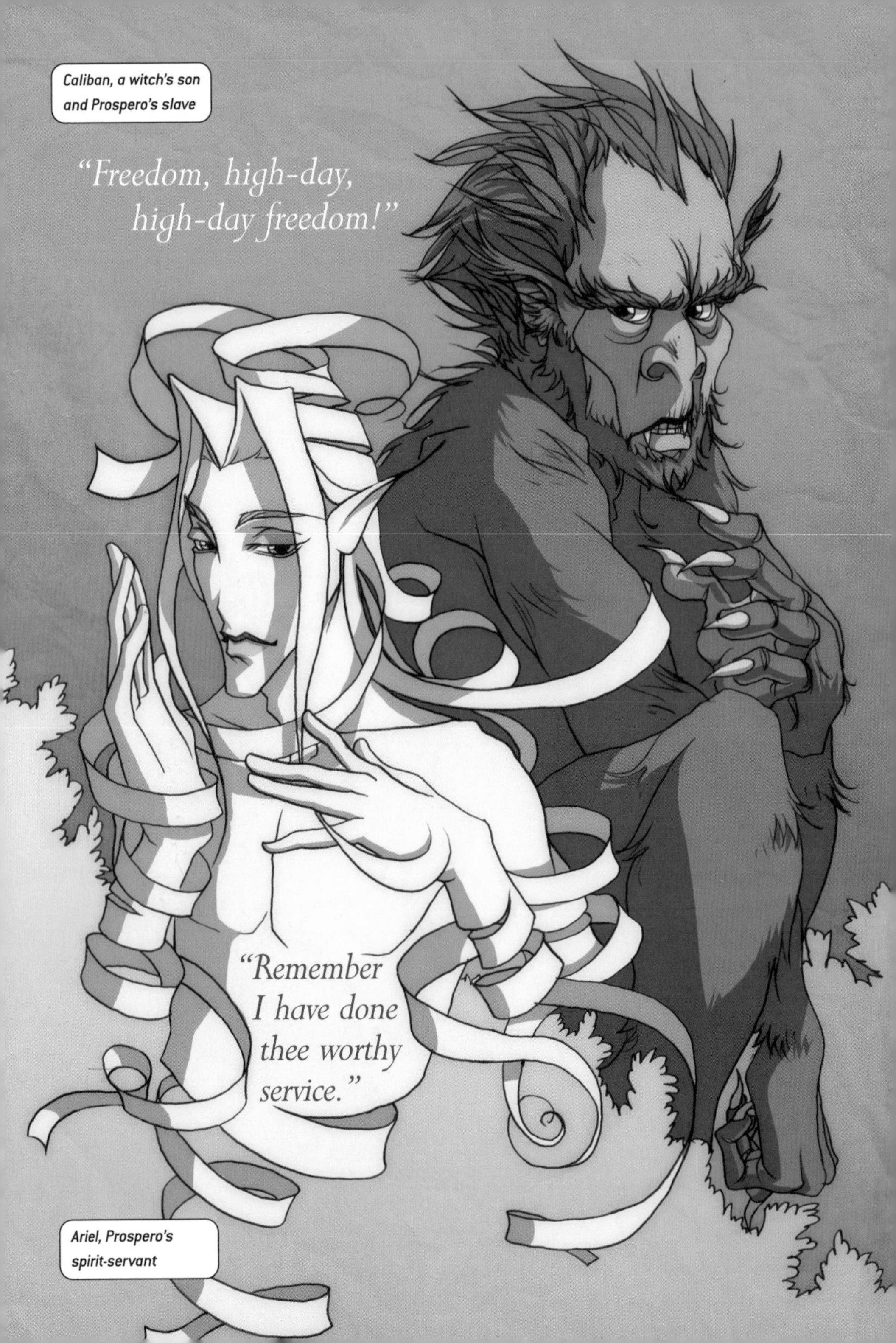
Caliban, a witch's son and Prospero's slave
"Freedom, high-day, high-day freedom!"
"Remember I have done thee worthy service."
Ariel, Prospero's spirit-servant

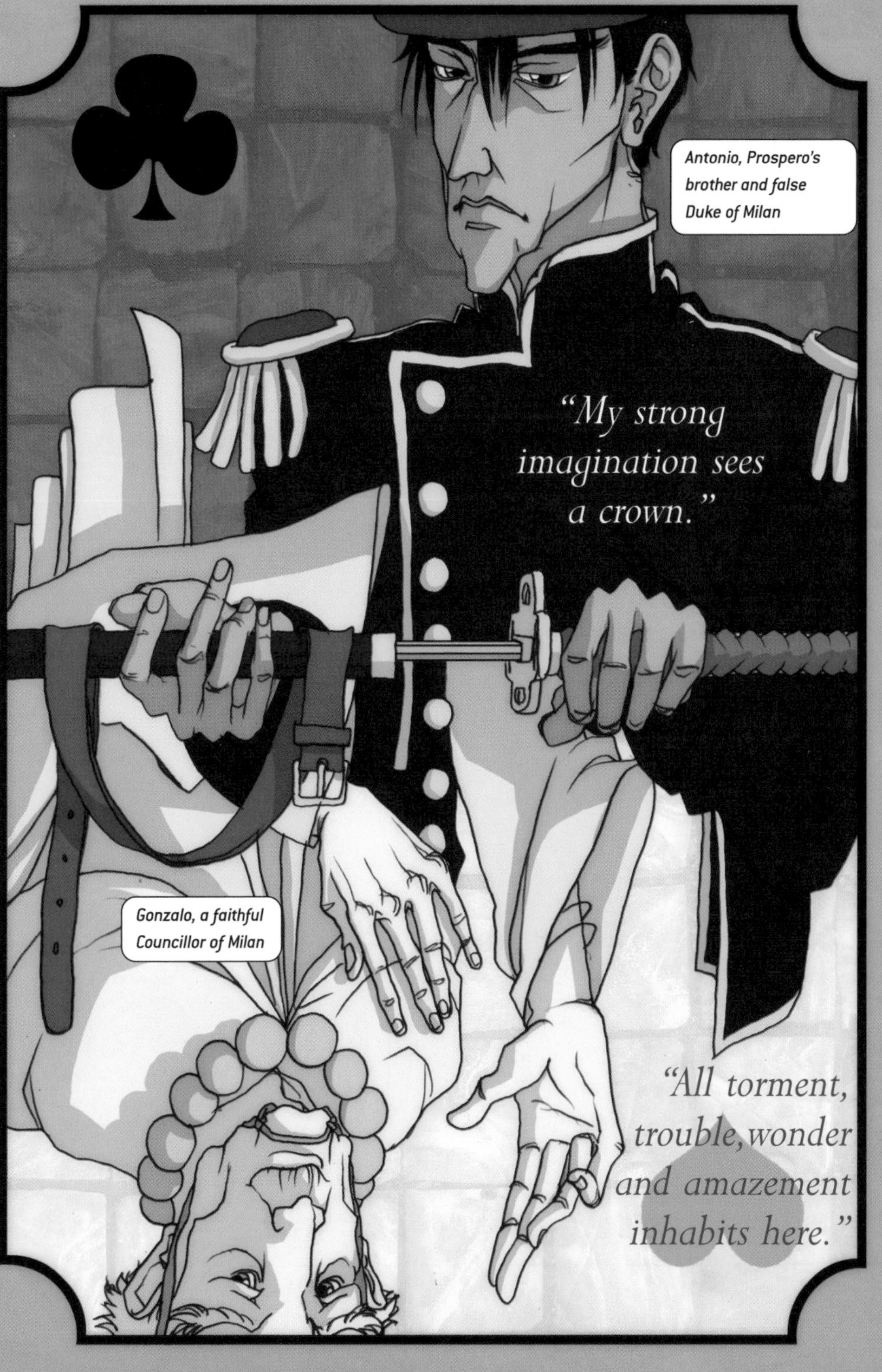
Antonio, Prospero's brother and false Duke of Milan
"My strong imagination sees a crown."
Gonzalo, a faithful Councillor of Milan
"All torment, trouble, wonder and amazement inhabits here."

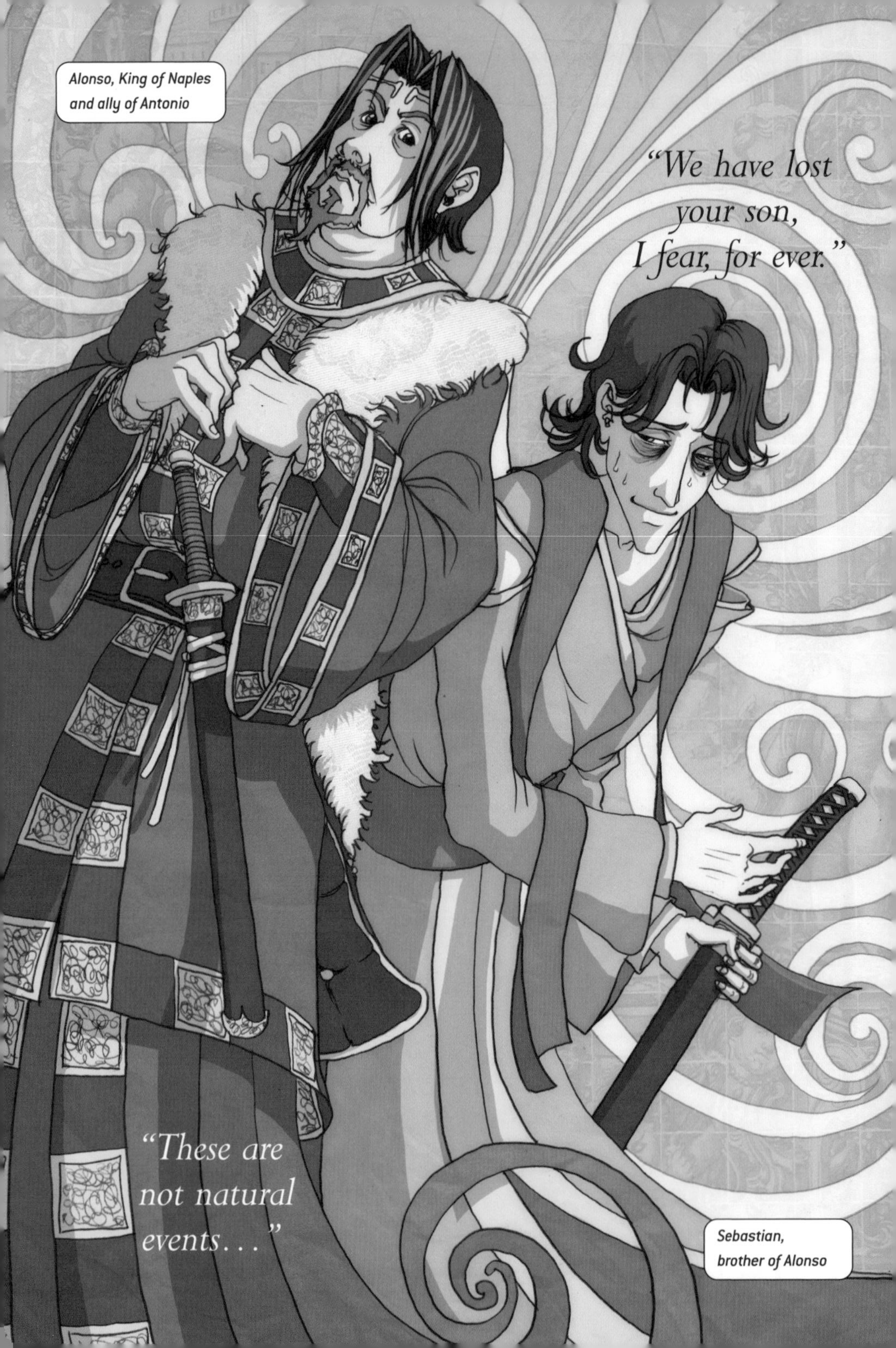
Alonso, King of Naples and ally of Antonio
"We have lost your son, I fear, for ever."
"These are not natural events. . ."
Sebastian, brother of Alonso

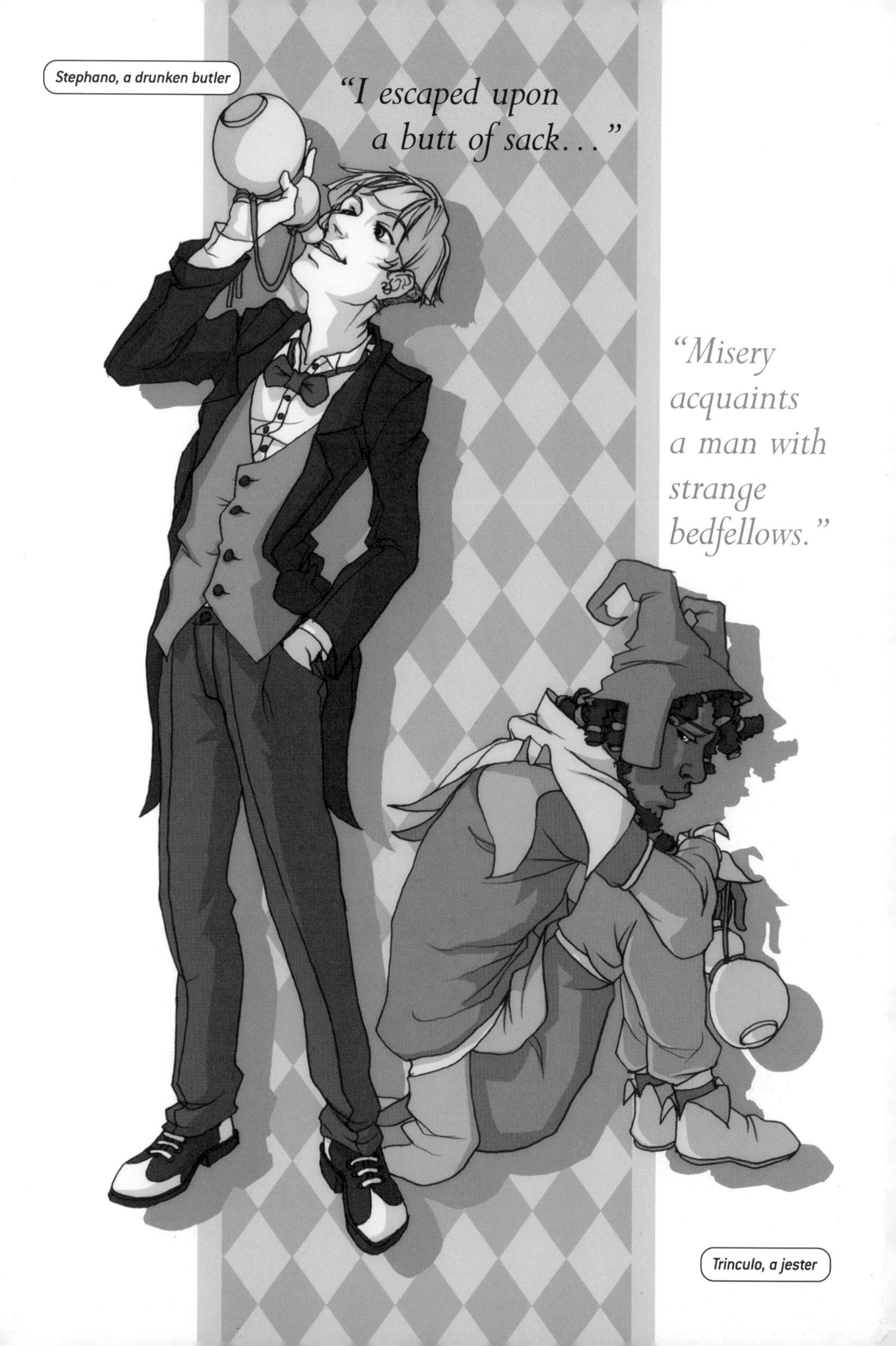
Stephano, a drunken butler
"I escaped upon a butt of sack…"
"Misery acquaints a man with strange bedfellows."
Trinculo, a jester

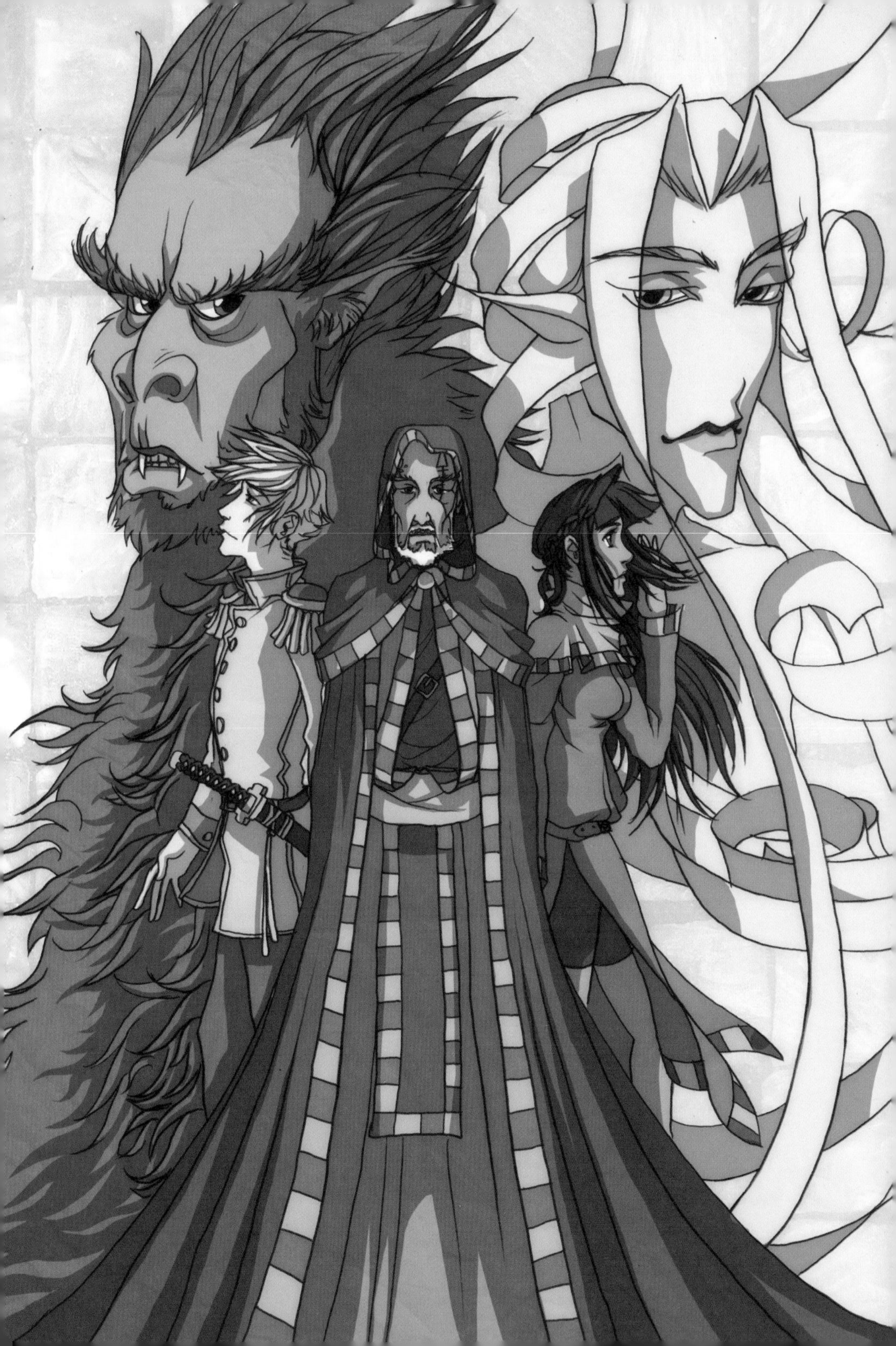

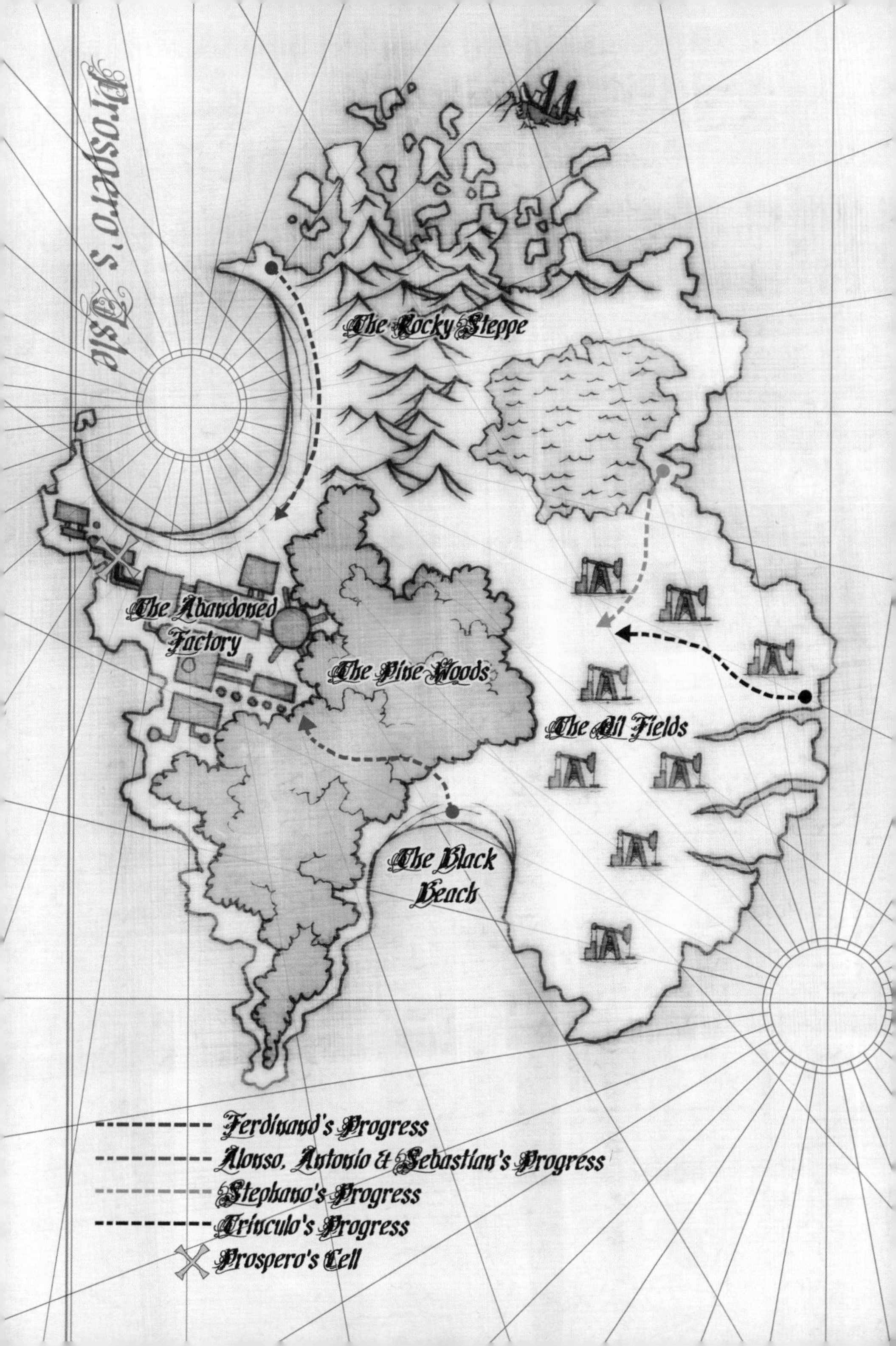
Prospero's Isle
The Rocky Steppe
The Abandoned Factory
The Pine Woods
The Oil Fields
The Black Beach
Ferdinand's Progress
Alonso, Antonio & Sebastian's Progress
Stephano's Progress
Trinculo's Progress
Prospero's Cell

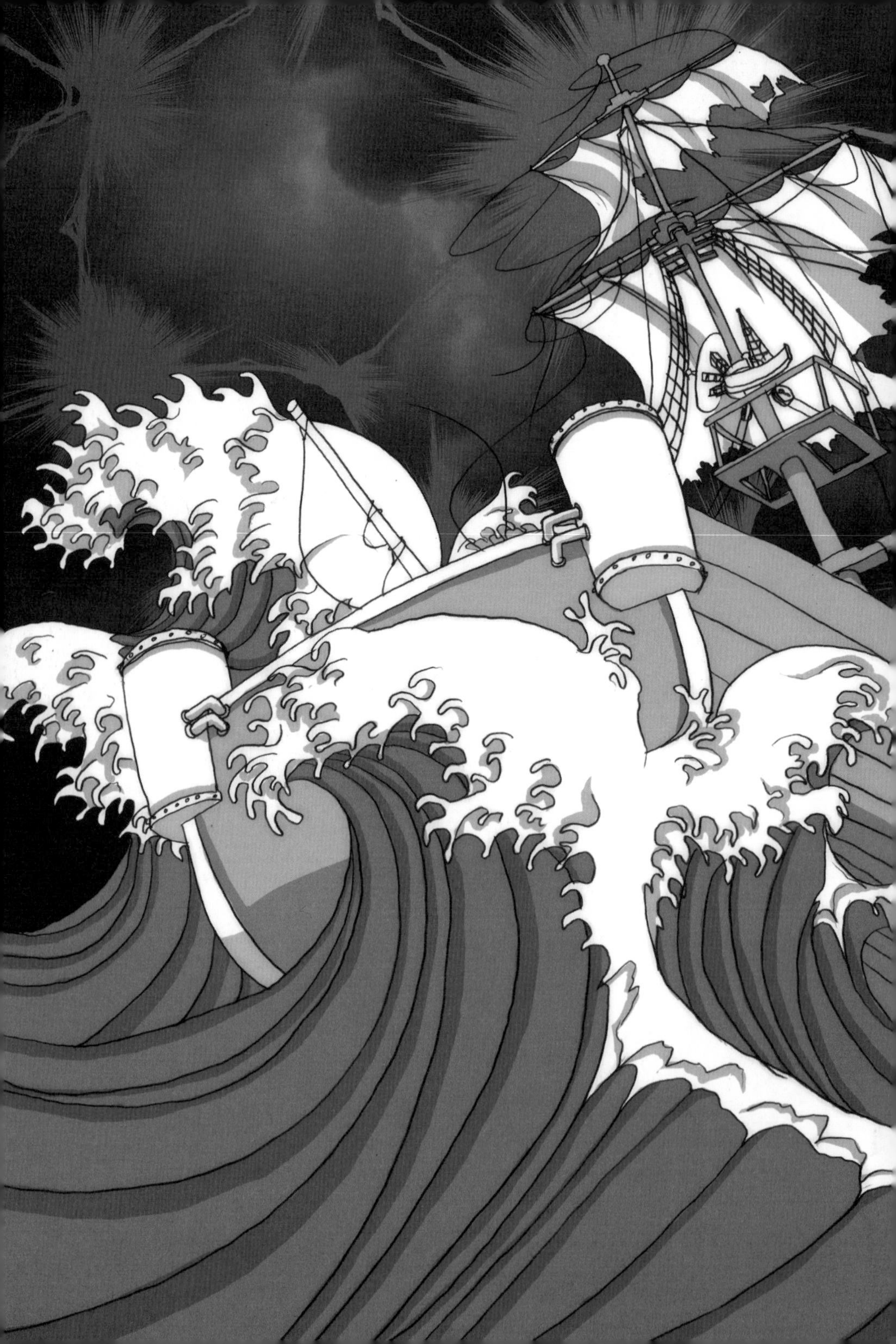

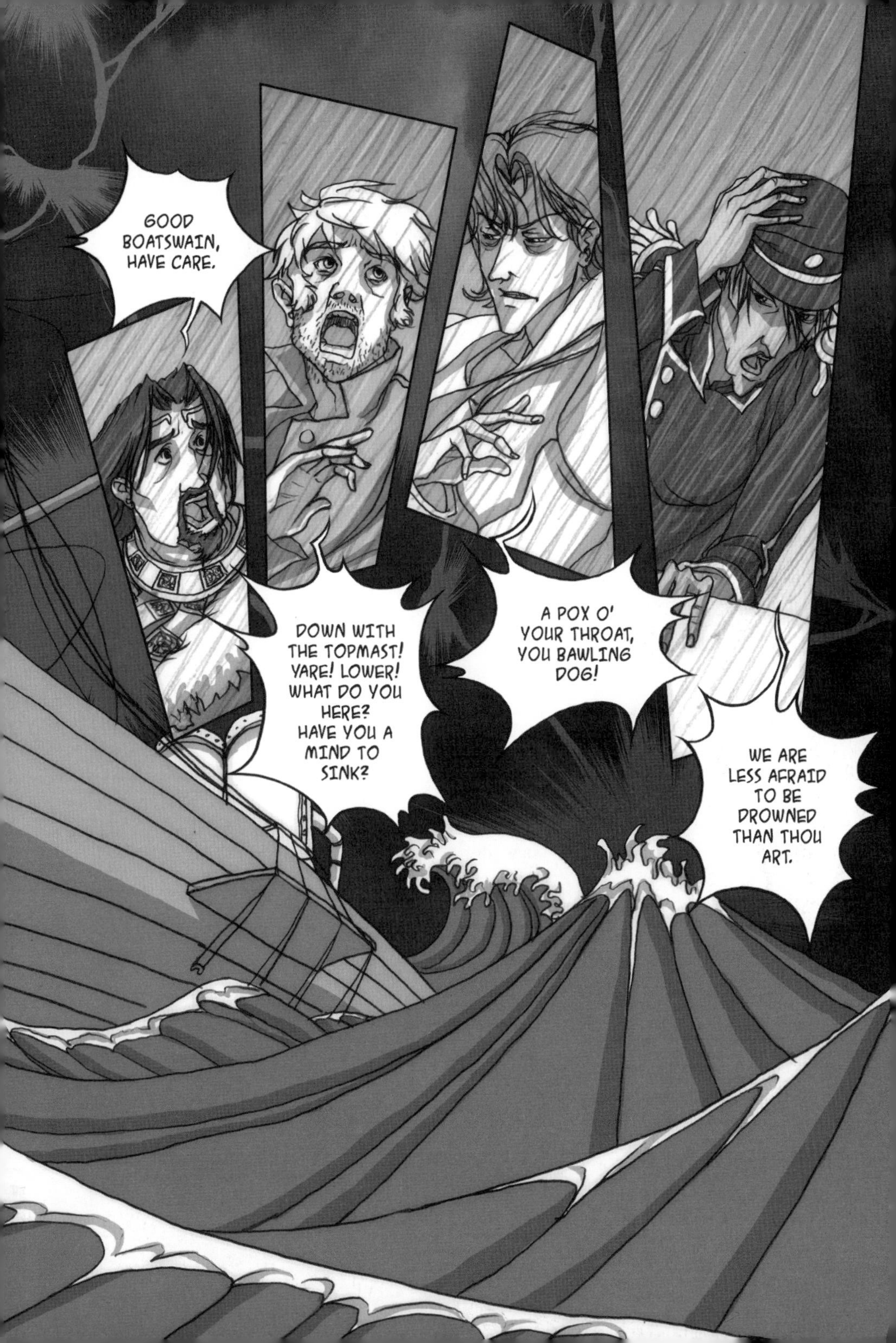
GOOD BOATSWAIN, HAVE CARE.
DOWN WITH THE TOPMAST! YARE! LOWER! WHAT DO YOU HERE? HAVE YOU A MIND TO SINK?
A POX O' YOUR THROAT, YOU BAWLING DOG!
WE ARE LESS AFRAID TO BE DROWNED THAN THOU ART.

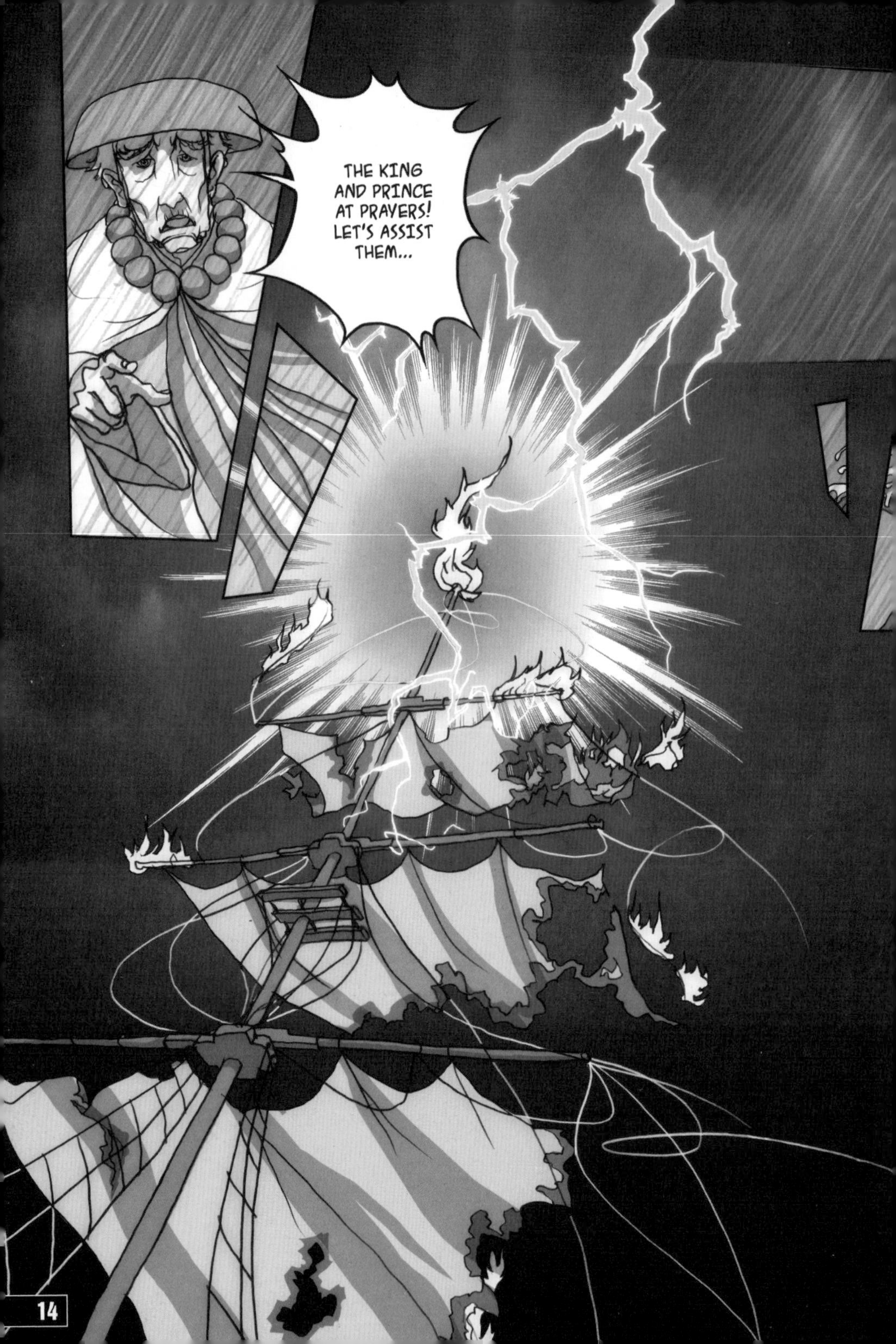
THE KING AND PRINCE AT PRAYERS! LET'S ASSIST THEM...

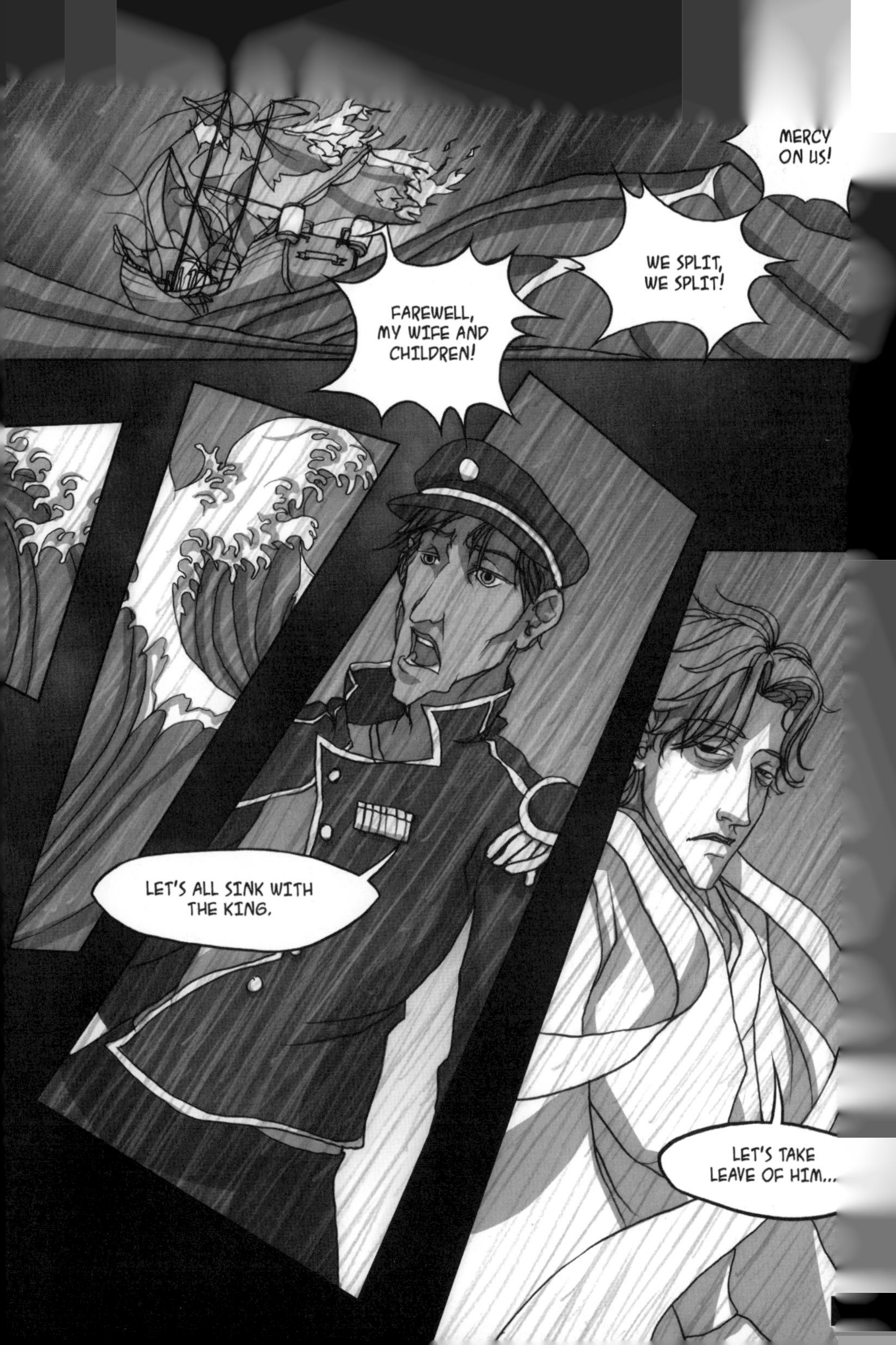
MERCY ON US!
WE SPLIT, WE SPLIT!
FAREWELL, MY WIFE AND CHILDREN!
LET'S ALL SINK WITH THE KING.
LET'S TAKE LEAVE OF HIM...

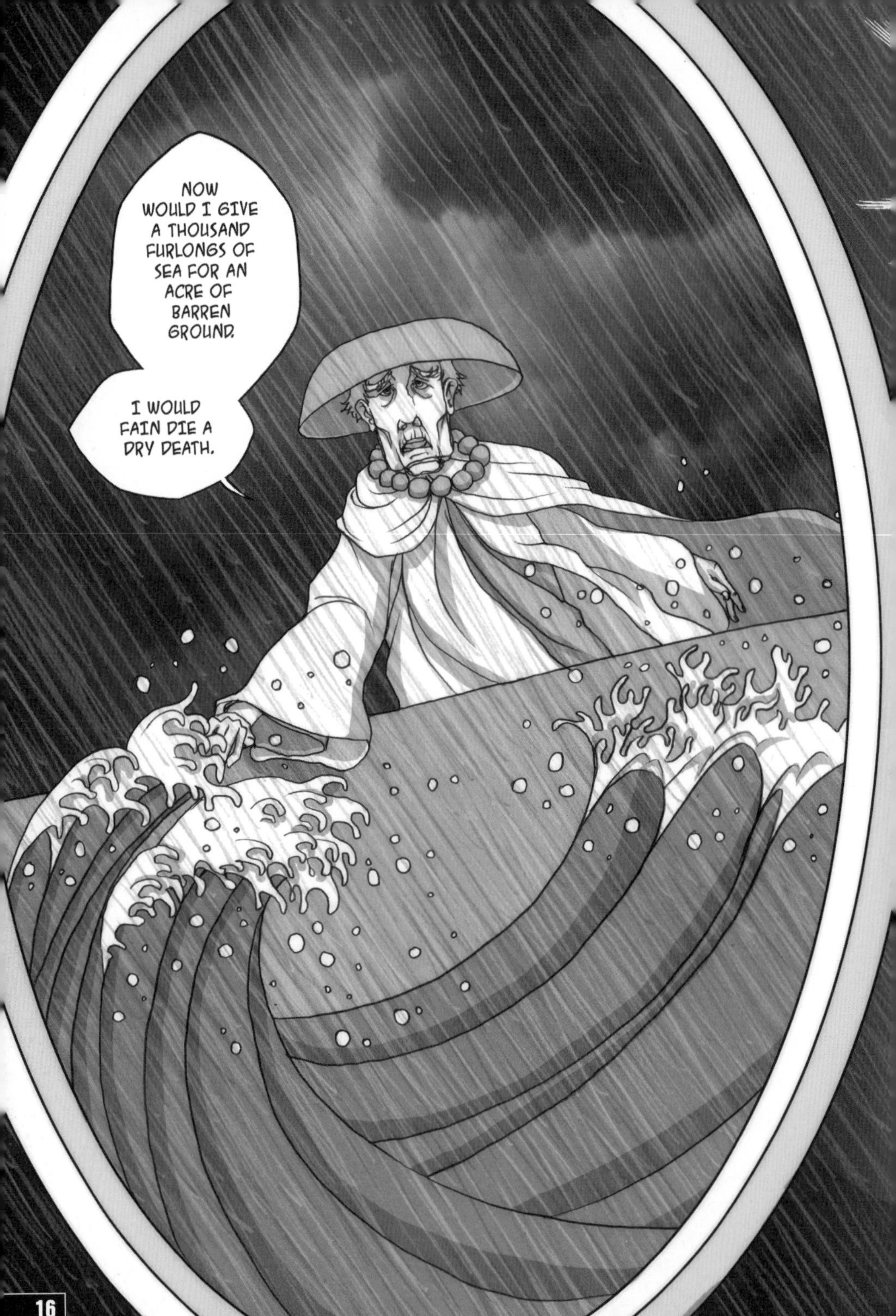
NOW WOULD I GIVE A THOUSAND FURLONGS OF SEA FOR AN ACRE OF BARREN GROUND.
I WOULD FAIN DIE A DRY DEATH.

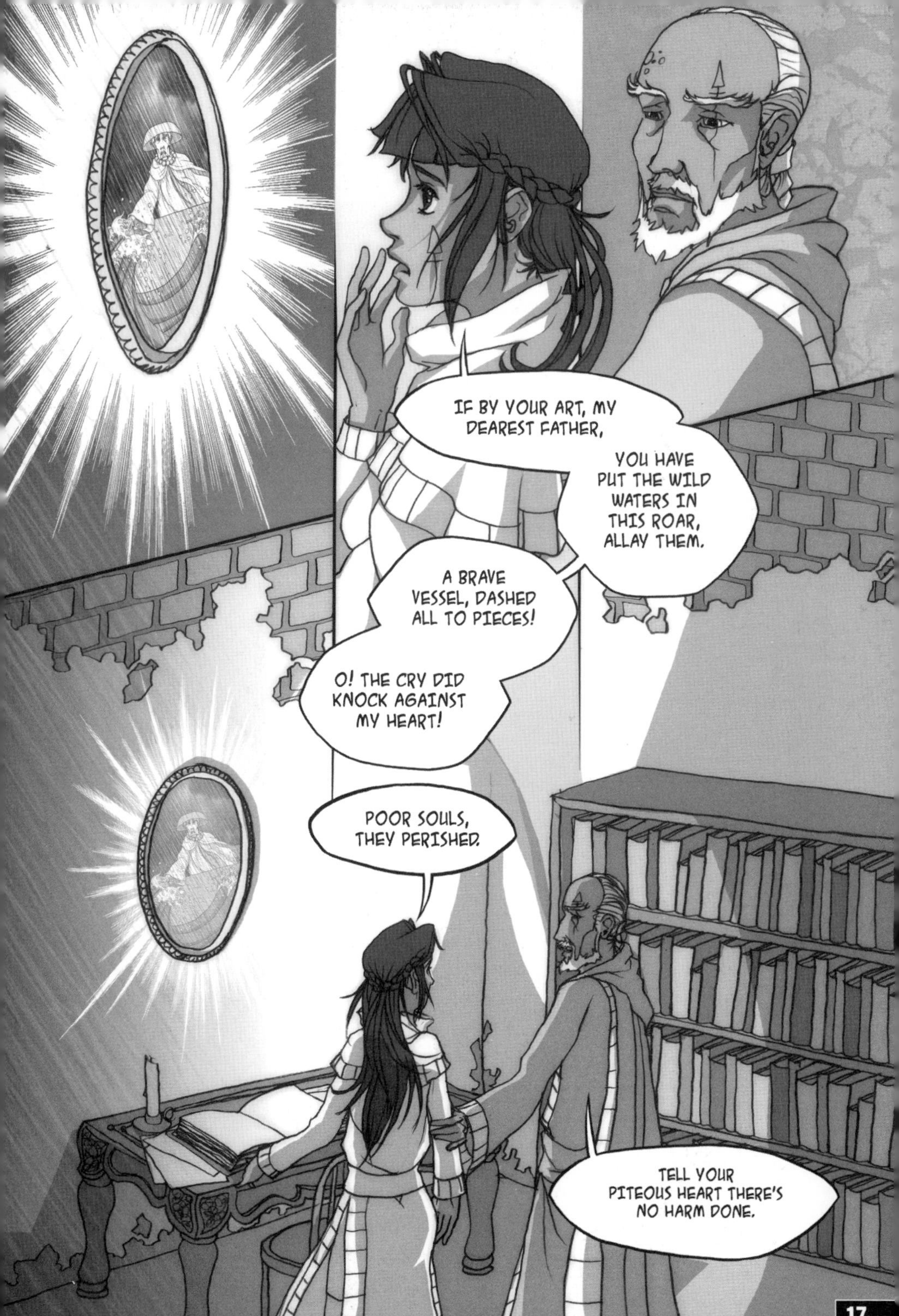
IF BY YOUR ART, MY DEAREST FATHER,
YOU HAVE PUT THE WILD WATERS IN THIS ROAR, ALLAY THEM.
A BRAVE VESSEL, DASHED ALL TO PIECES!
O! THE CRY DID KNOCK AGAINST MY HEART!
POOR SOULS, THEY PERISHED.
TELL YOUR PITEOUS HEART THERE'S NO HARM DONE.

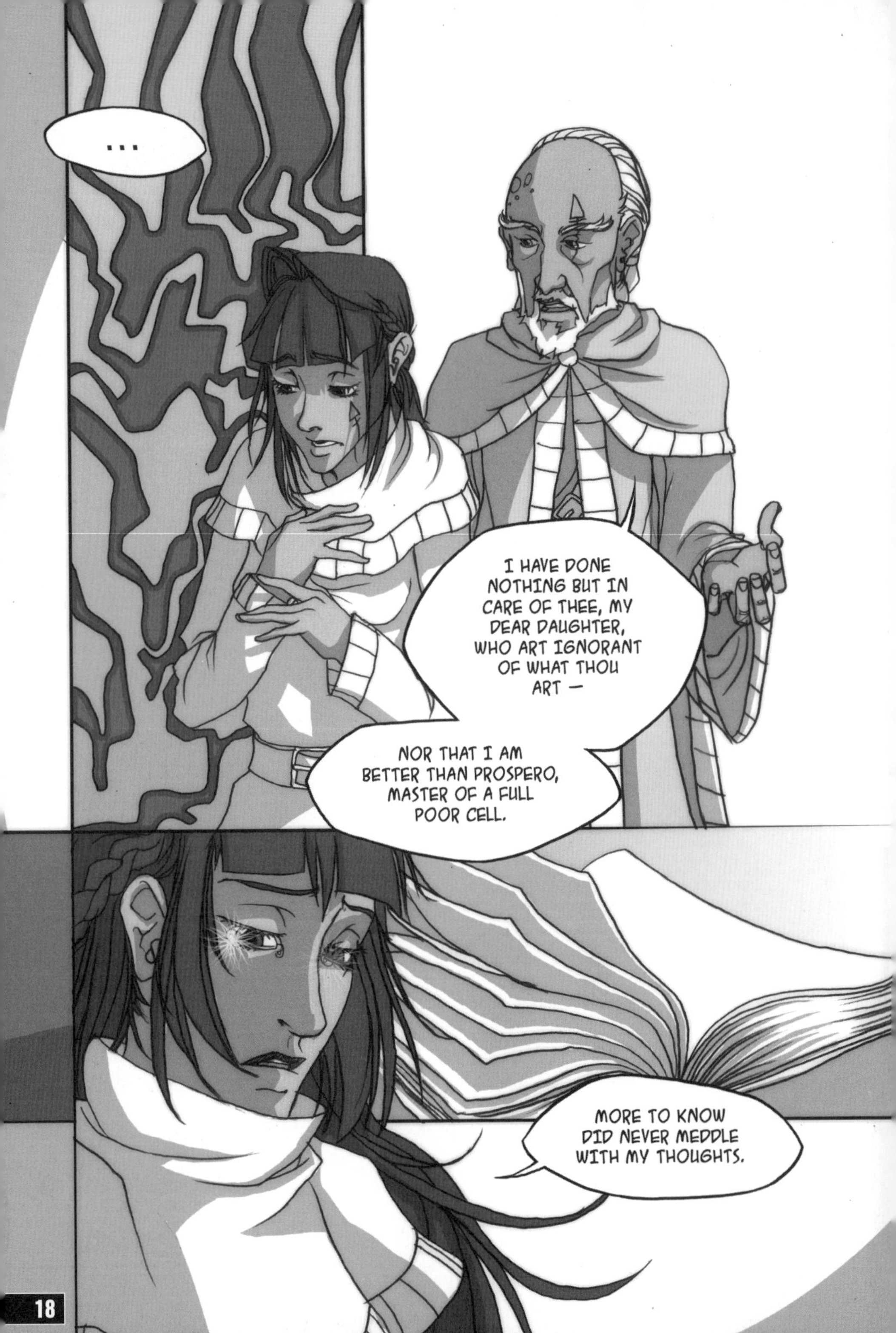
...
I HAVE DONE NOTHING BUT IN CARE OF THEE, MY DEAR DAUGHTER, WHO ART IGNORANT OF WHAT THOU ART —
NOR THAT I AM BETTER THAN PROSPERO, MASTER OF A FULL POOR CELL.
MORE TO KNOW DID NEVER MEDDLE WITH MY THOUGHTS.

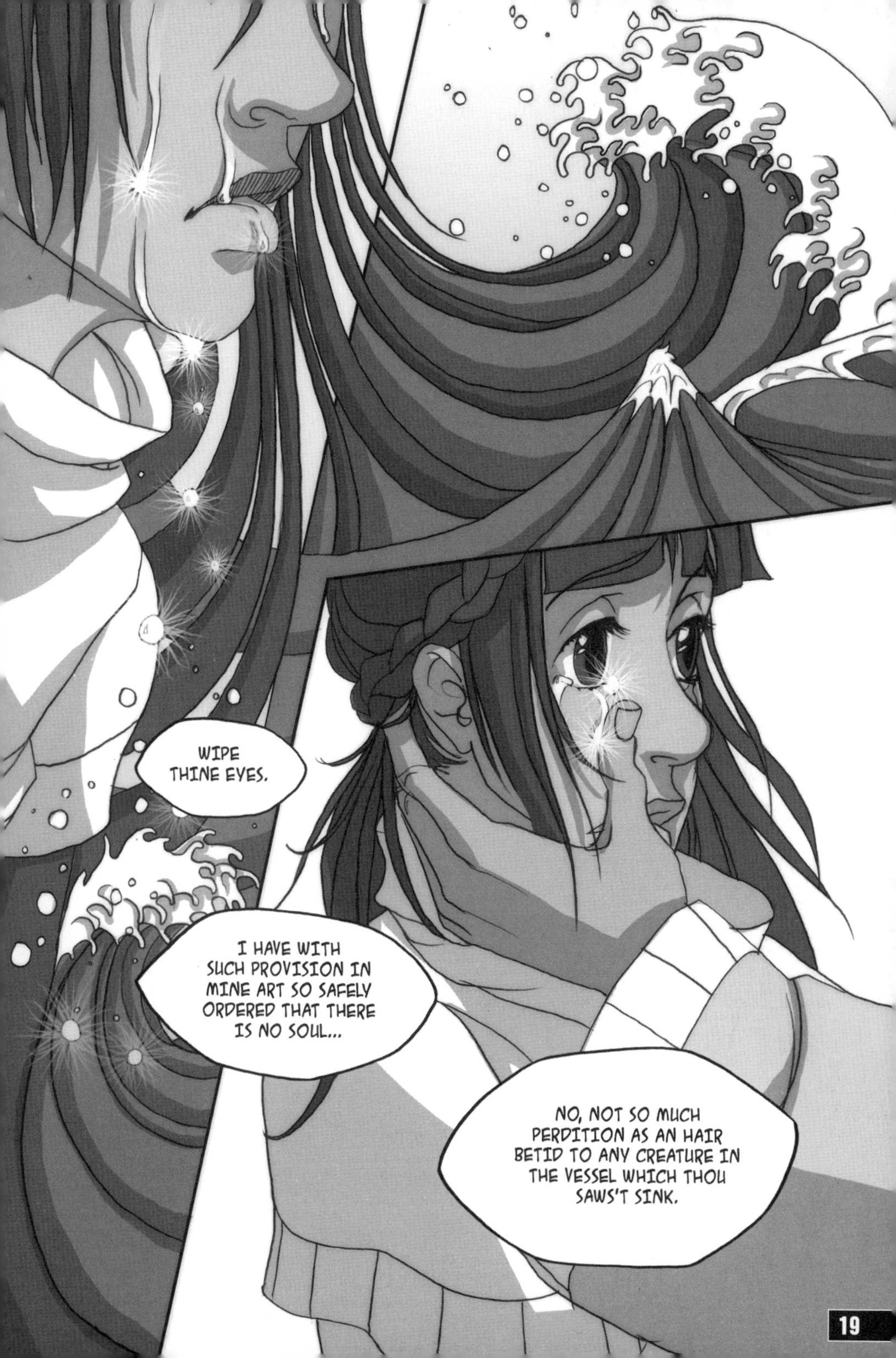
WIPE THINE EYES.
I HAVE WITH SUCH PROVISION IN MINE ART SO SAFELY ORDERED THAT THERE IS NO SOUL...
NO, NOT SO MUCH PERDITION AS AN HAIR BETID TO ANY CREATURE IN THE VESSEL WHICH THOU SAWS'T SINK.

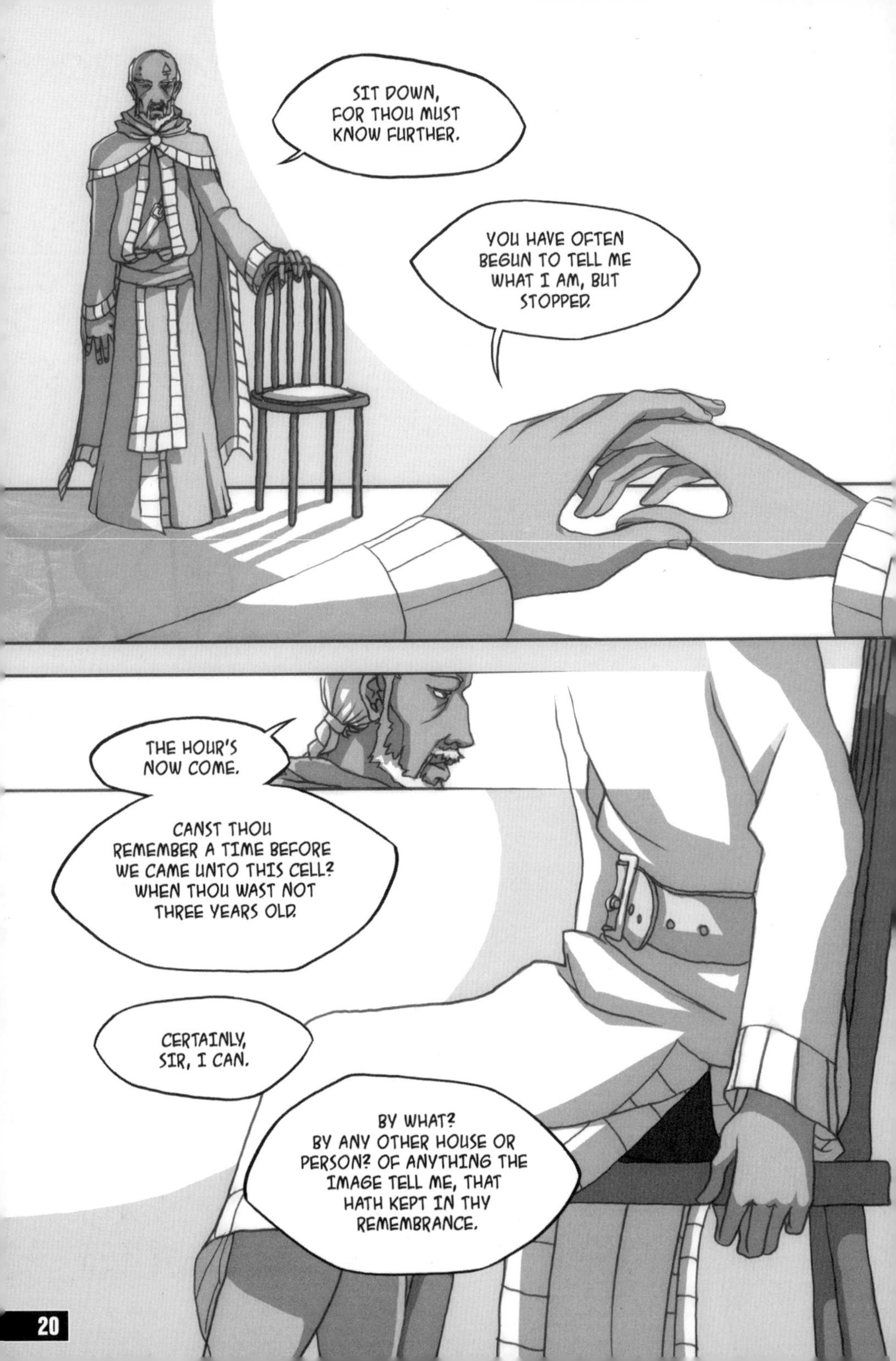
SIT DOWN, FOR THOU MUST KNOW FURTHER.
YOU HAVE OFTEN BEGUN TO TELL ME WHAT I AM, BUT STOPPED.
THE HOUR'S NOW COME.
CANST THOU REMEMBER A TIME BEFORE WE CAME UNTO THIS CELL? WHEN THOU WAST NOT THREE YEARS OLD.
CERTAINLY, SIR, I CAN.
BY WHAT? BY ANY OTHER HOUSE OR PERSON? OF ANYTHING THE IMAGE TELL ME, THAT HATH KEPT IN THY REMEMBRANCE.

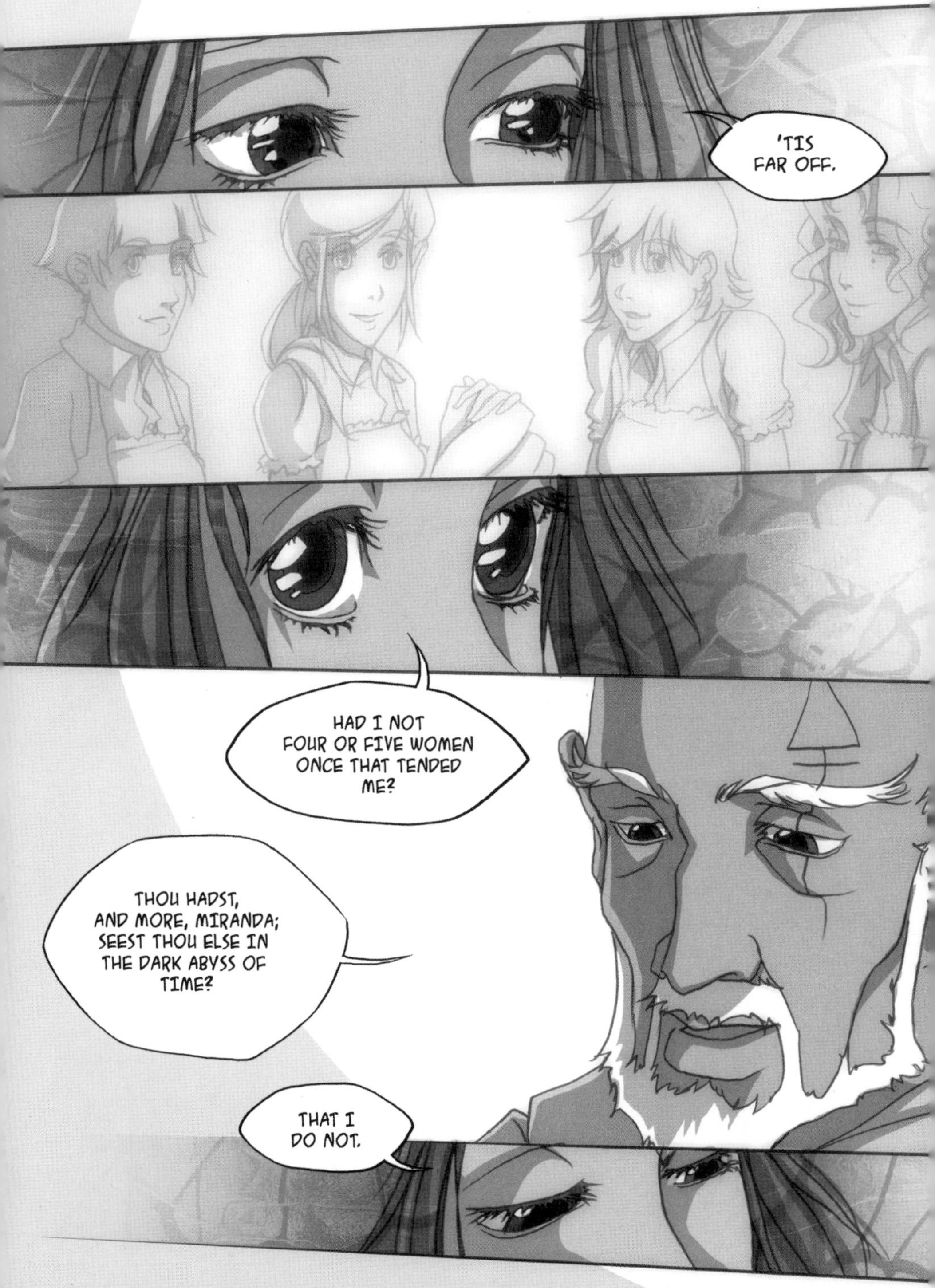
'TIS FAR OFF.
HAD I NOT FOUR OR FIVE WOMEN ONCE THAT TENDED ME?
THOU HADST, AND MORE, MIRANDA; SEEST THOU ELSE IN THE DARK ABYSS OF TIME?
THAT I DO NOT.

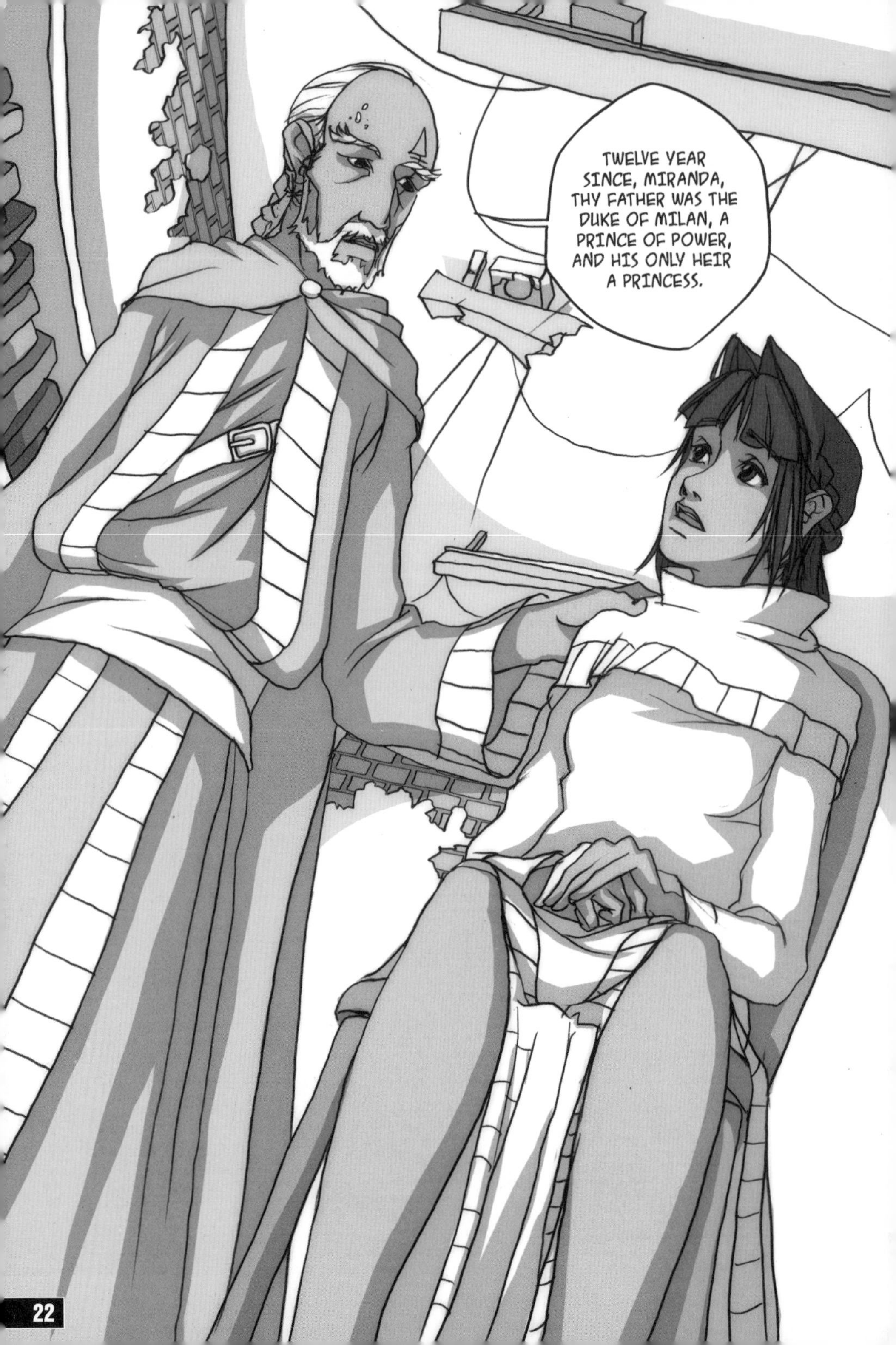
TWELVE YEAR SINCE, MIRANDA, THY FATHER WAS THE DUKE OF MILAN, A PRINCE OF POWER, AND HIS ONLY HEIR A PRINCESS.

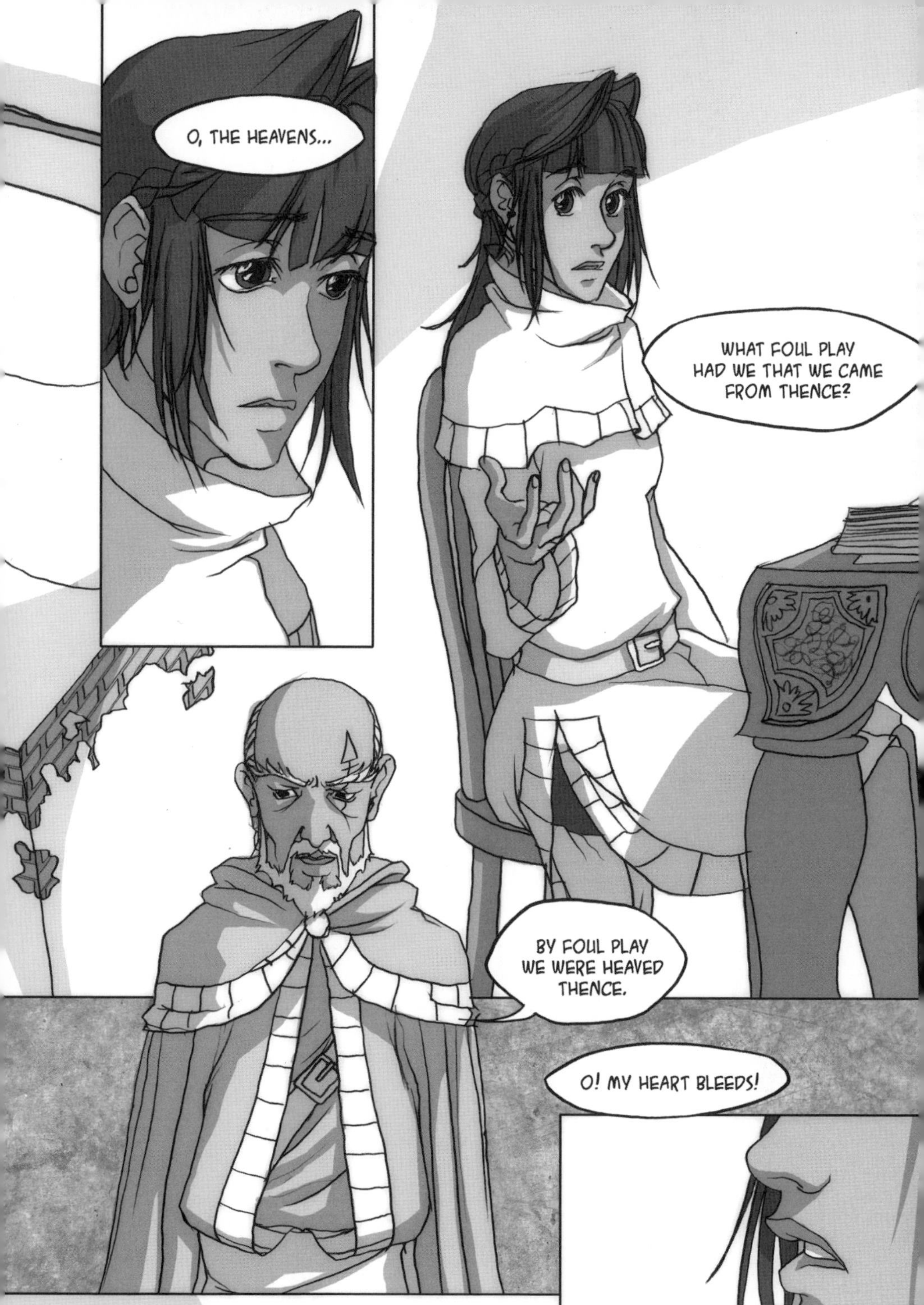
O, THE HEAVENS...
WHAT FOUL PLAY HAD WE THAT WE CAME FROM THENCE?
BY FOUL PLAY WE WERE HEAVED THENCE.
O! MY HEART BLEEDS!

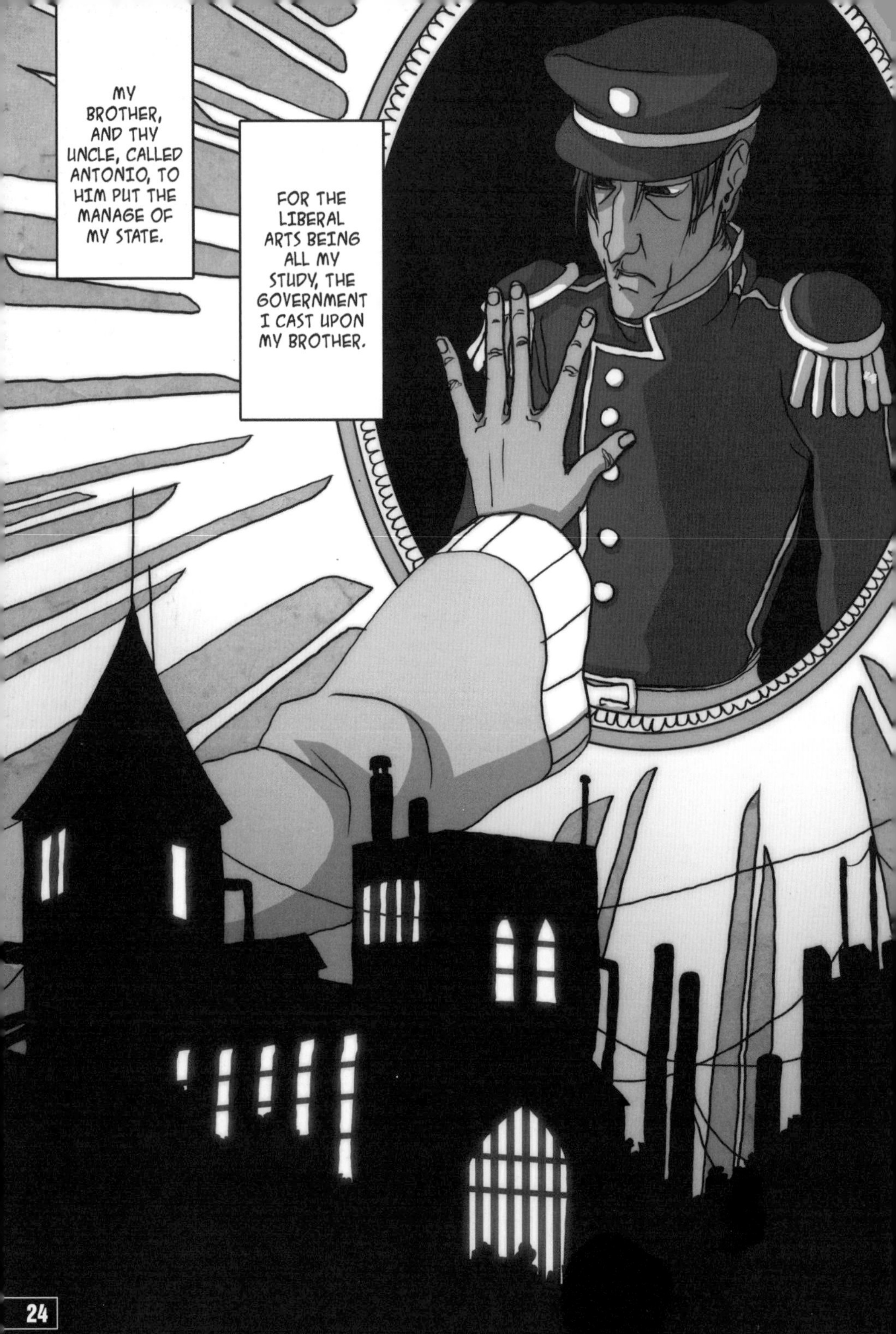
MY BROTHER, AND THY UNCLE, CALLED ANTONIO, TO HIM PUT THE MANAGE OF MY STATE.
FOR THE LIBERAL ARTS BEING ALL MY STUDY, THE GOVERNMENT I CAST UPON MY BROTHER.

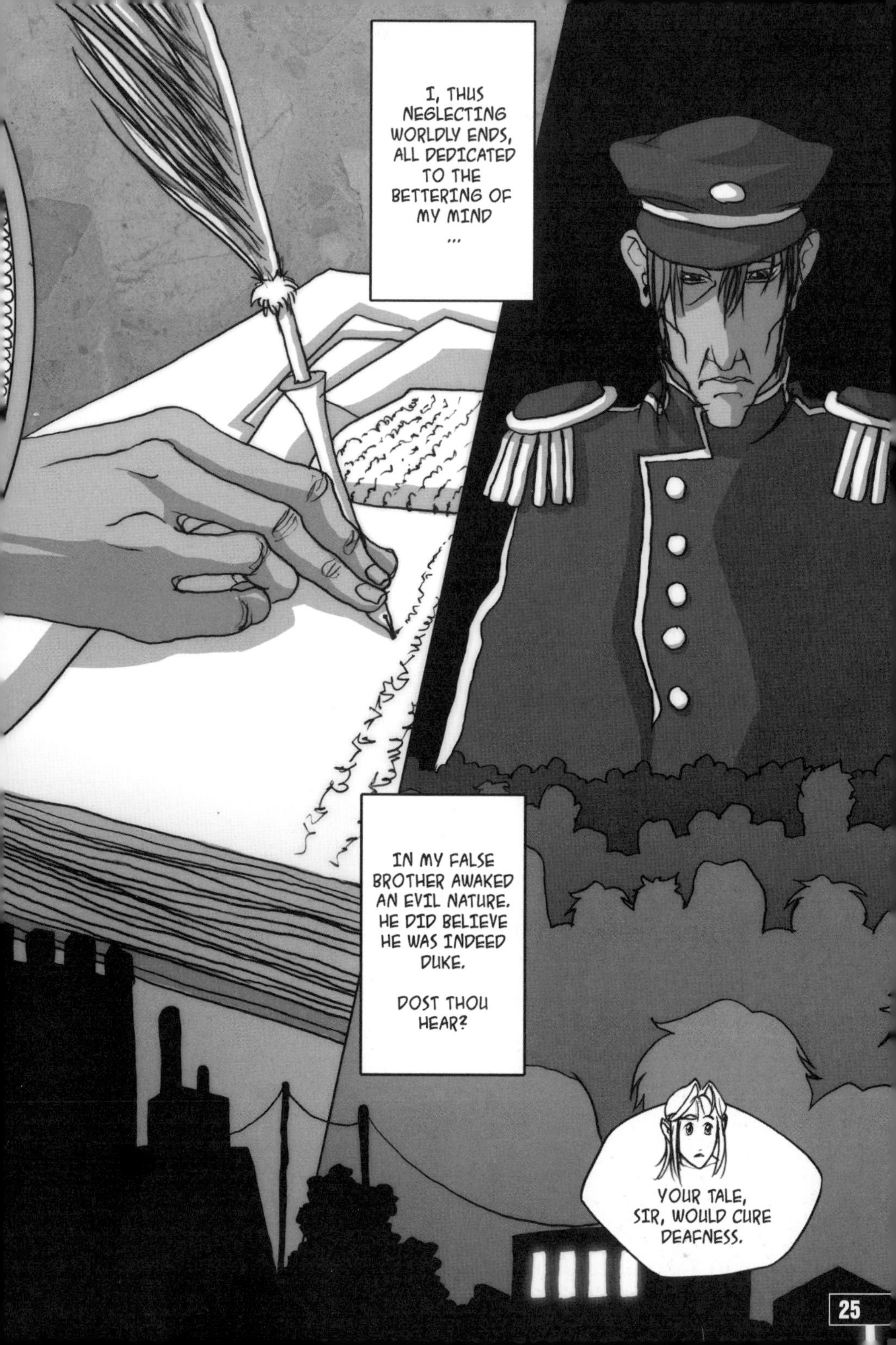
I, THUS NEGLECTING WORLDLY ENDS, ALL DEDICATED TO THE BETTERING OF MY MIND ...
IN MY FALSE BROTHER AWAKED AN EVIL NATURE. HE DID BELIEVE HE WAS INDEED DUKE.
DOST THOU HEAR?
YOUR TALE, SIR, WOULD CURE DEAFNESS.

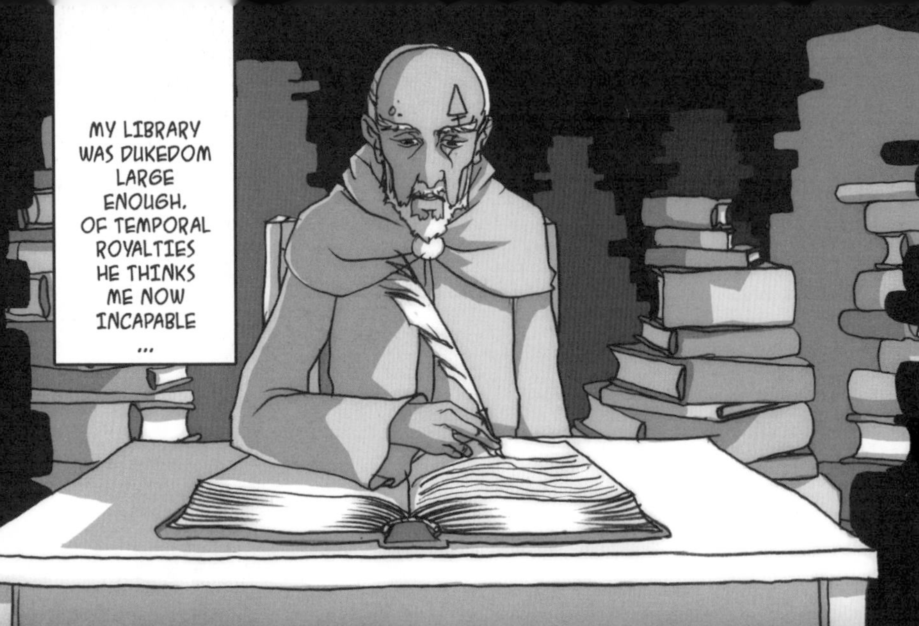
MY LIBRARY WAS DUKEDOM LARGE ENOUGH. OF TEMPORAL ROYALTIES HE THINKS ME NOW INCAPABLE ...

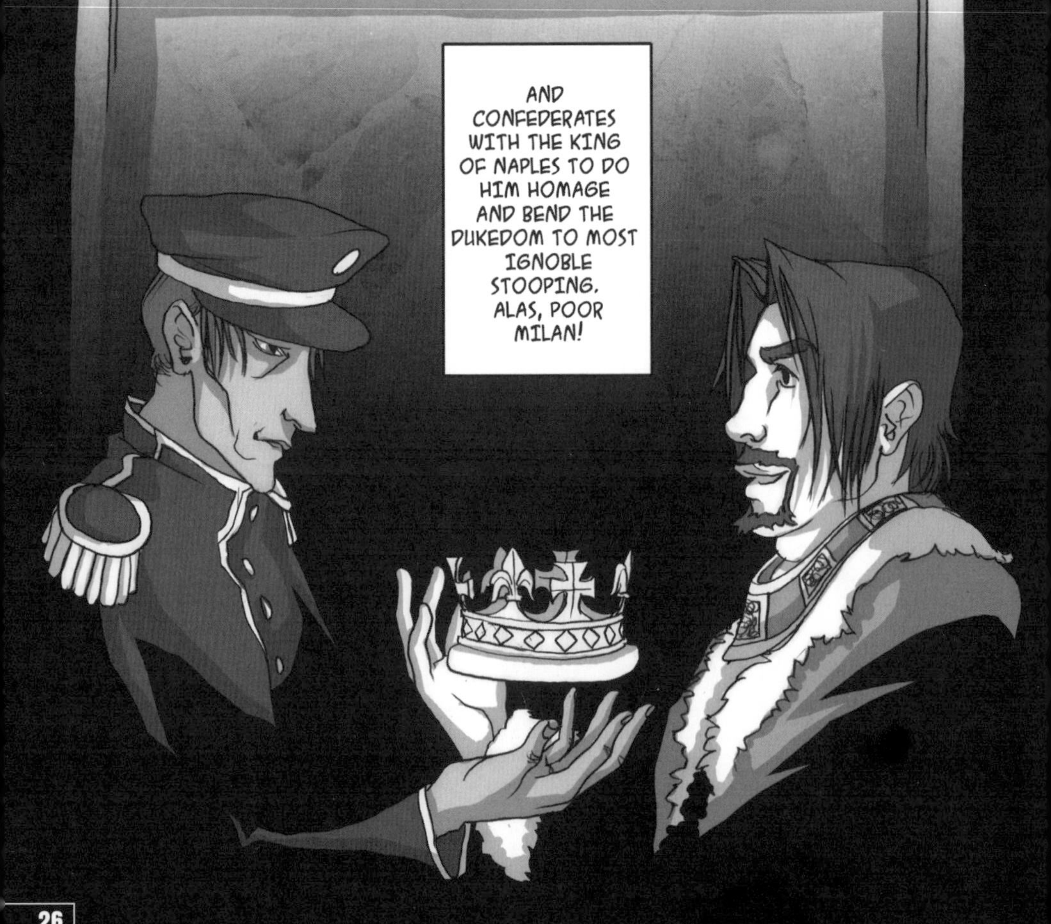
AND CONFEDERATES WITH THE KING OF NAPLES TO DO HIM HOMAGE AND BEND THE DUKEDOM TO MOST IGNOBLE STOOPING. ALAS, POOR MILAN!

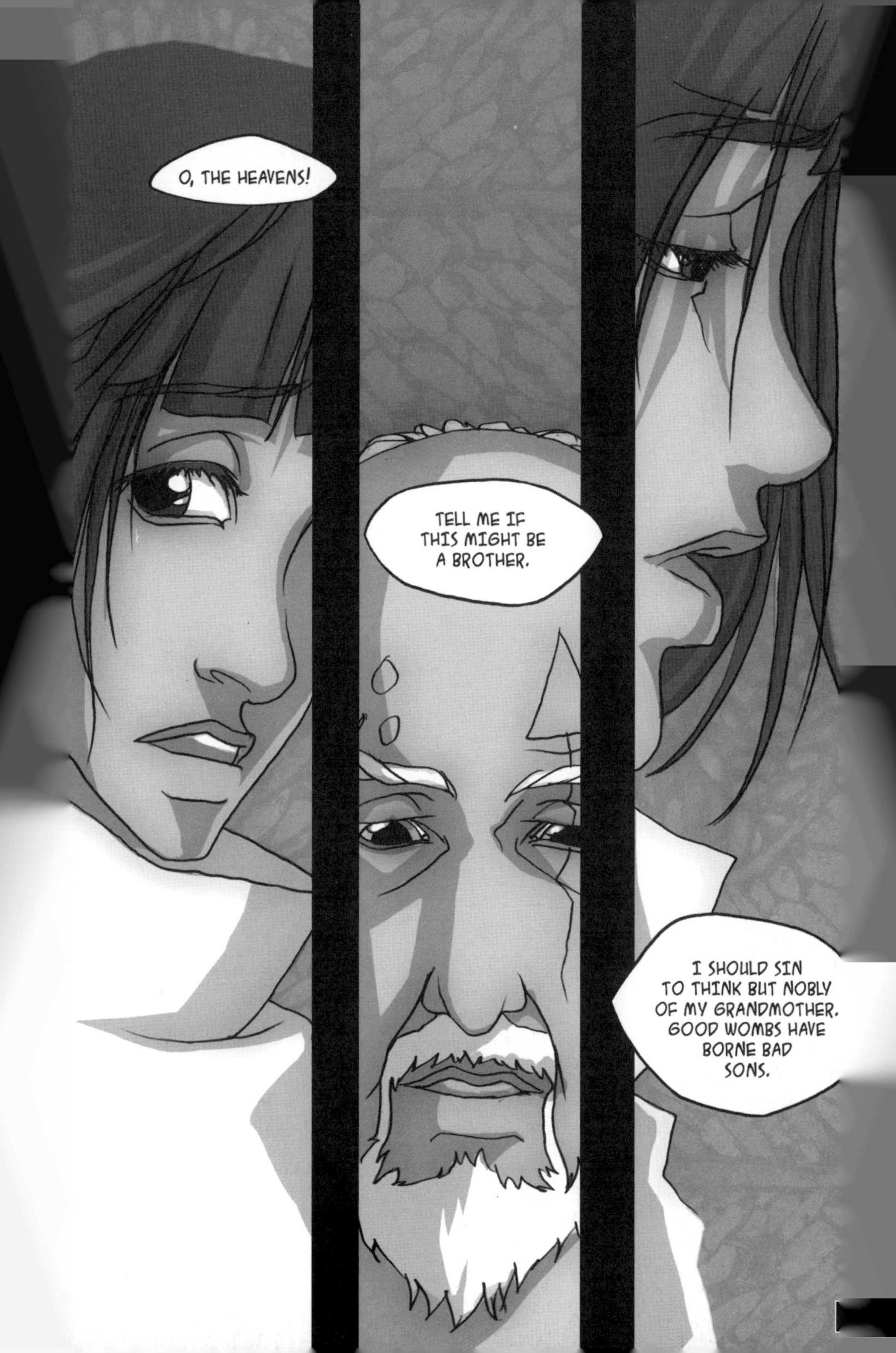
O, THE HEAVENS!
TELL ME IF THIS MIGHT BE A BROTHER.
I SHOULD SIN TO THINK BUT NOBLY OF MY GRANDMOTHER. GOOD WOMBS HAVE BORNE BAD SONS.

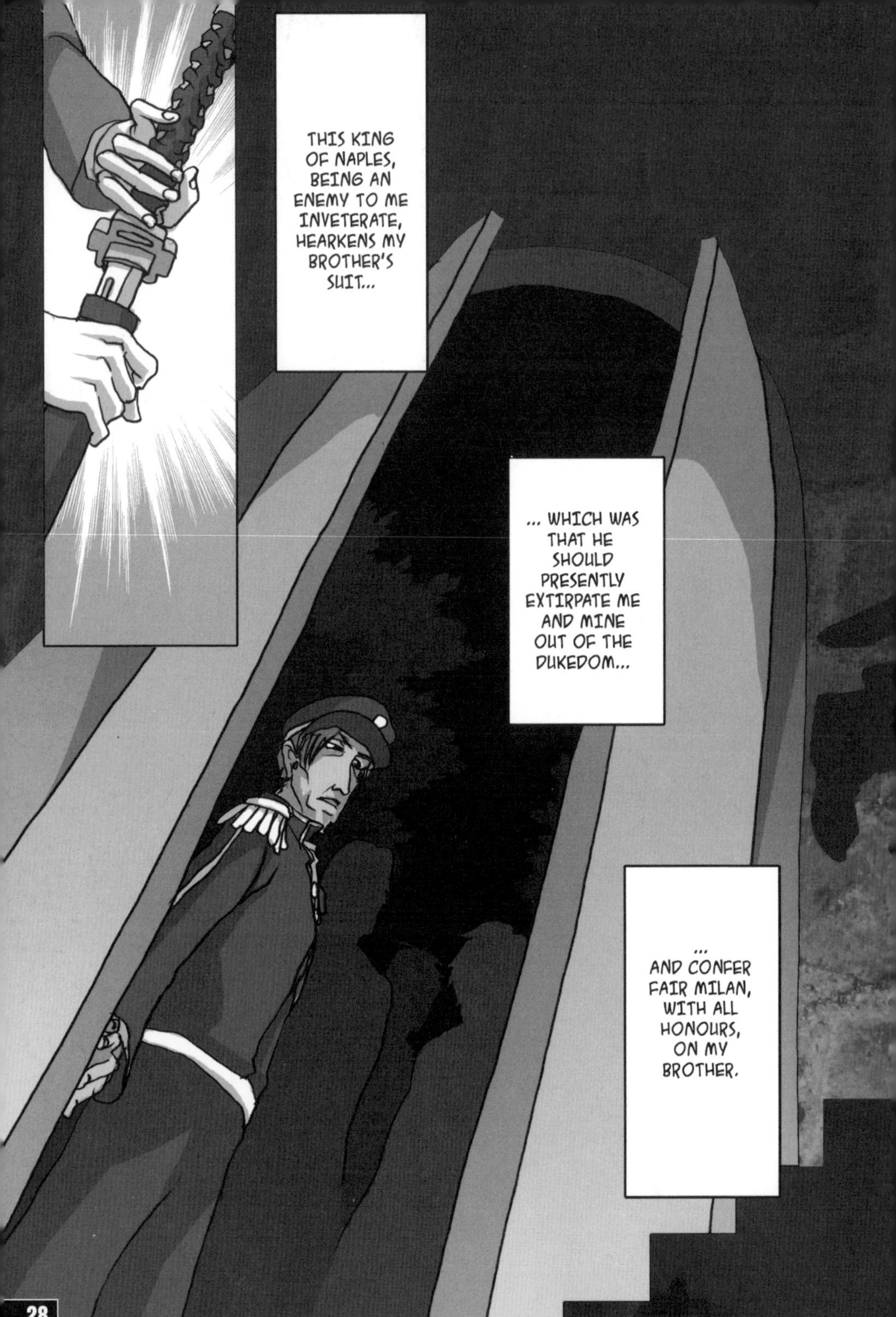
THIS KING OF NAPLES, BEING AN ENEMY TO ME INVETERATE, HEARKENS MY BROTHER'S SUIT...
... WHICH WAS THAT HE SHOULD PRESENTLY EXTIRPATE ME AND MINE OUT OF THE DUKEDOM...
... AND CONFER FAIR MILAN, WITH ALL HONOURS, ON MY BROTHER.

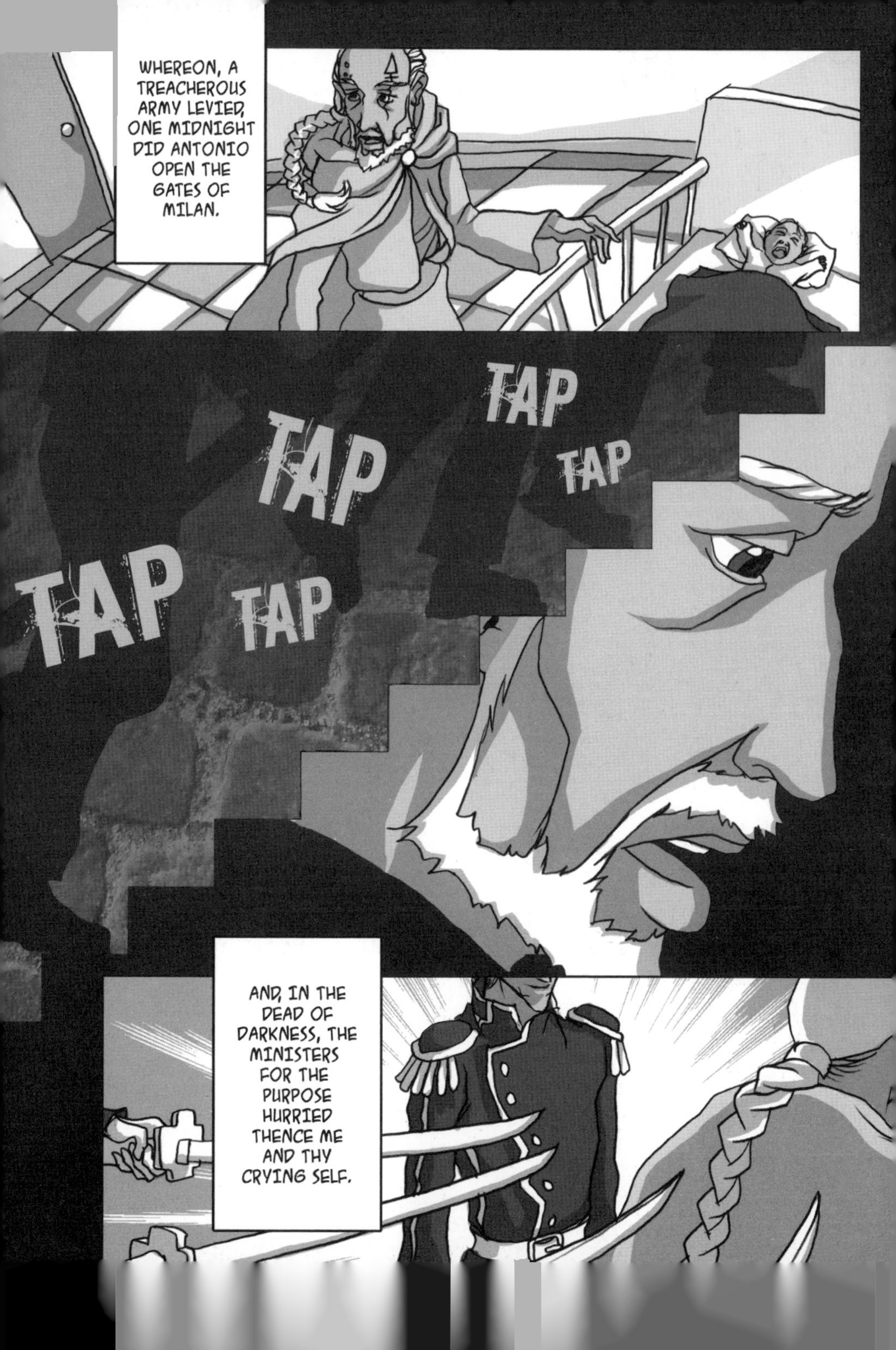
WHEREON, A TREACHEROUS ARMY LEVIED, ONE MIDNIGHT DID ANTONIO OPEN THE GATES OF MILAN.
TAP
TAP
TAP
TAP
TAP
AND, IN THE DEAD OF DARKNESS, THE MINISTERS FOR THE PURPOSE HURRIED THENCE ME AND THY CRYING SELF.

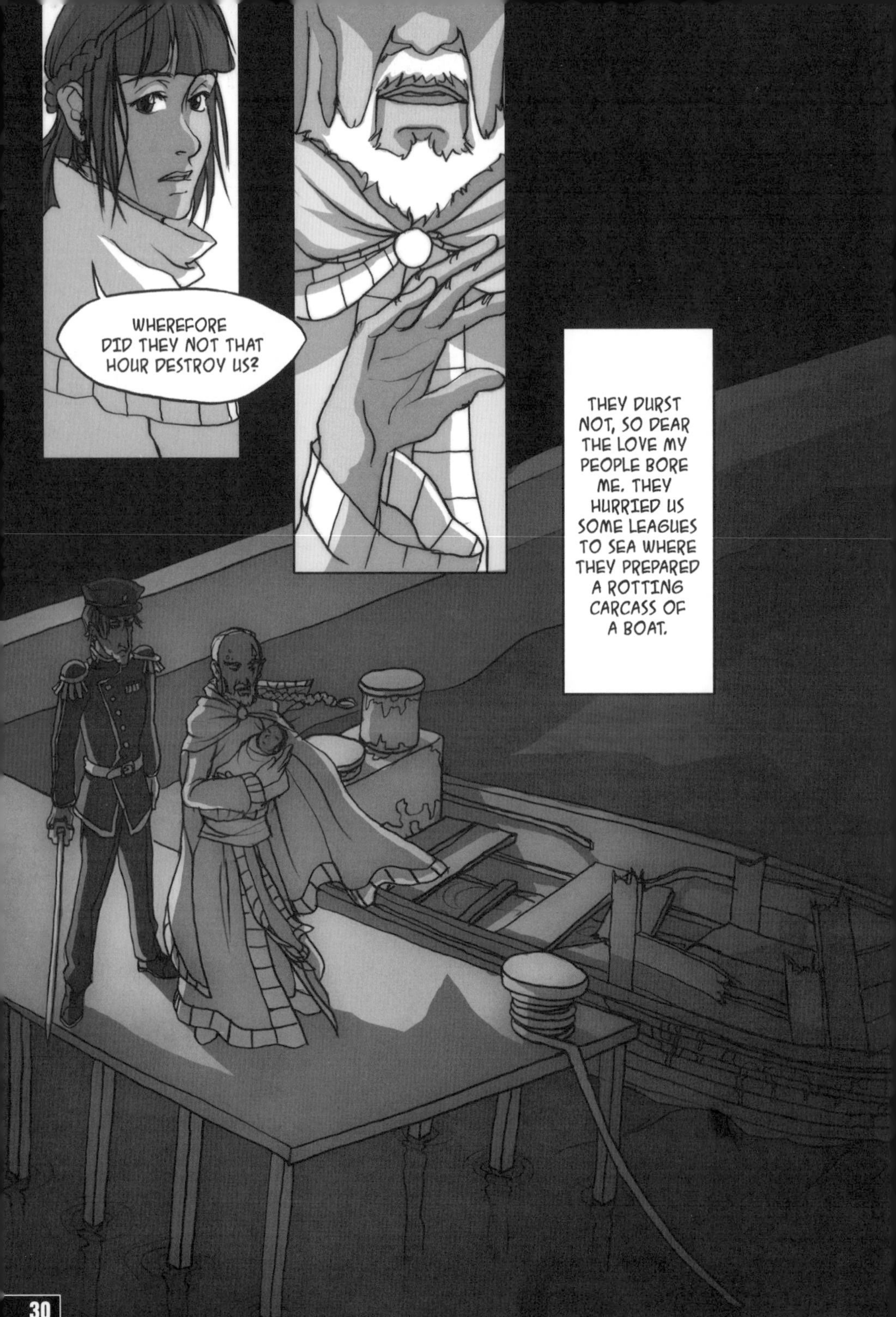
WHEREFORE DID THEY NOT THAT HOUR DESTROY US?
THEY DURST NOT, SO DEAR THE LOVE MY PEOPLE BORE ME. THEY HURRIED US SOME LEAGUES TO SEA WHERE THEY PREPARED A ROTTING CARCASS OF A BOAT.

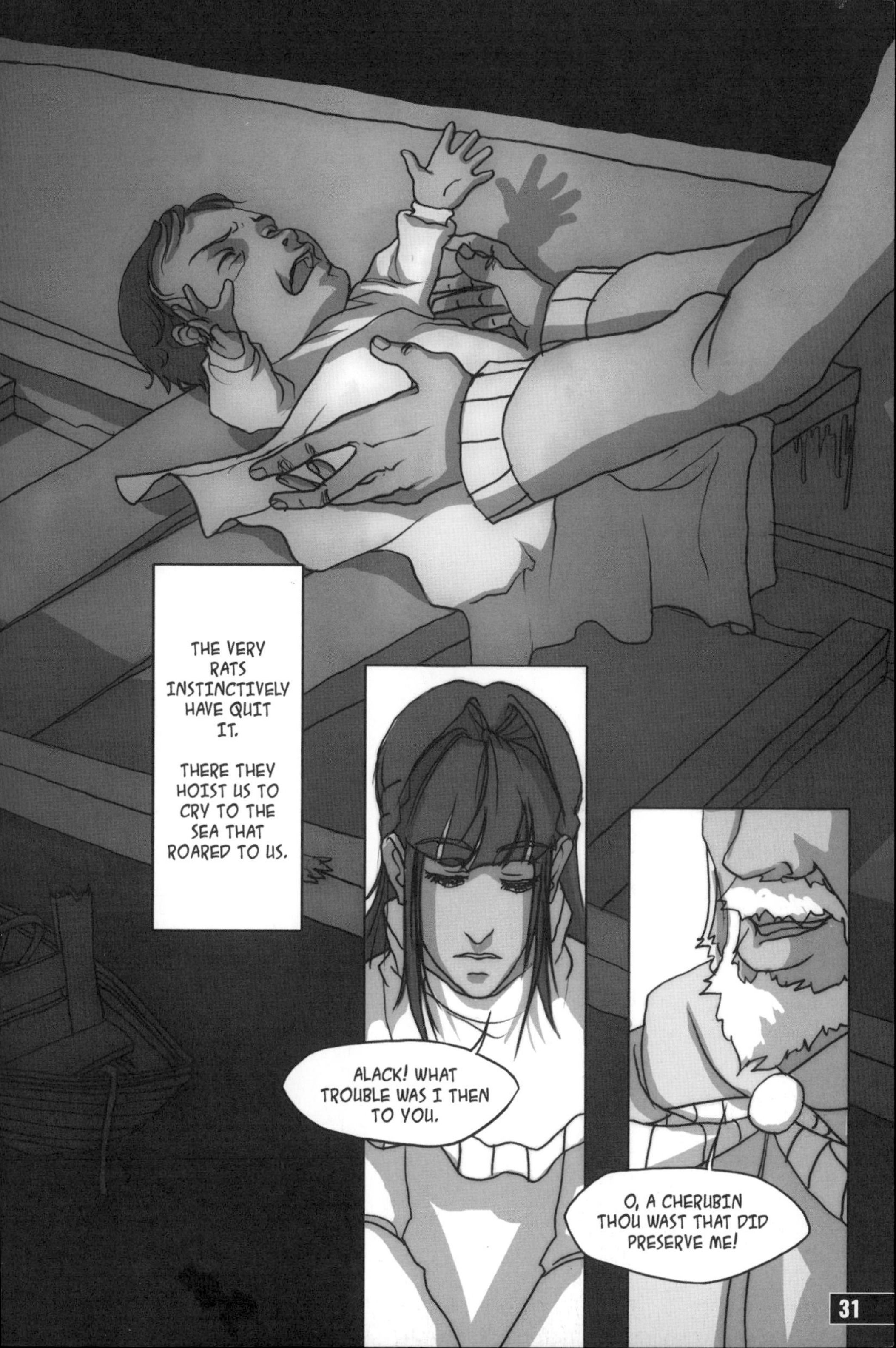
THE VERY RATS INSTINCTIVELY HAVE QUIT IT.
THERE THEY HOIST US TO CRY TO THE SEA THAT ROARED TO US.
ALACK! WHAT TROUBLE WAS I THEN TO YOU.
O, A CHERUBIN THOU WAST THAT DID PRESERVE ME!

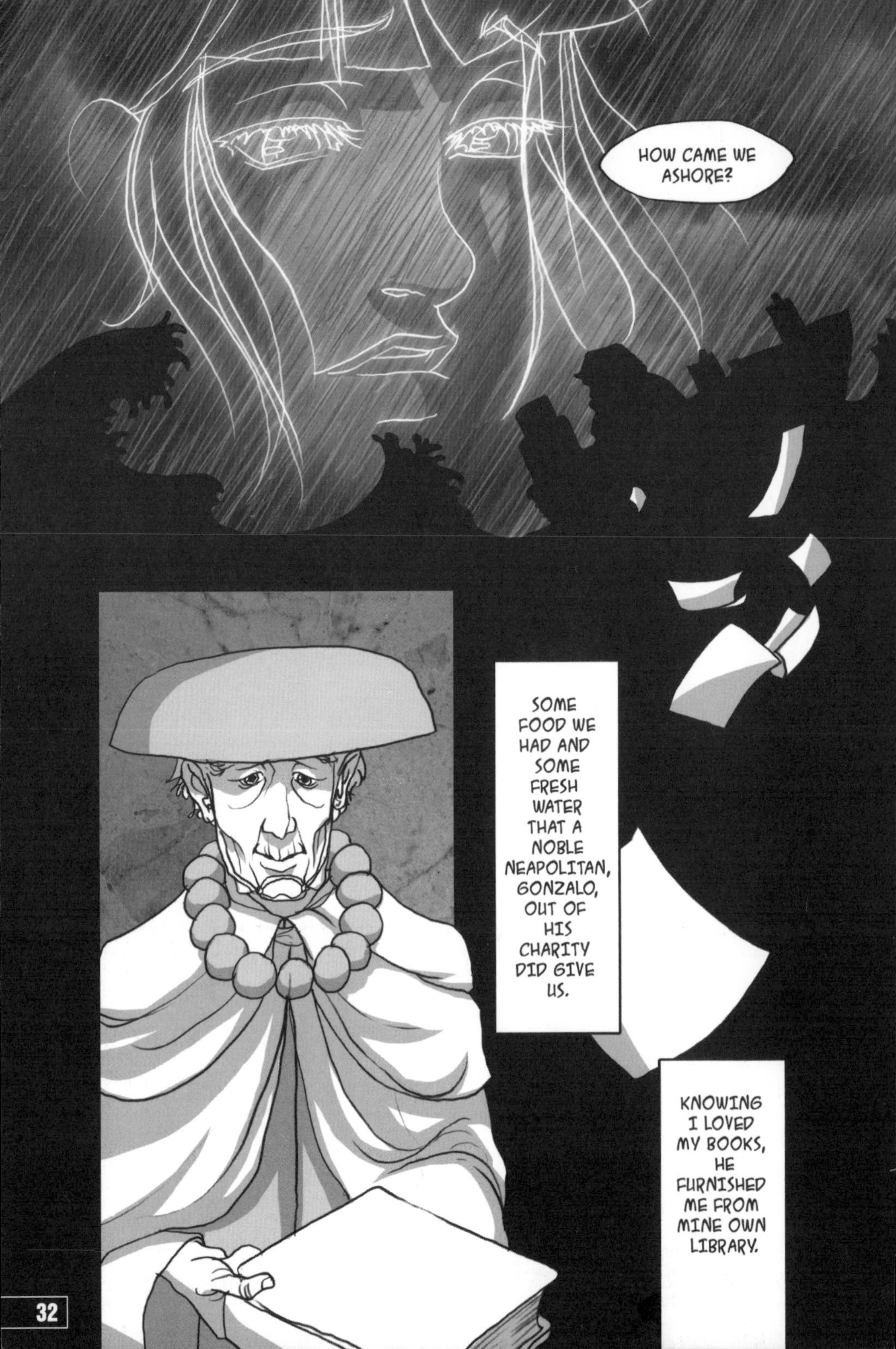
HOW CAME WE ASHORE?
SOME FOOD WE HAD AND SOME FRESH WATER THAT A NOBLE NEAPOLITAN, GONZALO, OUT OF HIS CHARITY DID GIVE US.
KNOWING I LOVED MY BOOKS, HE FURNISHED ME FROM MINE OWN LIBRARY.

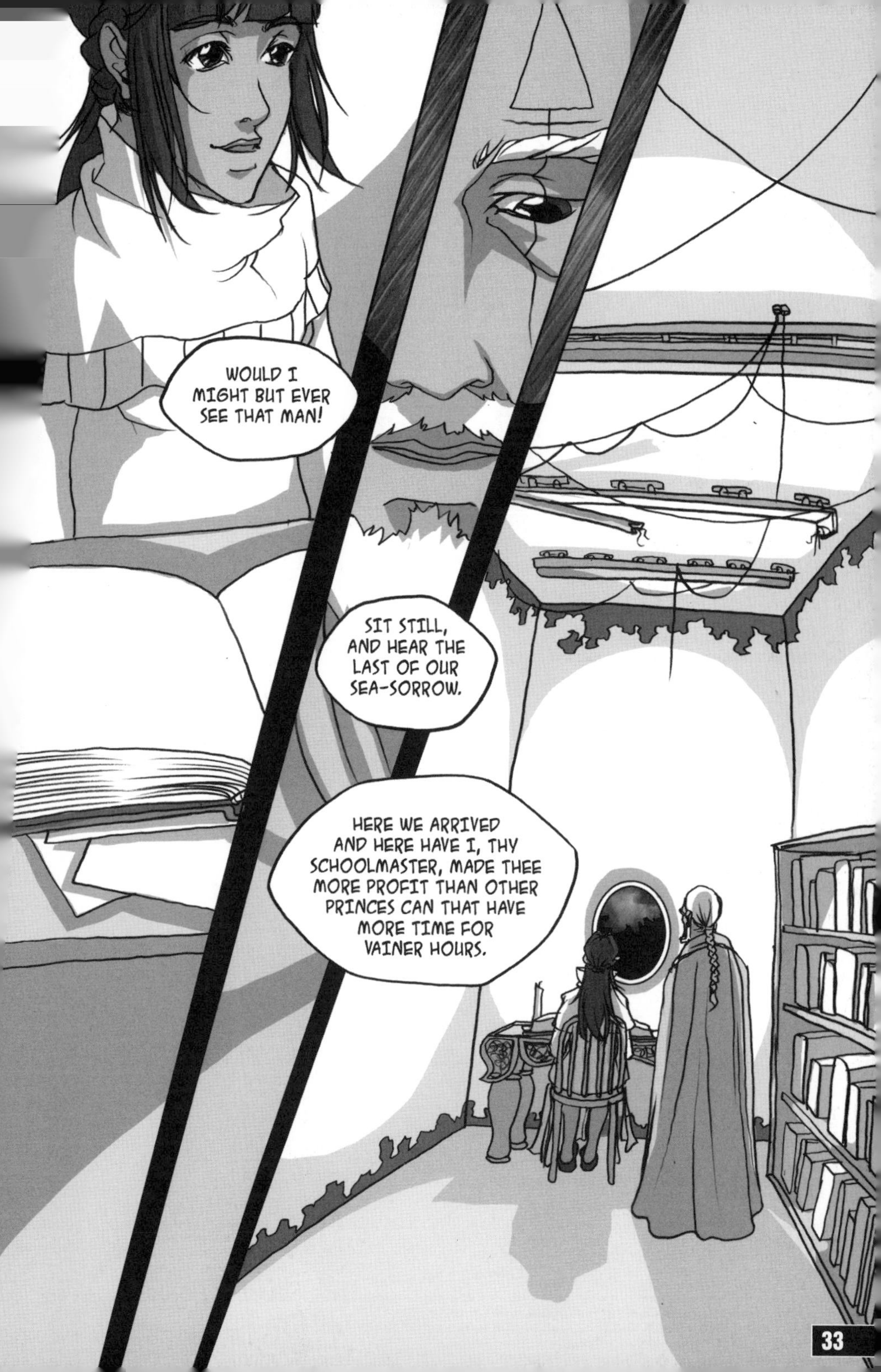
WOULD I MIGHT BUT EVER SEE THAT MAN!
SIT STILL, AND HEAR THE LAST OF OUR SEA-SORROW.
HERE WE ARRIVED AND HERE HAVE I, THY SCHOOLMASTER, MADE THEE MORE PROFIT THAN OTHER PRINCES CAN THAT HAVE MORE TIME FOR VAINER HOURS.

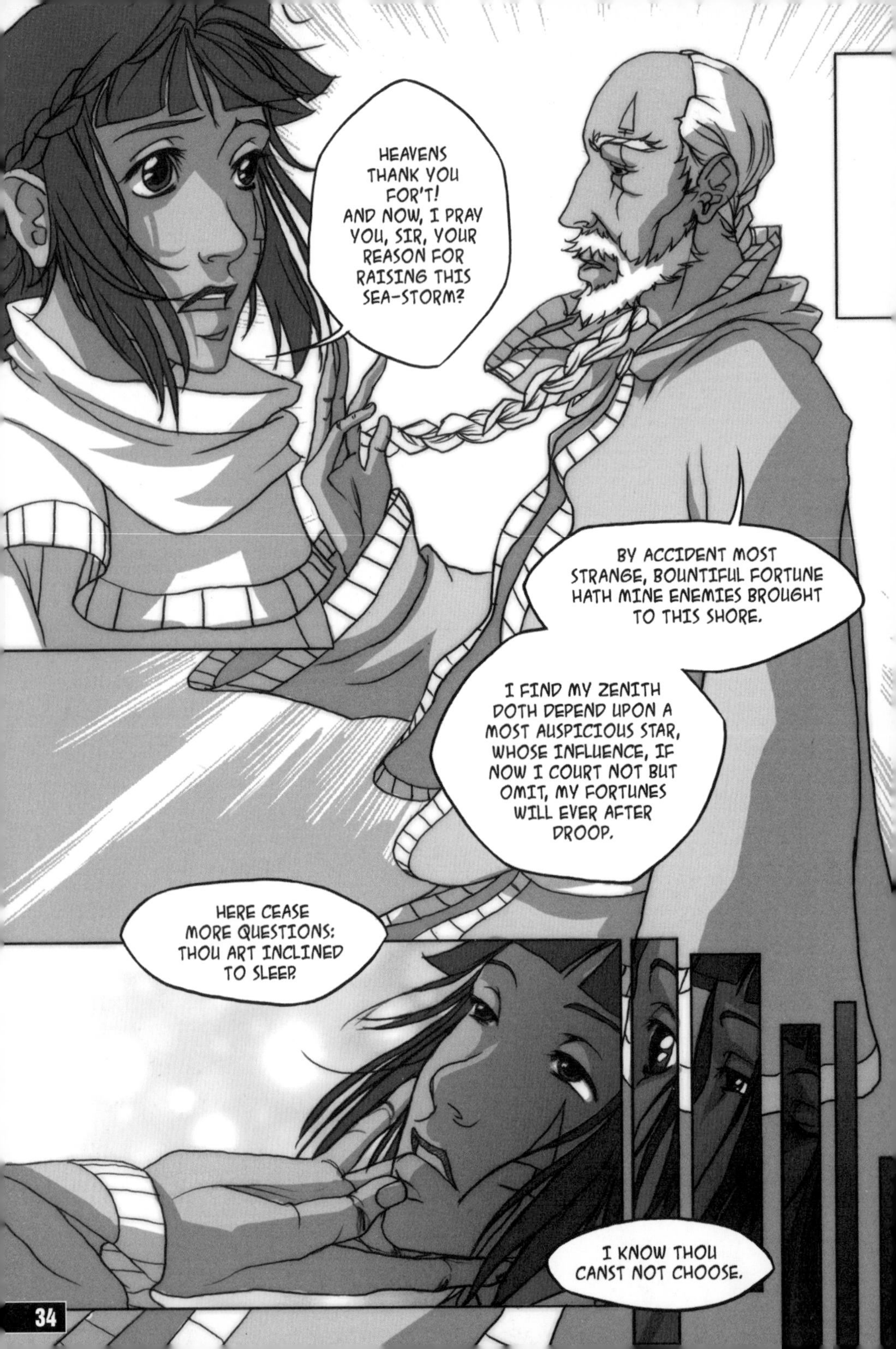
HEAVENS THANK YOU FOR'T! AND NOW, I PRAY YOU, SIR, YOUR REASON FOR RAISING THIS SEA-STORM?
BY ACCIDENT MOST STRANGE, BOUNTIFUL FORTUNE HATH MINE ENEMIES BROUGHT TO THIS SHORE.
I FIND MY ZENITH DOTH DEPEND UPON A MOST AUSPICIOUS STAR, WHOSE INFLUENCE, IF NOW I COURT NOT BUT OMIT, MY FORTUNES WILL EVER AFTER DROOP.
HERE CEASE MORE QUESTIONS: THOU ART INCLINED TO SLEEP.
I KNOW THOU CANST NOT CHOOSE.

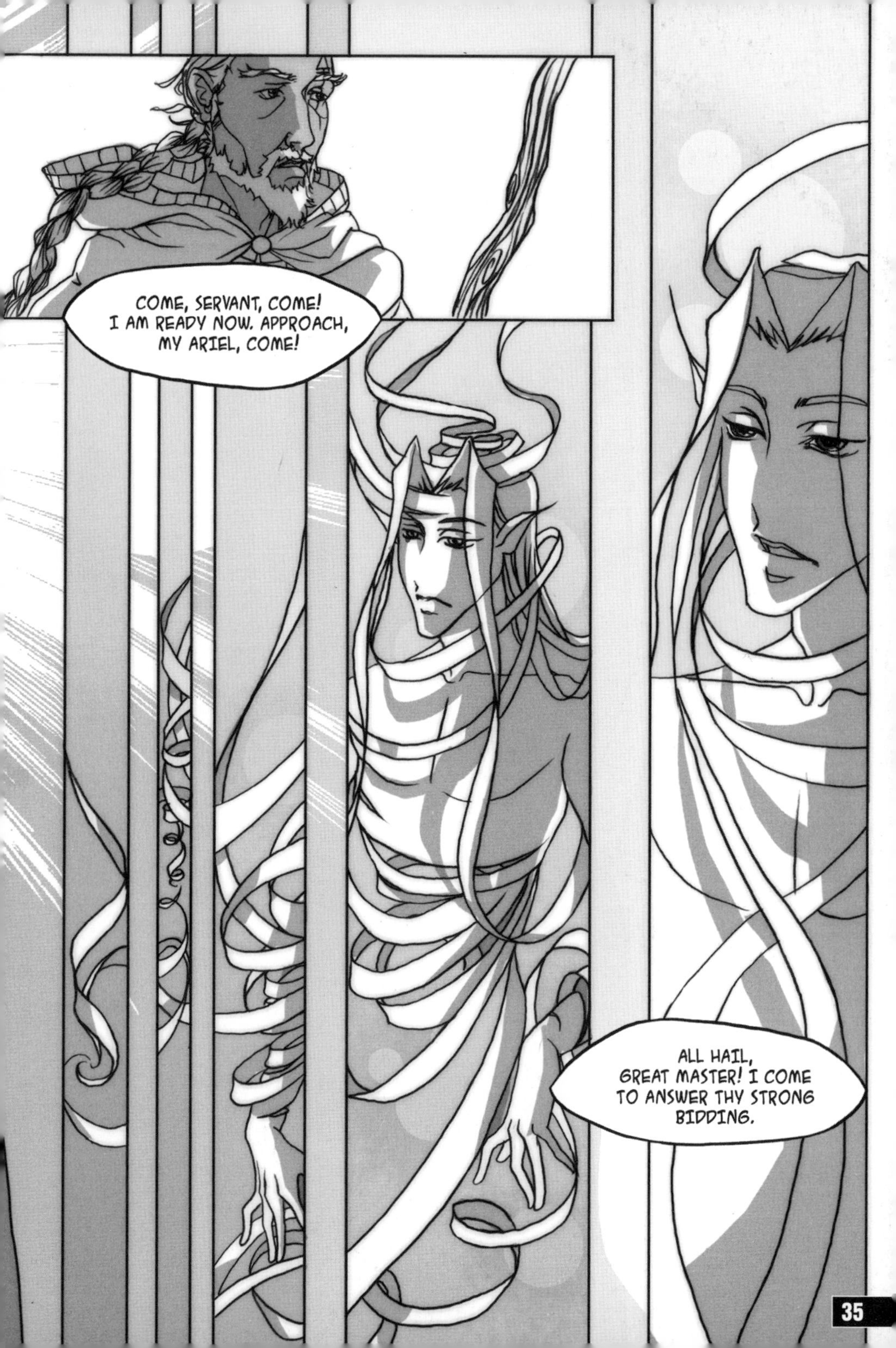
COME, SERVANT, COME! I AM READY NOW. APPROACH, MY ARIEL, COME!
ALL HAIL, GREAT MASTER! I COME TO ANSWER THY STRONG BIDDING.

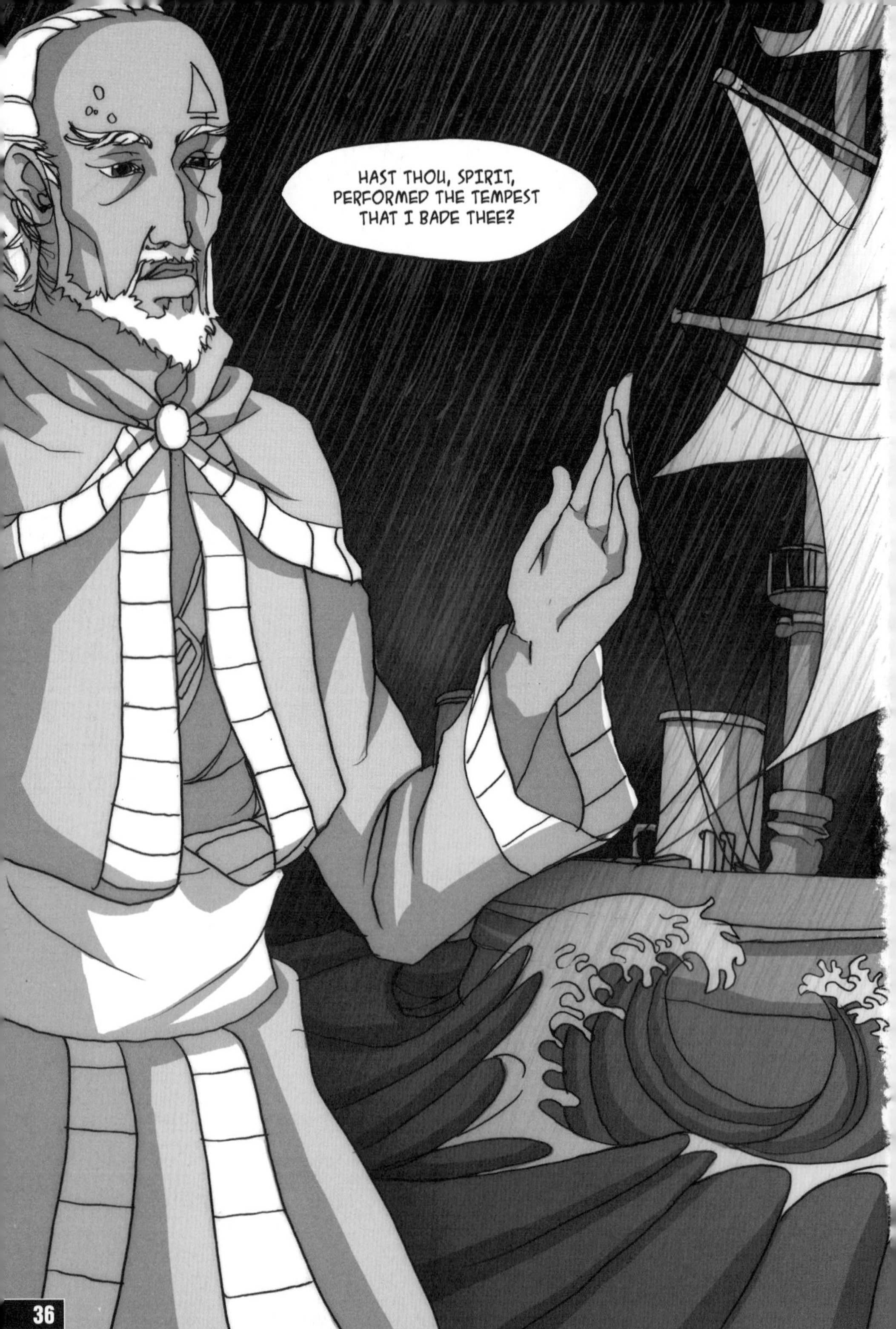
HAST THOU, SPIRIT, PERFORMED THE TEMPEST THAT I BADE THEE?

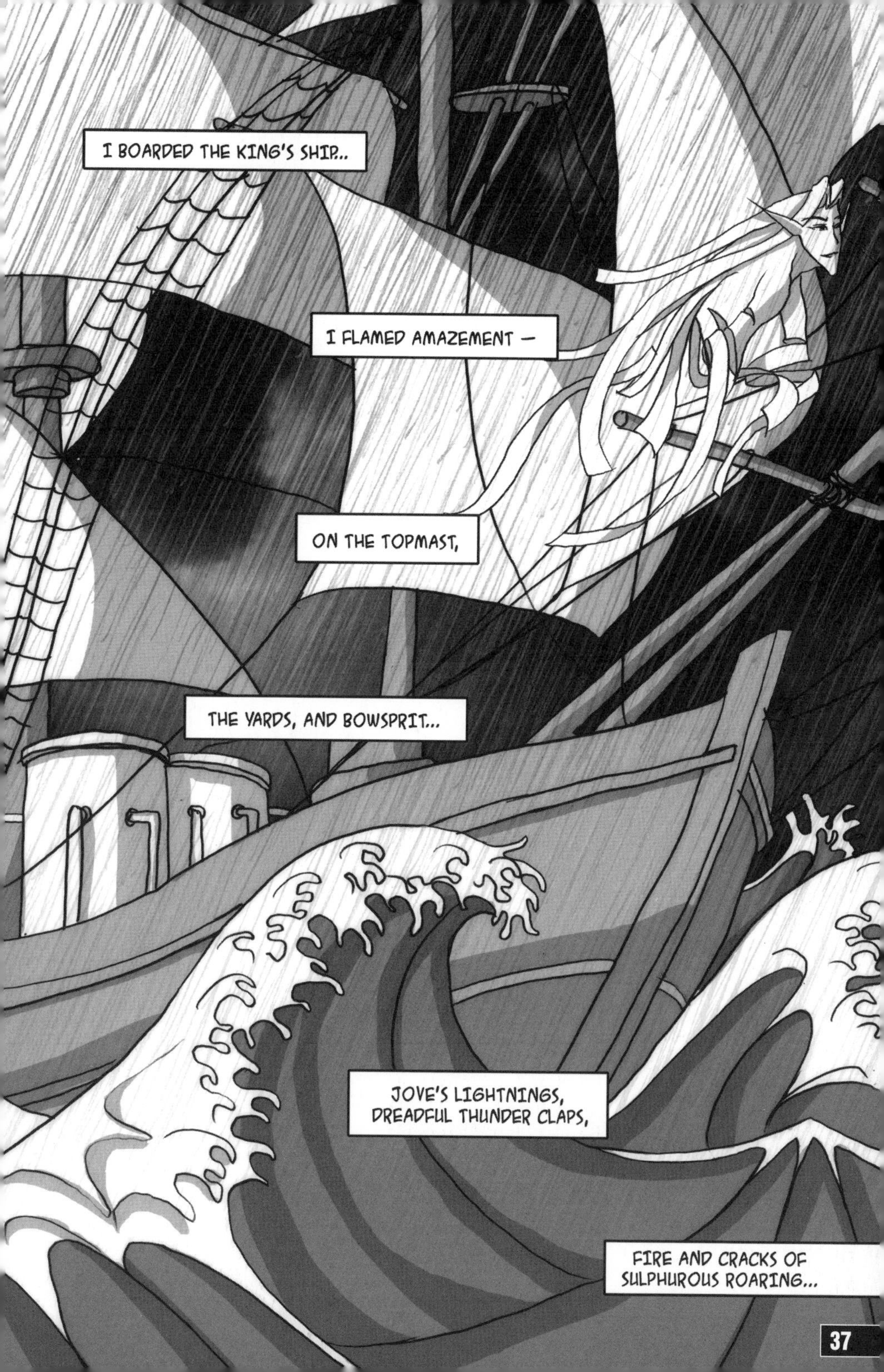
I BOARDED THE KING'S SHIP..
I FLAMED AMAZEMENT —
ON THE TOPMAST,
THE YARDS, AND BOWSPRIT...
JOVE'S LIGHTNINGS, DREADFUL THUNDER CLAPS,
FIRE AND CRACKS OF SULPHUROUS ROARING...

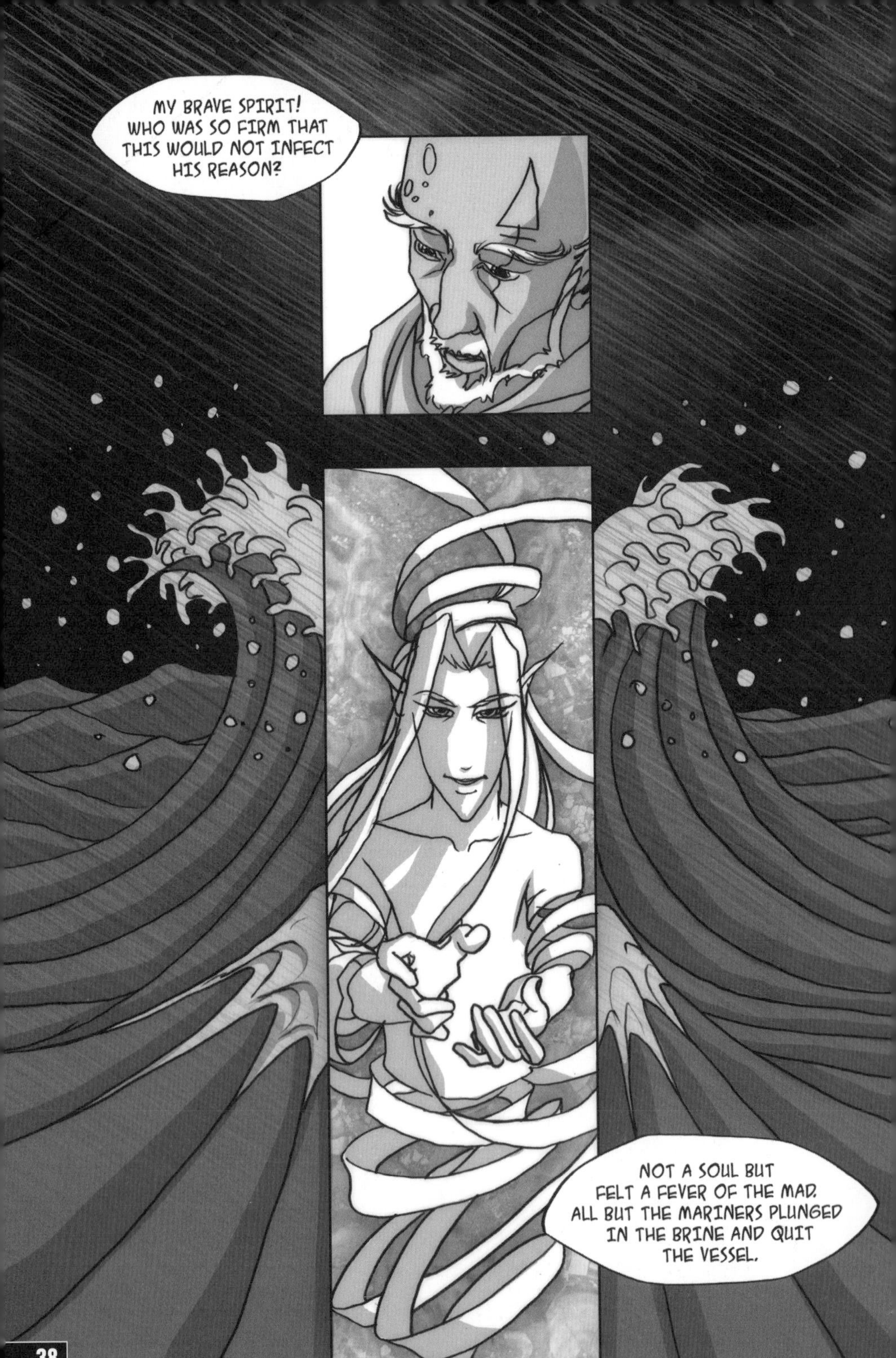
MY BRAVE SPIRIT! WHO WAS SO FIRM THAT THIS WOULD NOT INFECT HIS REASON?
NOT A SOUL BUT FELT A FEVER OF THE MAD. ALL BUT THE MARINERS PLUNGED IN THE BRINE AND QUIT THE VESSEL.

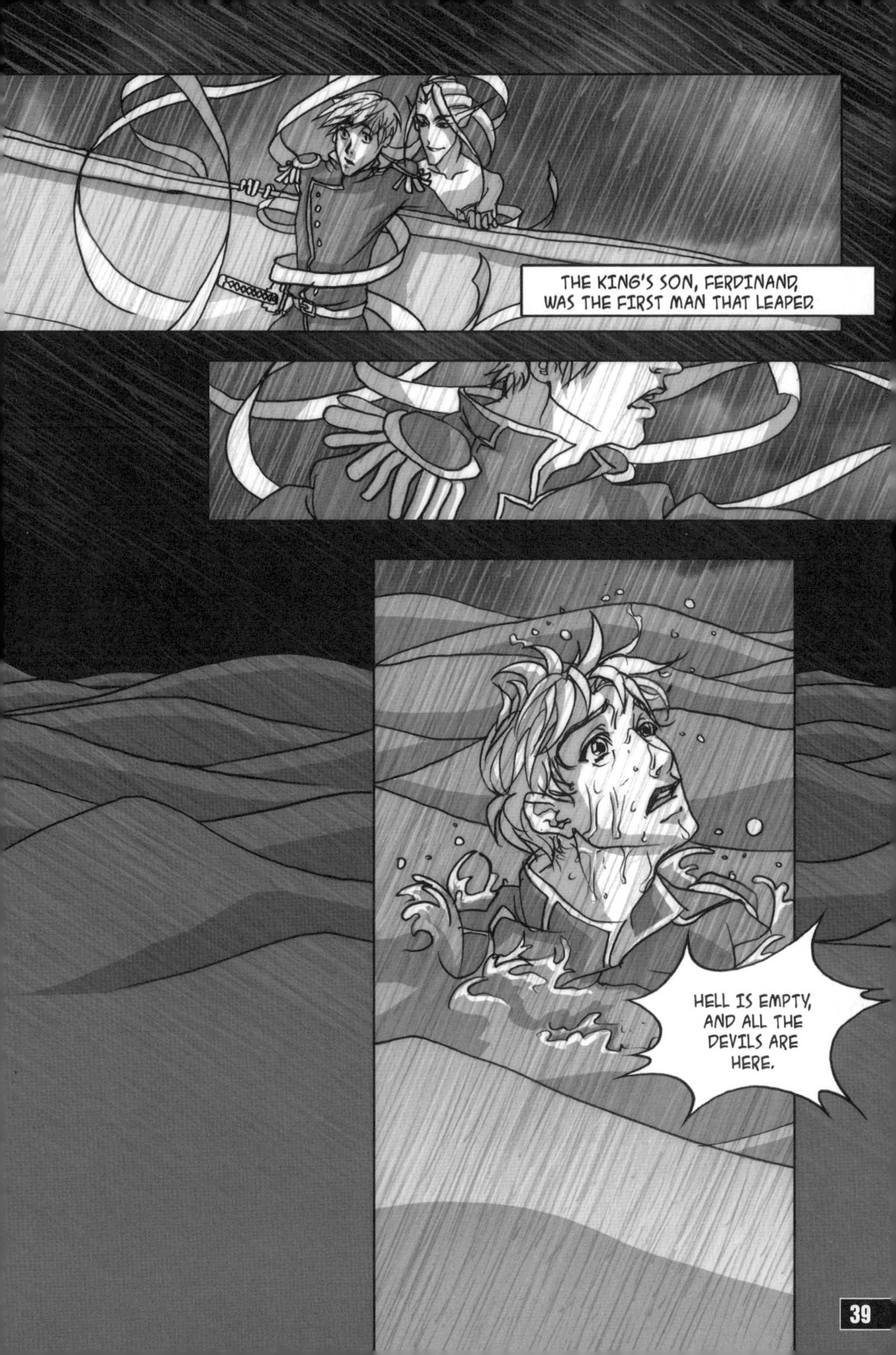
THE KING'S SON, FERDINAND,
WAS THE FIRST MAN THAT LEAPED.
HELL IS EMPTY, AND ALL THE DEVILS ARE HERE.

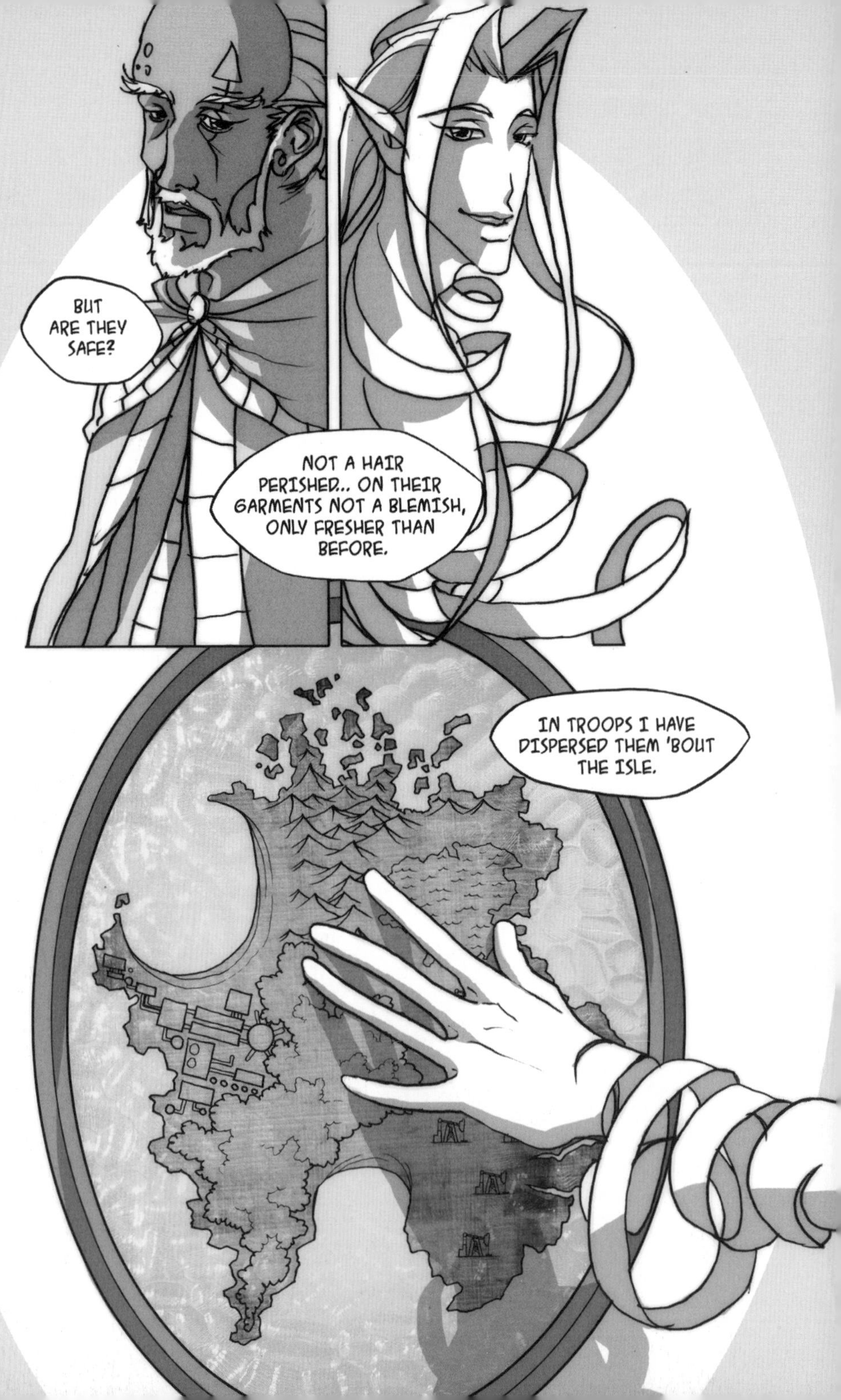
BUT ARE THEY SAFE?
NOT A HAIR PERISHED... ON THEIR GARMENTS NOT A BLEMISH, ONLY FRESHER THAN BEFORE.
IN TROOPS I HAVE DISPERSED THEM 'BOUT THE ISLE.

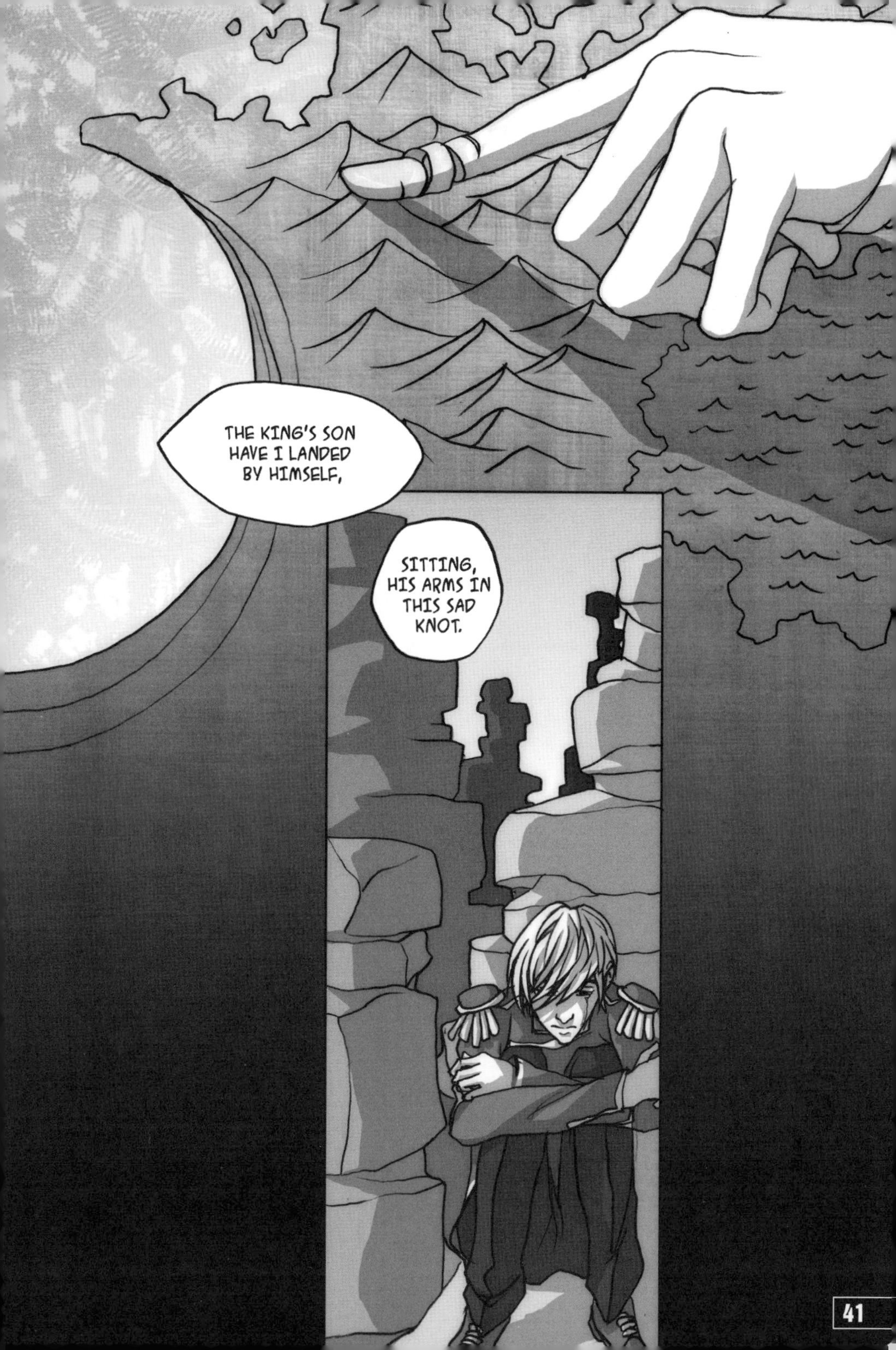
THE KING'S SON HAVE I LANDED BY HIMSELF,
SITTING, HIS ARMS IN THIS SAD KNOT.

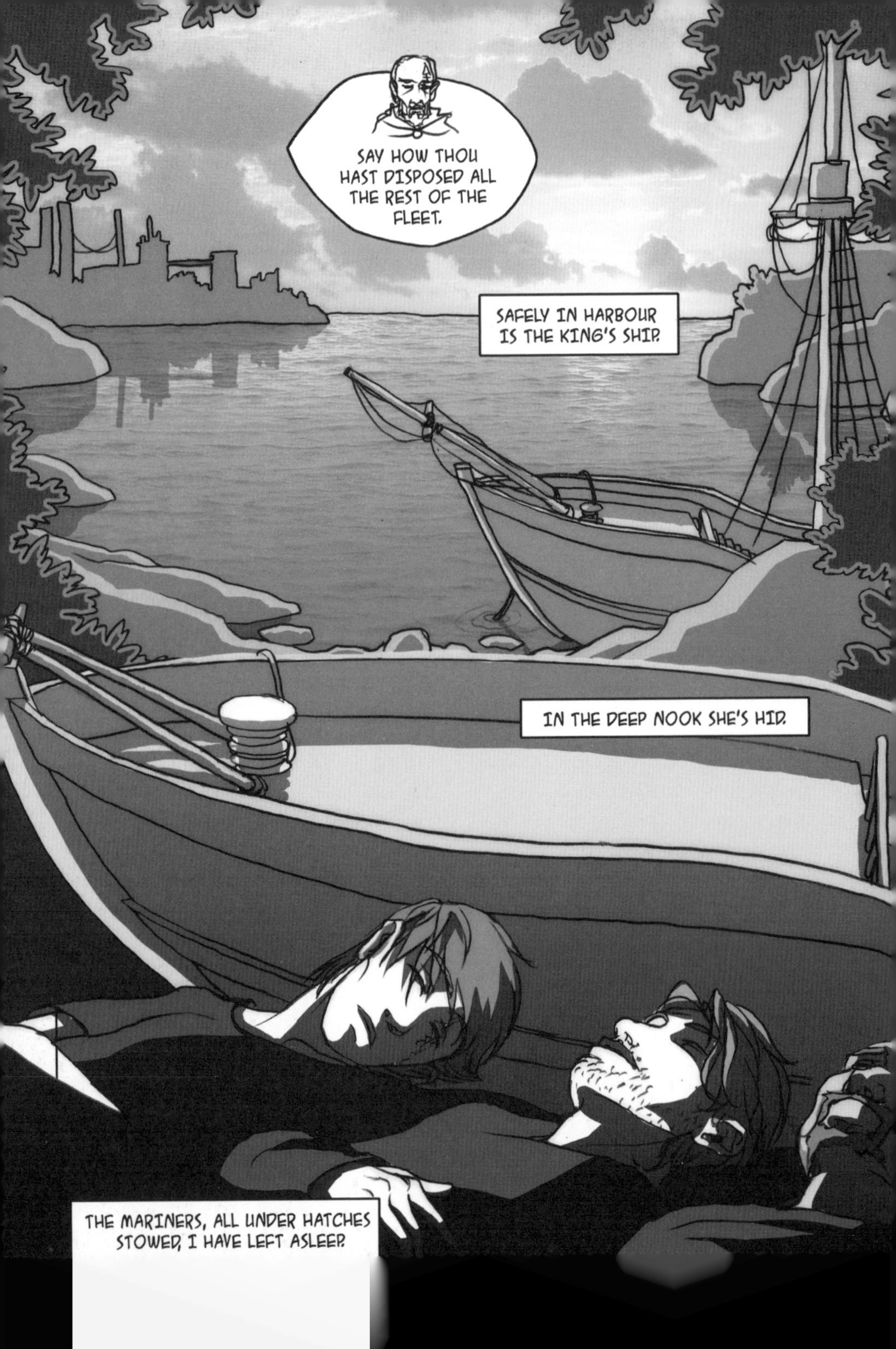
SAY HOW THOU HAST DISPOSED ALL THE REST OF THE FLEET.
SAFELY IN HARBOUR IS THE KING'S SHIP.
IN THE DEEP NOOK SHE'S HID.
THE MARINERS, ALL UNDER HATCHES STOWED, I HAVE LEFT ASLEEP.

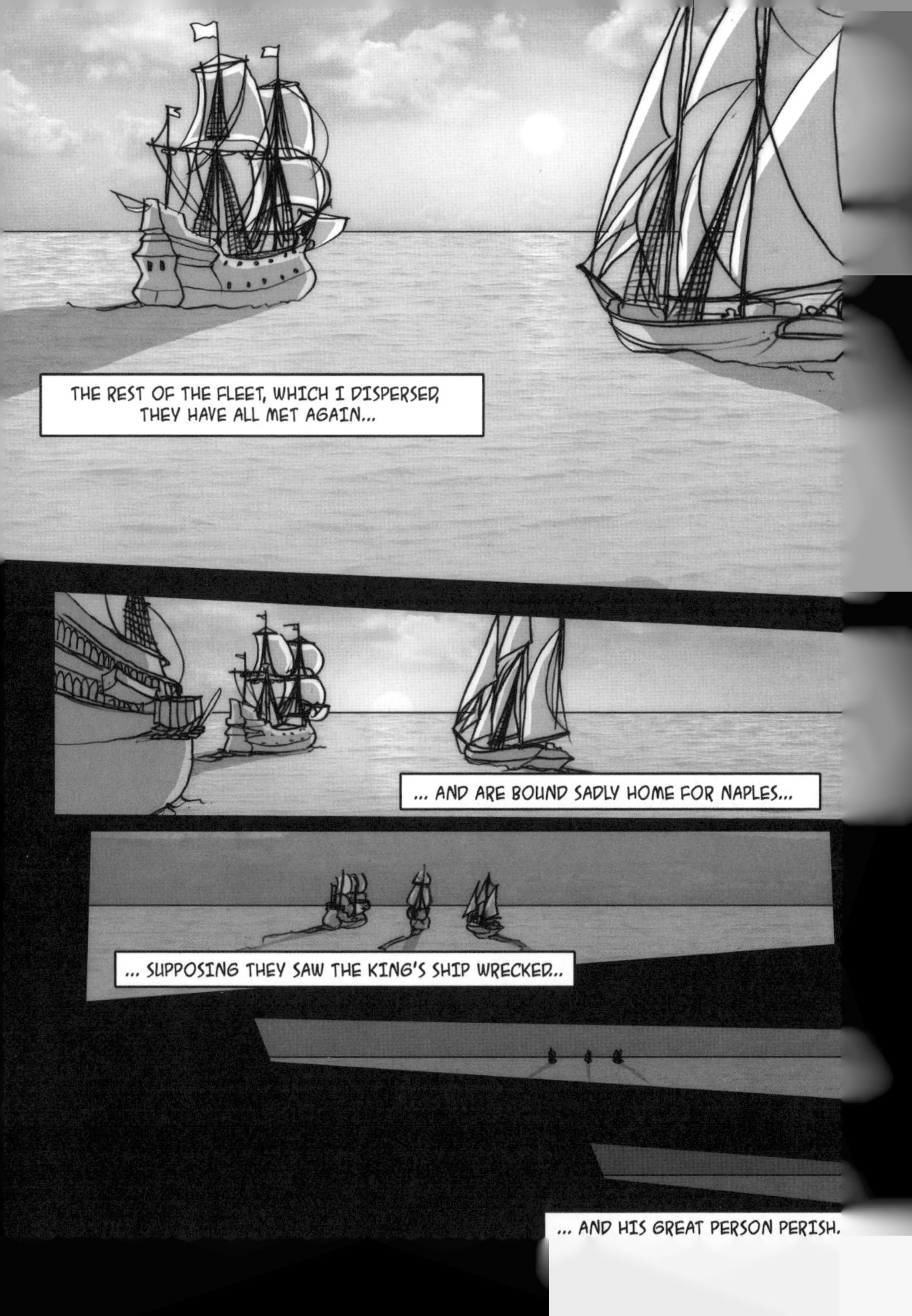
THE REST OF THE FLEET, WHICH I DISPERSED, THEY HAVE ALL MET AGAIN...
... AND ARE BOUND SADLY HOME FOR NAPLES...
... SUPPOSING THEY SAW THE KING'S SHIP WRECKED...
... AND HIS GREAT PERSON PERISH.

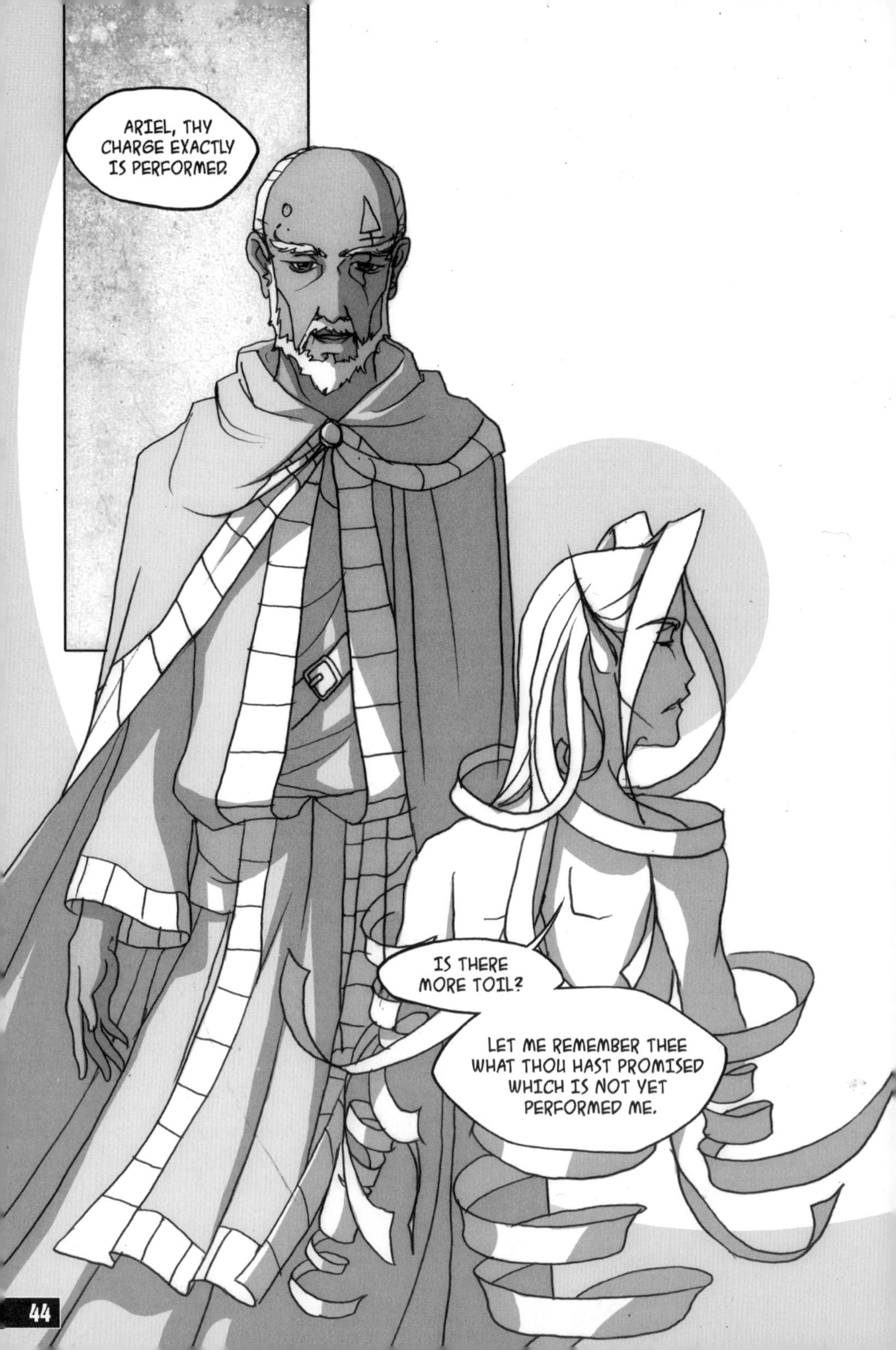
ARIEL, THY CHARGE EXACTLY IS PERFORMED.
IS THERE MORE TOIL?
LET ME REMEMBER THEE WHAT THOU HAST PROMISED WHICH IS NOT YET PERFORMED ME.

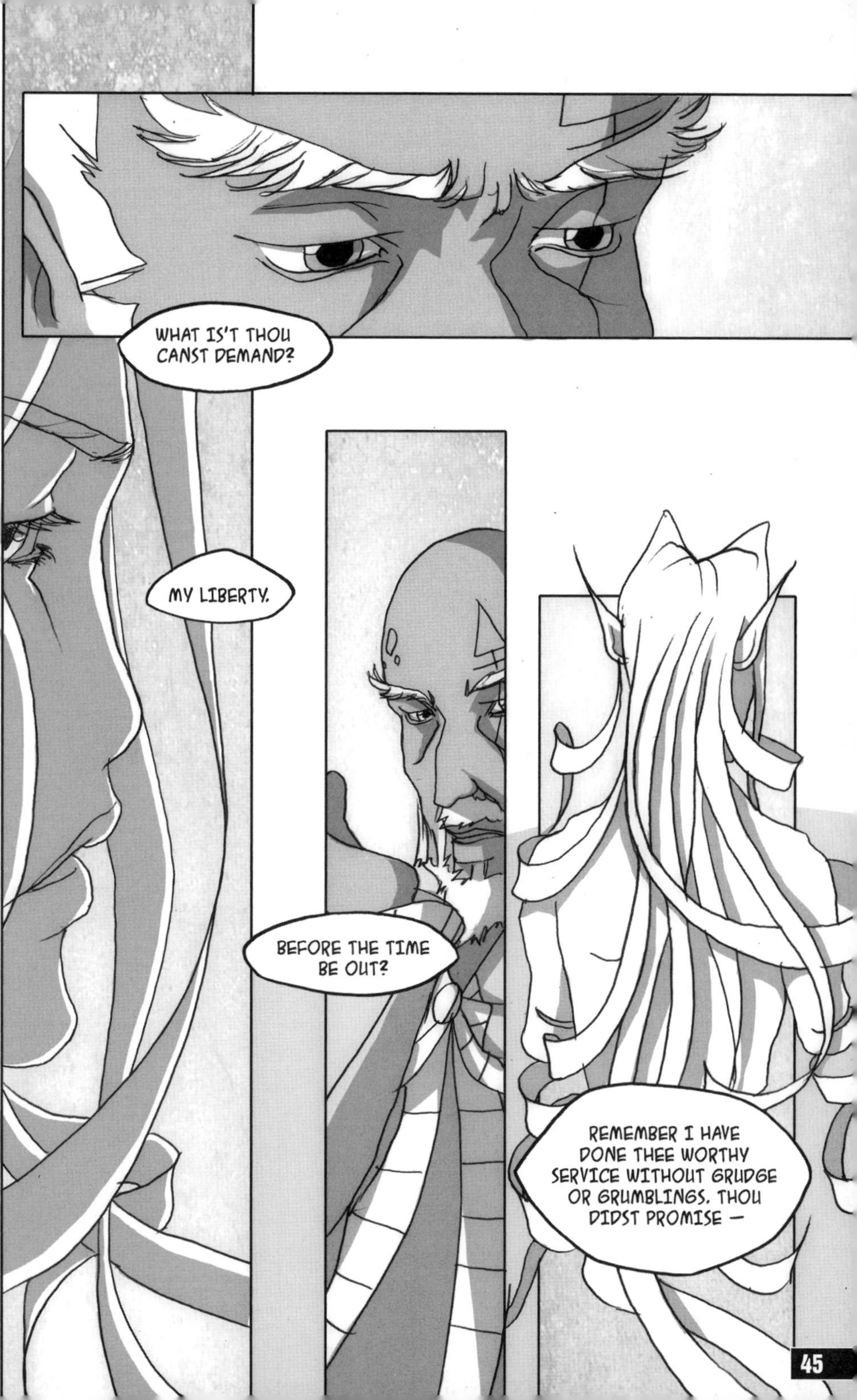
WHAT IS'T THOU CANST DEMAND?
MY LIBERTY.
BEFORE THE TIME BE OUT?
REMEMBER I HAVE DONE THEE WORTHY SERVICE WITHOUT GRUDGE OR GRUMBLINGS. THOU DIDST PROMISE —

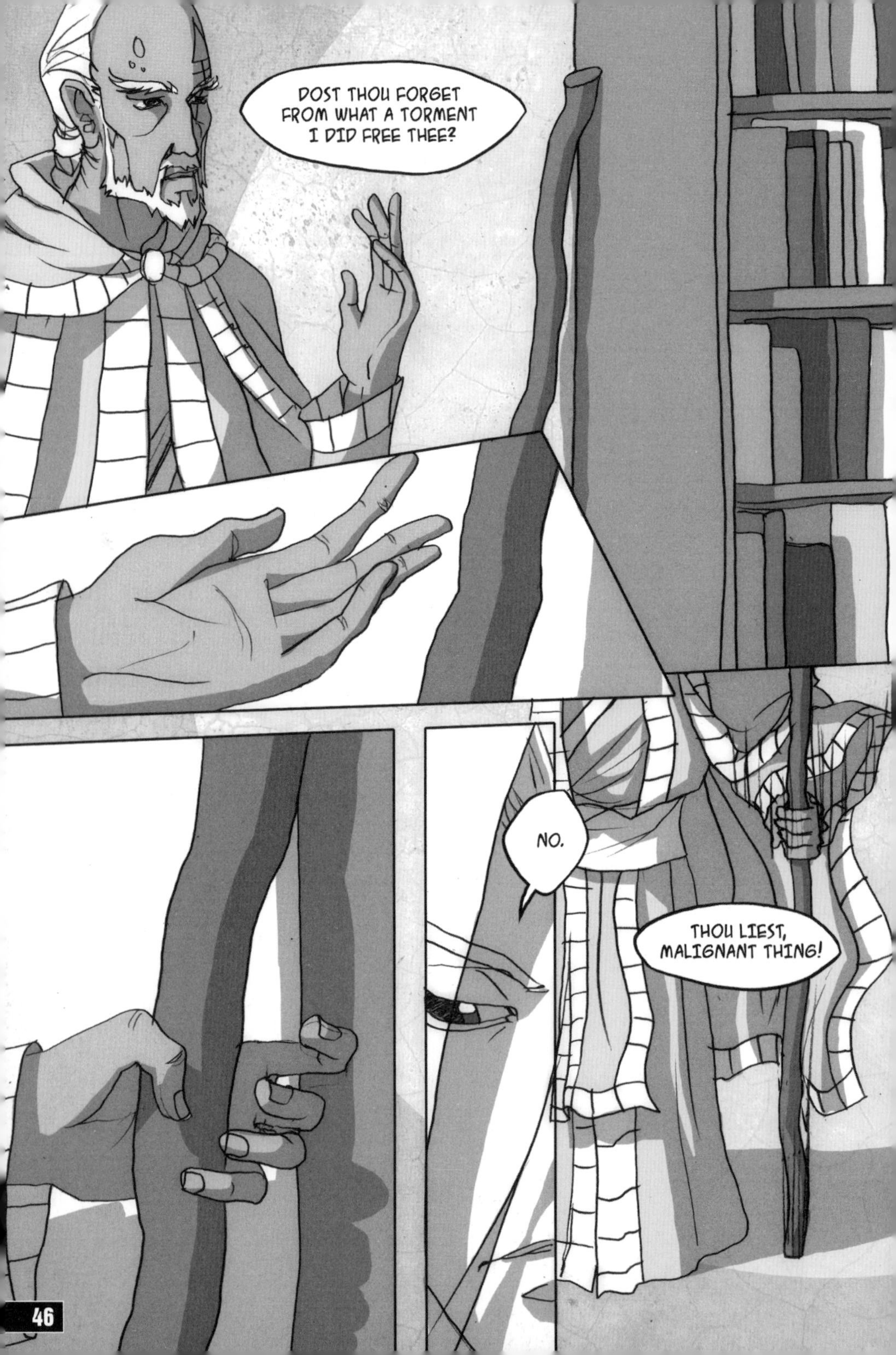
DOST THOU FORGET
FROM WHAT A TORMENT
I DID FREE THEE?
NO.
THOU LIEST,
MALIGNANT THING!

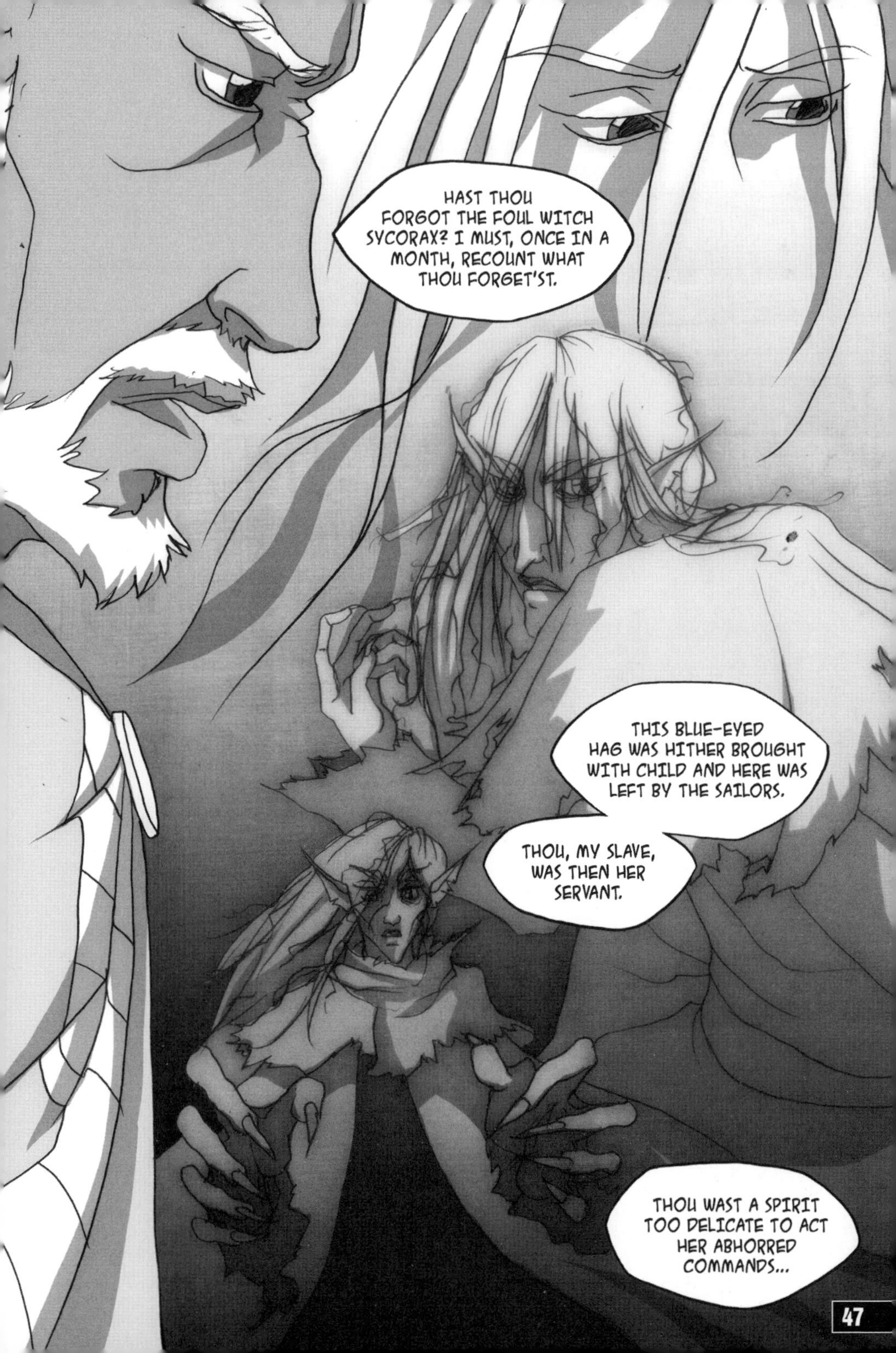
HAST THOU FORGOT THE FOUL WITCH SYCORAX? I MUST, ONCE IN A MONTH, RECOUNT WHAT THOU FORGET'ST.
THIS BLUE-EYED HAG WAS HITHER BROUGHT WITH CHILD AND HERE WAS LEFT BY THE SAILORS.
THOU, MY SLAVE, WAS THEN HER SERVANT.
THOU WAST A SPIRIT TOO DELICATE TO ACT HER ABHORRED COMMANDS...

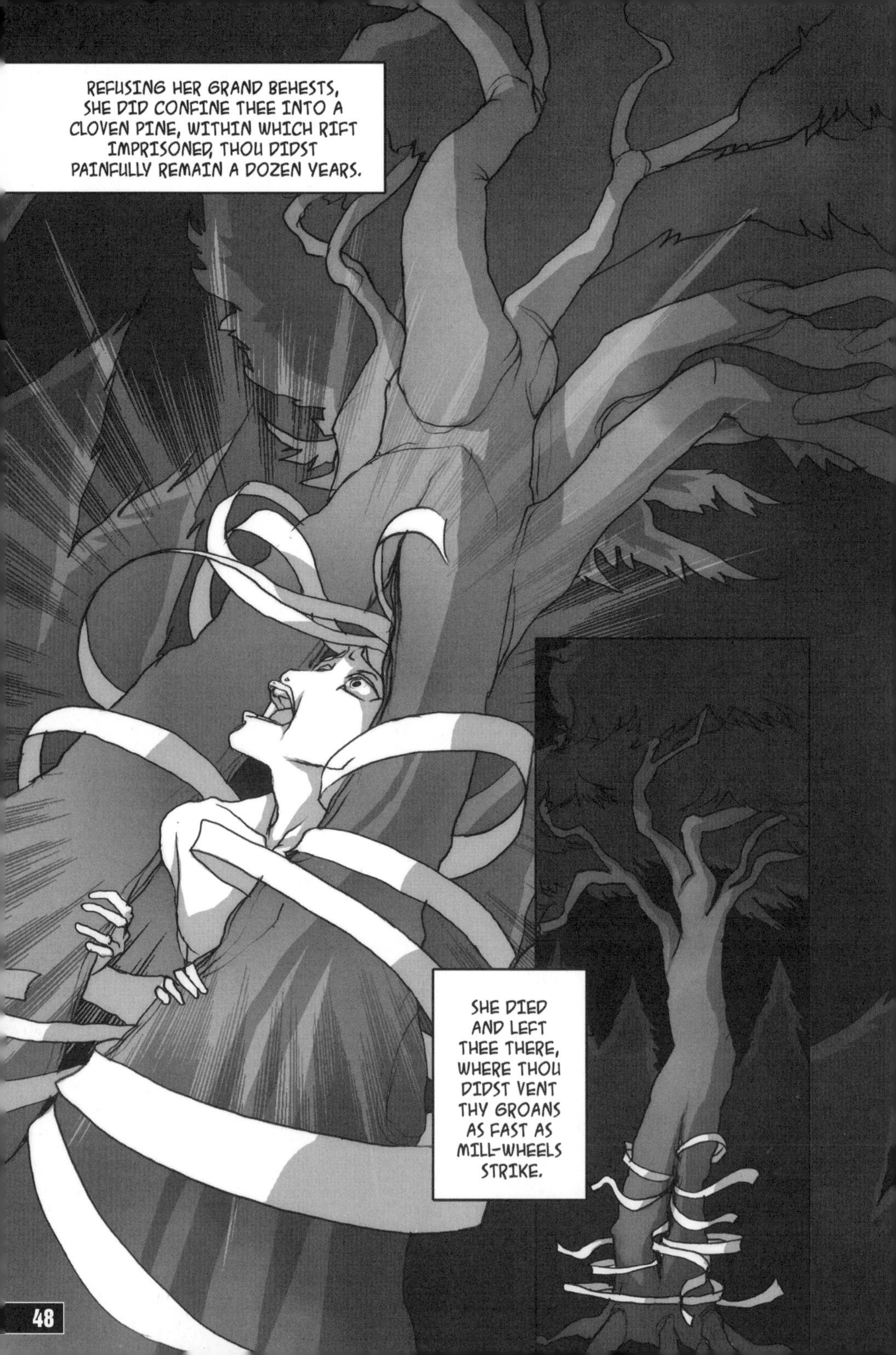
REFUSING HER GRAND BEHESTS, SHE DID CONFINE THEE INTO A CLOVEN PINE, WITHIN WHICH RIFT IMPRISONED, THOU DIDST PAINFULLY REMAIN A DOZEN YEARS.
SHE DIED AND LEFT THEE THERE, WHERE THOU DIDST VENT THY GROANS AS FAST AS MILL-WHEELS STRIKE.

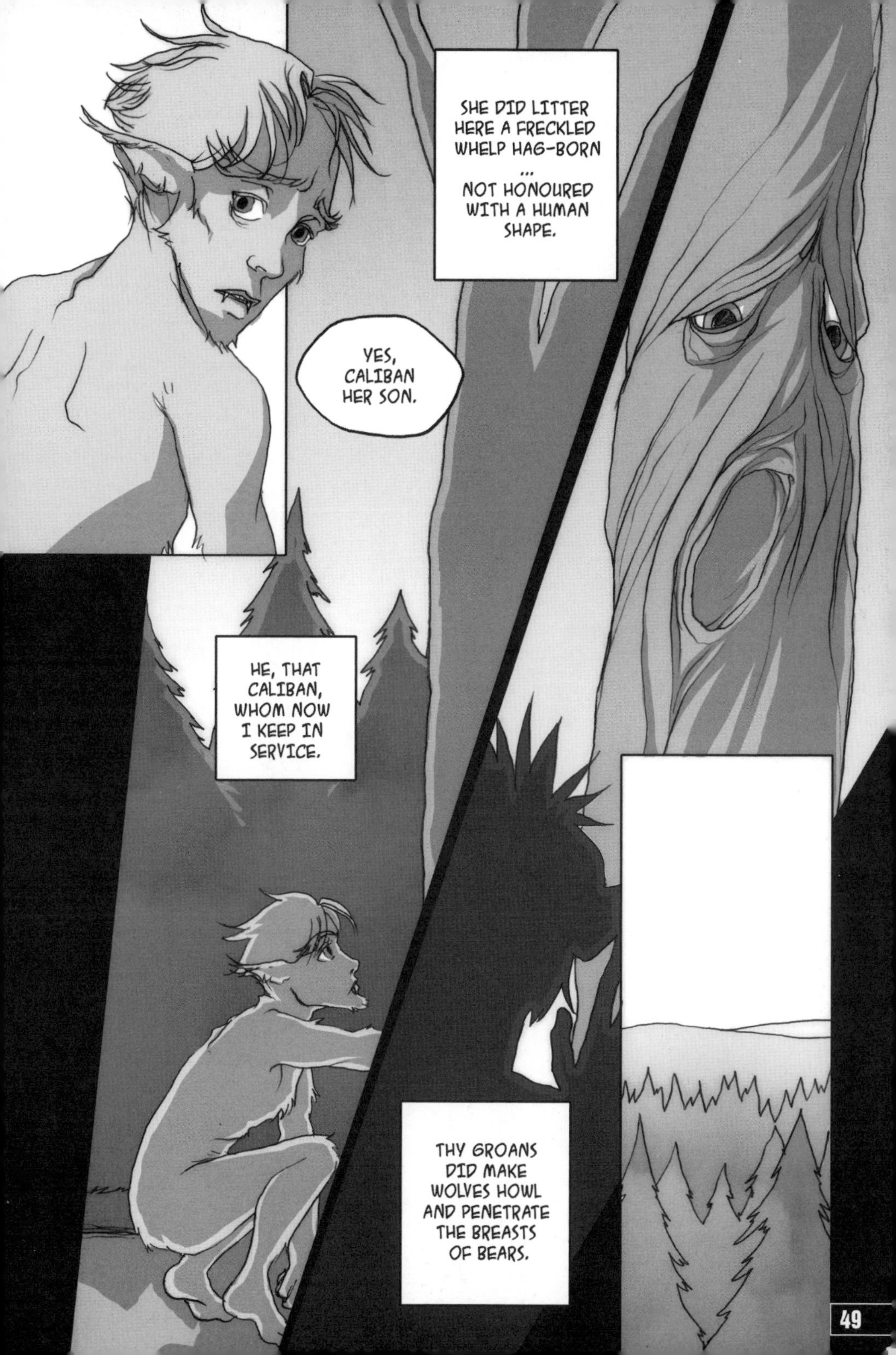
SHE DID LITTER HERE A FRECKLED WHELP HAG-BORN ... NOT HONOURED WITH A HUMAN SHAPE.
YES, CALIBAN HER SON.
HE, THAT CALIBAN, WHOM NOW I KEEP IN SERVICE.
THY GROANS DID MAKE WOLVES HOWL AND PENETRATE THE BREASTS OF BEARS.

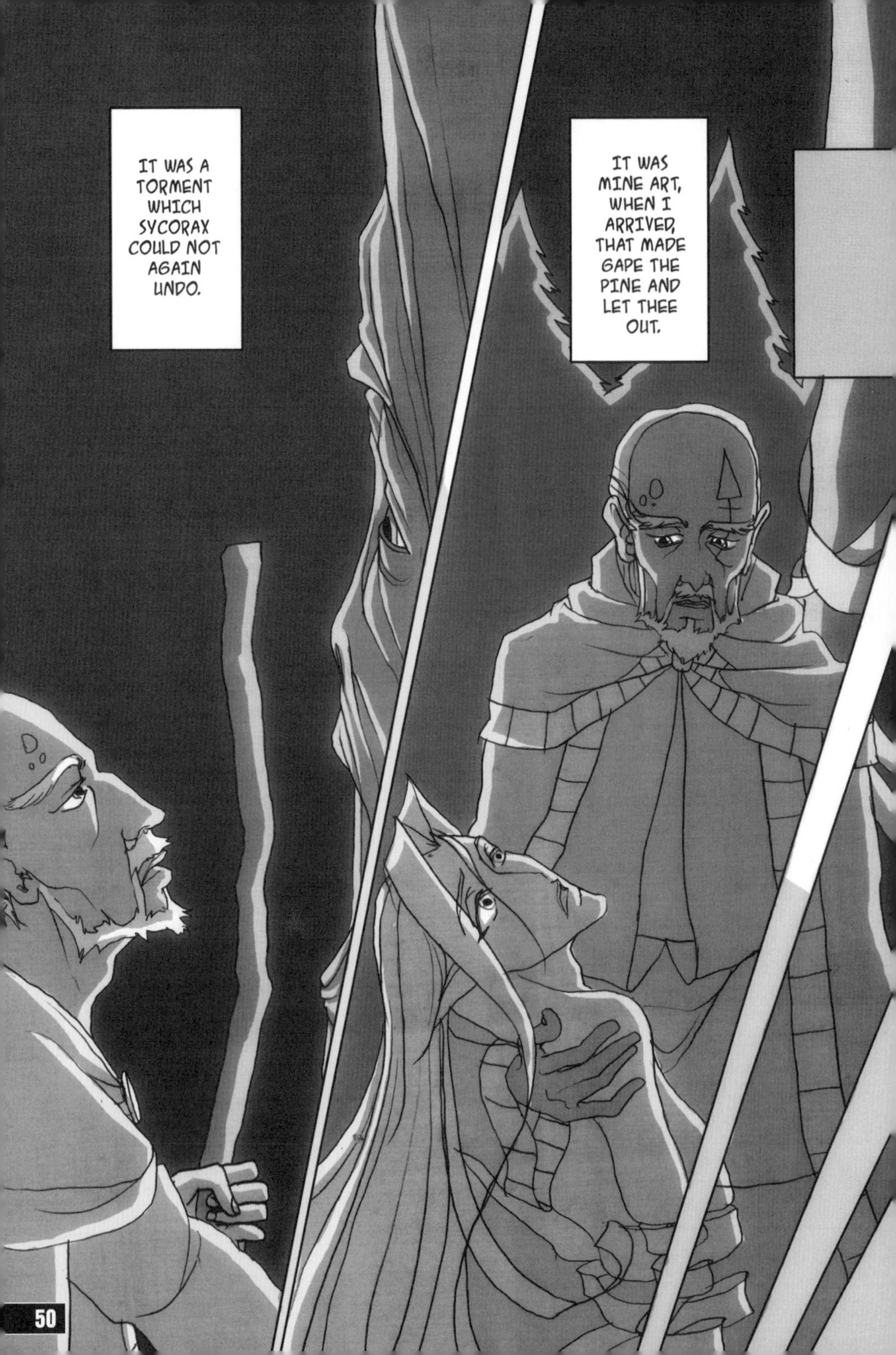
IT WAS A TORMENT WHICH SYCORAX COULD NOT AGAIN UNDO.
IT WAS MINE ART, WHEN I ARRIVED, THAT MADE GAPE THE PINE AND LET THEE OUT.

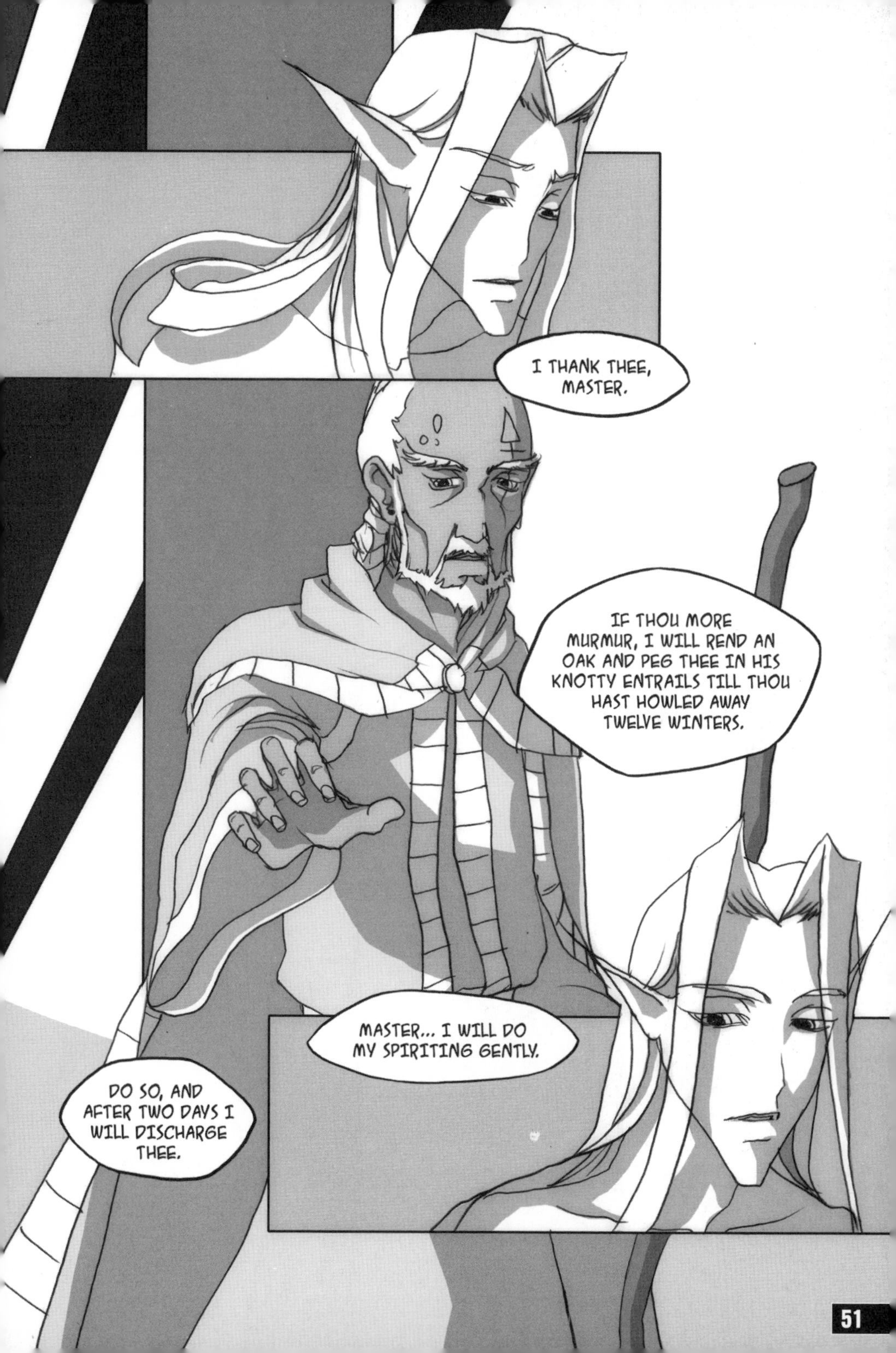
I THANK THEE, MASTER.
IF THOU MORE MURMUR, I WILL REND AN OAK AND PEG THEE IN HIS KNOTTY ENTRAILS TILL THOU HAST HOWLED AWAY TWELVE WINTERS.
MASTER... I WILL DO MY SPIRITING GENTLY.
DO SO, AND AFTER TWO DAYS I WILL DISCHARGE THEE.

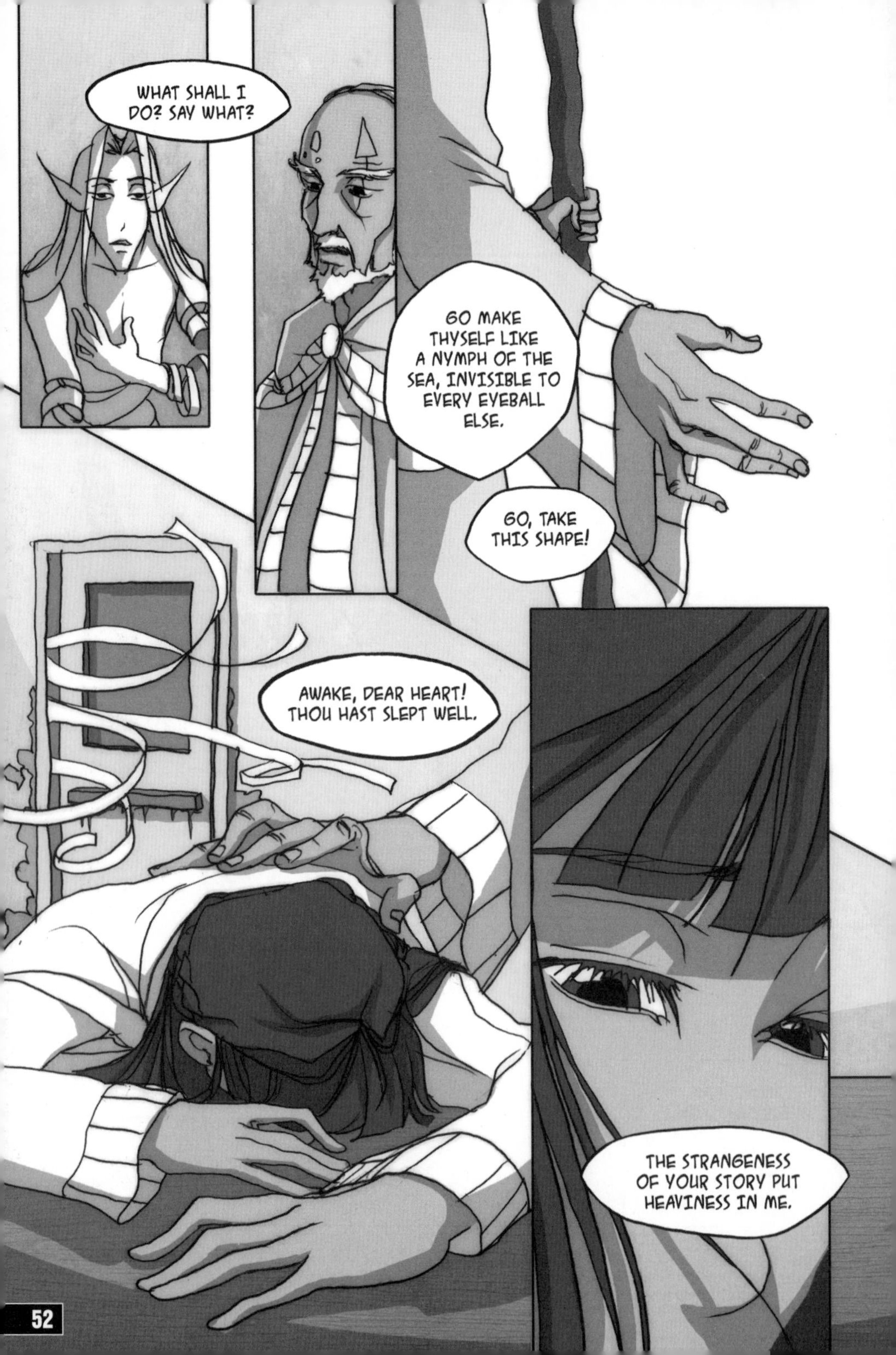
WHAT SHALL I DO? SAY WHAT?
GO MAKE THYSELF LIKE A NYMPH OF THE SEA, INVISIBLE TO EVERY EYEBALL ELSE.
GO, TAKE THIS SHAPE!
AWAKE, DEAR HEART! THOU HAST SLEPT WELL.
THE STRANGENESS OF YOUR STORY PUT HEAVINESS IN ME.

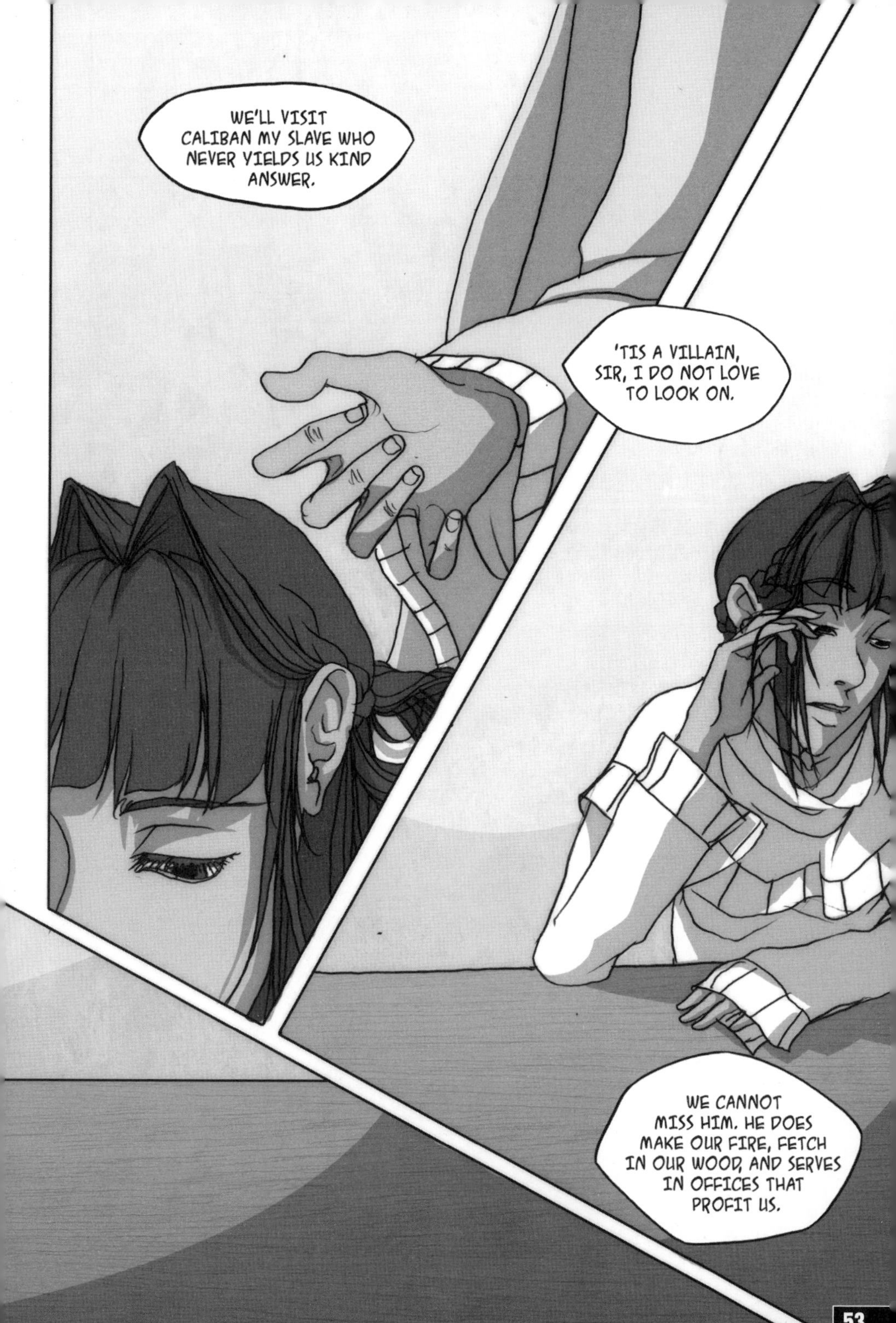
WE'LL VISIT CALIBAN MY SLAVE WHO NEVER YIELDS US KIND ANSWER.
'TIS A VILLAIN, SIR, I DO NOT LOVE TO LOOK ON.
WE CANNOT MISS HIM. HE DOES MAKE OUR FIRE, FETCH IN OUR WOOD, AND SERVES IN OFFICES THAT PROFIT US.

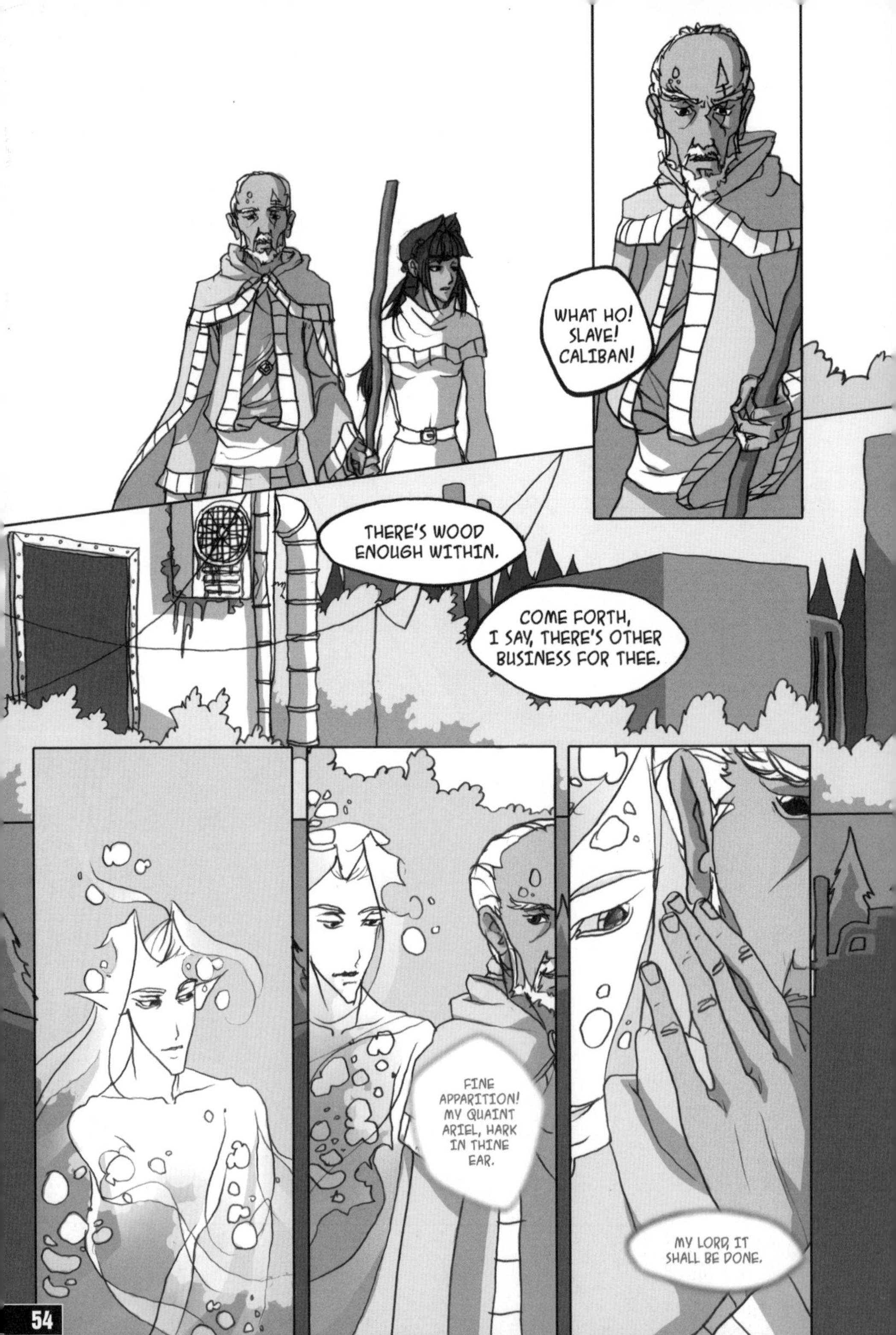
WHAT HO! SLAVE! CALIBAN!
THERE'S WOOD ENOUGH WITHIN.
COME FORTH, I SAY, THERE'S OTHER BUSINESS FOR THEE.
FINE APPARITION! MY QUAINT ARIEL, HARK IN THINE EAR.
MY LORD, IT SHALL BE DONE.

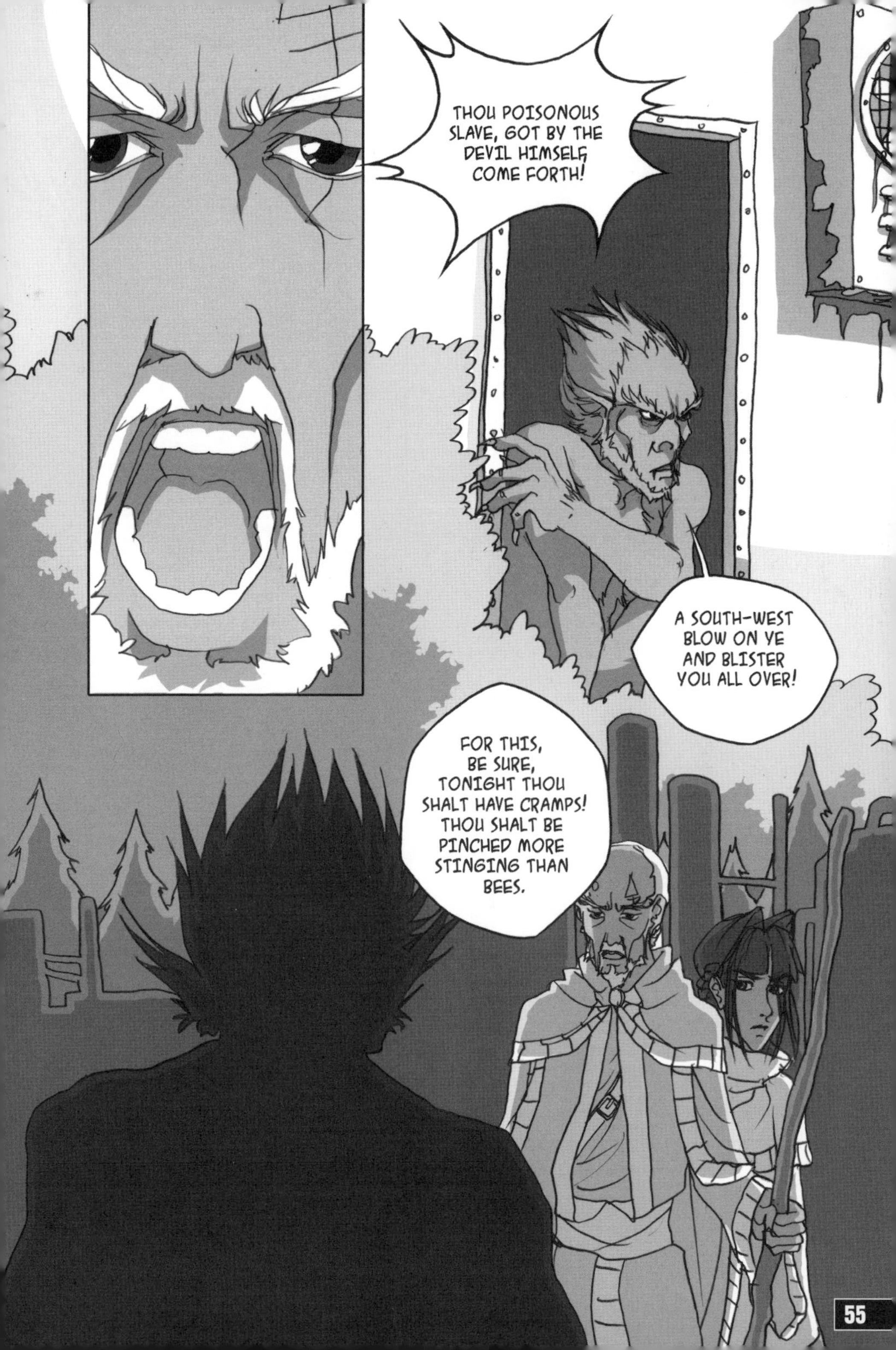
THOU POISONOUS SLAVE, GOT BY THE DEVIL HIMSELF, COME FORTH!
A SOUTH-WEST BLOW ON YE AND BLISTER YOU ALL OVER!
FOR THIS, BE SURE, TONIGHT THOU SHALT HAVE CRAMPS! THOU SHALT BE PINCHED MORE STINGING THAN BEES.

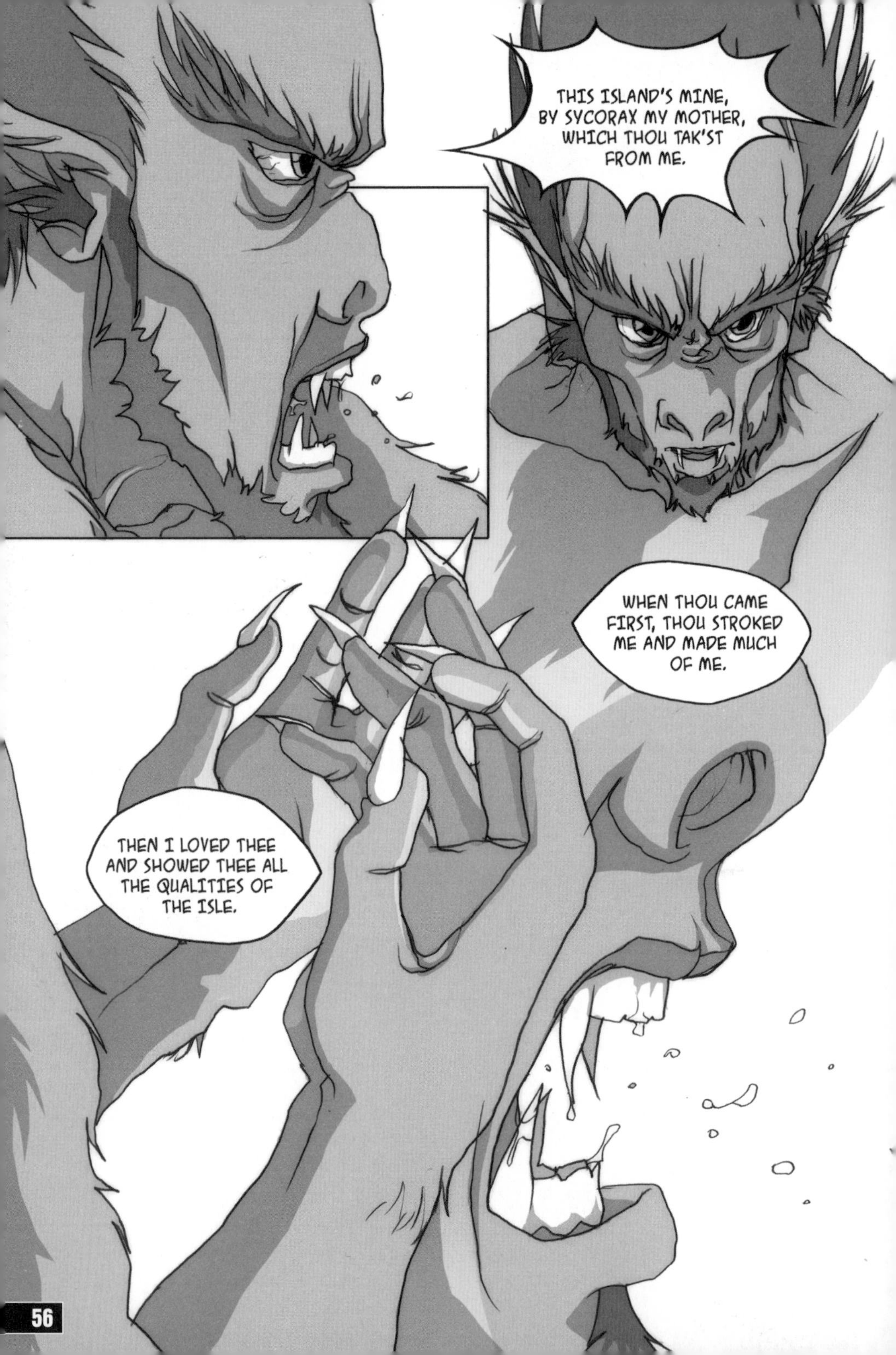
THIS ISLAND'S MINE, BY SYCORAX MY MOTHER, WHICH THOU TAK'ST FROM ME.
WHEN THOU CAME FIRST, THOU STROKED ME AND MADE MUCH OF ME.
THEN I LOVED THEE AND SHOWED THEE ALL THE QUALITIES OF THE ISLE.

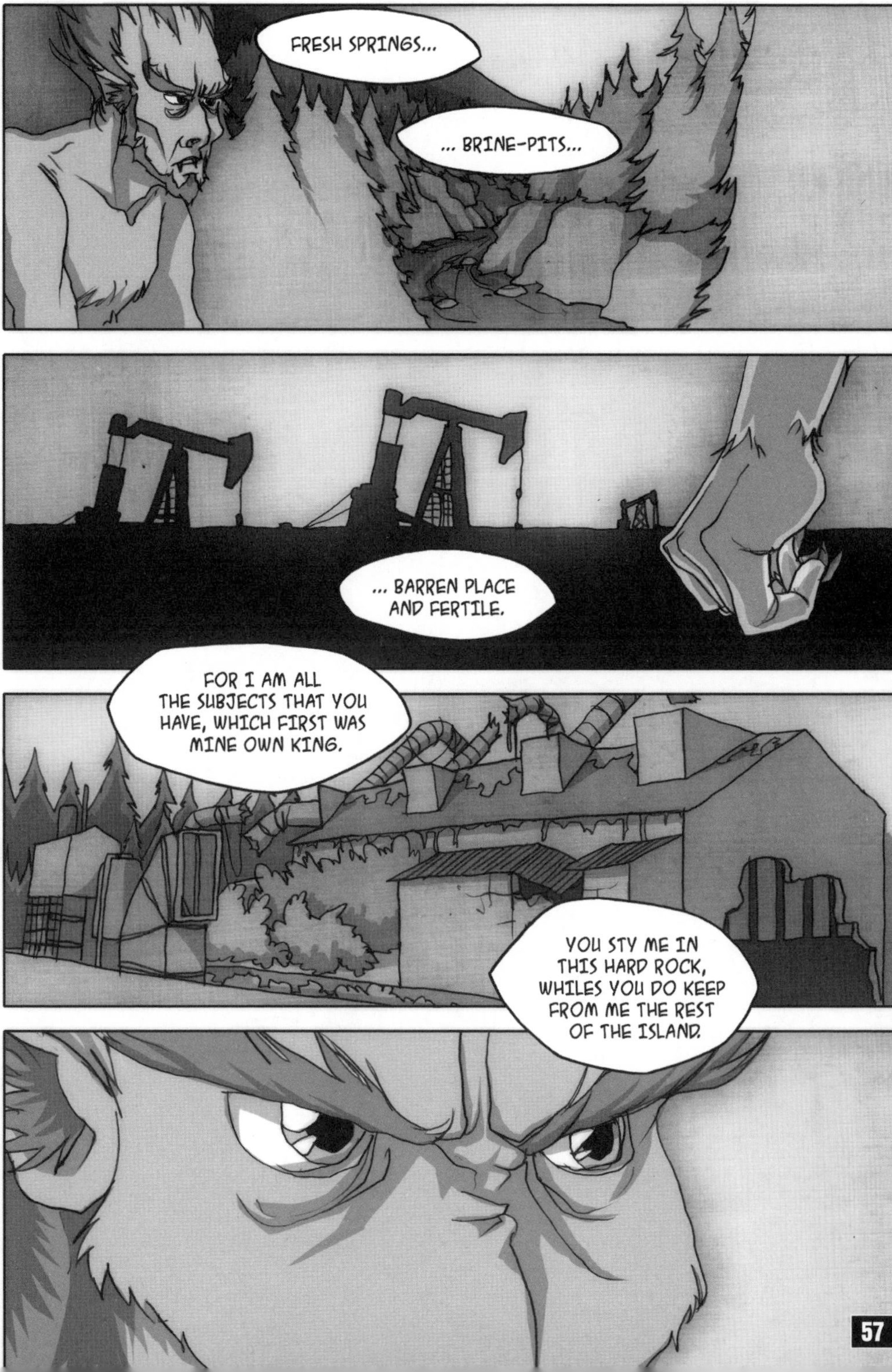
FRESH SPRINGS...
... BRINE-PITS...
... BARREN PLACE AND FERTILE.
FOR I AM ALL THE SUBJECTS THAT YOU HAVE, WHICH FIRST WAS MINE OWN KING.
YOU STY ME IN THIS HARD ROCK, WHILES YOU DO KEEP FROM ME THE REST OF THE ISLAND.

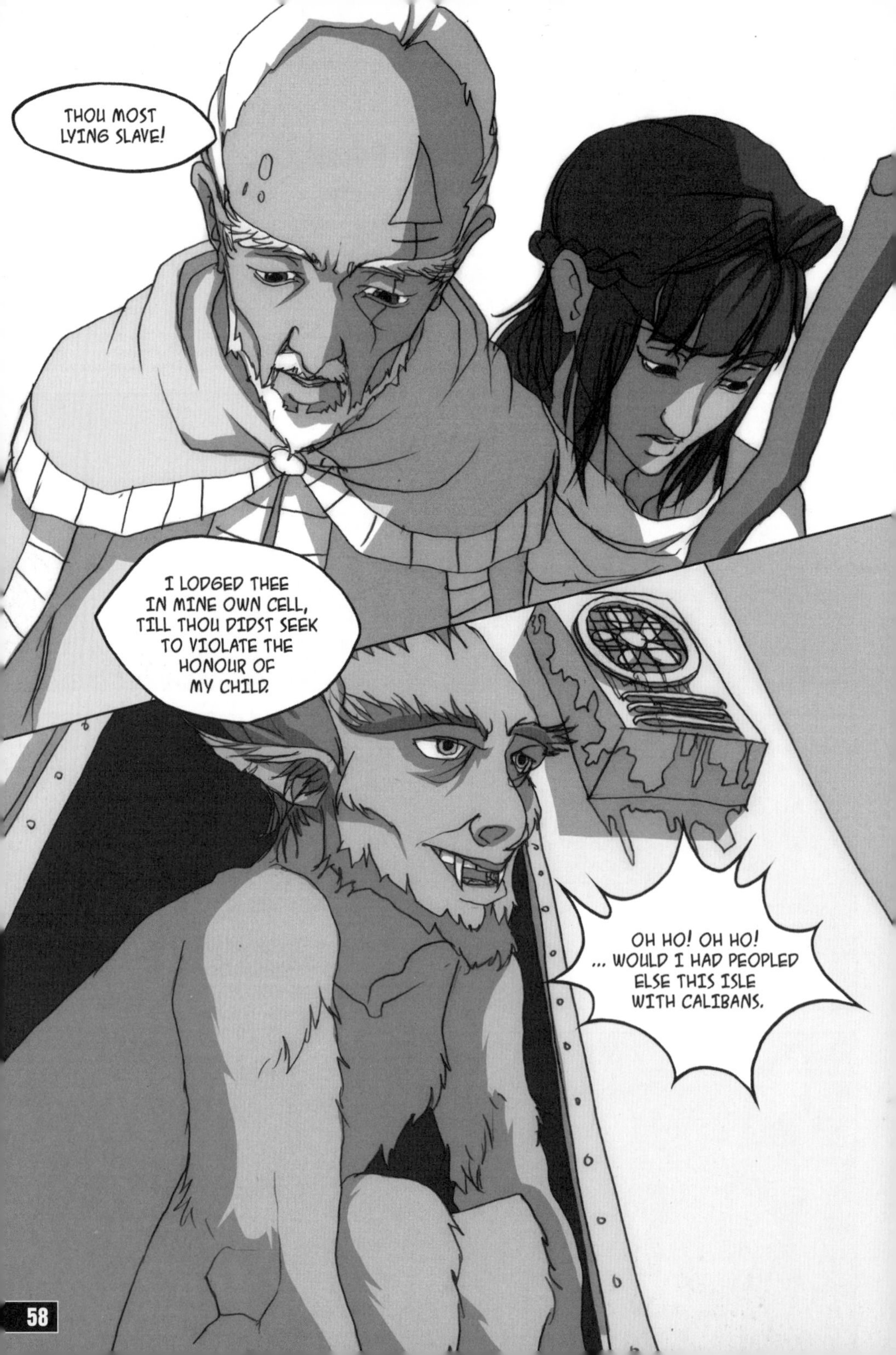
THOU MOST LYING SLAVE!
I LODGED THEE IN MINE OWN CELL, TILL THOU DIDST SEEK TO VIOLATE THE HONOUR OF MY CHILD.
OH HO! OH HO! ... WOULD I HAD PEOPLED ELSE THIS ISLE WITH CALIBANS.

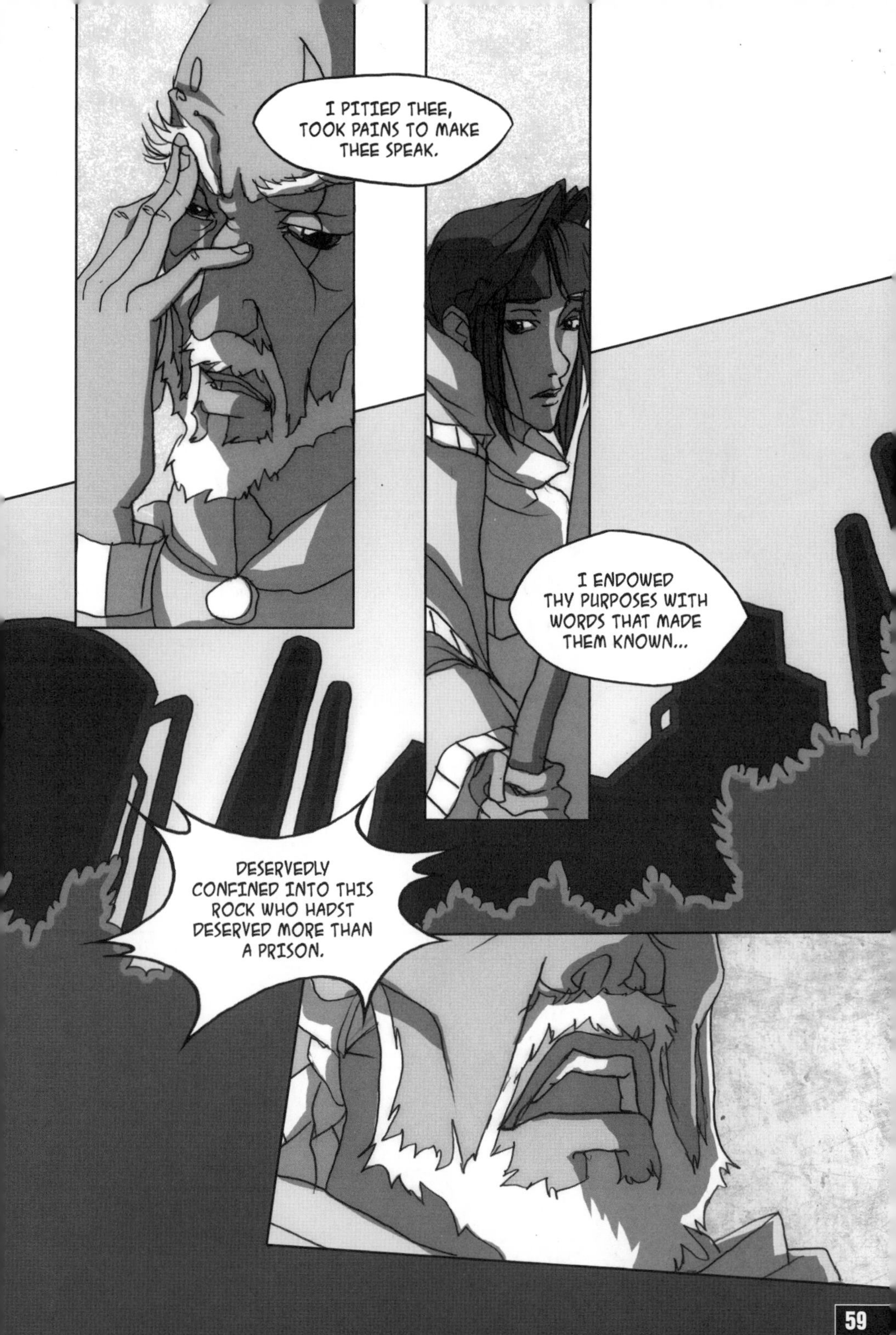
I PITIED THEE, TOOK PAINS TO MAKE THEE SPEAK.
I ENDOWED THY PURPOSES WITH WORDS THAT MADE THEM KNOWN...
DESERVEDLY CONFINED INTO THIS ROCK WHO HADST DESERVED MORE THAN A PRISON.

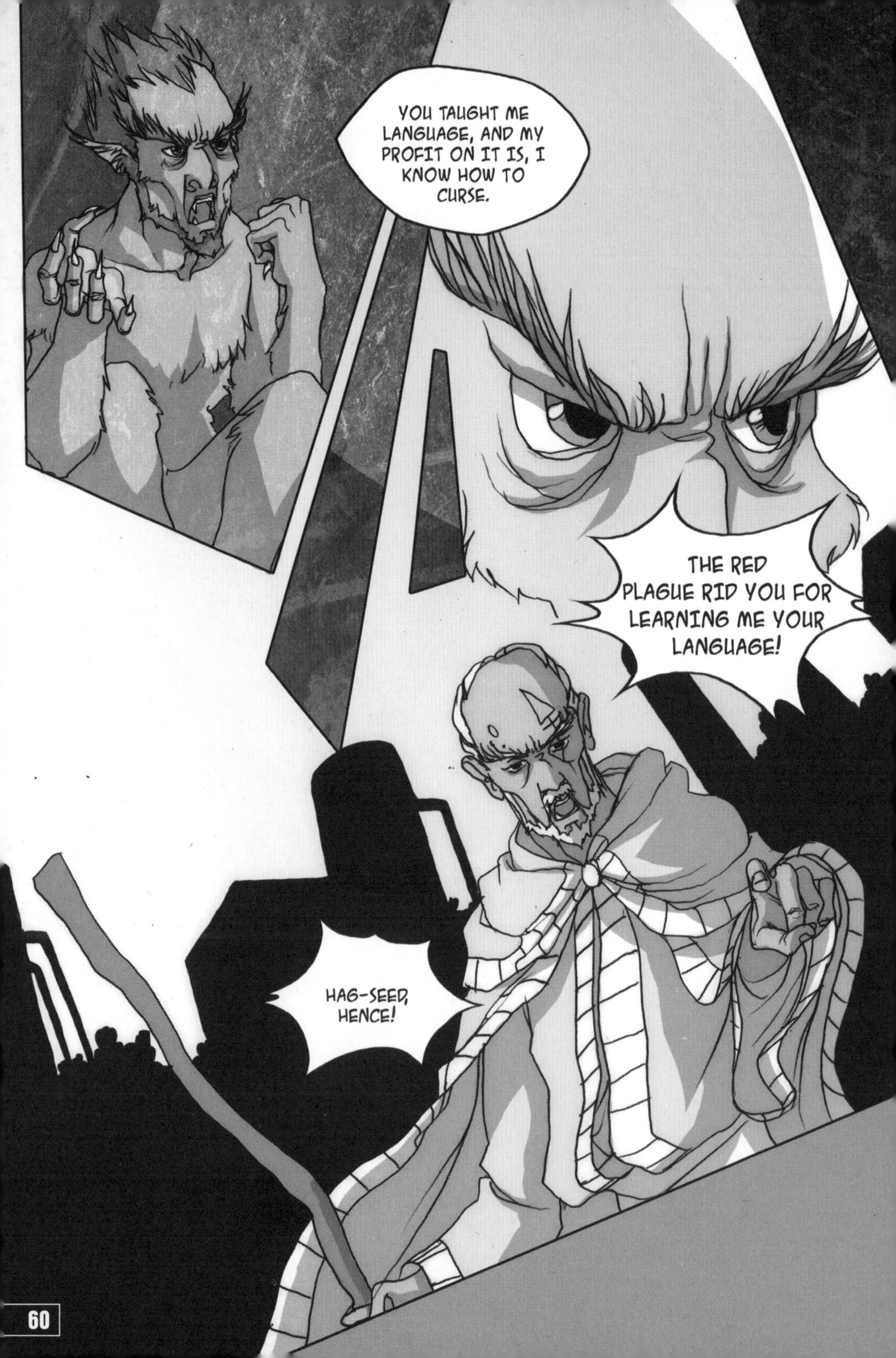
YOU TAUGHT ME LANGUAGE, AND MY PROFIT ON IT IS, I KNOW HOW TO CURSE.
THE RED PLAGUE RID YOU FOR LEARNING ME YOUR LANGUAGE!
HAG-SEED, HENCE!

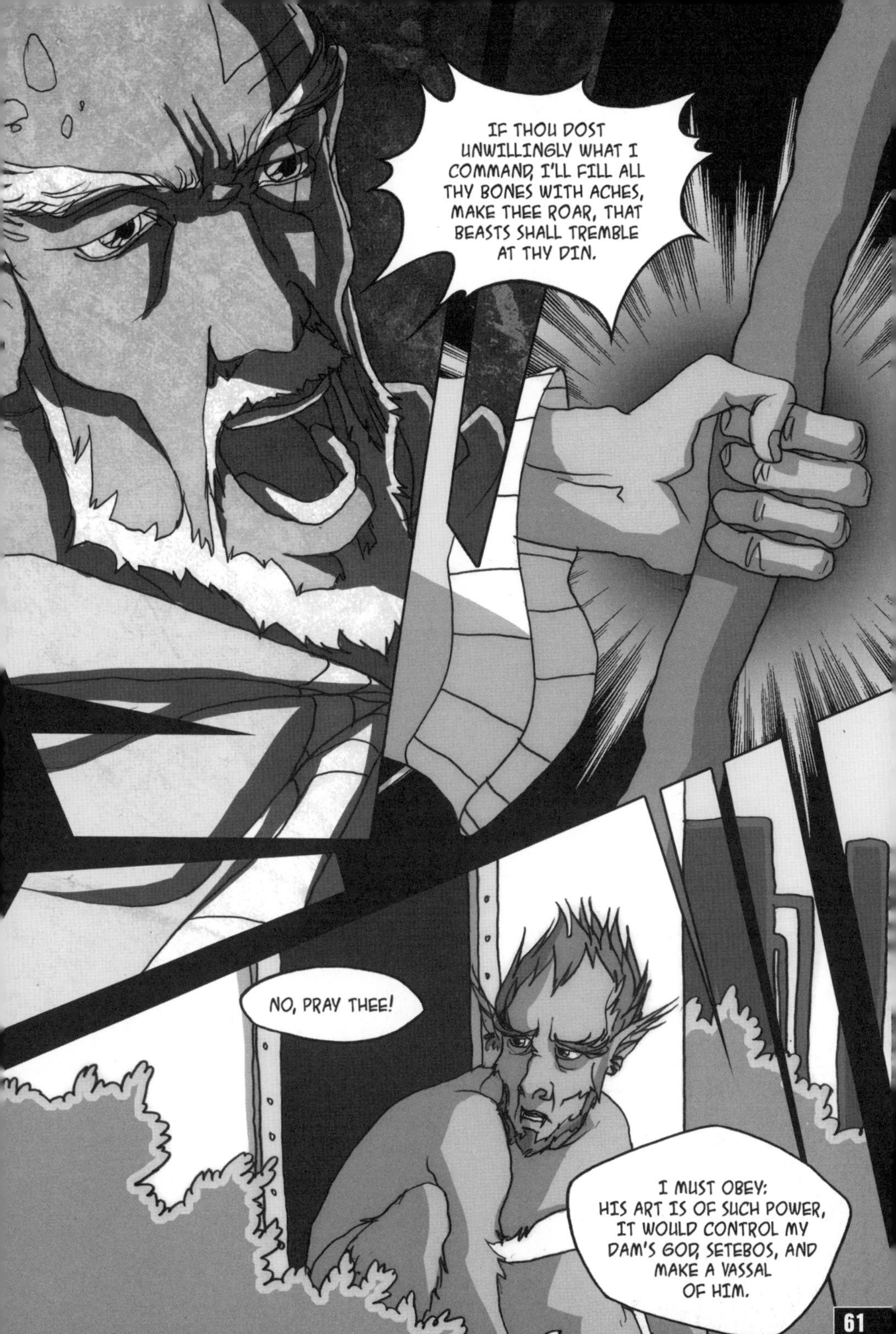
IF THOU DOST UNWILLINGLY WHAT I COMMAND, I'LL FILL ALL THY BONES WITH ACHES, MAKE THEE ROAR, THAT BEASTS SHALL TREMBLE AT THY DIN.
NO, PRAY THEE!
I MUST OBEY: HIS ART IS OF SUCH POWER, IT WOULD CONTROL MY DAM'S GOD, SETEBOS, AND MAKE A VASSAL OF HIM.

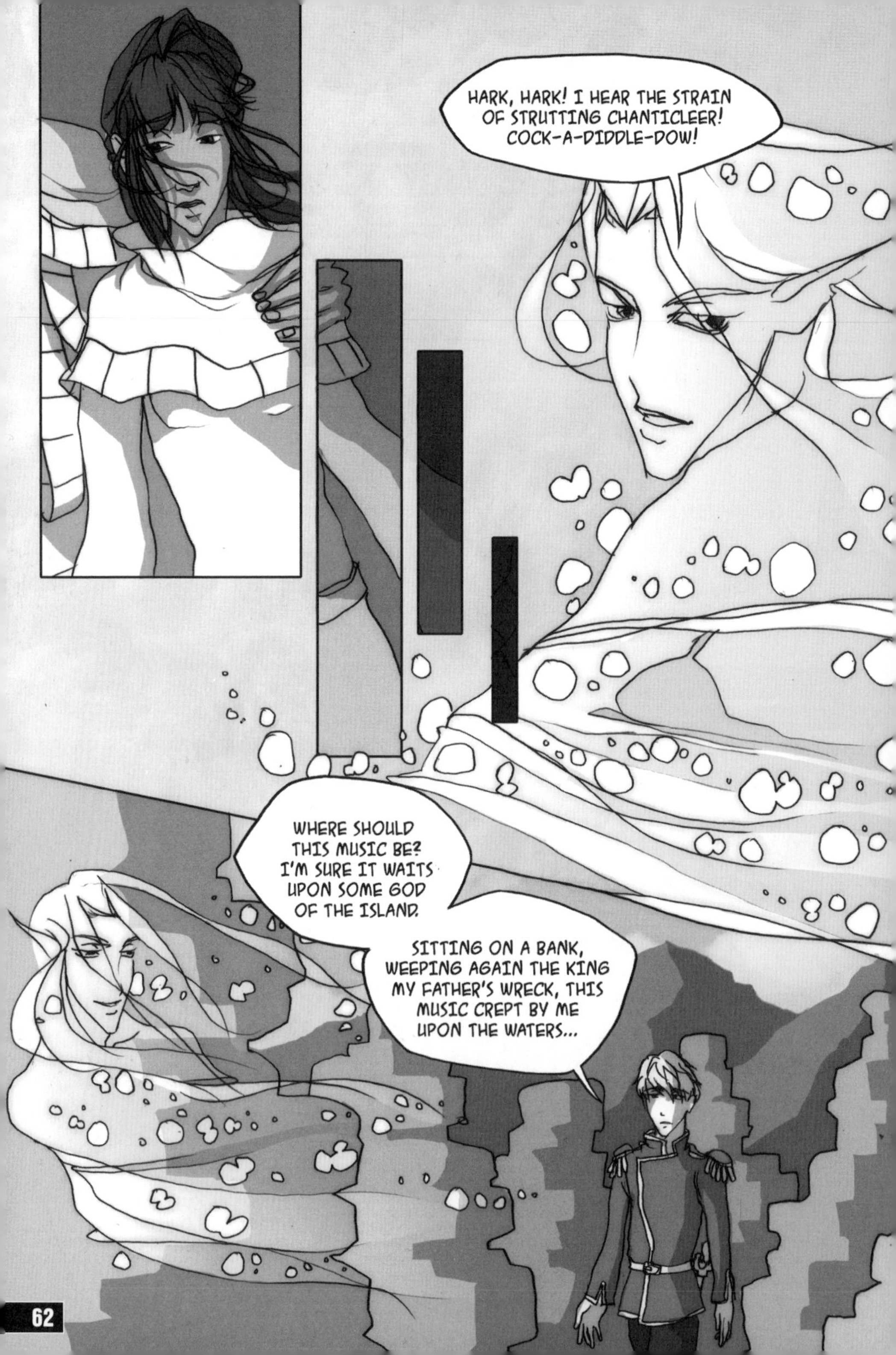
HARK, HARK! I HEAR THE STRAIN OF STRUTTING CHANTICLEER! COCK-A-DIDDLE-DOW!
WHERE SHOULD THIS MUSIC BE? I'M SURE IT WAITS UPON SOME GOD OF THE ISLAND.
SITTING ON A BANK, WEEPING AGAIN THE KING MY FATHER'S WRECK, THIS MUSIC CREPT BY ME UPON THE WATERS...

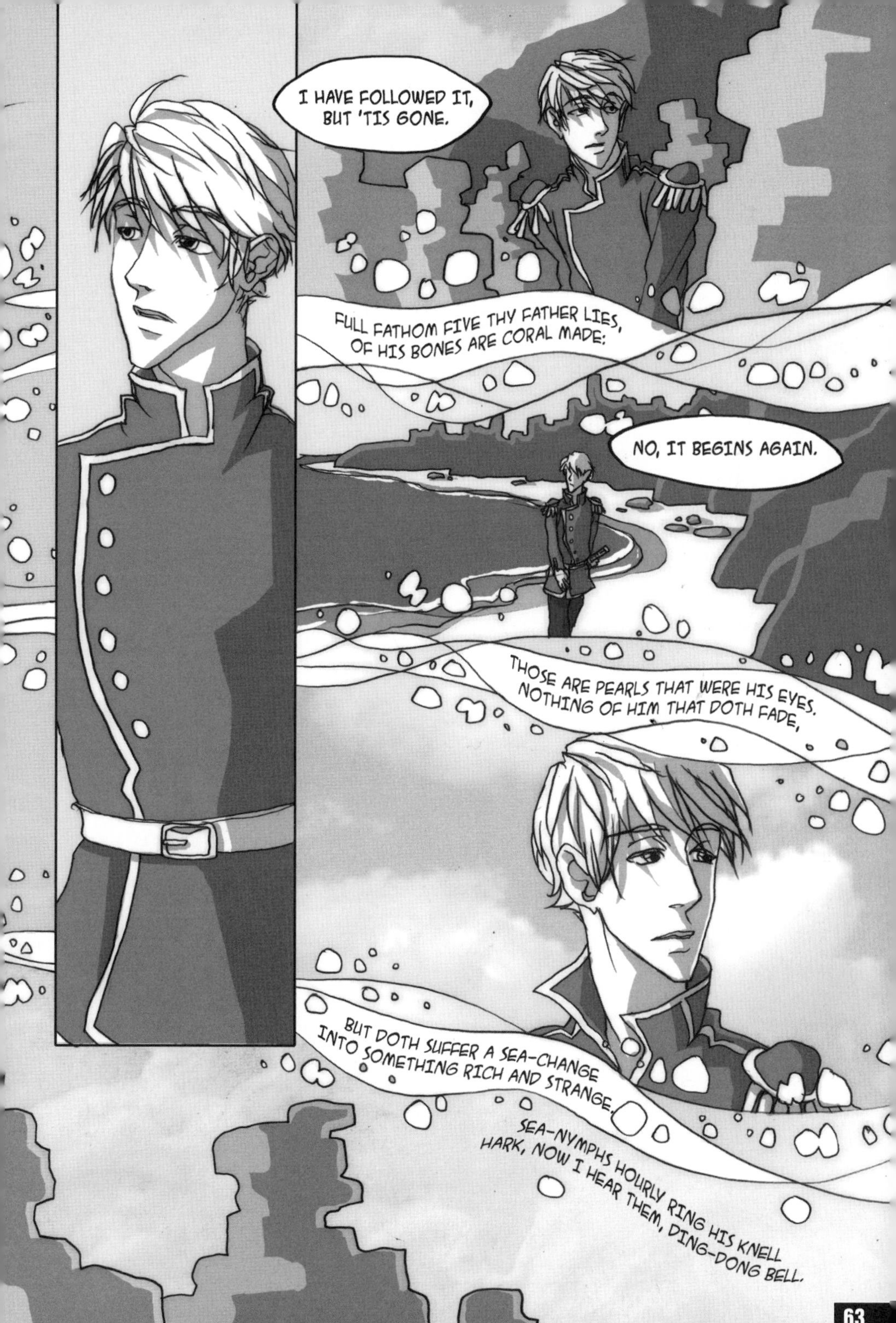
I HAVE FOLLOWED IT, BUT 'TIS GONE.
FULL FATHOM FIVE THY FATHER LIES, OF HIS BONES ARE CORAL MADE:
NO, IT BEGINS AGAIN.
THOSE ARE PEARLS THAT WERE HIS EYES. NOTHING OF HIM THAT DOTH FADE,
BUT DOTH SUFFER A SEA-CHANGE INTO SOMETHING RICH AND STRANGE.
SEA-NYMPHS HOURLY RING HIS KNELL HARK, NOW I HEAR THEM, DING-DONG BELL.

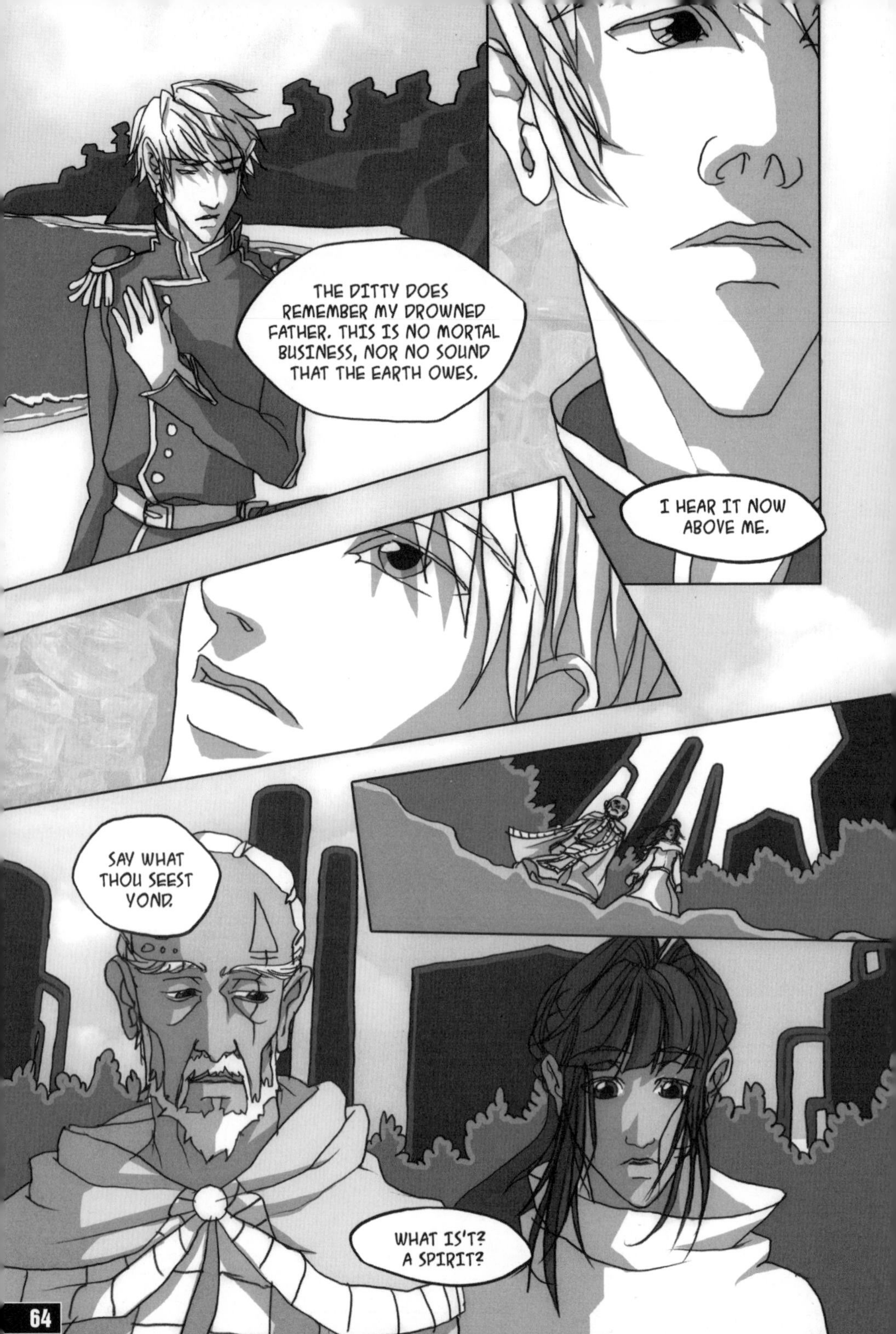
THE DITTY DOES REMEMBER MY DROWNED FATHER. THIS IS NO MORTAL BUSINESS, NOR NO SOUND THAT THE EARTH OWES.
I HEAR IT NOW ABOVE ME.
SAY WHAT THOU SEEST YOND.
WHAT IS'T? A SPIRIT?

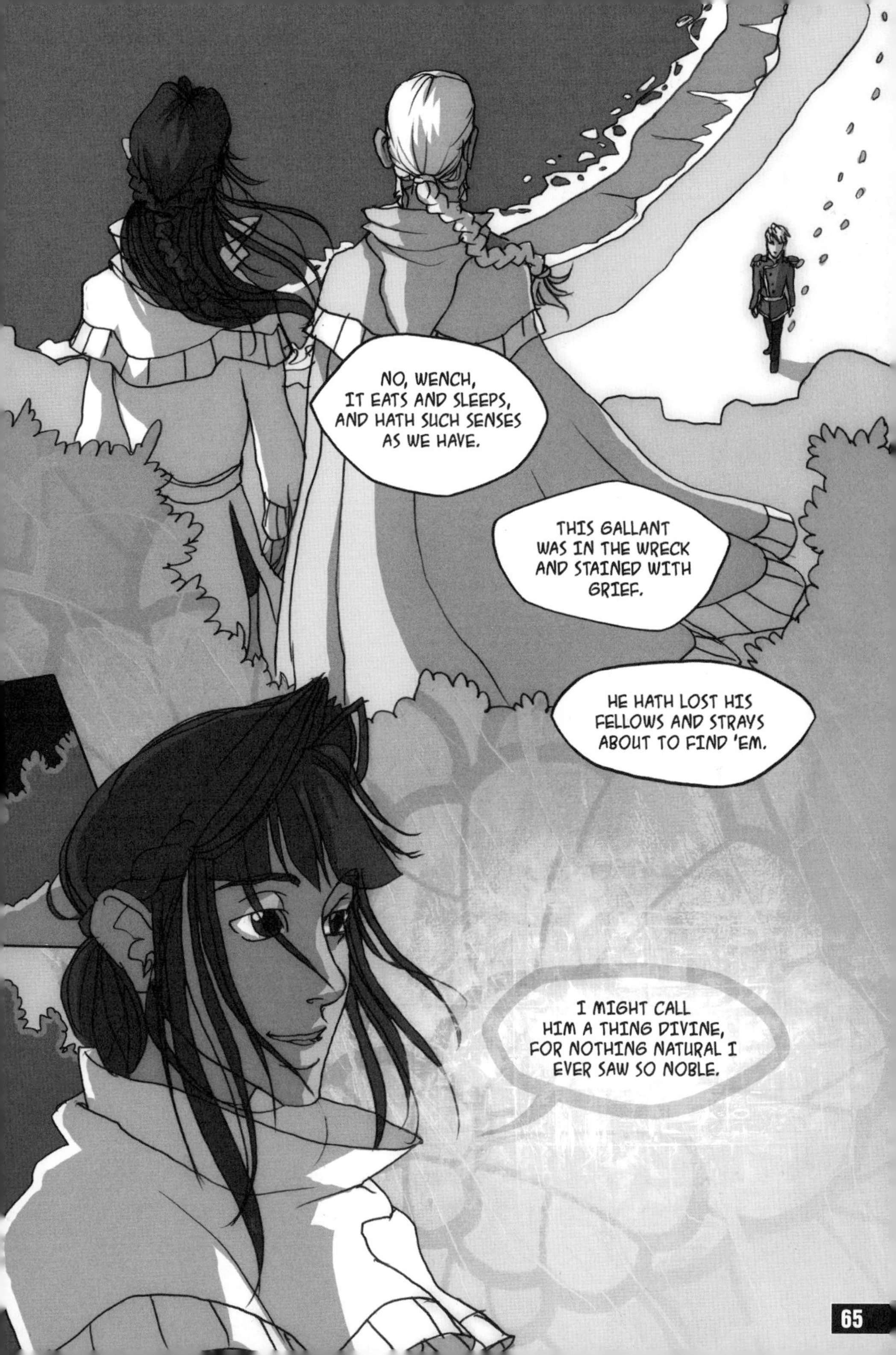
NO, WENCH, IT EATS AND SLEEPS, AND HATH SUCH SENSES AS WE HAVE.
THIS GALLANT WAS IN THE WRECK AND STAINED WITH GRIEF.
HE HATH LOST HIS FELLOWS AND STRAYS ABOUT TO FIND 'EM.
I MIGHT CALL HIM A THING DIVINE, FOR NOTHING NATURAL I EVER SAW SO NOBLE.

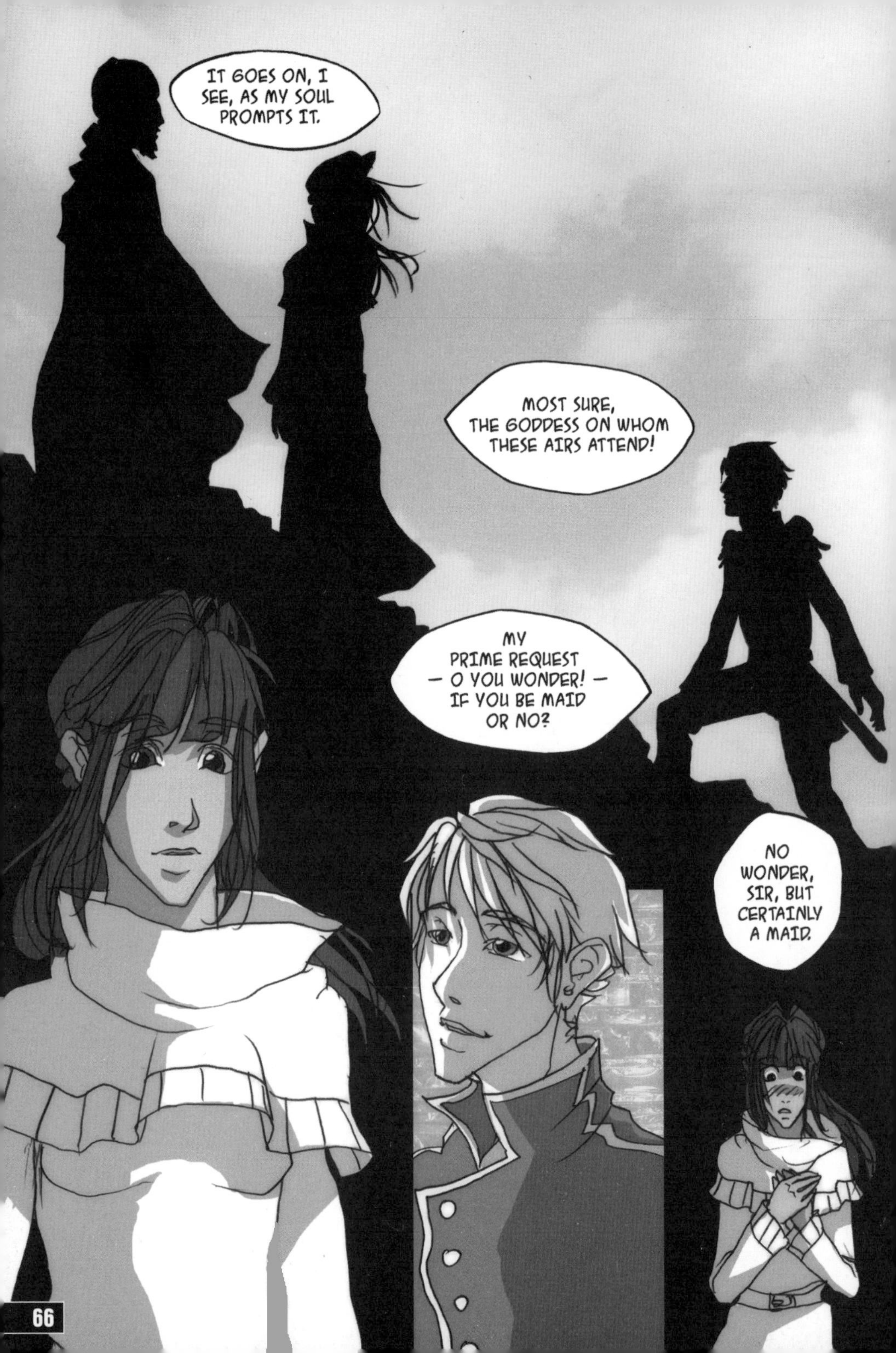
IT GOES ON, I SEE, AS MY SOUL PROMPTS IT.
MOST SURE, THE GODDESS ON WHOM THESE AIRS ATTEND!
MY PRIME REQUEST — O YOU WONDER! — IF YOU BE MAID OR NO?
NO WONDER, SIR, BUT CERTAINLY A MAID.

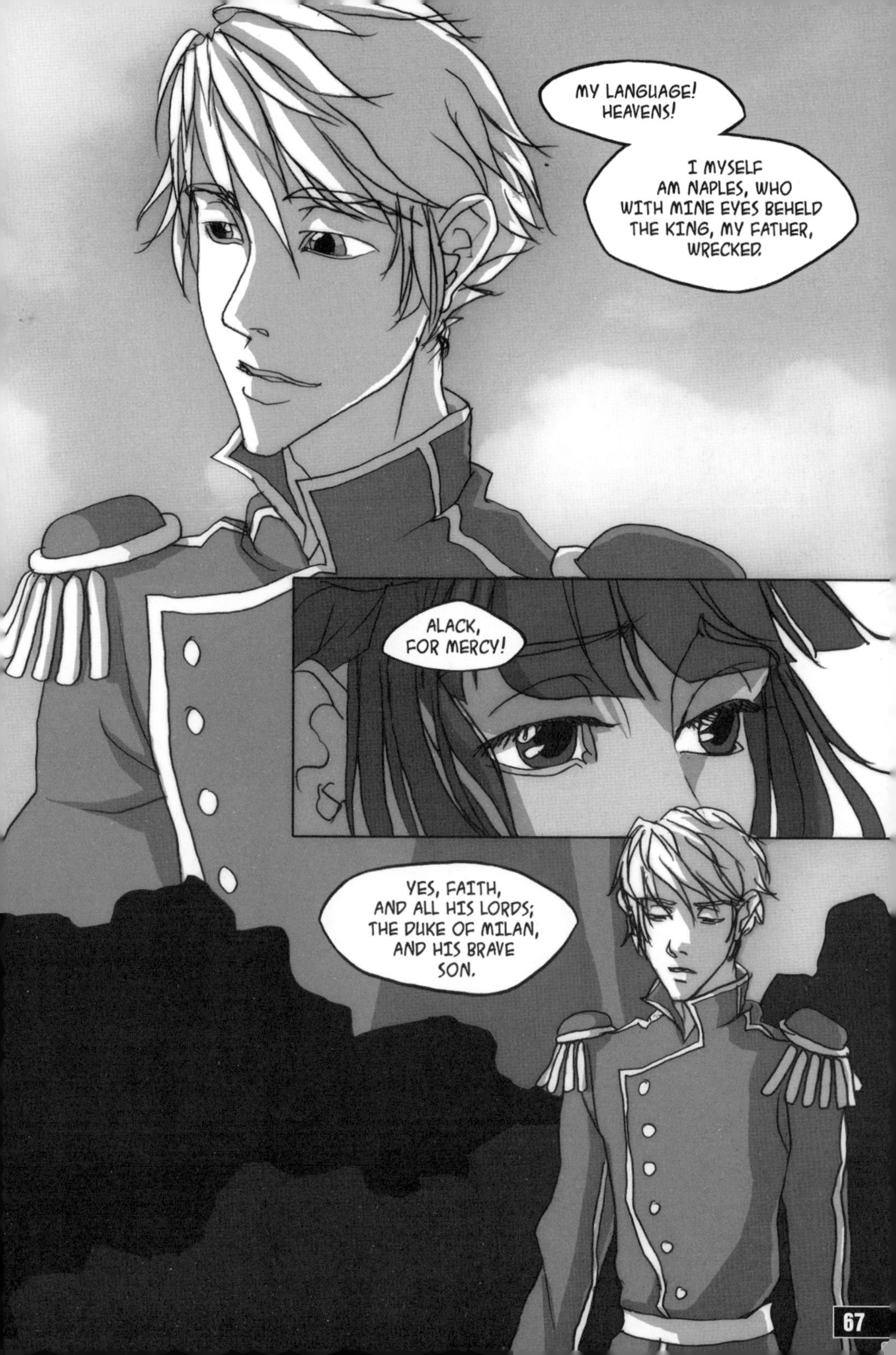
MY LANGUAGE! HEAVENS!
I MYSELF AM NAPLES, WHO WITH MINE EYES BEHELD THE KING, MY FATHER, WRECKED.
ALACK, FOR MERCY!
YES, FAITH, AND ALL HIS LORDS; THE DUKE OF MILAN, AND HIS BRAVE SON.

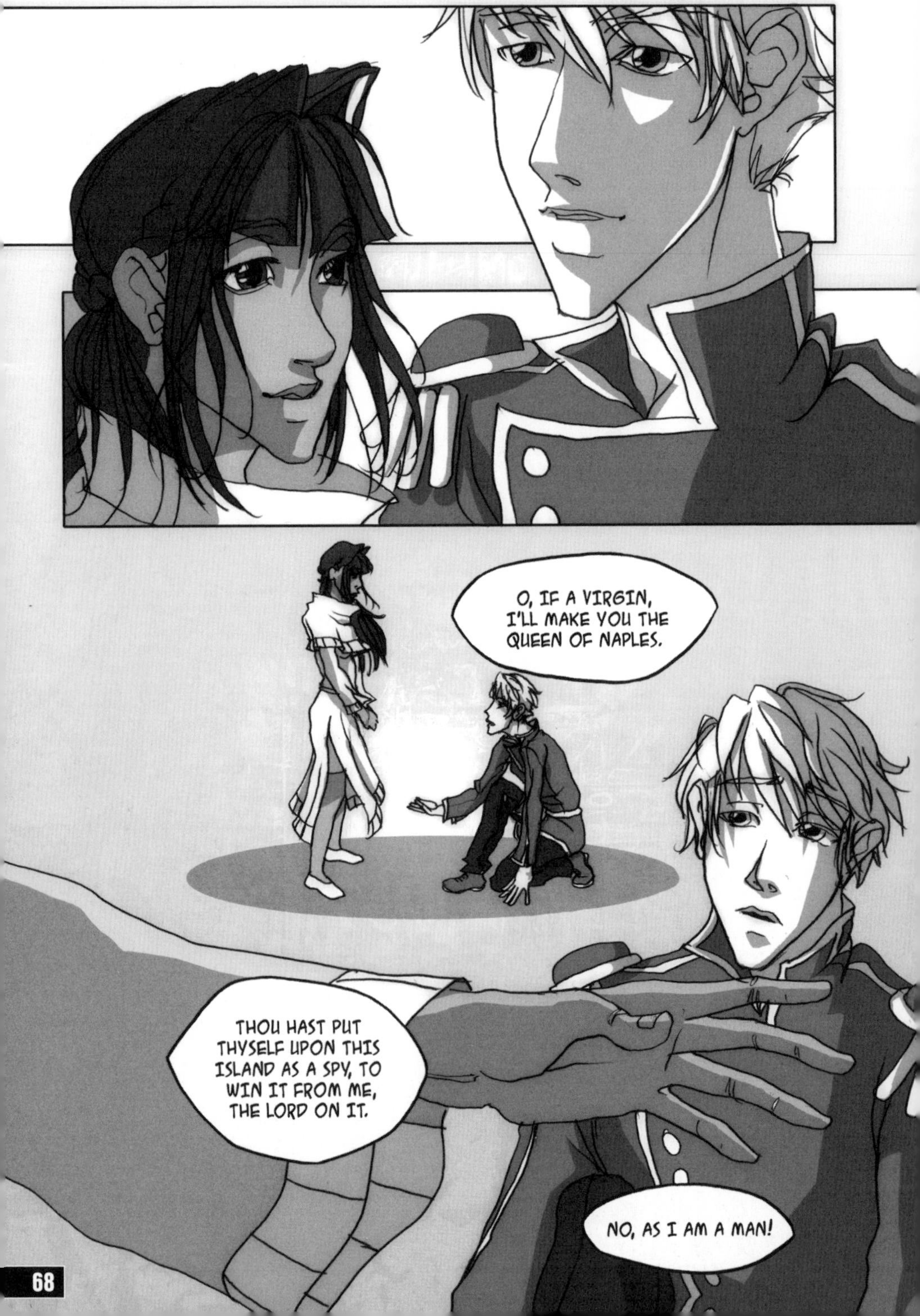
O, IF A VIRGIN, I'LL MAKE YOU THE QUEEN OF NAPLES.
THOU HAST PUT THYSELF UPON THIS ISLAND AS A SPY, TO WIN IT FROM ME, THE LORD ON IT.
NO, AS I AM A MAN!

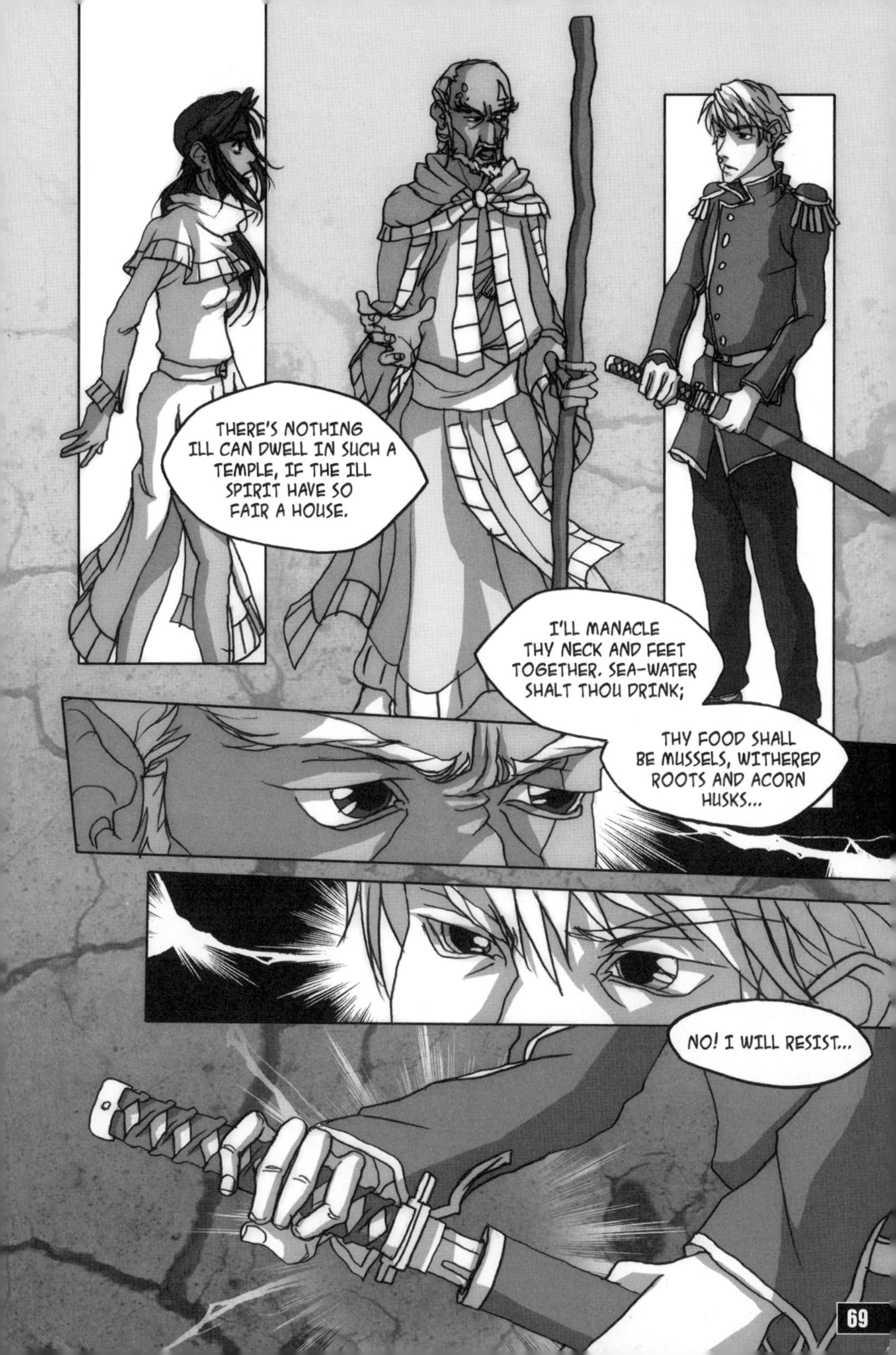

THERE'S NOTHING ILL CAN DWELL IN SUCH A TEMPLE, IF THE ILL SPIRIT HAVE SO FAIR A HOUSE.
I'LL MANACLE THY NECK AND FEET TOGETHER. SEA-WATER SHALT THOU DRINK;
THY FOOD SHALL BE MUSSELS, WITHERED ROOTS AND ACORN HUSKS...
NO! I WILL RESIST...

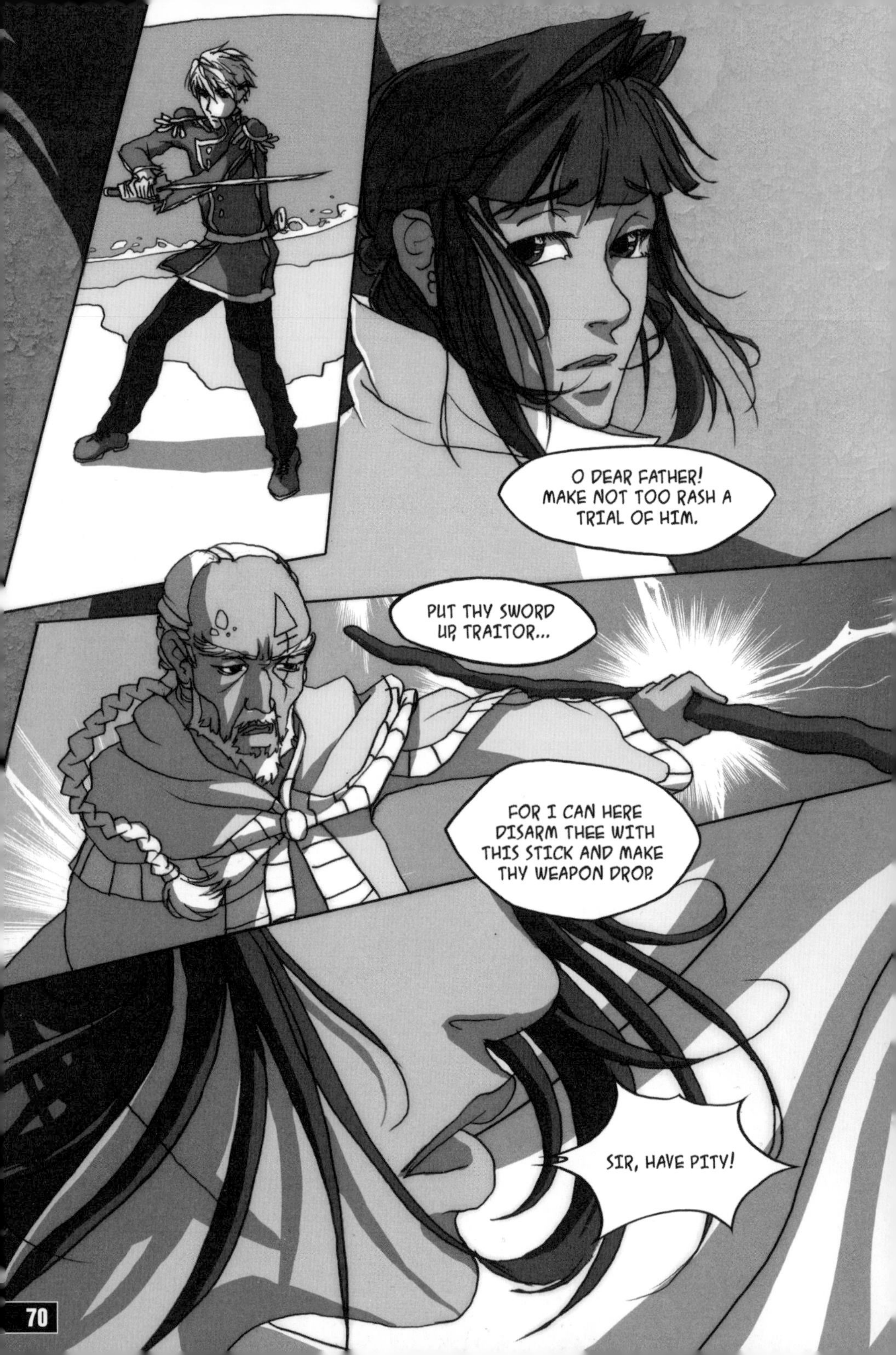

O DEAR FATHER! MAKE NOT TOO RASH A TRIAL OF HIM.
PUT THY SWORD UP, TRAITOR...
FOR I CAN HERE DISARM THEE WITH THIS STICK AND MAKE THY WEAPON DROP.
SIR, HAVE PITY!

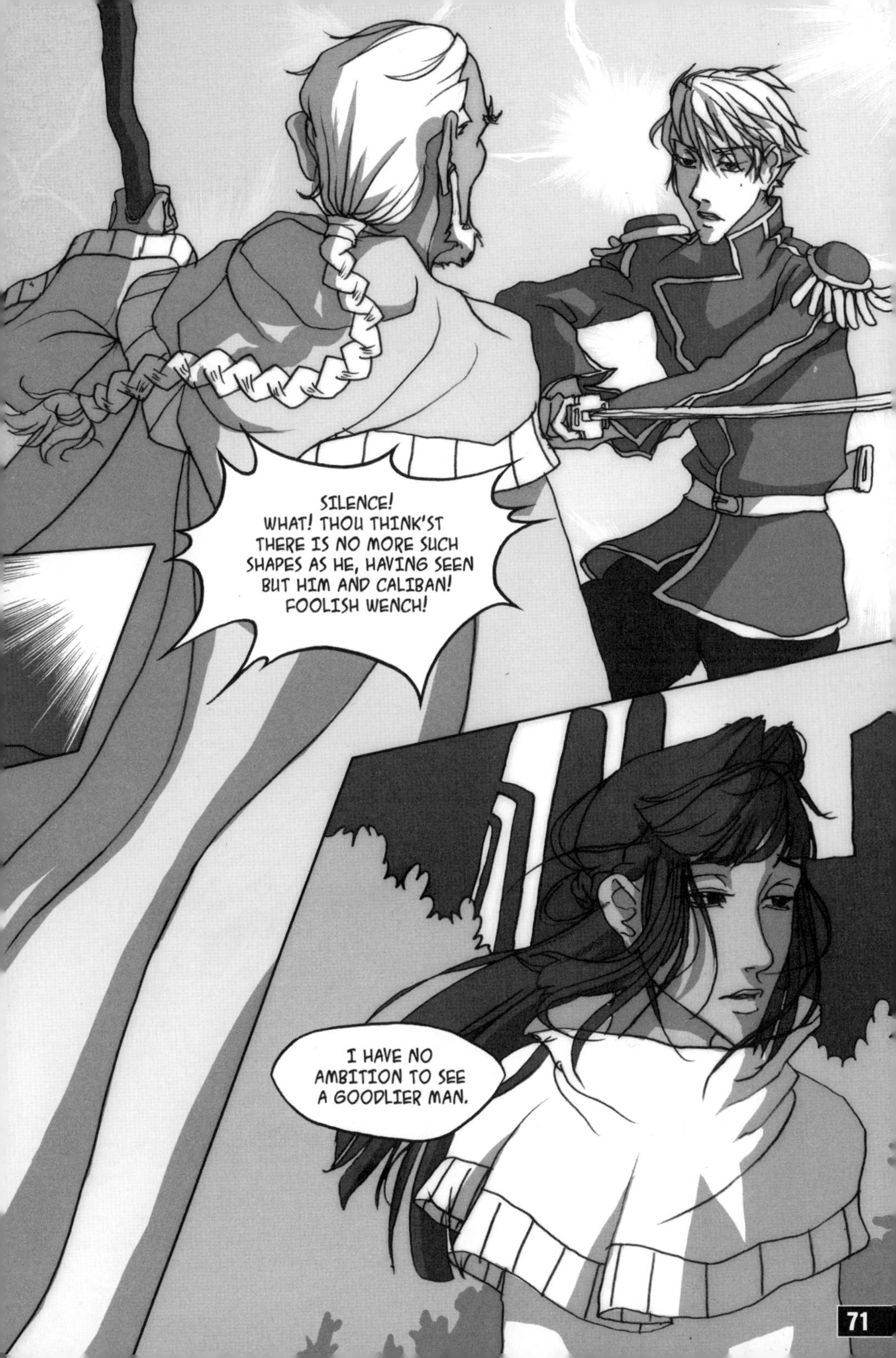
SILENCE! WHAT! THOU THINK'ST THERE IS NO MORE SUCH SHAPES AS HE, HAVING SEEN BUT HIM AND CALIBAN! FOOLISH WENCH!
I HAVE NO AMBITION TO SEE A GOODLIER MAN.

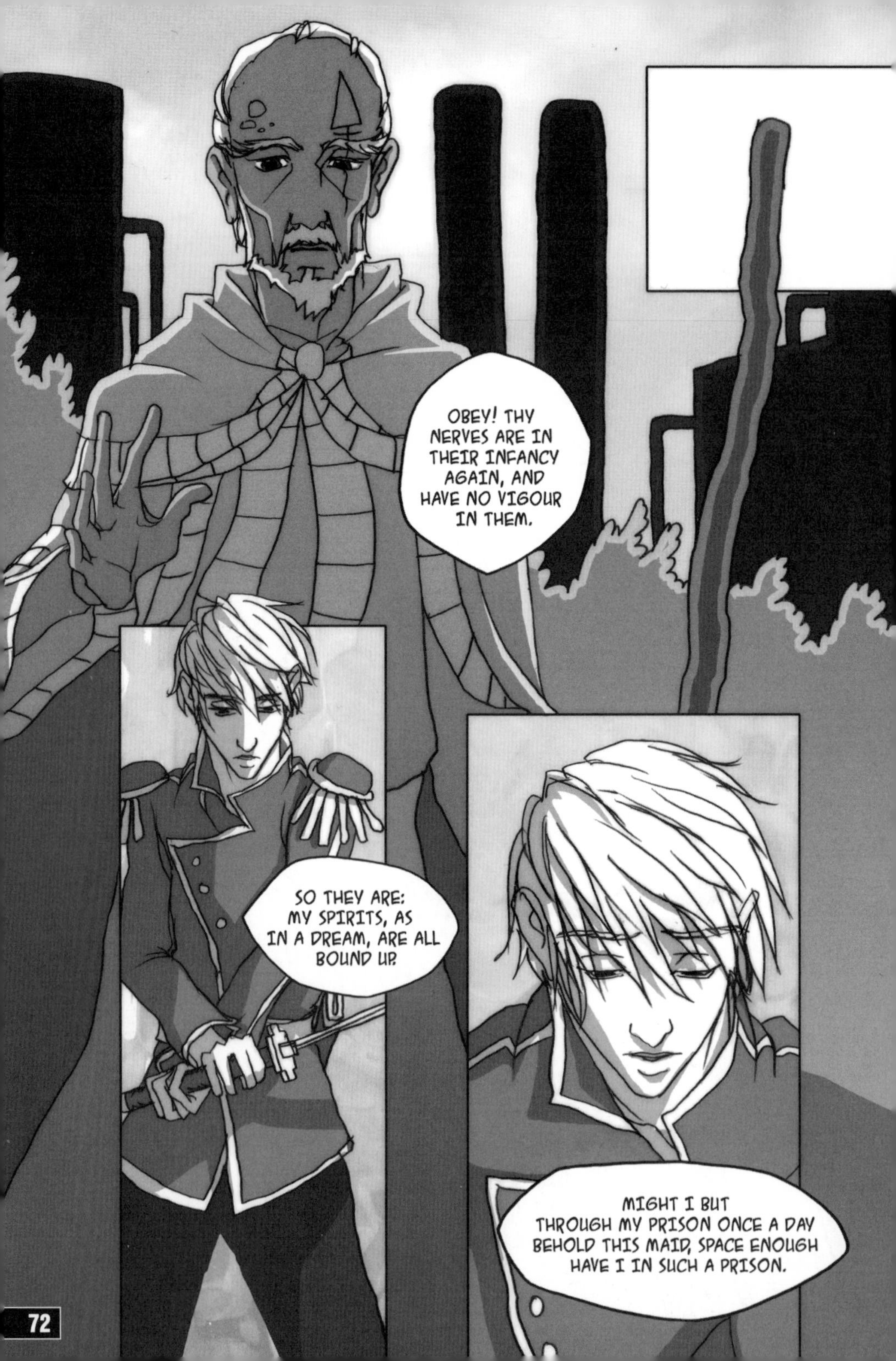
OBEY! THY NERVES ARE IN THEIR INFANCY AGAIN, AND HAVE NO VIGOUR IN THEM.
SO THEY ARE: MY SPIRITS, AS IN A DREAM, ARE ALL BOUND UP.
MIGHT I BUT THROUGH MY PRISON ONCE A DAY BEHOLD THIS MAID, SPACE ENOUGH HAVE I IN SUCH A PRISON.

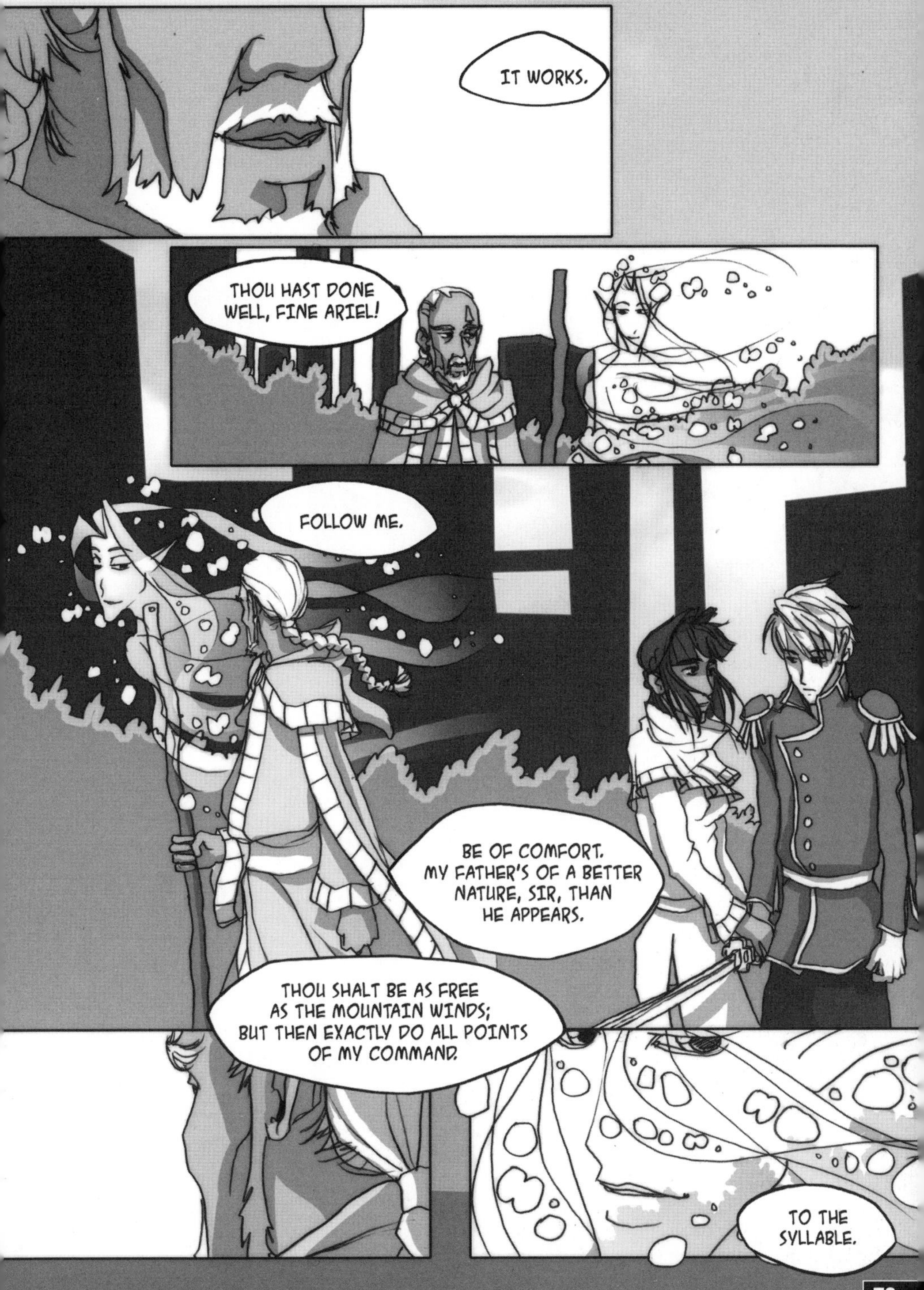
IT WORKS.
THOU HAST DONE WELL, FINE ARIEL!
FOLLOW ME.
BE OF COMFORT. MY FATHER'S OF A BETTER NATURE, SIR, THAN HE APPEARS.
THOU SHALT BE AS FREE AS THE MOUNTAIN WINDS; BUT THEN EXACTLY DO ALL POINTS OF MY COMMAND.
TO THE SYLLABLE.

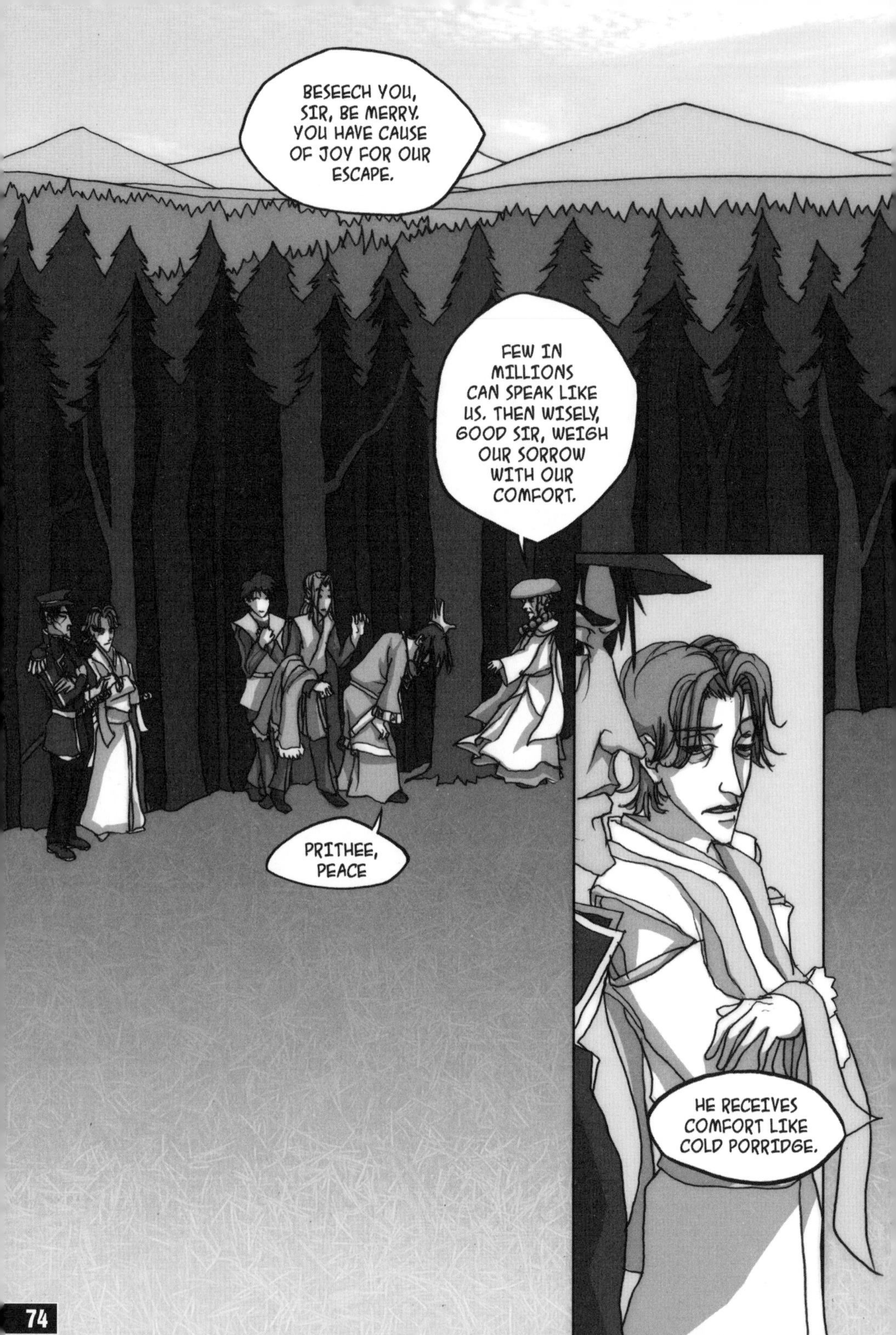
BESEECH YOU, SIR, BE MERRY. YOU HAVE CAUSE OF JOY FOR OUR ESCAPE.
FEW IN MILLIONS CAN SPEAK LIKE US. THEN WISELY, GOOD SIR, WEIGH OUR SORROW WITH OUR COMFORT.
PRITHEE, PEACE
HE RECEIVES COMFORT LIKE COLD PORRIDGE.

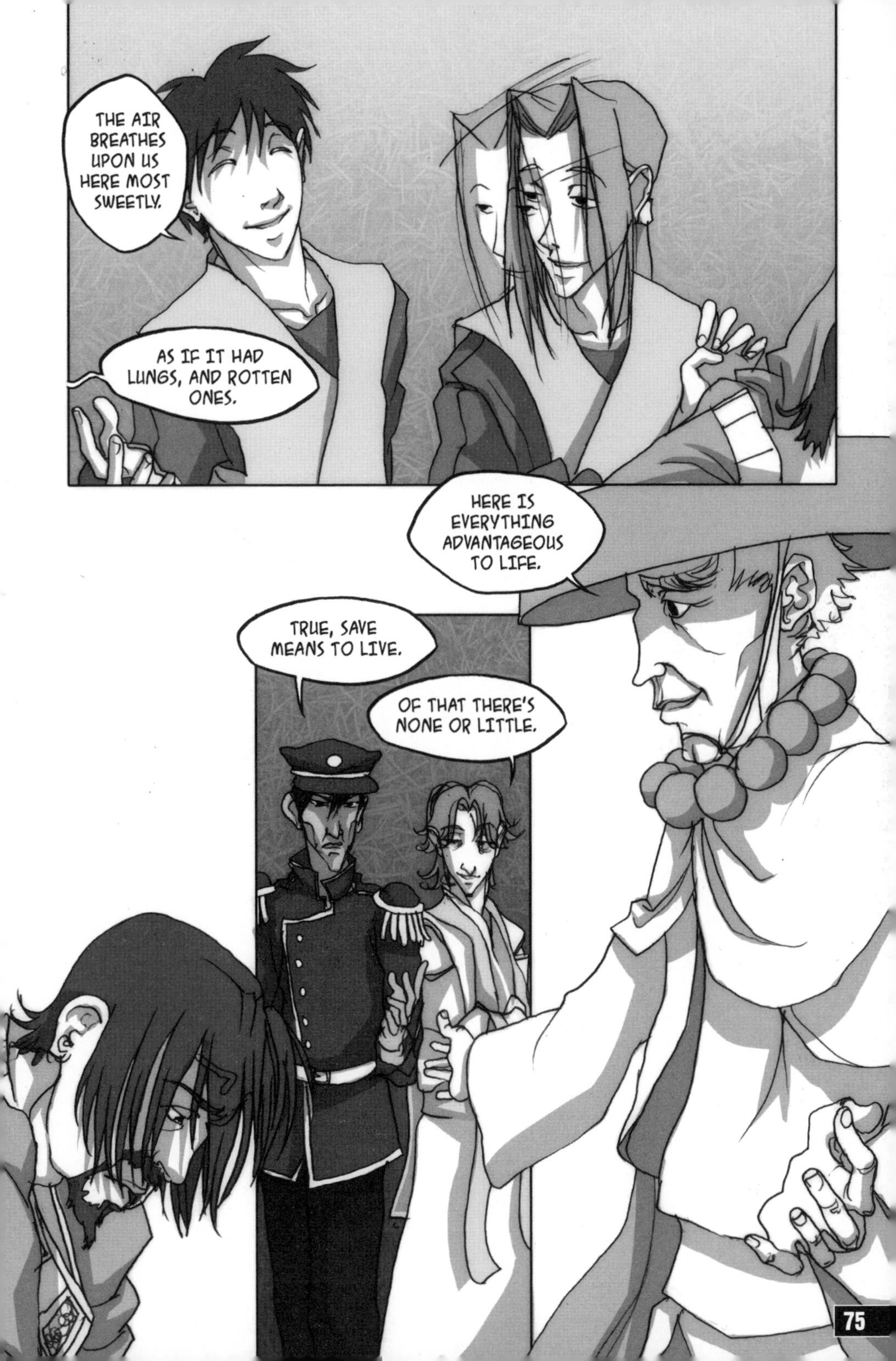
THE AIR BREATHES UPON US HERE MOST SWEETLY.
AS IF IT HAD LUNGS, AND ROTTEN ONES.
HERE IS EVERYTHING ADVANTAGEOUS TO LIFE.
TRUE, SAVE MEANS TO LIVE.
OF THAT THERE'S NONE OR LITTLE.

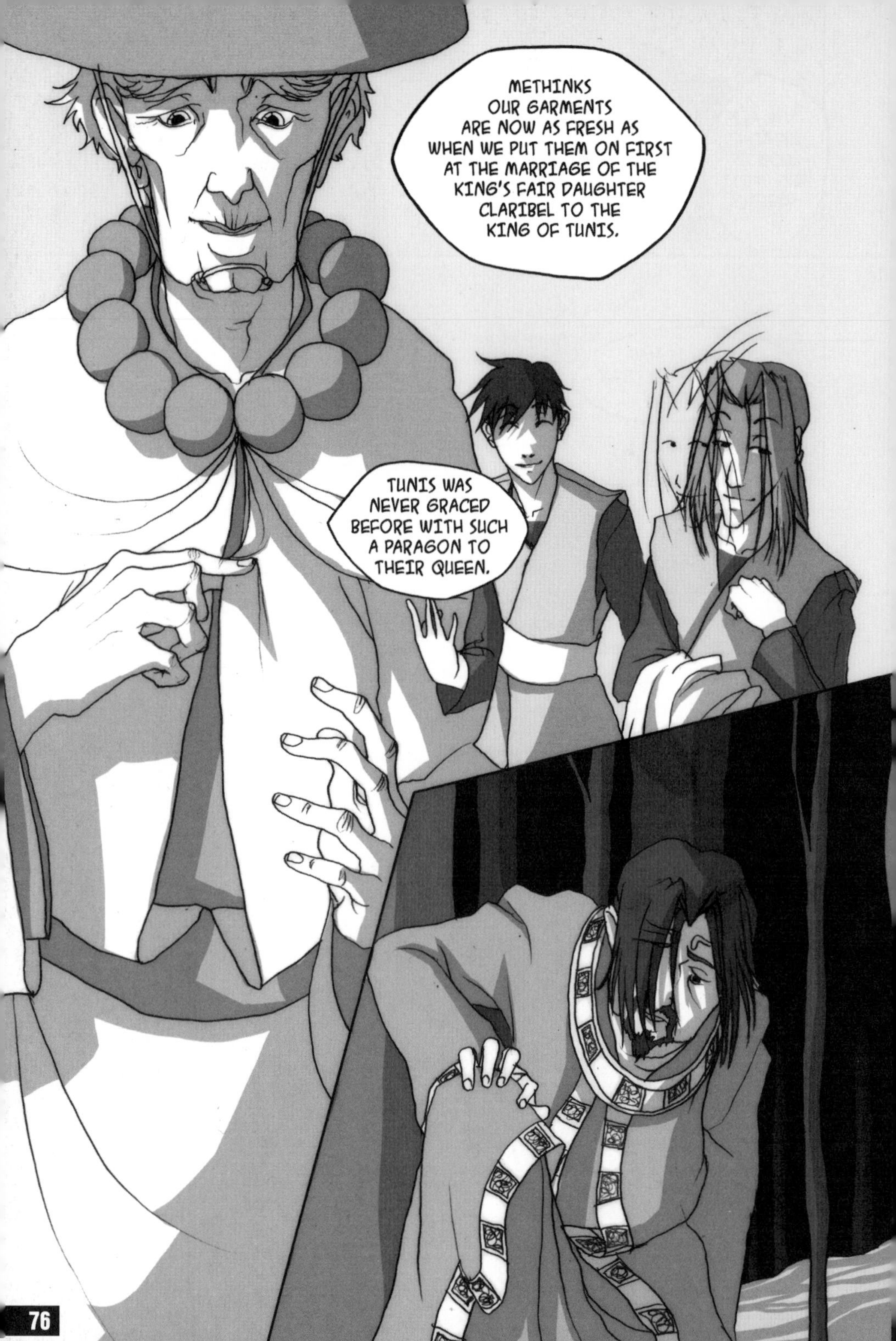
METHINKS OUR GARMENTS ARE NOW AS FRESH AS WHEN WE PUT THEM ON FIRST AT THE MARRIAGE OF THE KING'S FAIR DAUGHTER CLARIBEL TO THE KING OF TUNIS.
TUNIS WAS NEVER GRACED BEFORE WITH SUCH A PARAGON TO THEIR QUEEN.

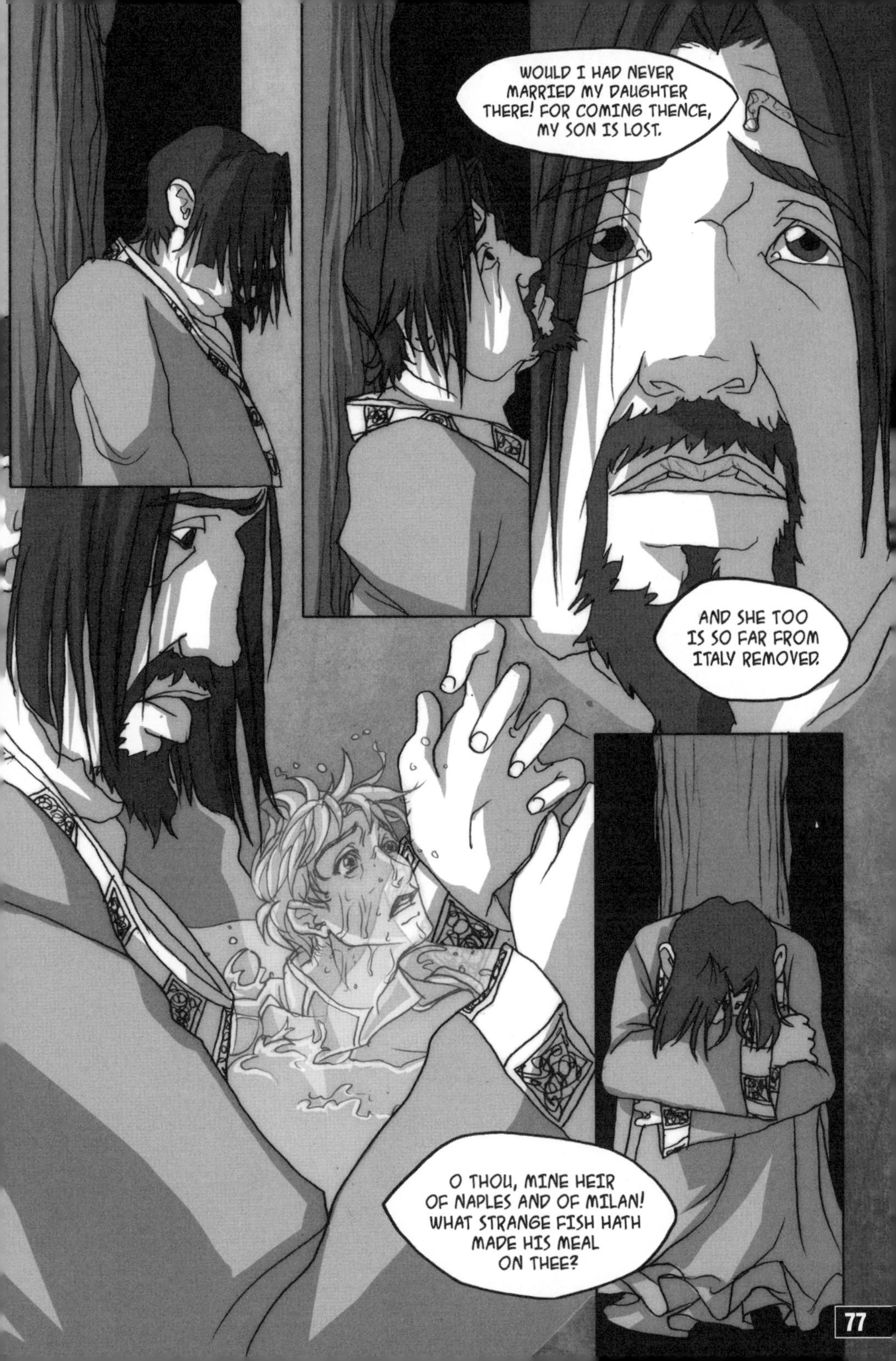
WOULD I HAD NEVER MARRIED MY DAUGHTER THERE! FOR COMING THENCE, MY SON IS LOST.
AND SHE TOO IS SO FAR FROM ITALY REMOVED.
O THOU, MINE HEIR OF NAPLES AND OF MILAN! WHAT STRANGE FISH HATH MADE HIS MEAL ON THEE?

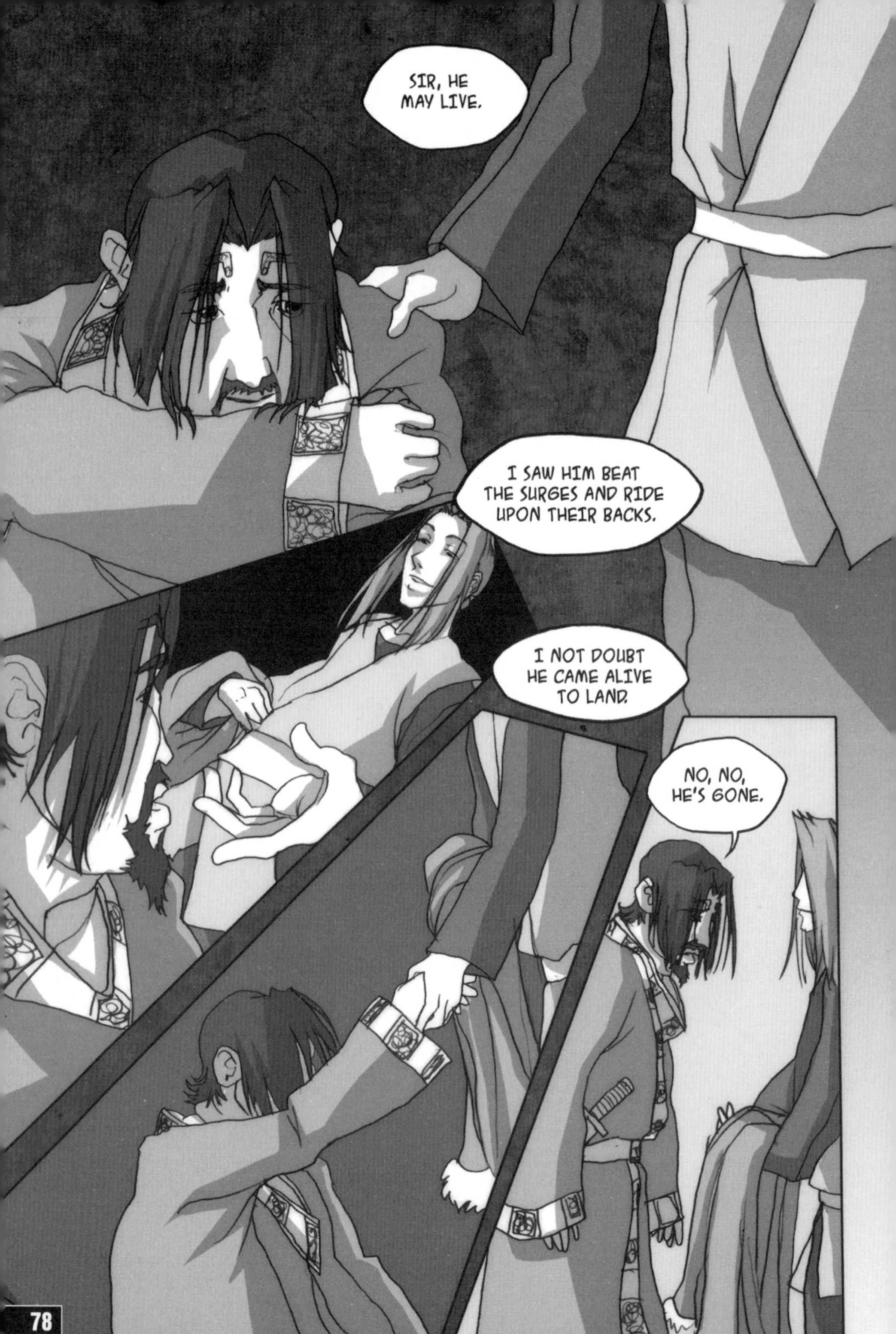
SIR, HE MAY LIVE.
I SAW HIM BEAT THE SURGES AND RIDE UPON THEIR BACKS.
I NOT DOUBT HE CAME ALIVE TO LAND.
NO, NO, HE'S GONE.

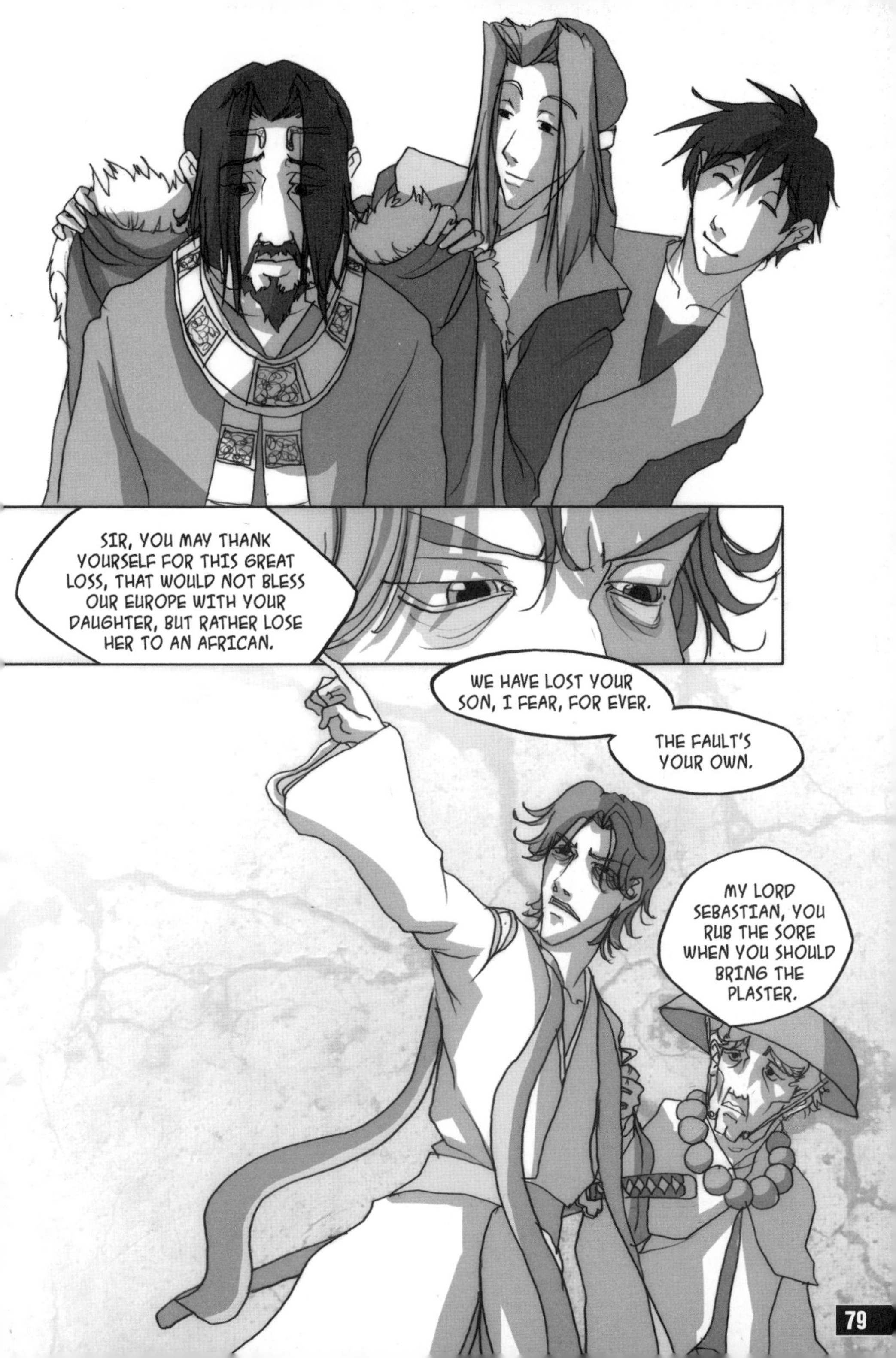

SIR, YOU MAY THANK YOURSELF FOR THIS GREAT LOSS, THAT WOULD NOT BLESS OUR EUROPE WITH YOUR DAUGHTER, BUT RATHER LOSE HER TO AN AFRICAN.
WE HAVE LOST YOUR SON, I FEAR, FOR EVER.
THE FAULT'S YOUR OWN.
MY LORD SEBASTIAN, YOU RUB THE SORE WHEN YOU SHOULD BRING THE PLASTER.

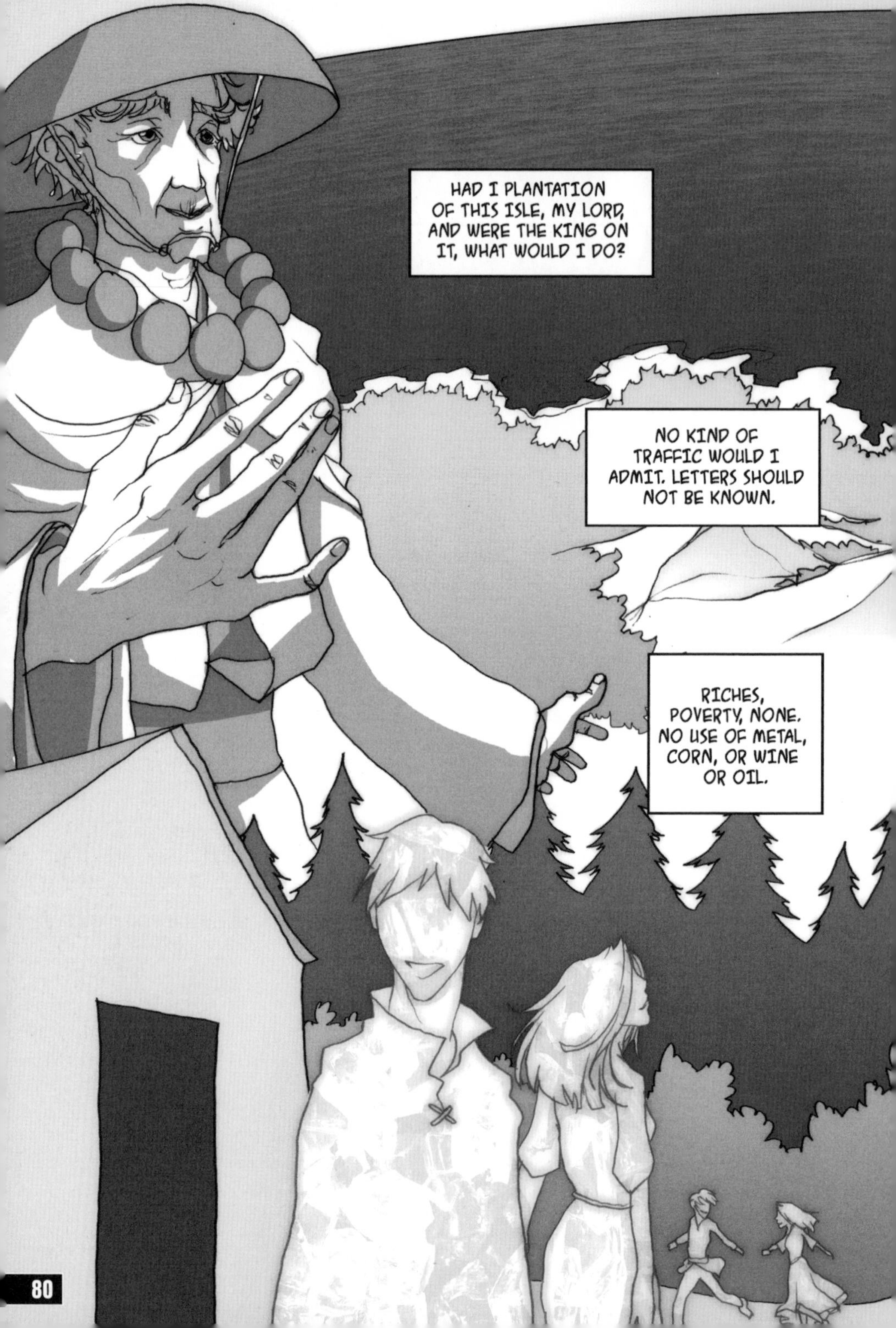
HAD I PLANTATION OF THIS ISLE, MY LORD, AND WERE THE KING ON IT, WHAT WOULD I DO?
NO KIND OF TRAFFIC WOULD I ADMIT. LETTERS SHOULD NOT BE KNOWN.
RICHES, POVERTY, NONE. NO USE OF METAL, CORN, OR WINE OR OIL.

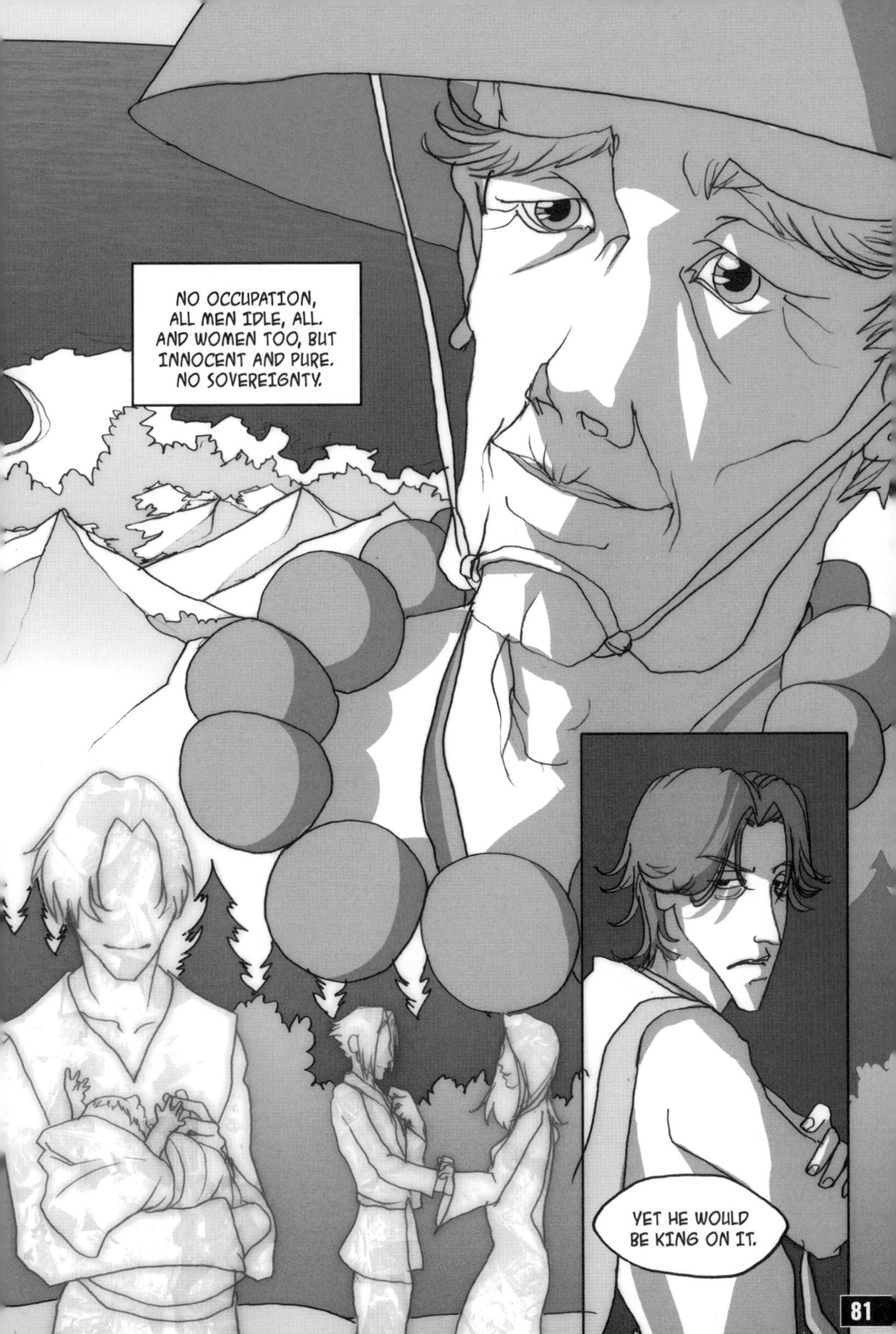
NO OCCUPATION, ALL MEN IDLE, ALL. AND WOMEN TOO, BUT INNOCENT AND PURE. NO SOVEREIGNTY.
YET HE WOULD BE KING ON IT.

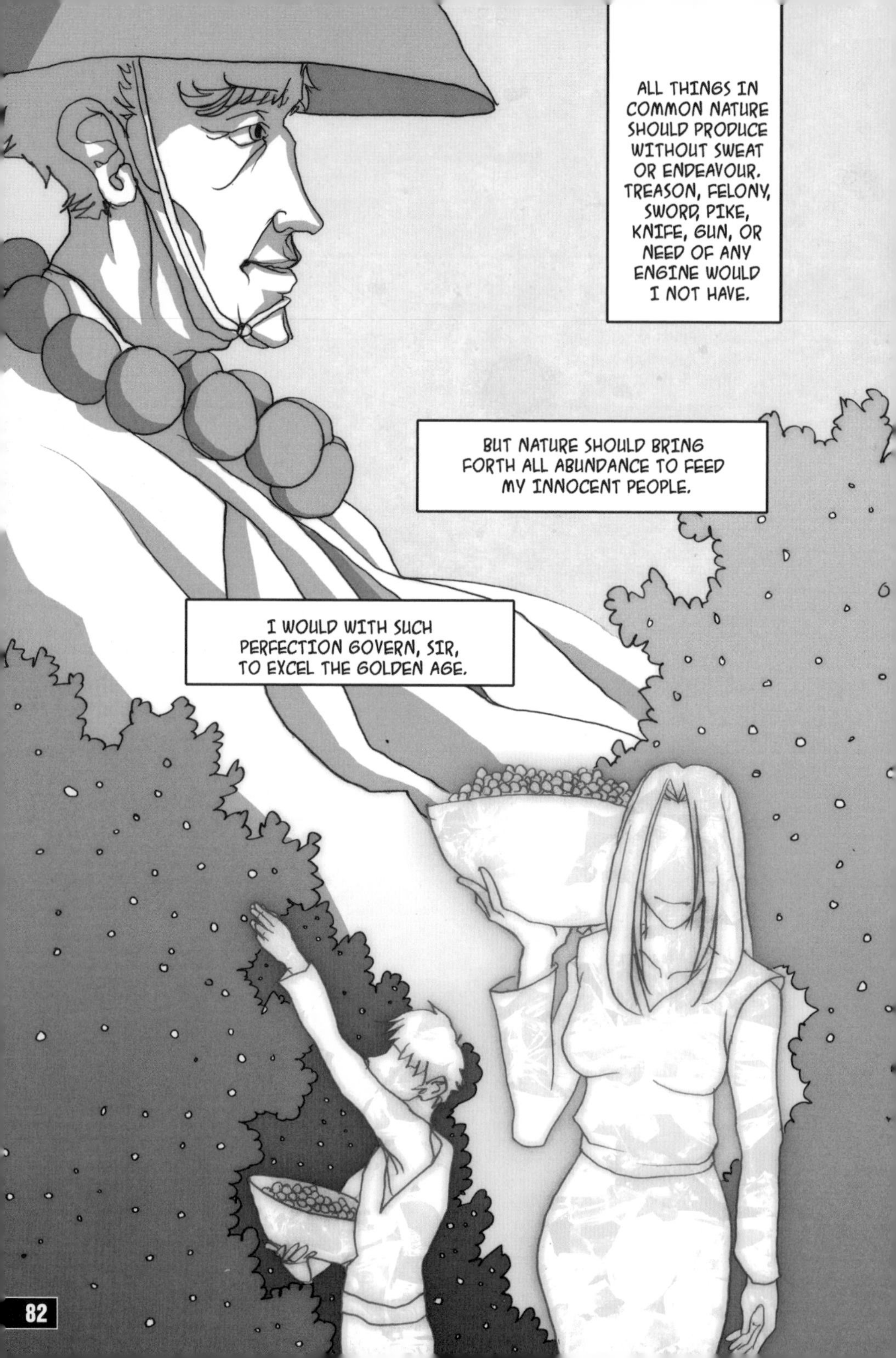
ALL THINGS IN COMMON NATURE SHOULD PRODUCE WITHOUT SWEAT OR ENDEAVOUR. TREASON, FELONY, SWORD, PIKE, KNIFE, GUN, OR NEED OF ANY ENGINE WOULD I NOT HAVE.
BUT NATURE SHOULD BRING FORTH ALL ABUNDANCE TO FEED MY INNOCENT PEOPLE.
I WOULD WITH SUCH PERFECTION GOVERN, SIR, TO EXCEL THE GOLDEN AGE.

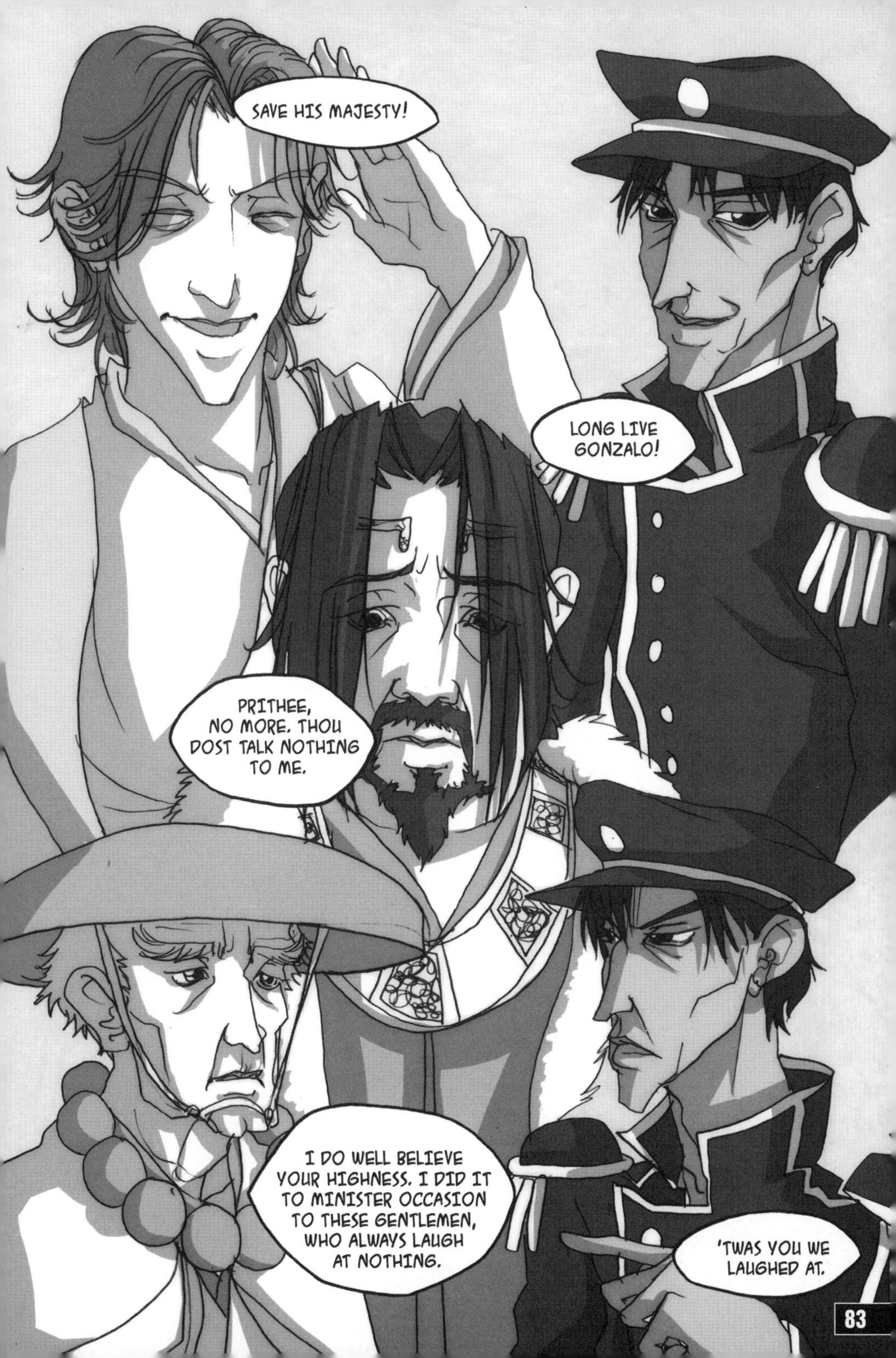
SAVE HIS MAJESTY!
LONG LIVE GONZALO!
PRITHEE, NO MORE. THOU DOST TALK NOTHING TO ME.
I DO WELL BELIEVE YOUR HIGHNESS. I DID IT TO MINISTER OCCASION TO THESE GENTLEMEN, WHO ALWAYS LAUGH AT NOTHING.
'TWAS YOU WE LAUGHED AT.

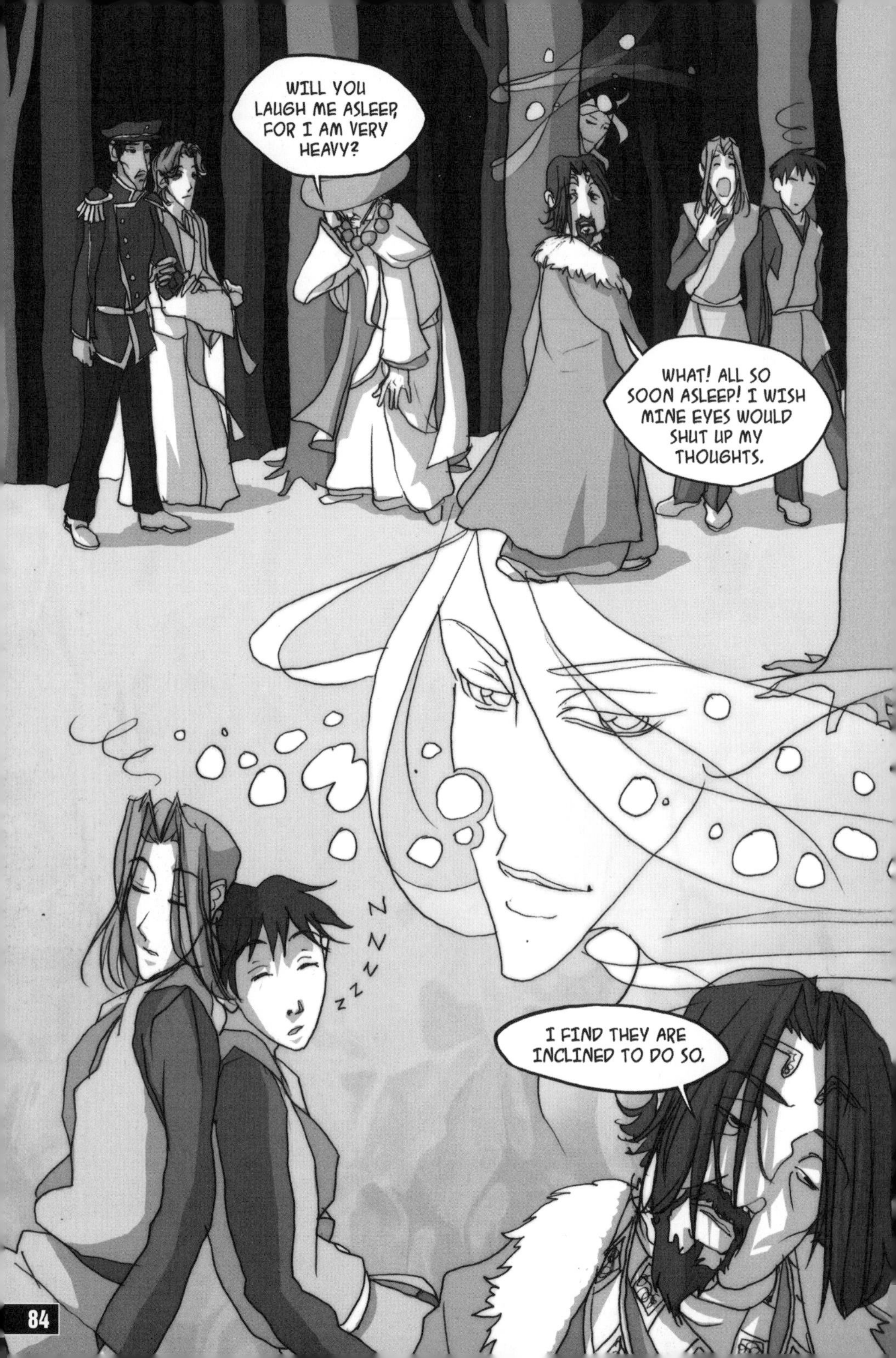
WILL YOU LAUGH ME ASLEEP, FOR I AM VERY HEAVY?
WHAT! ALL SO SOON ASLEEP! I WISH MINE EYES WOULD SHUT UP MY THOUGHTS.
N N N Z Z Z
I FIND THEY ARE INCLINED TO DO SO.

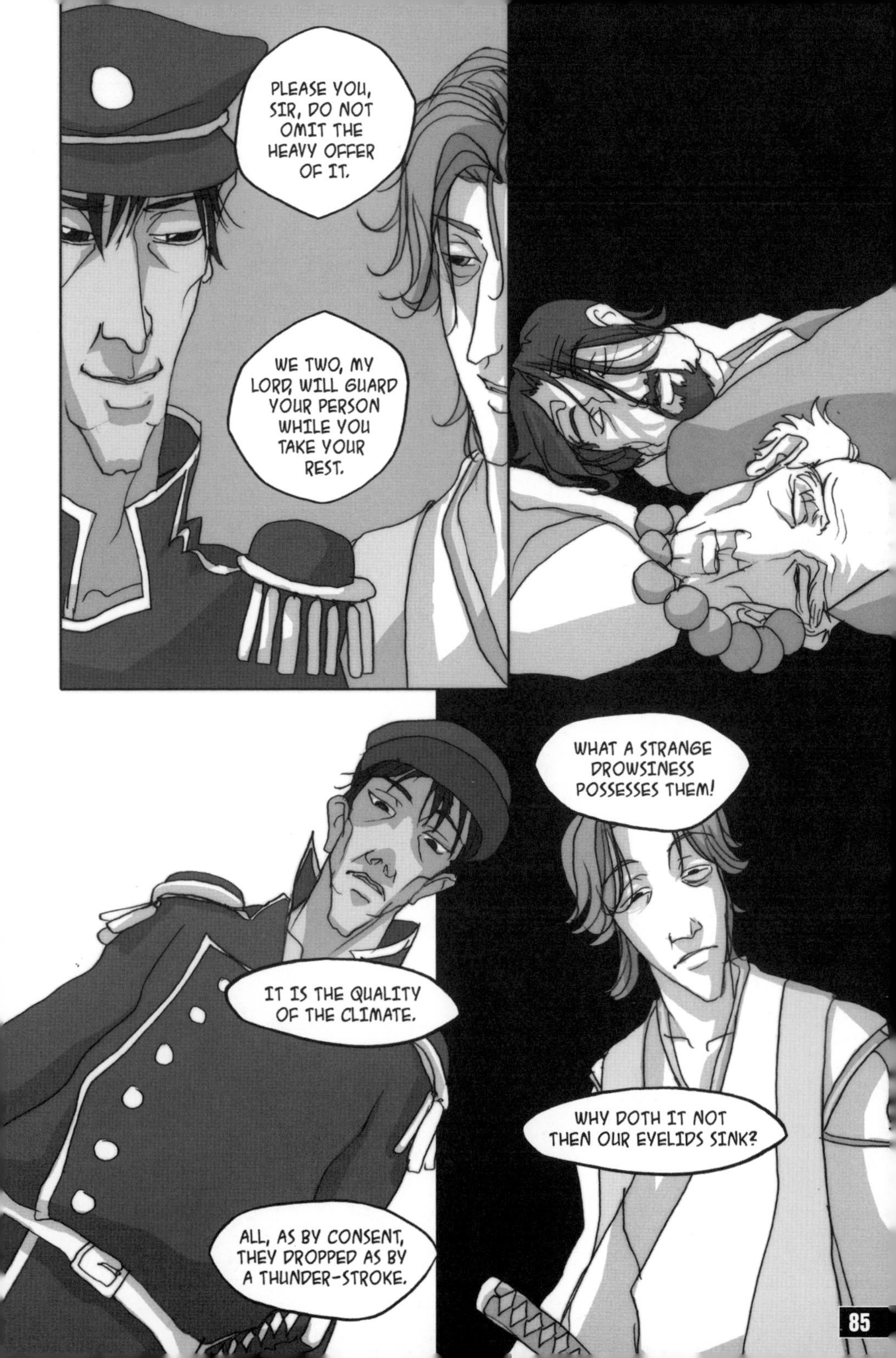
PLEASE YOU, SIR, DO NOT OMIT THE HEAVY OFFER OF IT.
WE TWO, MY LORD, WILL GUARD YOUR PERSON WHILE YOU TAKE YOUR REST.
WHAT A STRANGE DROWSINESS POSSESSES THEM!
IT IS THE QUALITY OF THE CLIMATE.
WHY DOTH IT NOT THEN OUR EYELIDS SINK?
ALL, AS BY CONSENT, THEY DROPPED AS BY A THUNDER-STROKE.

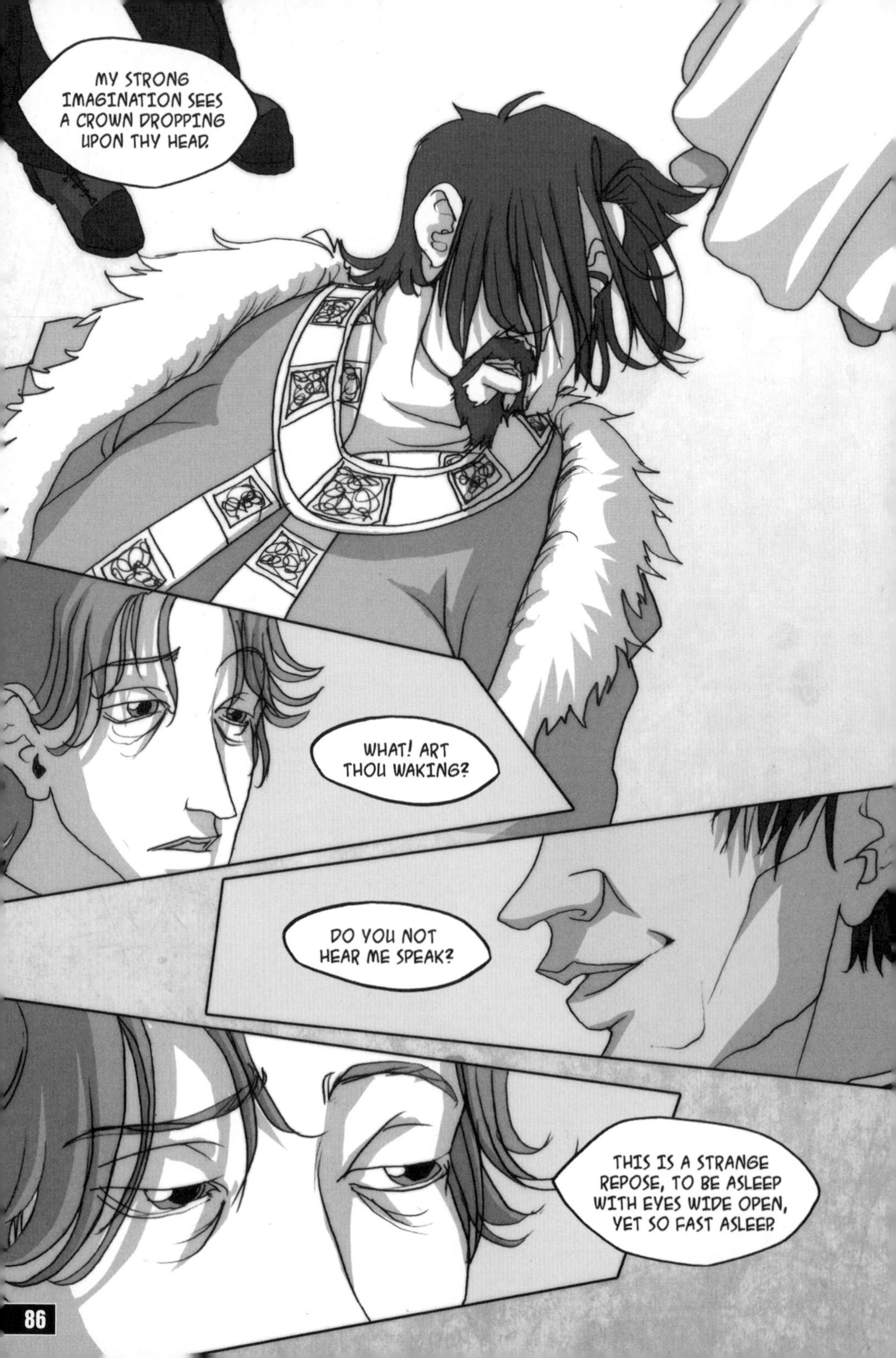
MY STRONG IMAGINATION SEES A CROWN DROPPING UPON THY HEAD.
WHAT! ART THOU WAKING?
DO YOU NOT HEAR ME SPEAK?
THIS IS A STRANGE REPOSE, TO BE ASLEEP WITH EYES WIDE OPEN, YET SO FAST ASLEEP.

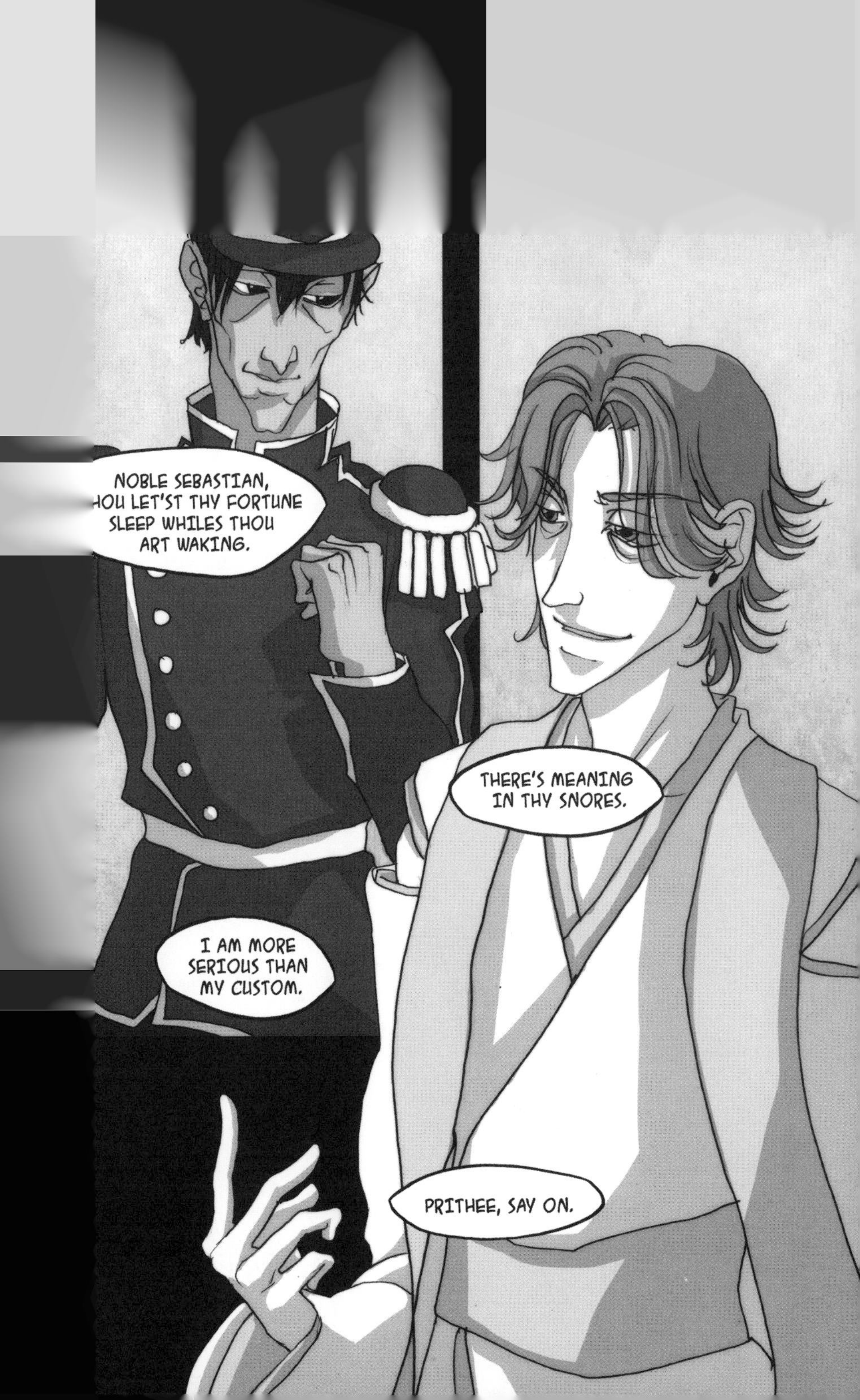
NOBLE SEBASTIAN, HOU LET'ST THY FORTUNE SLEEP WHILES THOU ART WAKING.
THERE'S MEANING IN THY SNORES.
I AM MORE SERIOUS THAN MY CUSTOM.
PRITHEE, SAY ON.

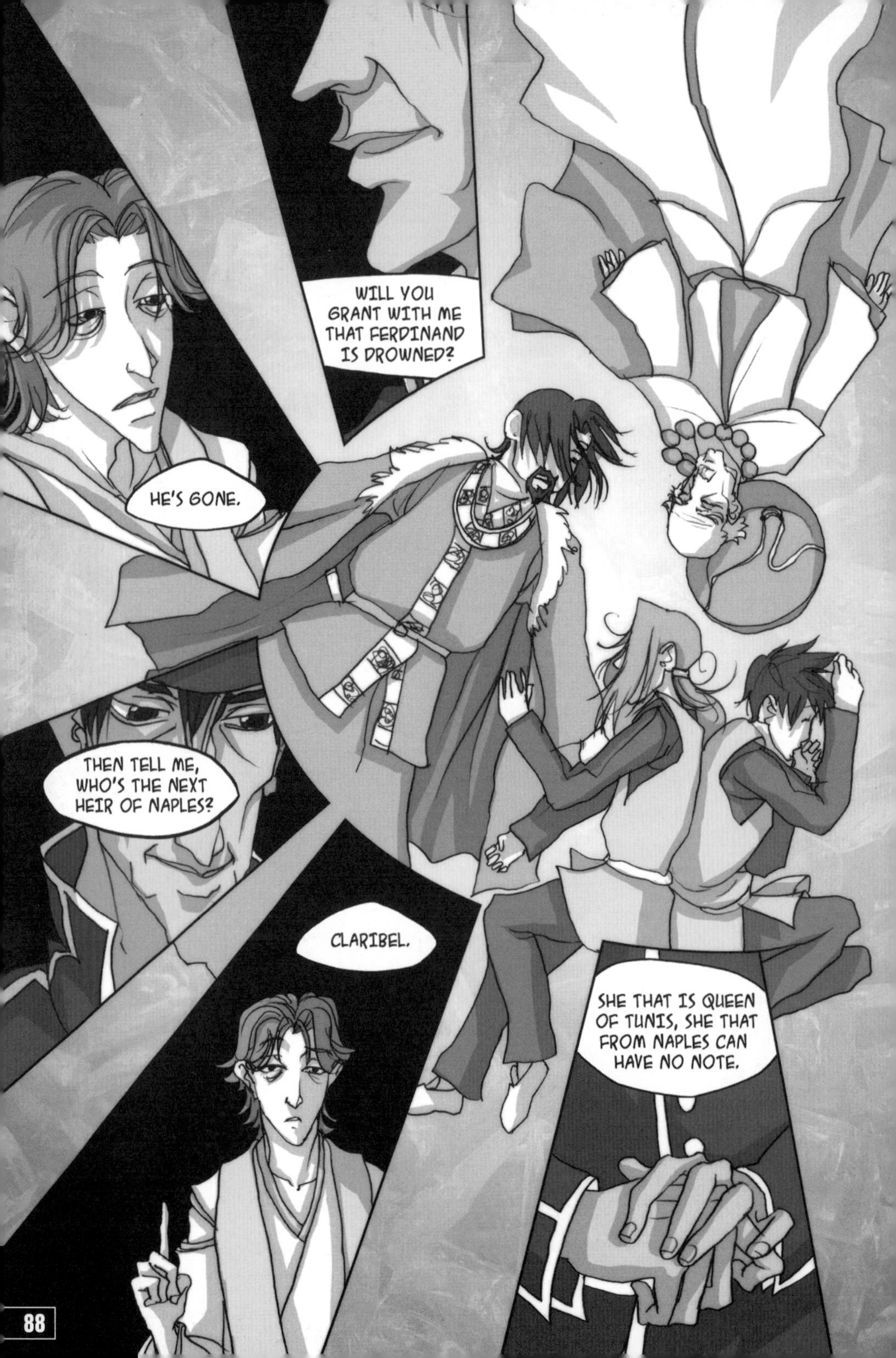
WILL YOU GRANT WITH ME THAT FERDINAND IS DROWNED?
HE'S GONE.
THEN TELL ME, WHO'S THE NEXT HEIR OF NAPLES?
CLARIBEL.
SHE THAT IS QUEEN OF TUNIS, SHE THAT FROM NAPLES CAN HAVE NO NOTE.

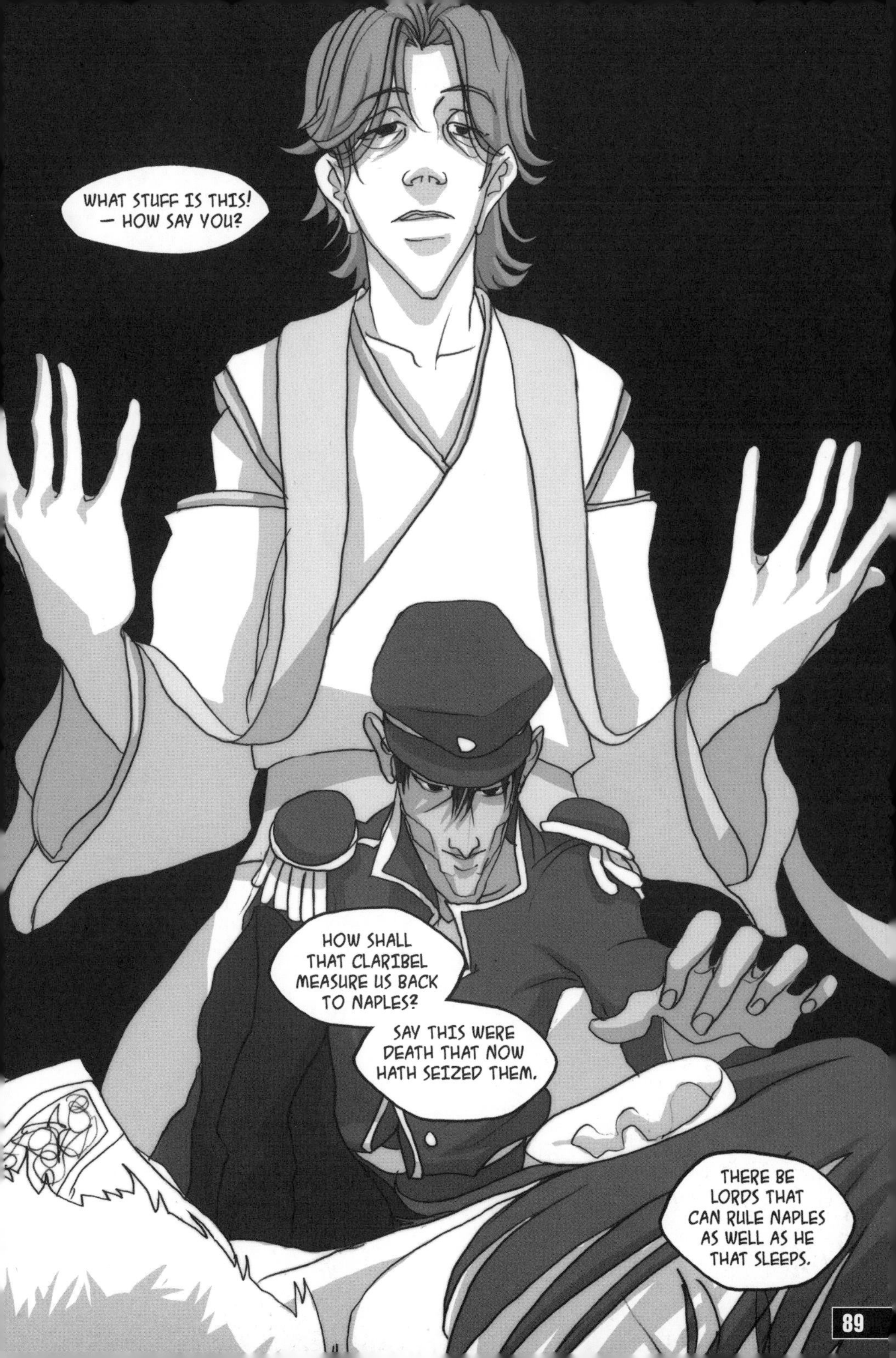
WHAT STUFF IS THIS! — HOW SAY YOU?
HOW SHALL THAT CLARIBEL MEASURE US BACK TO NAPLES?
SAY THIS WERE DEATH THAT NOW HATH SEIZED THEM.
THERE BE LORDS THAT CAN RULE NAPLES AS WELL AS HE THAT SLEEPS.

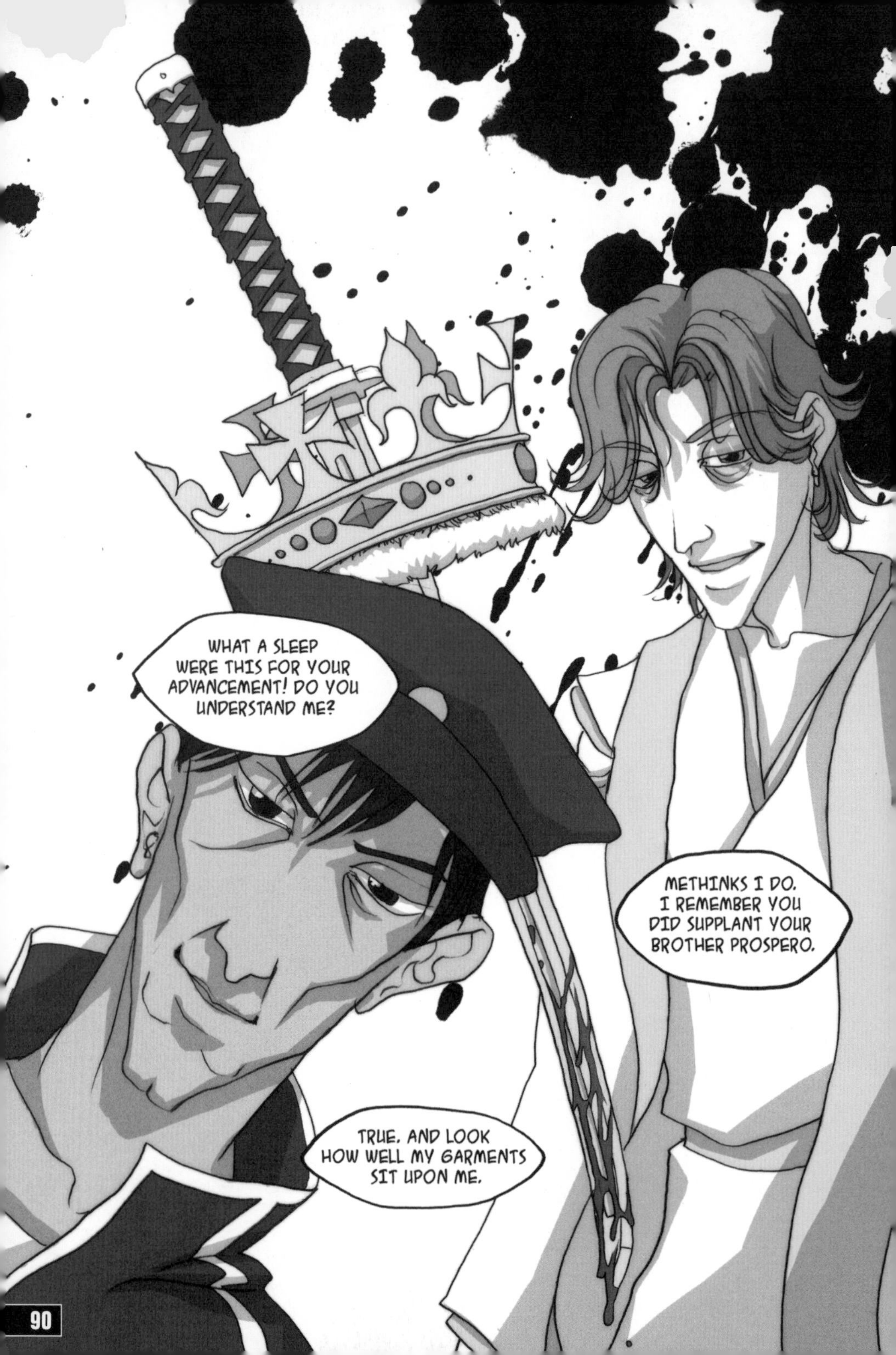
WHAT A SLEEP WERE THIS FOR YOUR ADVANCEMENT! DO YOU UNDERSTAND ME?
METHINKS I DO. I REMEMBER YOU DID SUPPLANT YOUR BROTHER PROSPERO.
TRUE. AND LOOK HOW WELL MY GARMENTS SIT UPON ME.

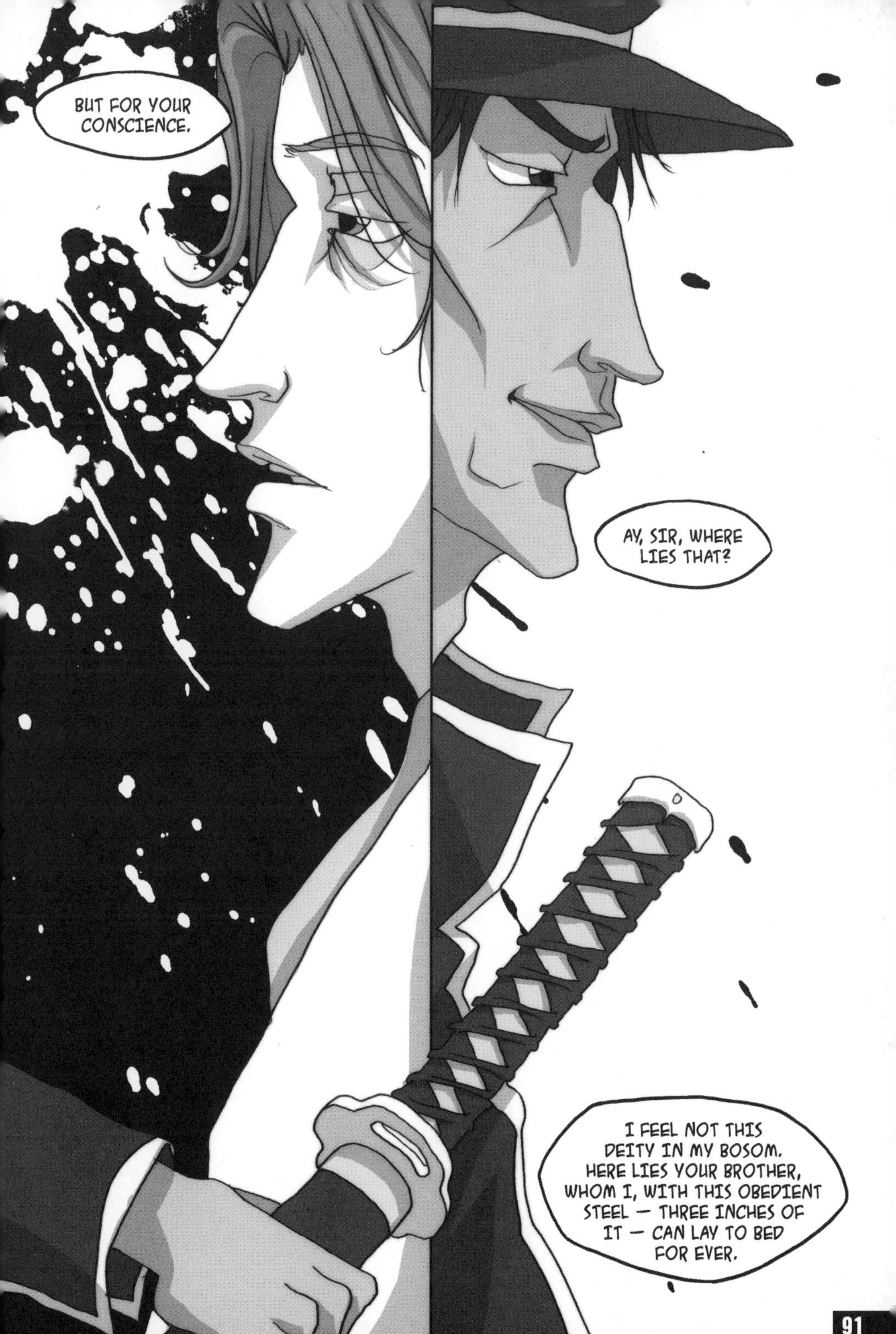
BUT FOR YOUR CONSCIENCE.
AY, SIR, WHERE LIES THAT?
I FEEL NOT THIS DEITY IN MY BOSOM. HERE LIES YOUR BROTHER, WHOM I, WITH THIS OBEDIENT STEEL — THREE INCHES OF IT — CAN LAY TO BED FOR EVER.

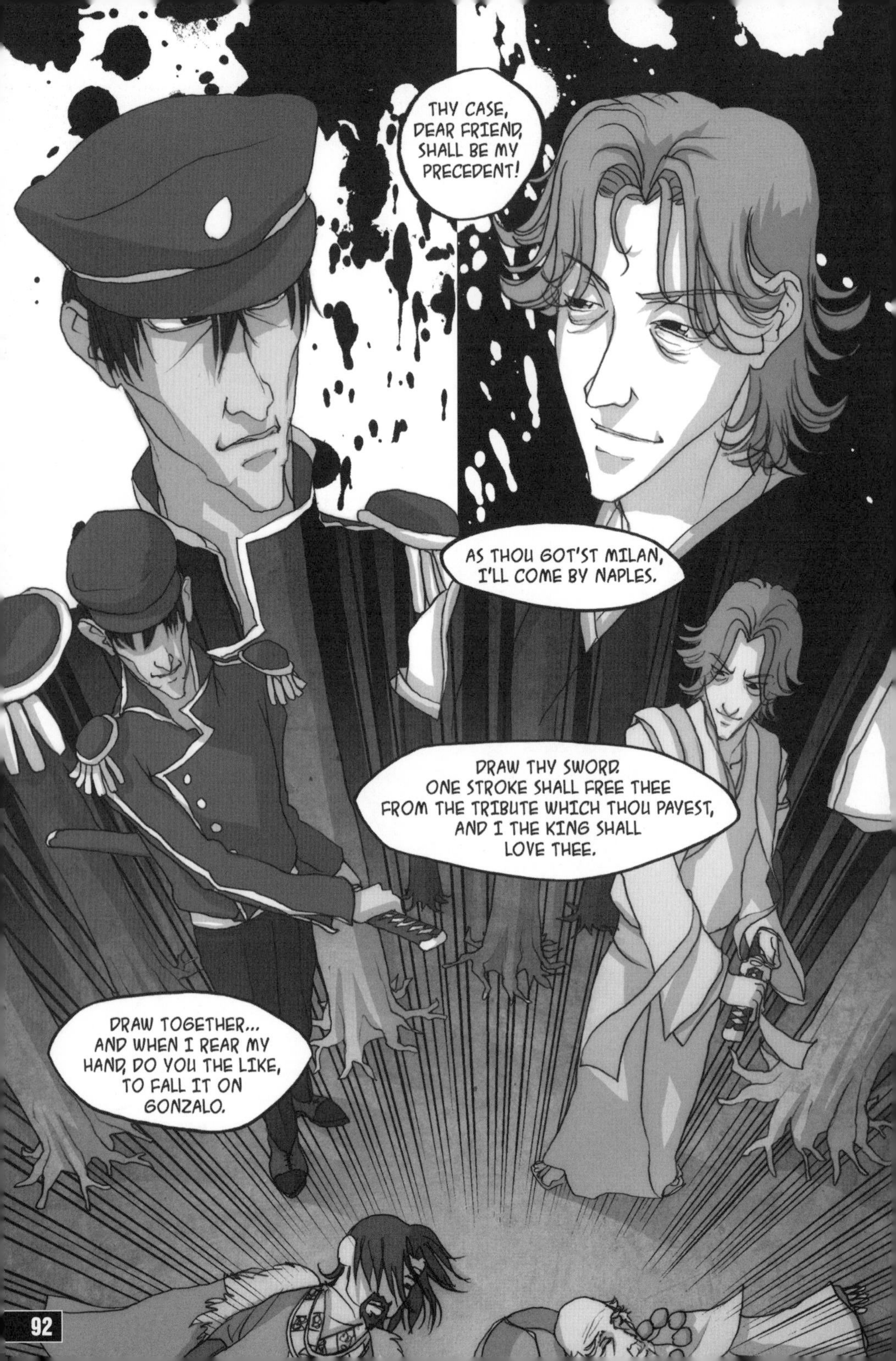
THY CASE, DEAR FRIEND, SHALL BE MY PRECEDENT!
AS THOU GOT'ST MILAN, I'LL COME BY NAPLES.
DRAW THY SWORD. ONE STROKE SHALL FREE THEE FROM THE TRIBUTE WHICH THOU PAYEST, AND I THE KING SHALL LOVE THEE.
DRAW TOGETHER... AND WHEN I REAR MY HAND, DO YOU THE LIKE, TO FALL IT ON GONZALO.

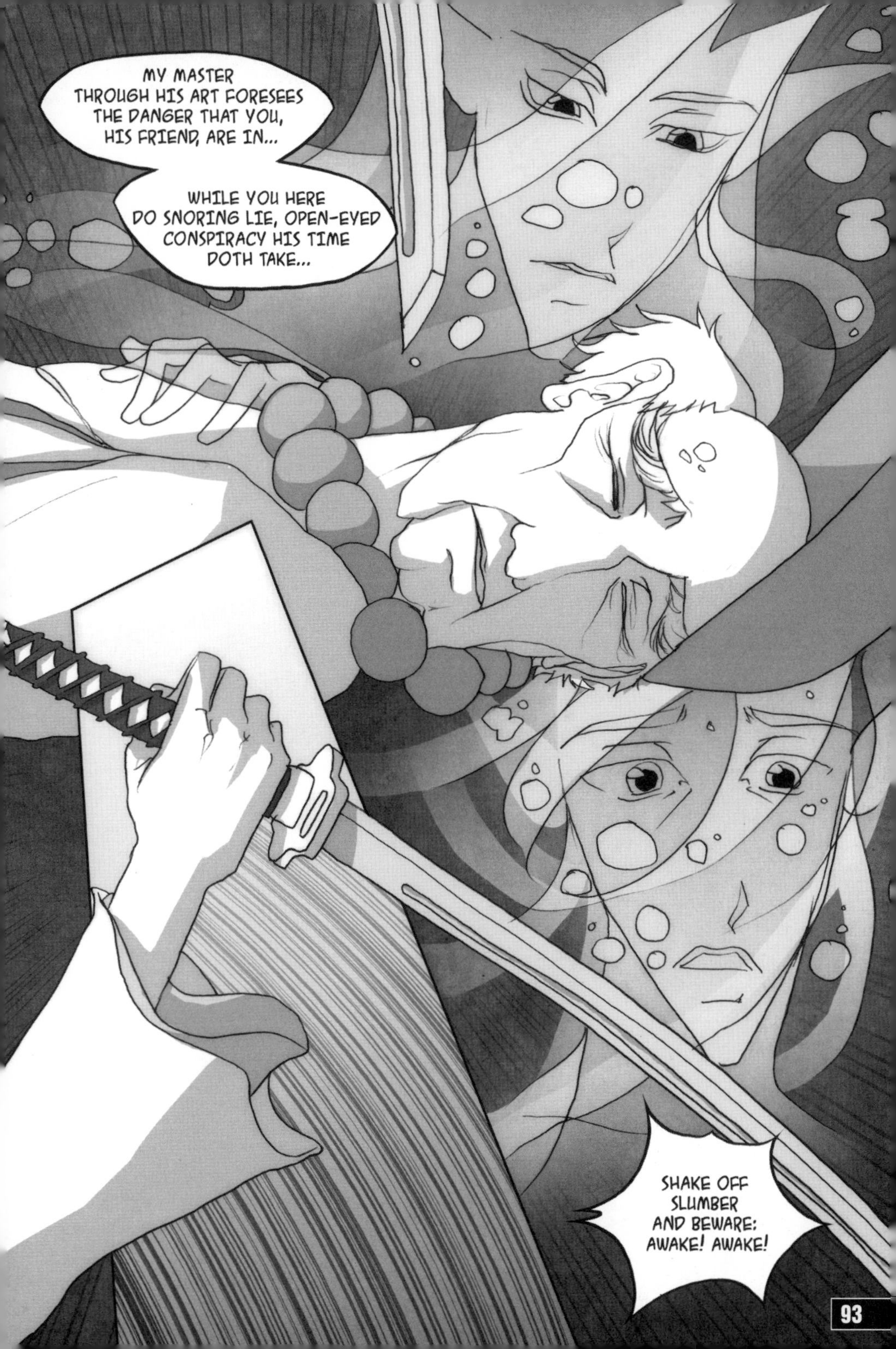
MY MASTER THROUGH HIS ART FORESEES THE DANGER THAT YOU, HIS FRIEND, ARE IN...
WHILE YOU HERE DO SNORING LIE, OPEN-EYED CONSPIRACY HIS TIME DOTH TAKE...
SHAKE OFF SLUMBER AND BEWARE: AWAKE! AWAKE!

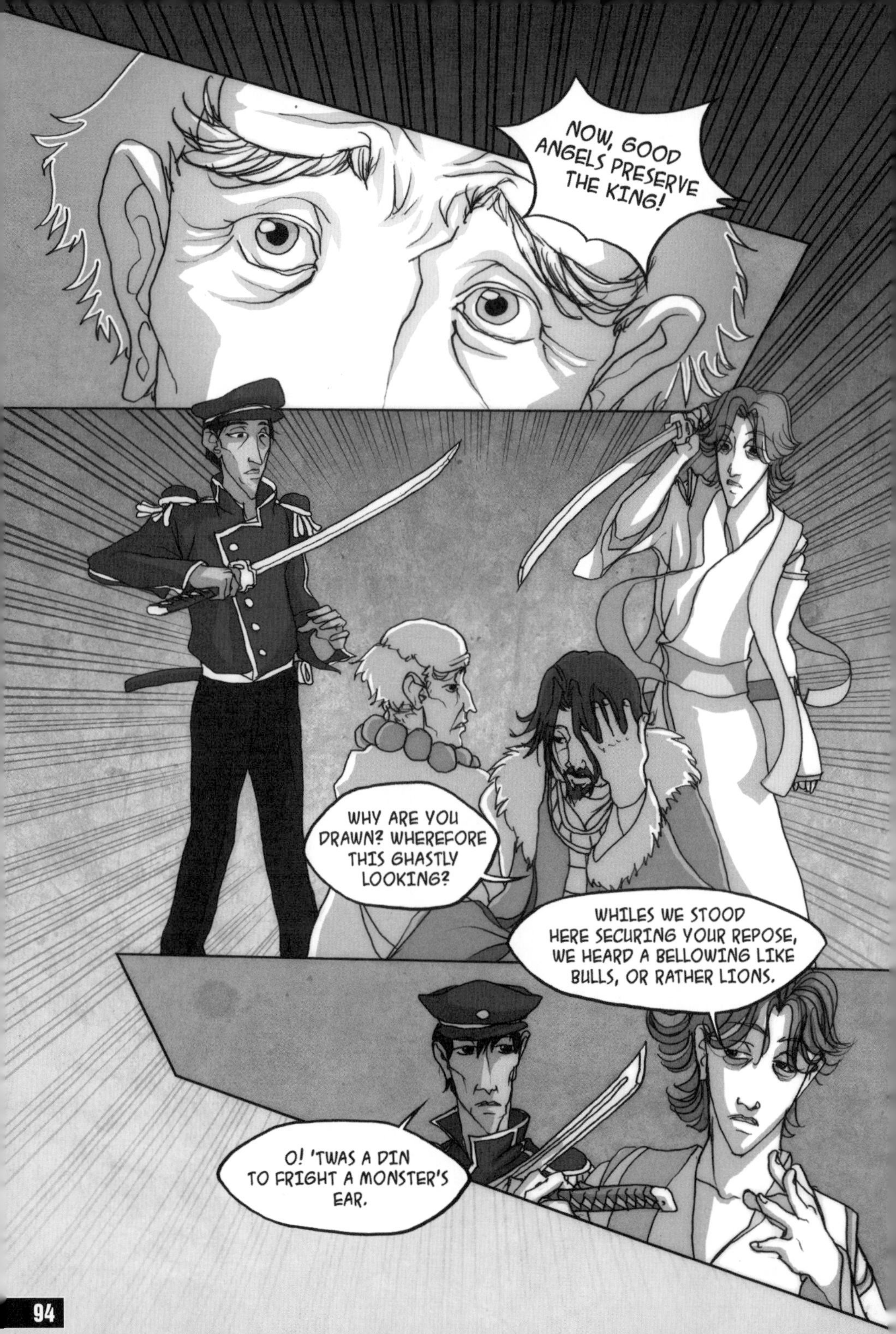
NOW, GOOD ANGELS PRESERVE THE KING!
WHY ARE YOU DRAWN? WHEREFORE THIS GHASTLY LOOKING?
WHILES WE STOOD HERE SECURING YOUR REPOSE, WE HEARD A BELLOWING LIKE BULLS, OR RATHER LIONS.
O! 'TWAS A DIN TO FRIGHT A MONSTER'S EAR.

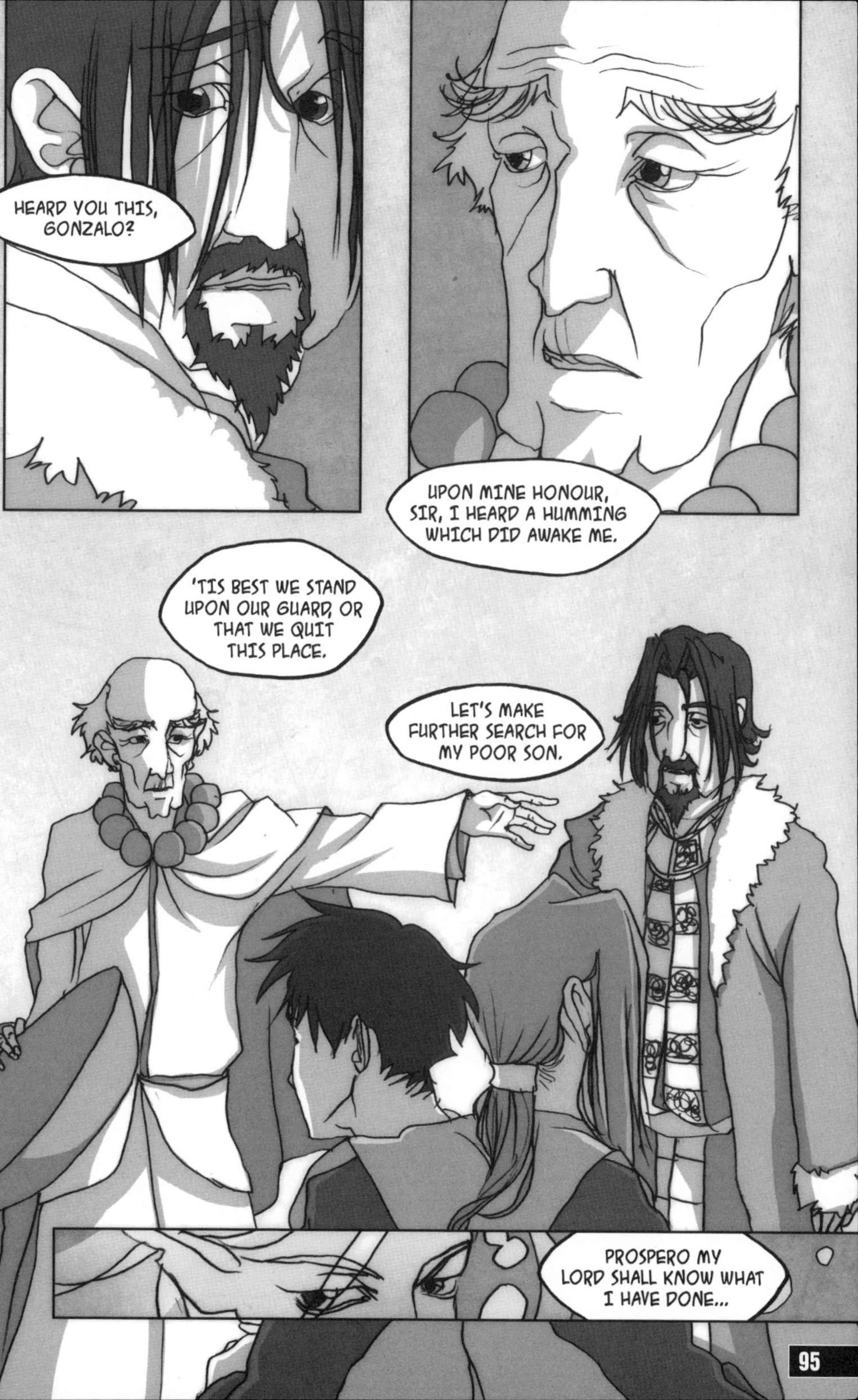
HEARD YOU THIS, GONZALO?
UPON MINE HONOUR, SIR, I HEARD A HUMMING WHICH DID AWAKE ME.
'TIS BEST WE STAND UPON OUR GUARD, OR THAT WE QUIT THIS PLACE.
LET'S MAKE FURTHER SEARCH FOR MY POOR SON.
PROSPERO MY LORD SHALL KNOW WHAT I HAVE DONE...

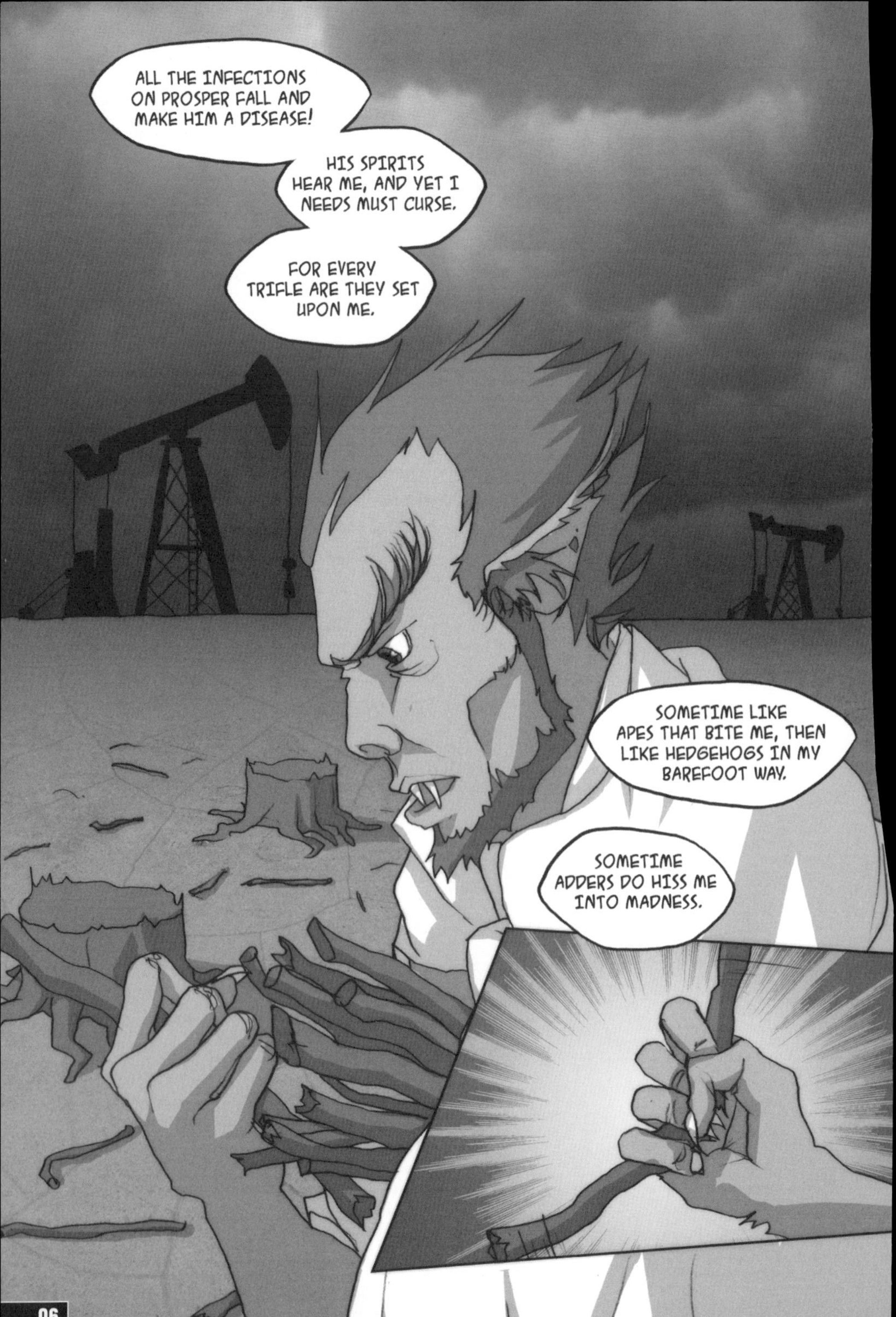
ALL THE INFECTIONS ON PROSPER FALL AND MAKE HIM A DISEASE!
HIS SPIRITS HEAR ME, AND YET I NEEDS MUST CURSE.
FOR EVERY TRIFLE ARE THEY SET UPON ME.
SOMETIME LIKE APES THAT BITE ME, THEN LIKE HEDGEHOGS IN MY BAREFOOT WAY.
SOMETIME ADDERS DO HISS ME INTO MADNESS.

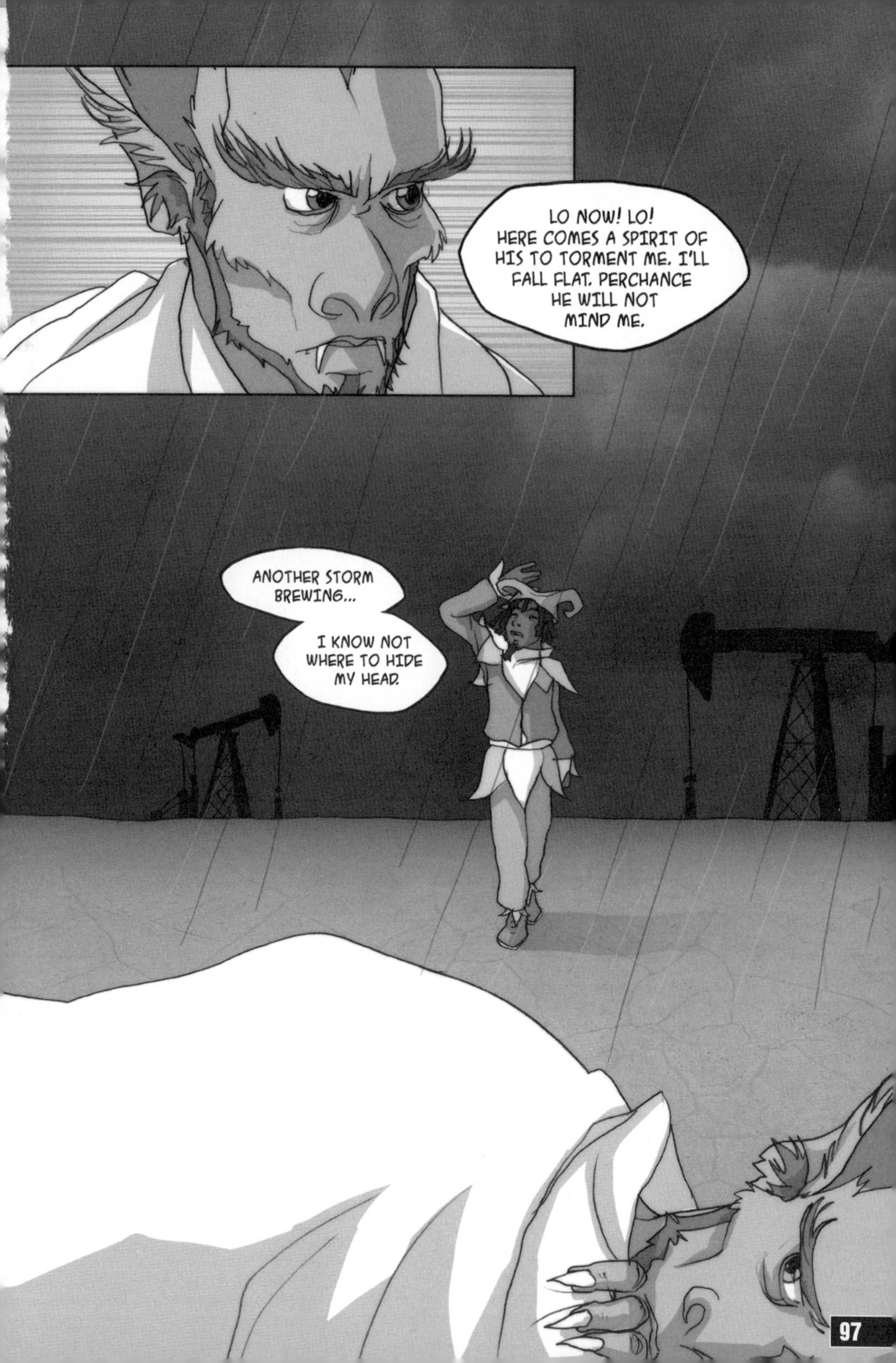
LO NOW! LO! HERE COMES A SPIRIT OF HIS TO TORMENT ME. I'LL FALL FLAT. PERCHANCE HE WILL NOT MIND ME.
ANOTHER STORM BREWING...
I KNOW NOT WHERE TO HIDE MY HEAD.

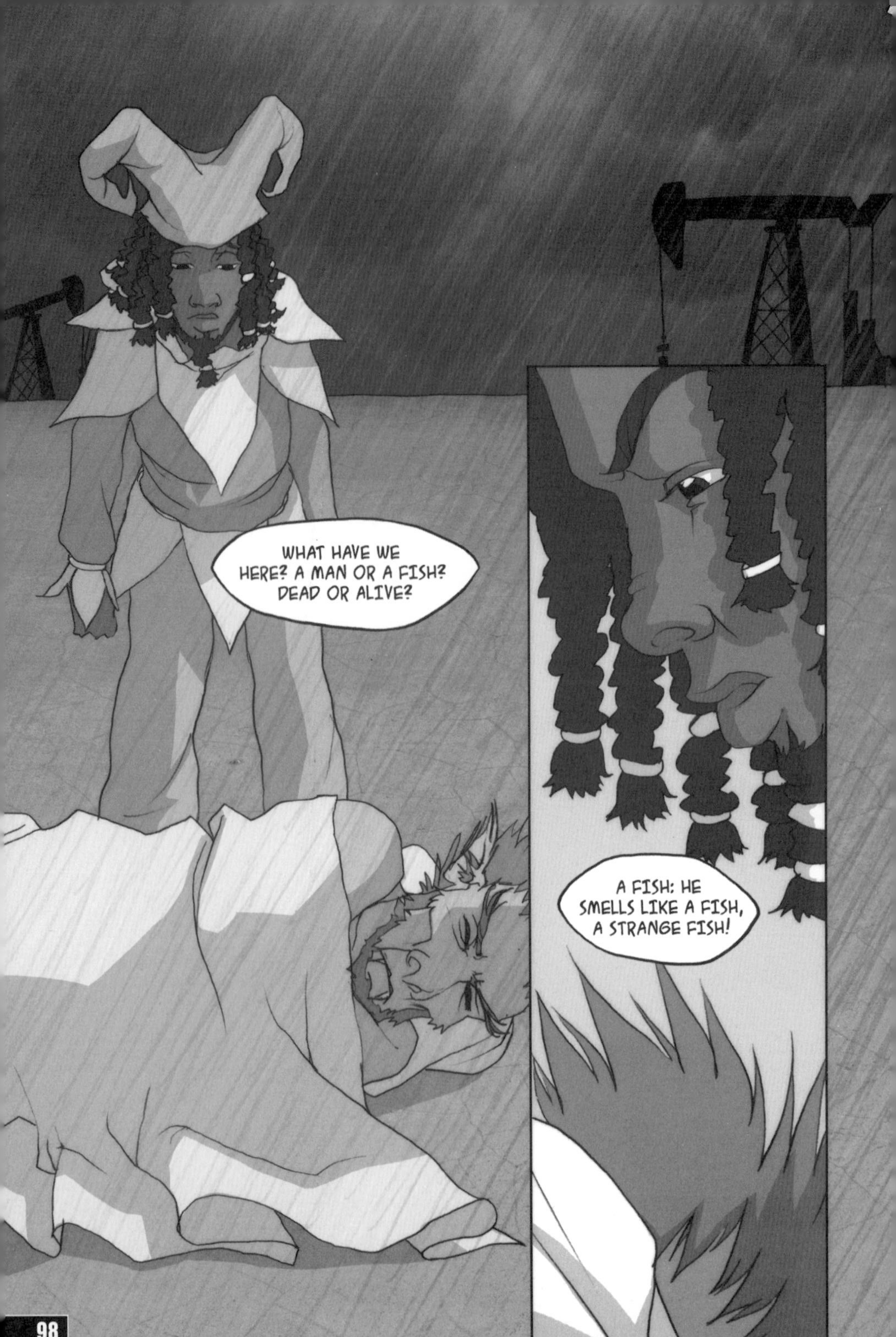

WHAT HAVE WE HERE? A MAN OR A FISH? DEAD OR ALIVE?
A FISH: HE SMELLS LIKE A FISH, A STRANGE FISH!

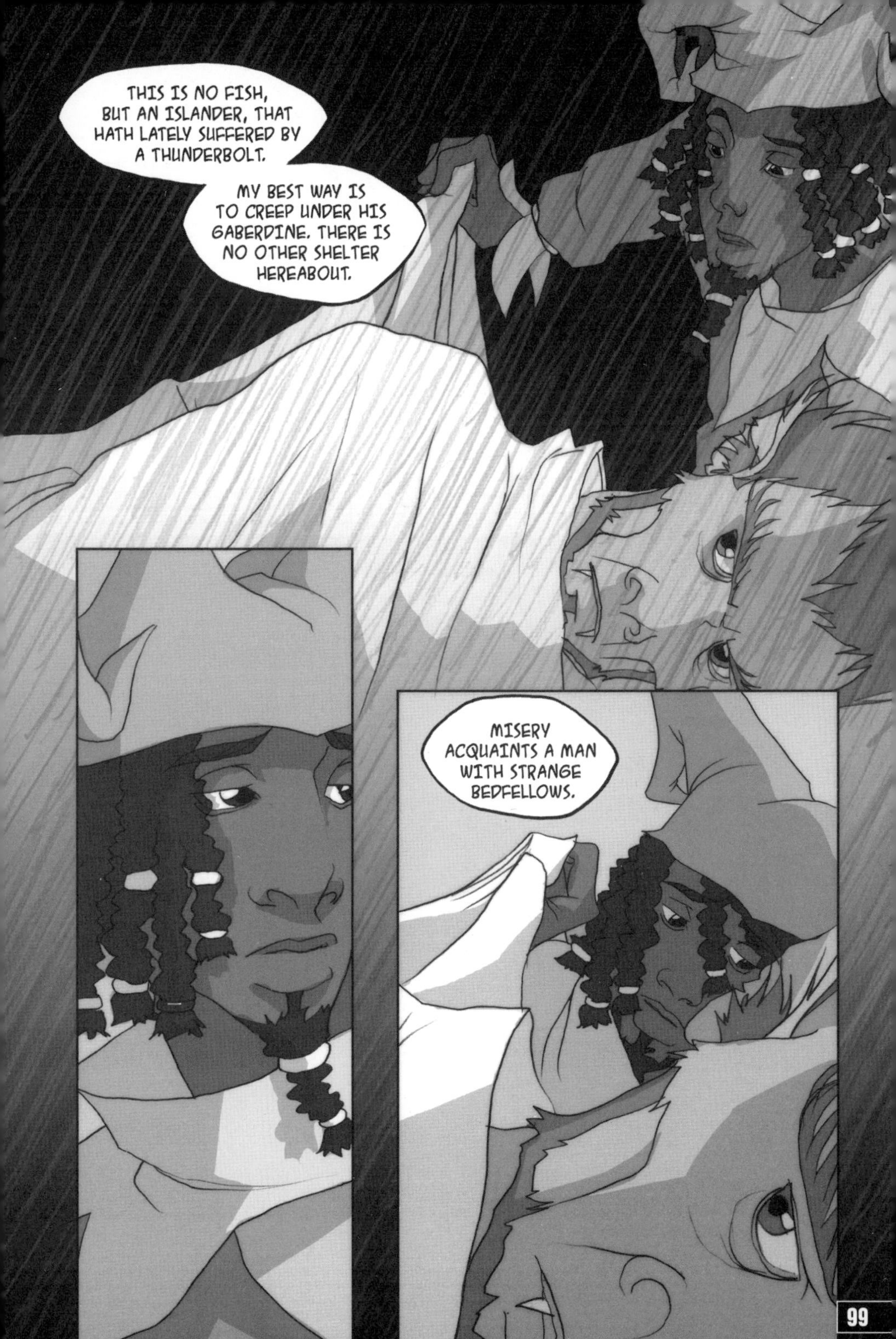
THIS IS NO FISH, BUT AN ISLANDER, THAT HATH LATELY SUFFERED BY A THUNDERBOLT.
MY BEST WAY IS TO CREEP UNDER HIS GABERDINE. THERE IS NO OTHER SHELTER HEREABOUT.
MISERY ACQUAINTS A MAN WITH STRANGE BEDFELLOWS.

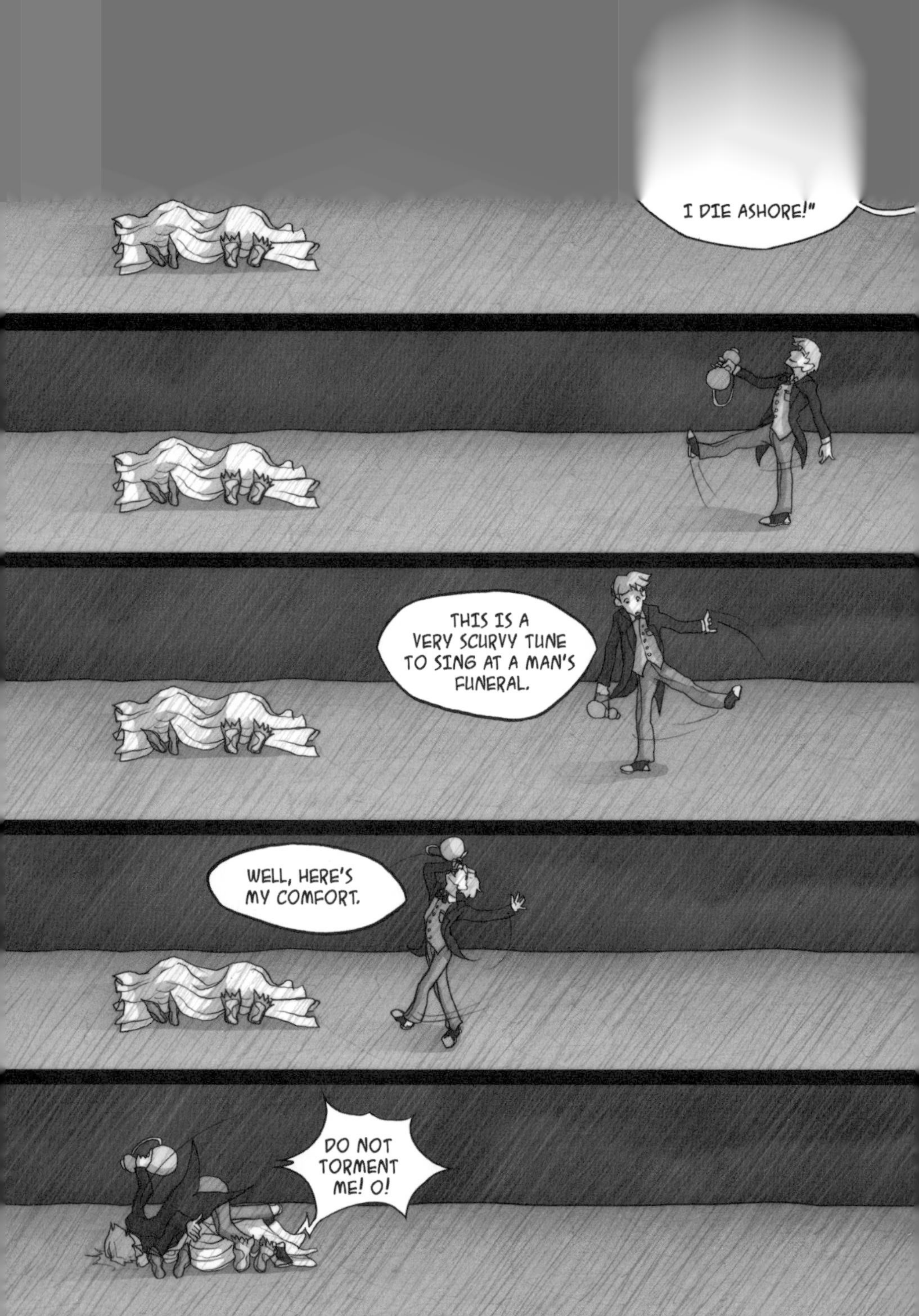
I DIE ASHORE!"
THIS IS A VERY SCURVY TUNE TO SING AT A MAN'S FUNERAL.
WELL, HERE'S MY COMFORT.
DO NOT TORMENT ME! O!

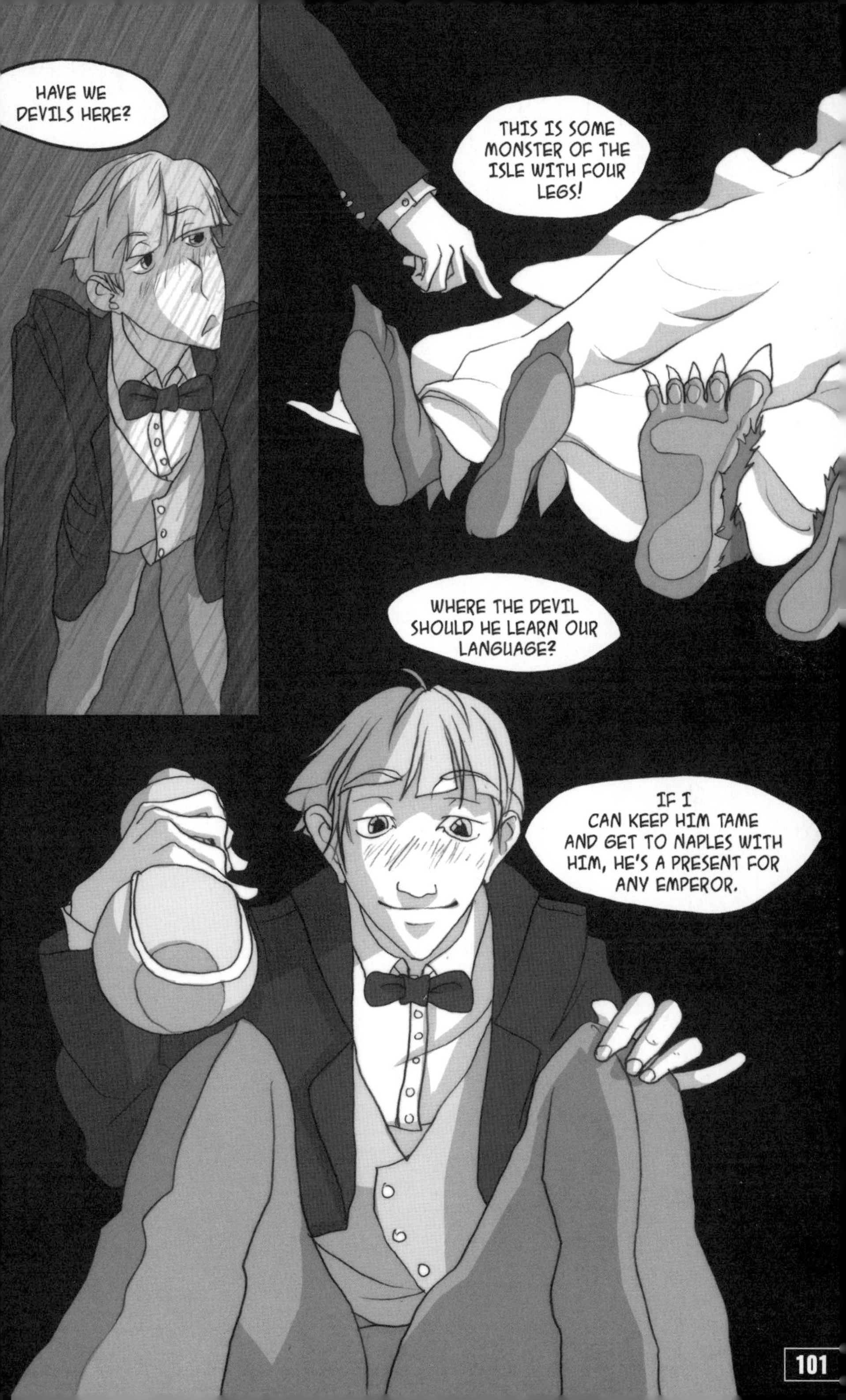
HAVE WE DEVILS HERE?
THIS IS SOME MONSTER OF THE ISLE WITH FOUR LEGS!
WHERE THE DEVIL SHOULD HE LEARN OUR LANGUAGE?
IF I CAN KEEP HIM TAME AND GET TO NAPLES WITH HIM, HE'S A PRESENT FOR ANY EMPEROR.

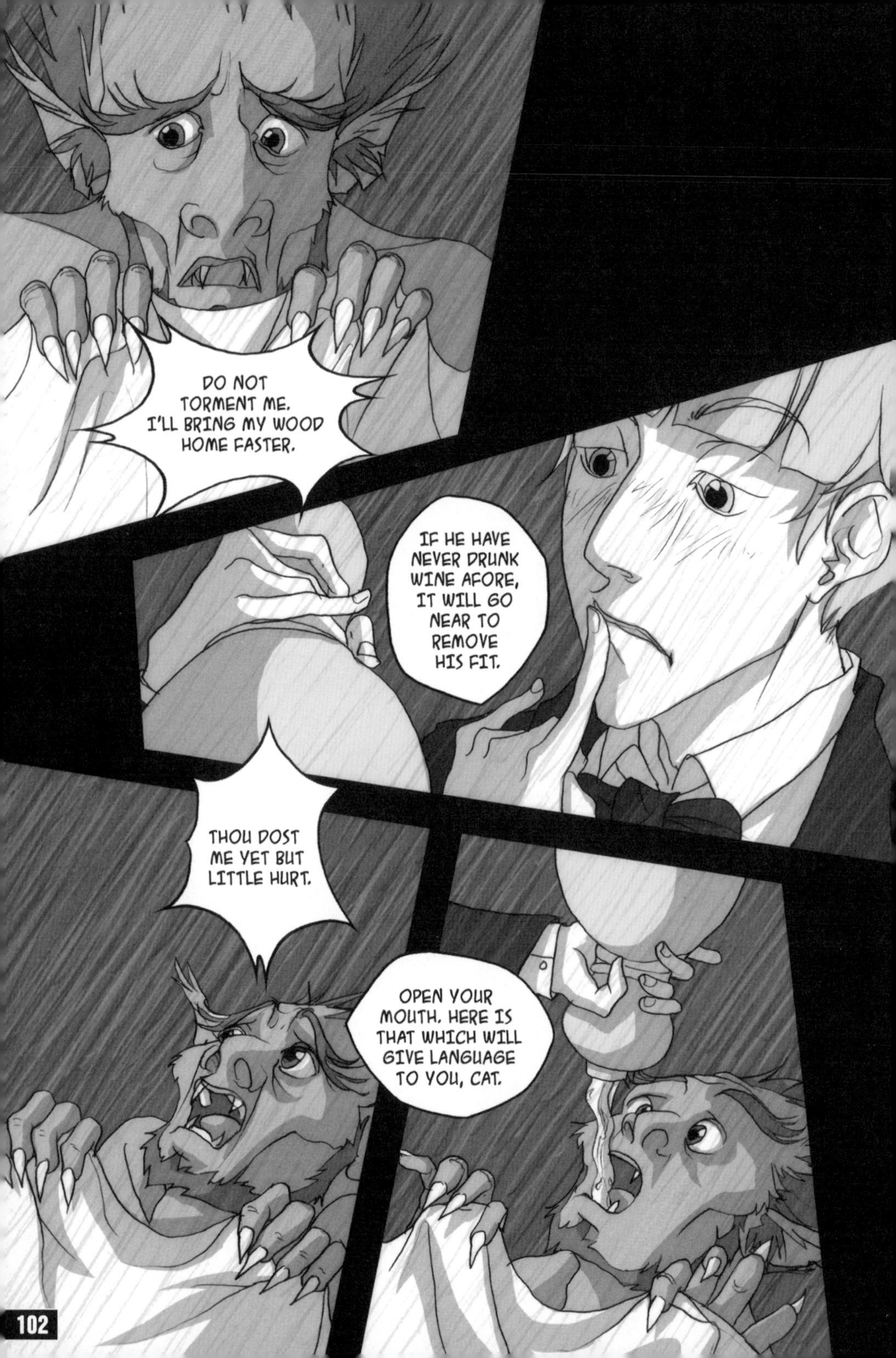
DO NOT TORMENT ME. I'LL BRING MY WOOD HOME FASTER.
IF HE HAVE NEVER DRUNK WINE AFORE, IT WILL GO NEAR TO REMOVE HIS FIT.
THOU DOST ME YET BUT LITTLE HURT.
OPEN YOUR MOUTH. HERE IS THAT WHICH WILL GIVE LANGUAGE TO YOU, CAT.

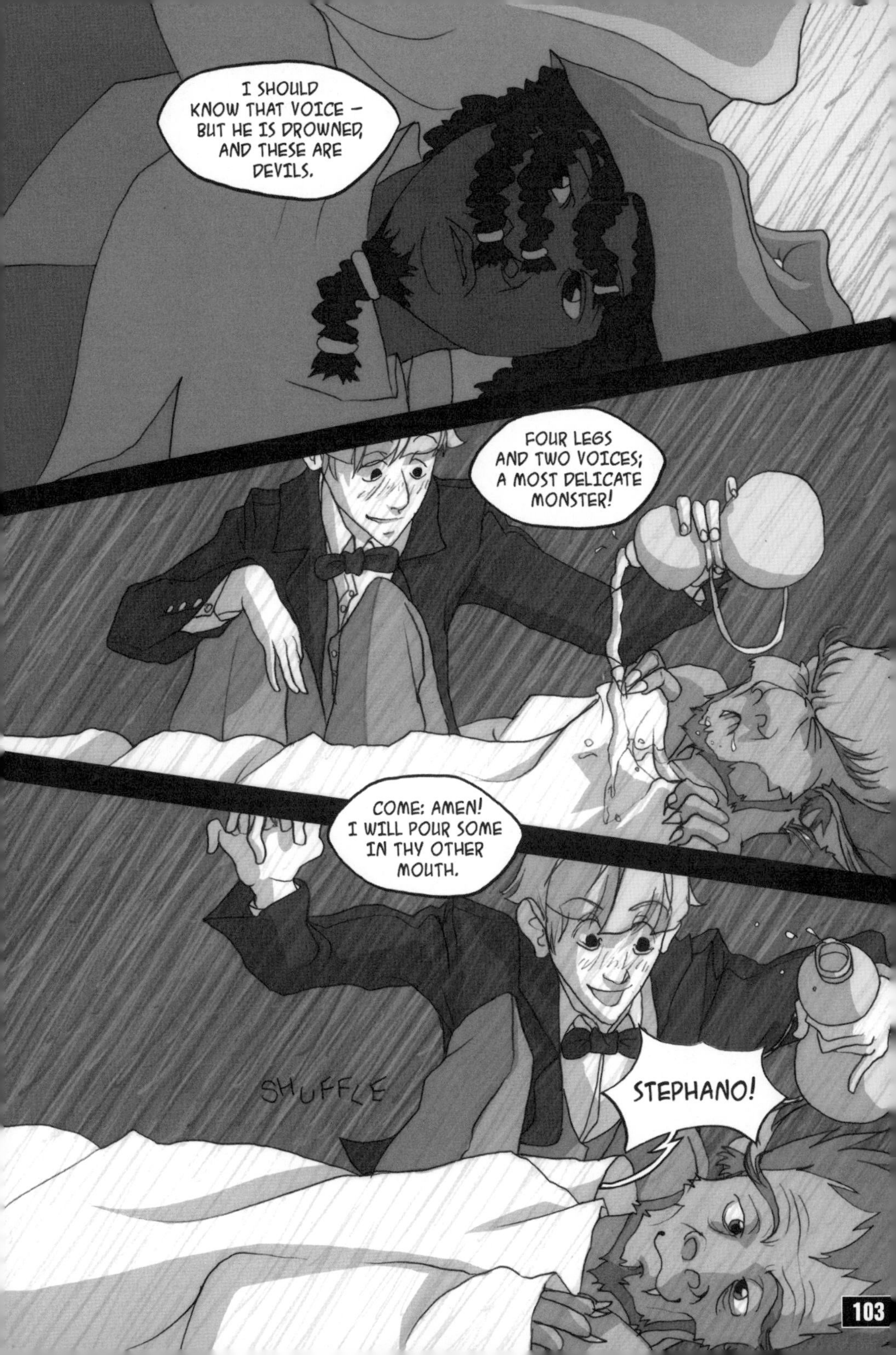
I SHOULD KNOW THAT VOICE – BUT HE IS DROWNED, AND THESE ARE DEVILS.
FOUR LEGS AND TWO VOICES; A MOST DELICATE MONSTER!
COME: AMEN! I WILL POUR SOME IN THY OTHER MOUTH.
SHUFFLE
STEPHANO!

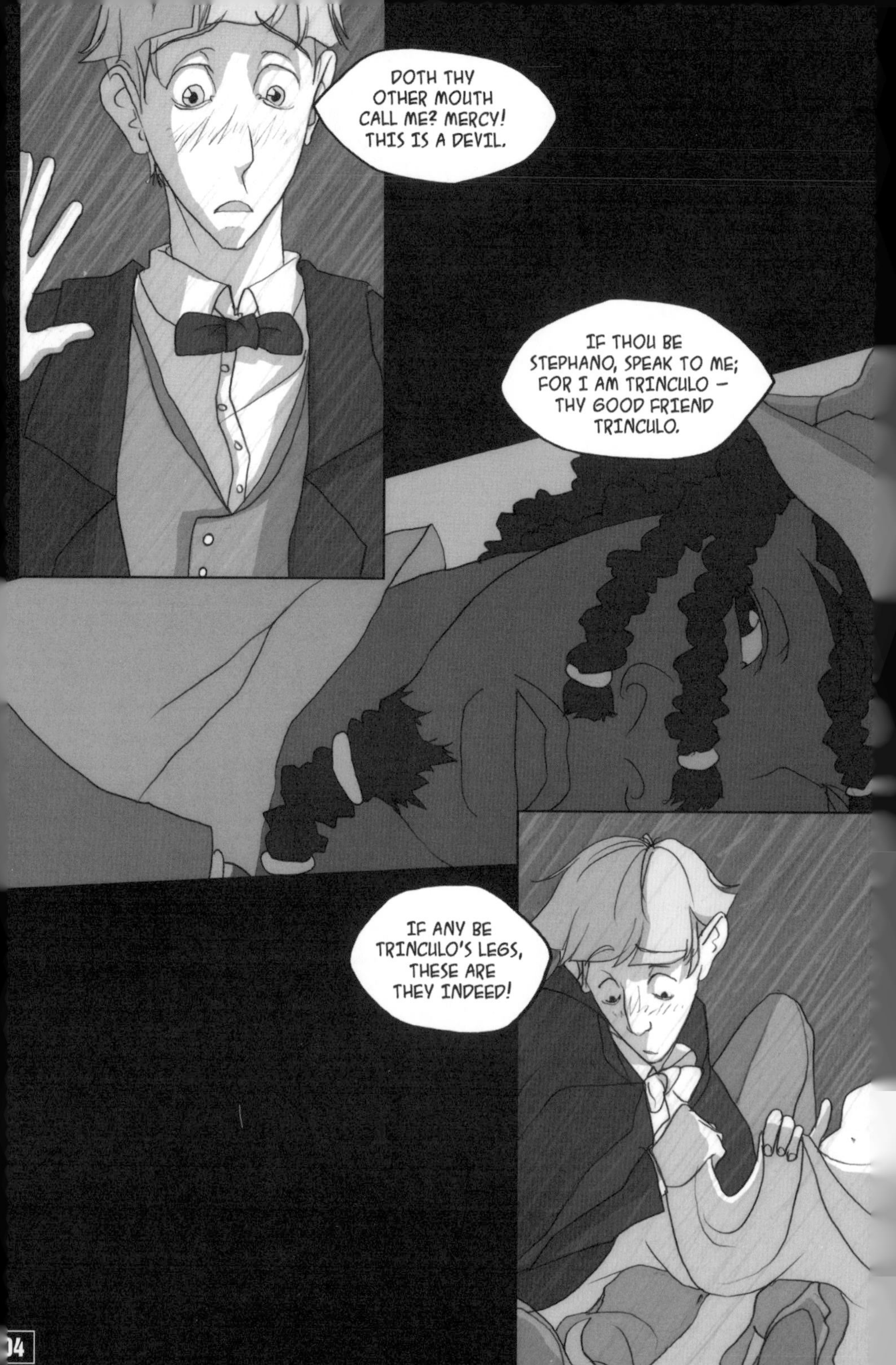
DOTH THY OTHER MOUTH CALL ME? MERCY! THIS IS A DEVIL.
IF THOU BE STEPHANO, SPEAK TO ME; FOR I AM TRINCULO — THY GOOD FRIEND TRINCULO.
IF ANY BE TRINCULO'S LEGS, THESE ARE THEY INDEED!

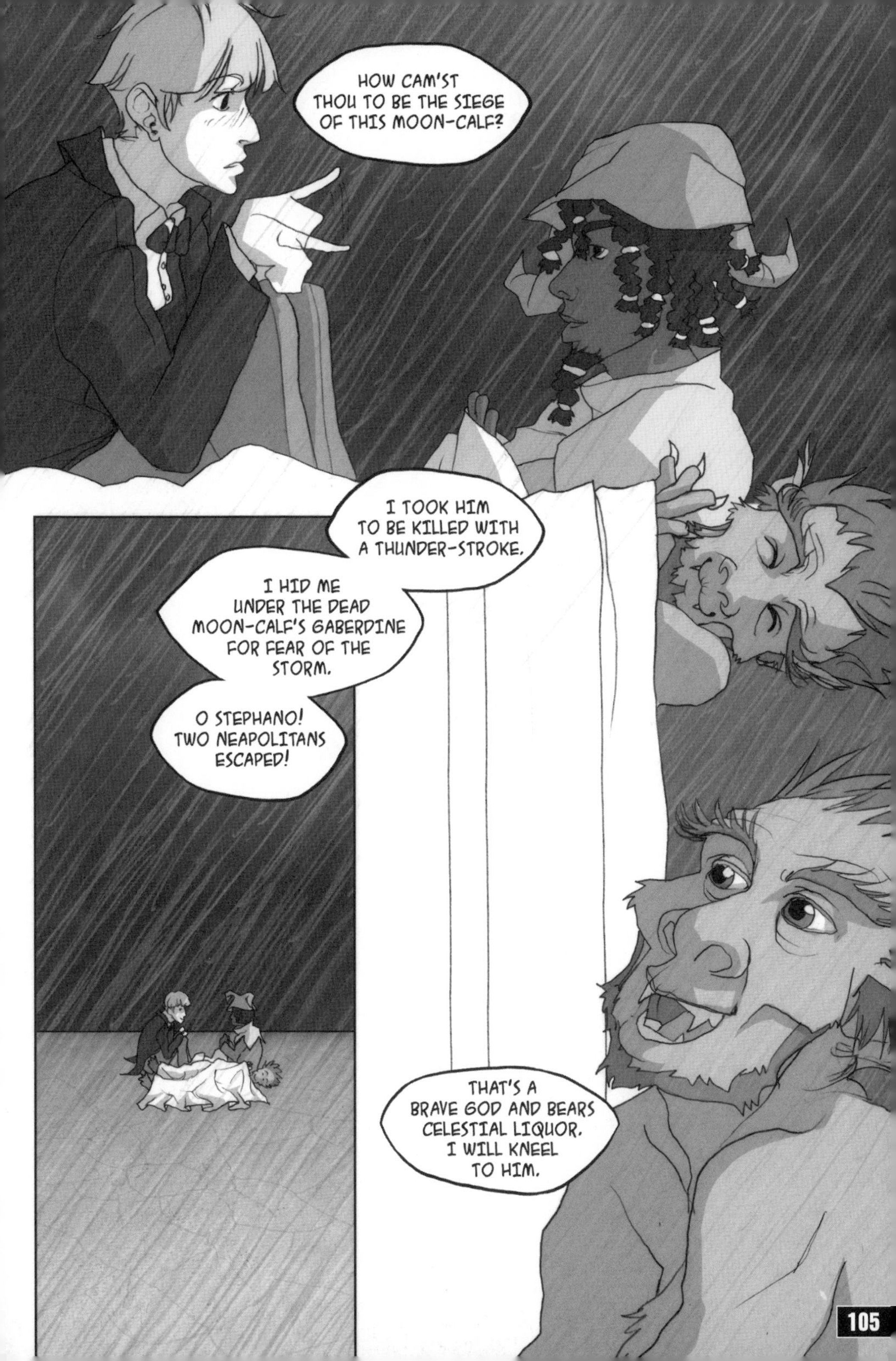
HOW CAM'ST THOU TO BE THE SIEGE OF THIS MOON-CALF?
I TOOK HIM TO BE KILLED WITH A THUNDER-STROKE.
I HID ME UNDER THE DEAD MOON-CALF'S GABERDINE FOR FEAR OF THE STORM.
O STEPHANO! TWO NEAPOLITANS ESCAPED!
THAT'S A BRAVE GOD AND BEARS CELESTIAL LIQUOR. I WILL KNEEL TO HIM.

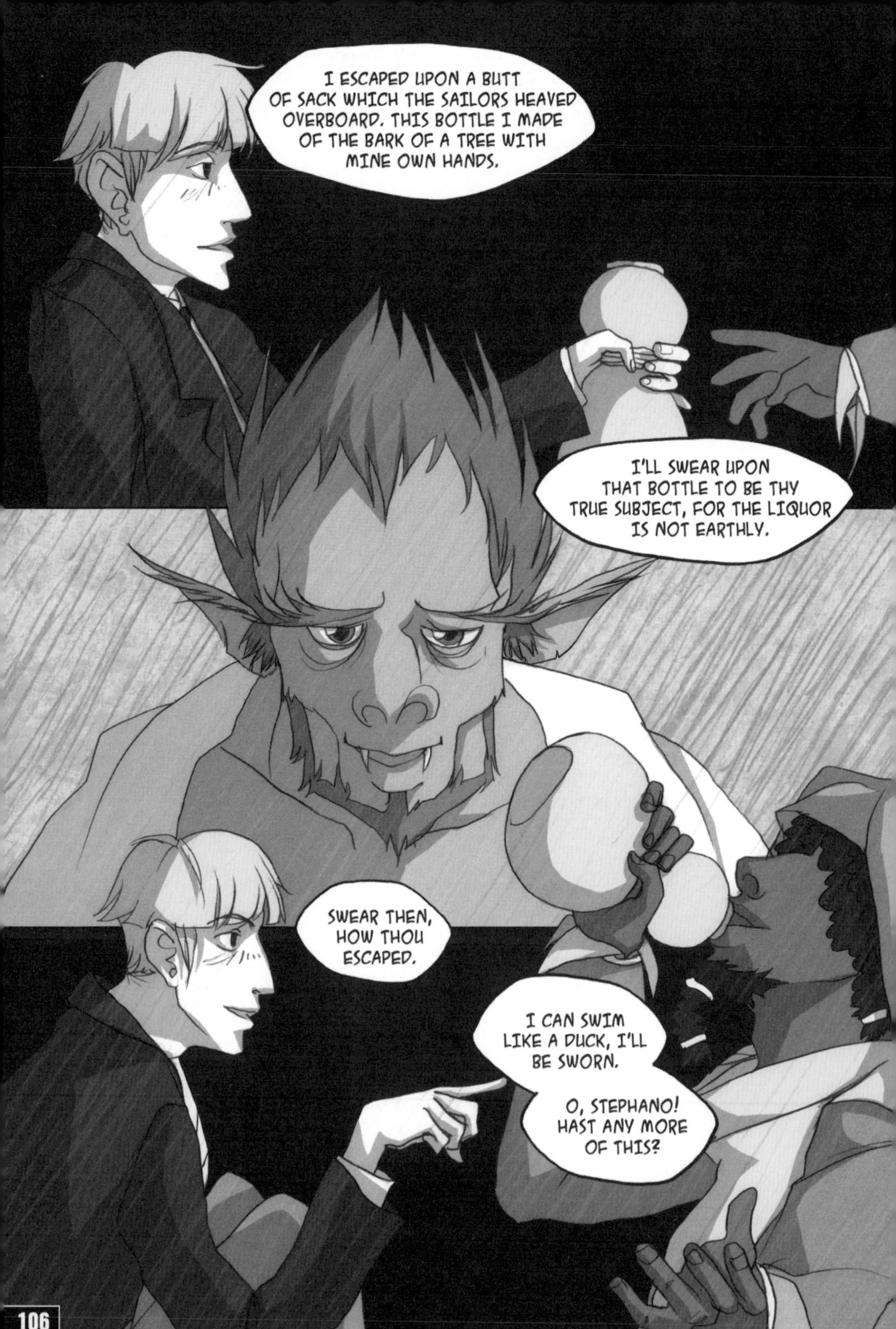
I ESCAPED UPON A BUTT OF SACK WHICH THE SAILORS HEAVED OVERBOARD. THIS BOTTLE I MADE OF THE BARK OF A TREE WITH MINE OWN HANDS.
I'LL SWEAR UPON THAT BOTTLE TO BE THY TRUE SUBJECT, FOR THE LIQUOR IS NOT EARTHLY.
SWEAR THEN, HOW THOU ESCAPED.
I CAN SWIM LIKE A DUCK, I'LL BE SWORN.
O, STEPHANO! HAST ANY MORE OF THIS?

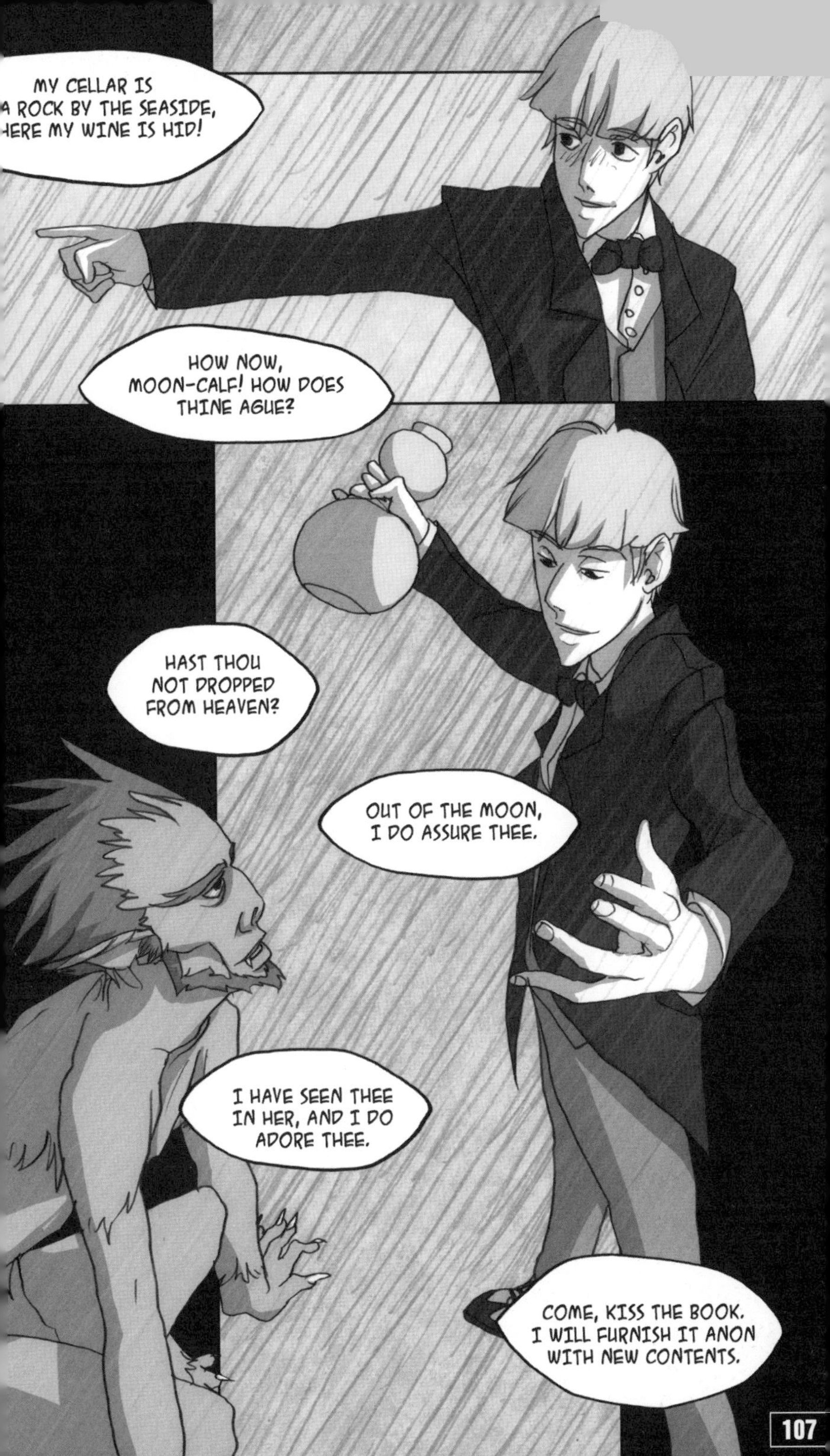
MY CELLAR IS A ROCK BY THE SEASIDE, HERE MY WINE IS HID!
HOW NOW, MOON-CALF! HOW DOES THINE AGUE?
HAST THOU NOT DROPPED FROM HEAVEN?
OUT OF THE MOON, I DO ASSURE THEE.
I HAVE SEEN THEE IN HER, AND I DO ADORE THEE.
COME, KISS THE BOOK. I WILL FURNISH IT ANON WITH NEW CONTENTS.

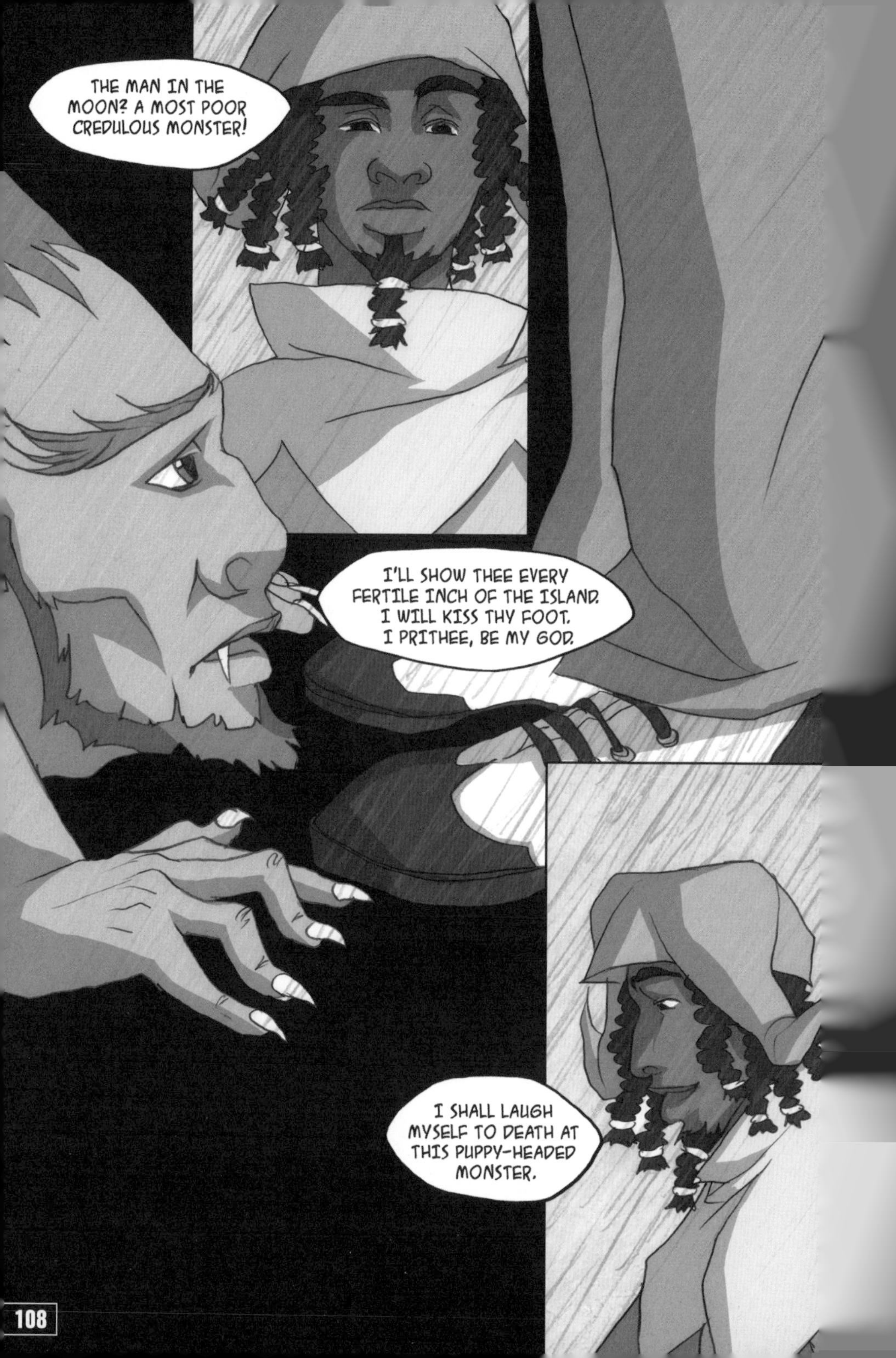
THE MAN IN THE MOON? A MOST POOR CREDULOUS MONSTER!
I'LL SHOW THEE EVERY FERTILE INCH OF THE ISLAND. I WILL KISS THY FOOT. I PRITHEE, BE MY GOD.
I SHALL LAUGH MYSELF TO DEATH AT THIS PUPPY-HEADED MONSTER.

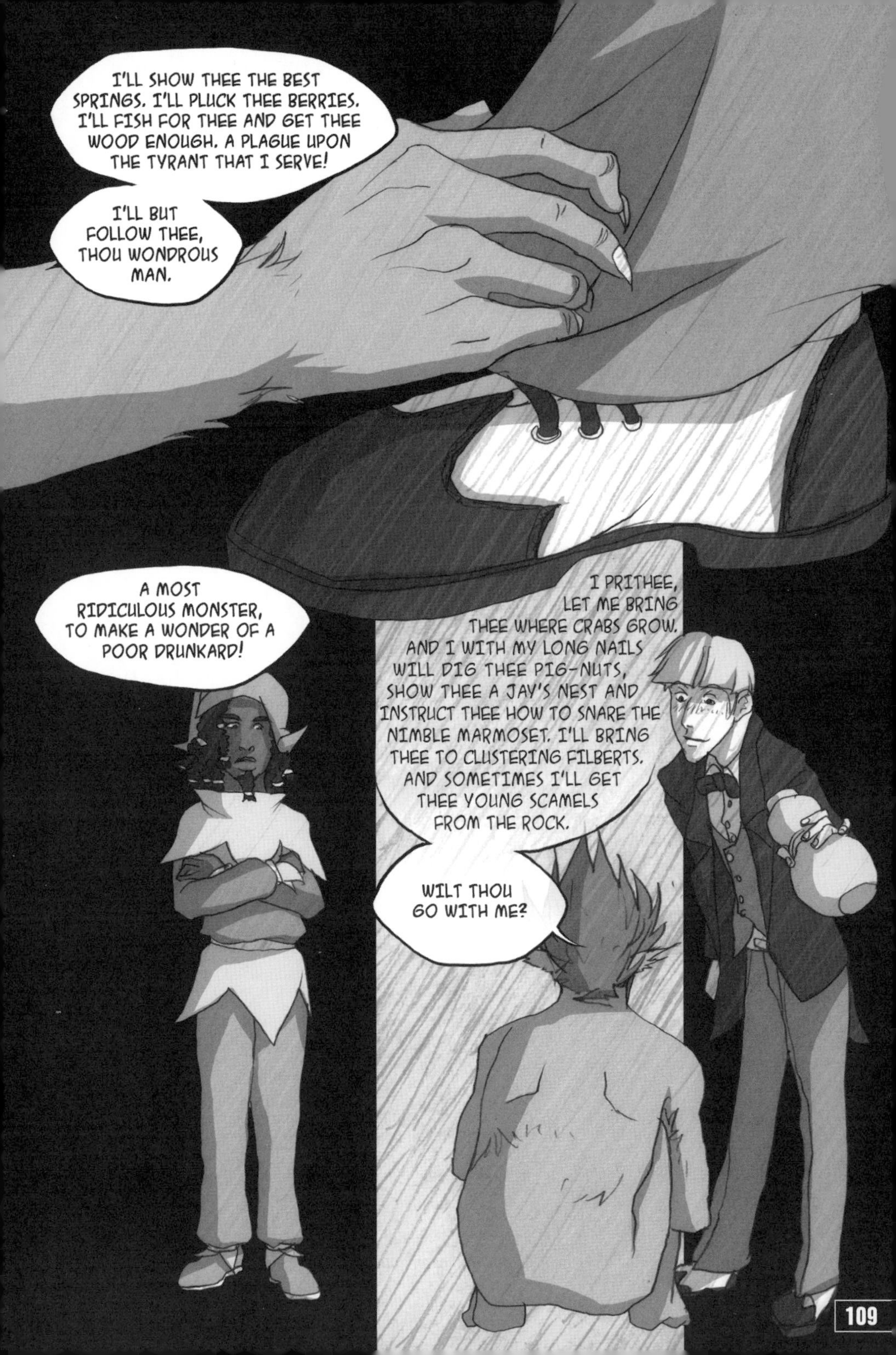
I'LL SHOW THEE THE BEST SPRINGS. I'LL PLUCK THEE BERRIES. I'LL FISH FOR THEE AND GET THEE WOOD ENOUGH. A PLAGUE UPON THE TYRANT THAT I SERVE!
I'LL BUT FOLLOW THEE, THOU WONDROUS MAN.
A MOST RIDICULOUS MONSTER, TO MAKE A WONDER OF A POOR DRUNKARD!
I PRITHEE, LET ME BRING THEE WHERE CRABS GROW. AND I WITH MY LONG NAILS WILL DIG THEE PIG-NUTS, SHOW THEE A JAY'S NEST AND INSTRUCT THEE HOW TO SNARE THE NIMBLE MARMOSET. I'LL BRING THEE TO CLUSTERING FILBERTS. AND SOMETIMES I'LL GET THEE YOUNG SCAMELS FROM THE ROCK.
WILT THOU GO WITH ME?

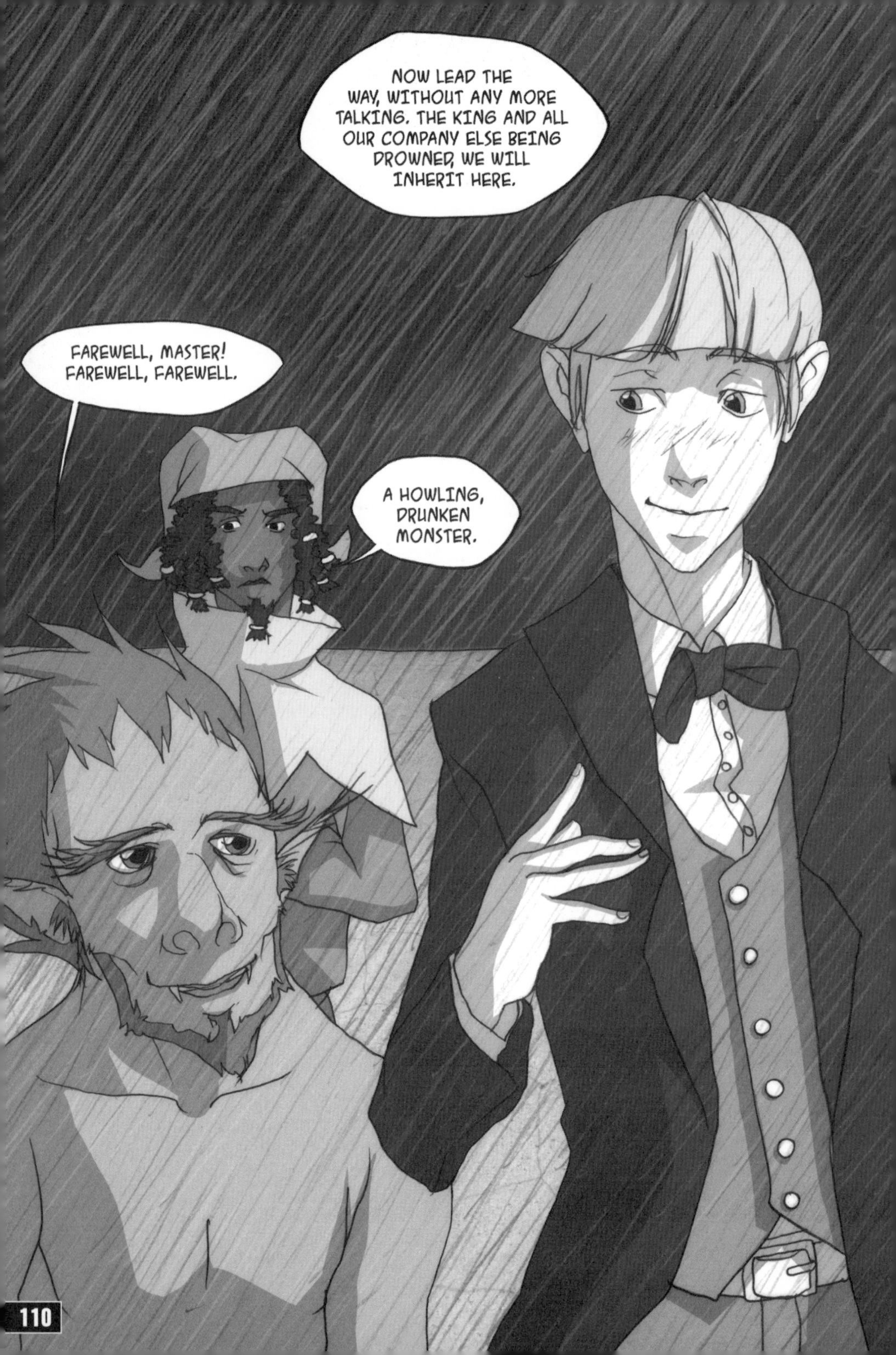
NOW LEAD THE WAY, WITHOUT ANY MORE TALKING. THE KING AND ALL OUR COMPANY ELSE BEING DROWNED, WE WILL INHERIT HERE.
FAREWELL, MASTER! FAREWELL, FAREWELL.
A HOWLING, DRUNKEN MONSTER.

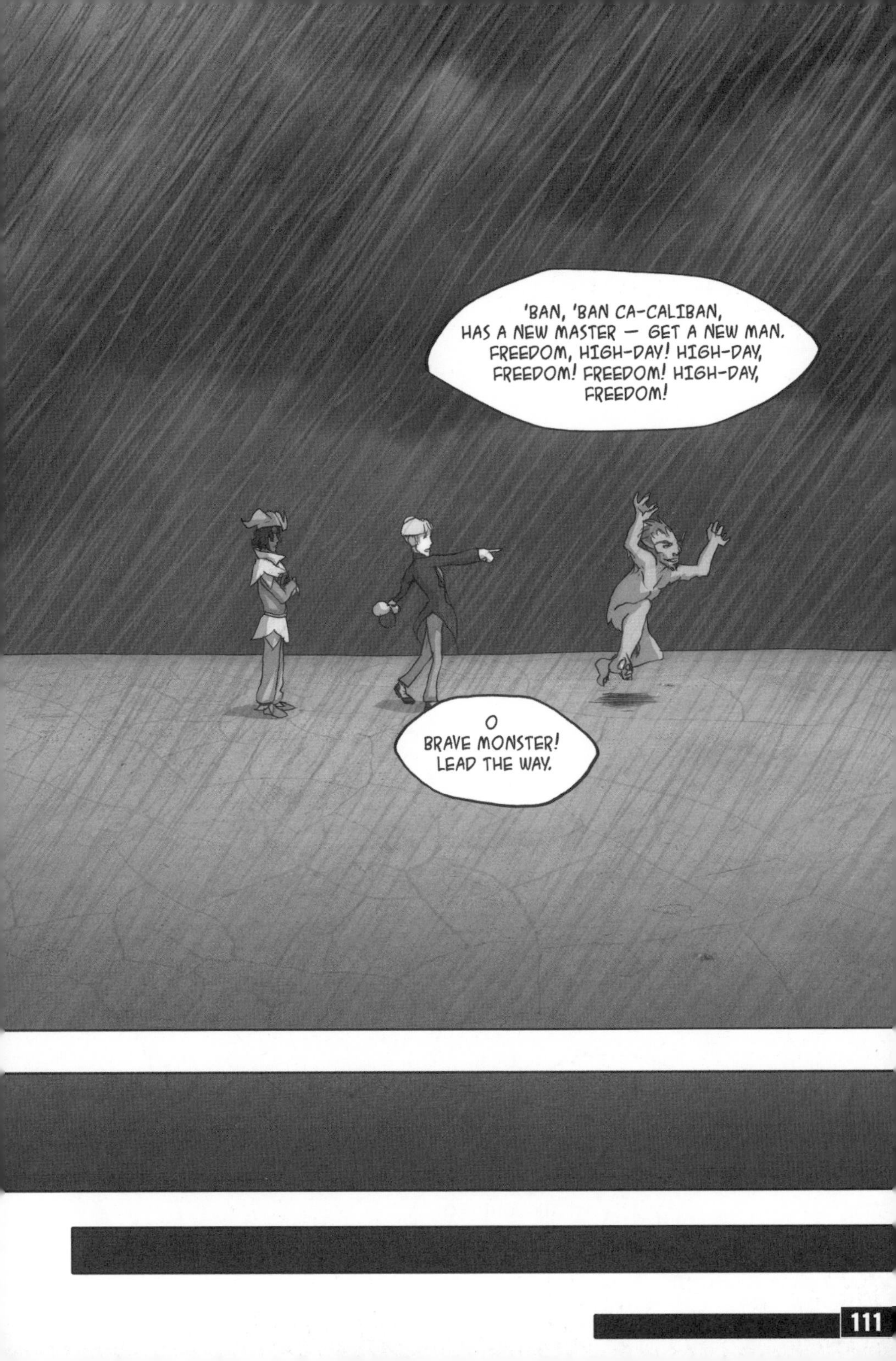
'BAN, 'BAN CA-CALIBAN, HAS A NEW MASTER — GET A NEW MAN. FREEDOM, HIGH-DAY! HIGH-DAY, FREEDOM! FREEDOM! HIGH-DAY, FREEDOM!
O BRAVE MONSTER! LEAD THE WAY.

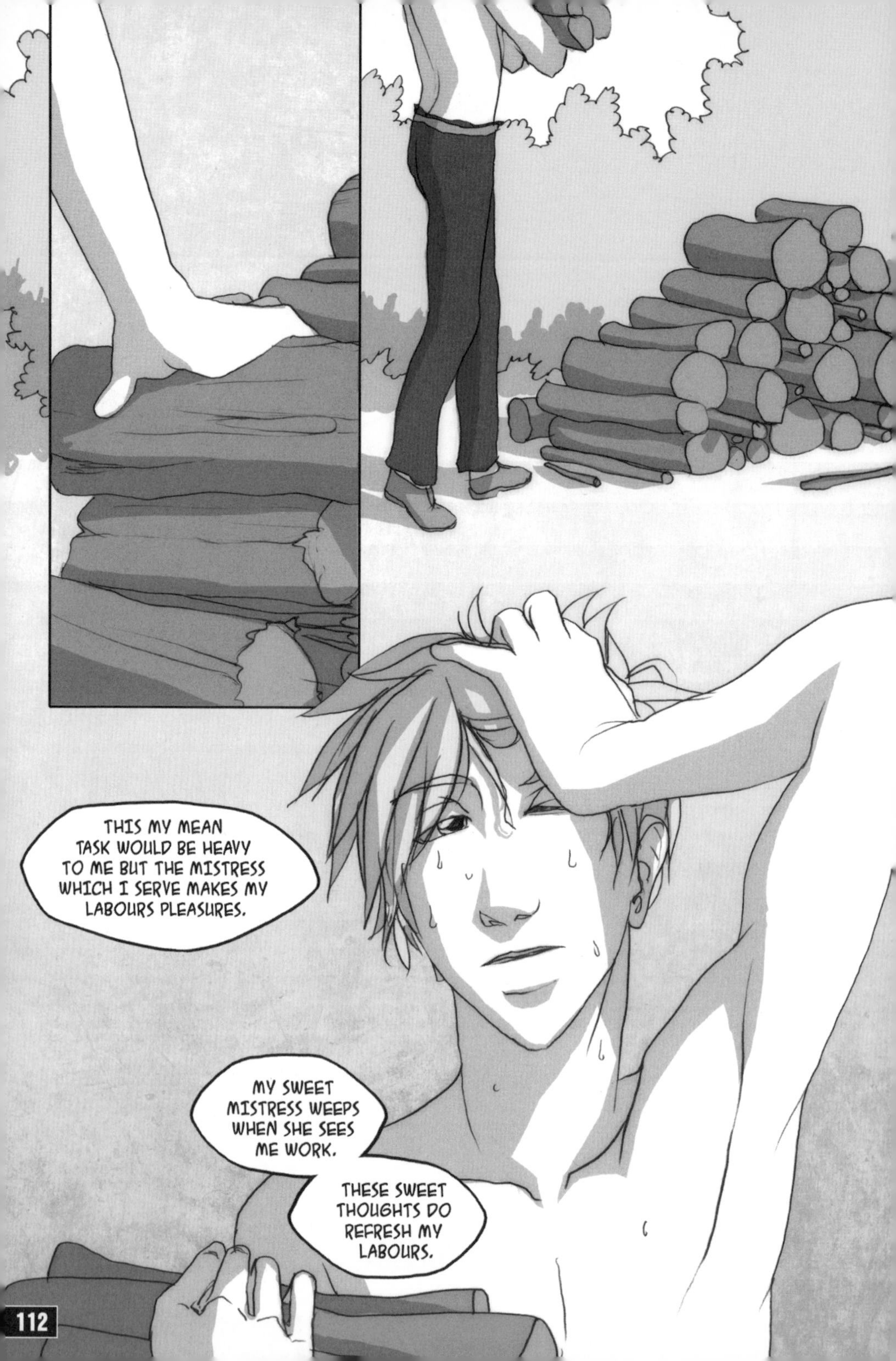
THIS MY MEAN TASK WOULD BE HEAVY TO ME BUT THE MISTRESS WHICH I SERVE MAKES MY LABOURS PLEASURES.
MY SWEET MISTRESS WEEPS WHEN SHE SEES ME WORK.
THESE SWEET THOUGHTS DO REFRESH MY LABOURS.

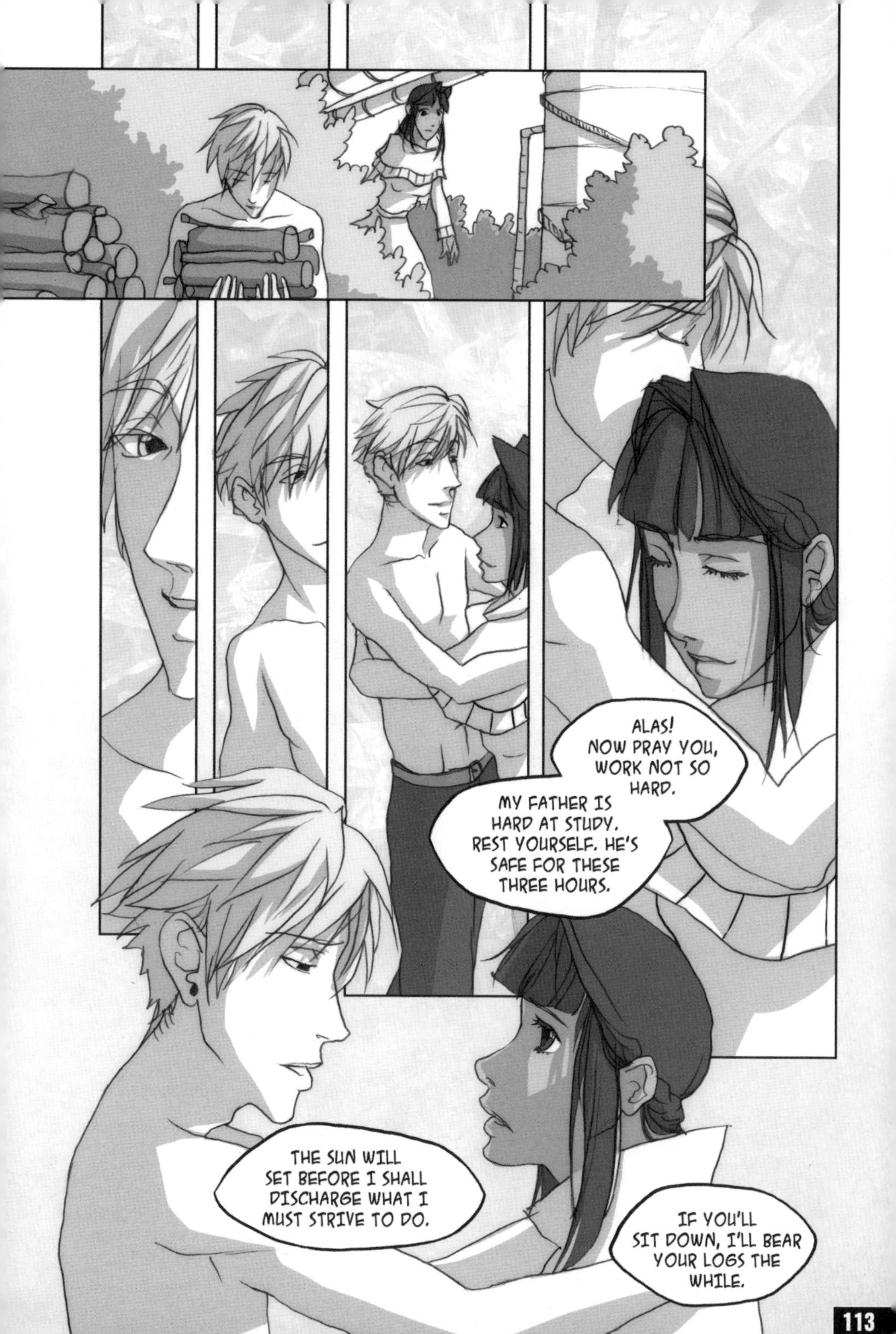
ALAS! NOW PRAY YOU, WORK NOT SO HARD.
MY FATHER IS HARD AT STUDY. REST YOURSELF. HE'S SAFE FOR THESE THREE HOURS.
THE SUN WILL SET BEFORE I SHALL DISCHARGE WHAT I MUST STRIVE TO DO.
IF YOU'LL SIT DOWN, I'LL BEAR YOUR LOGS THE WHILE.

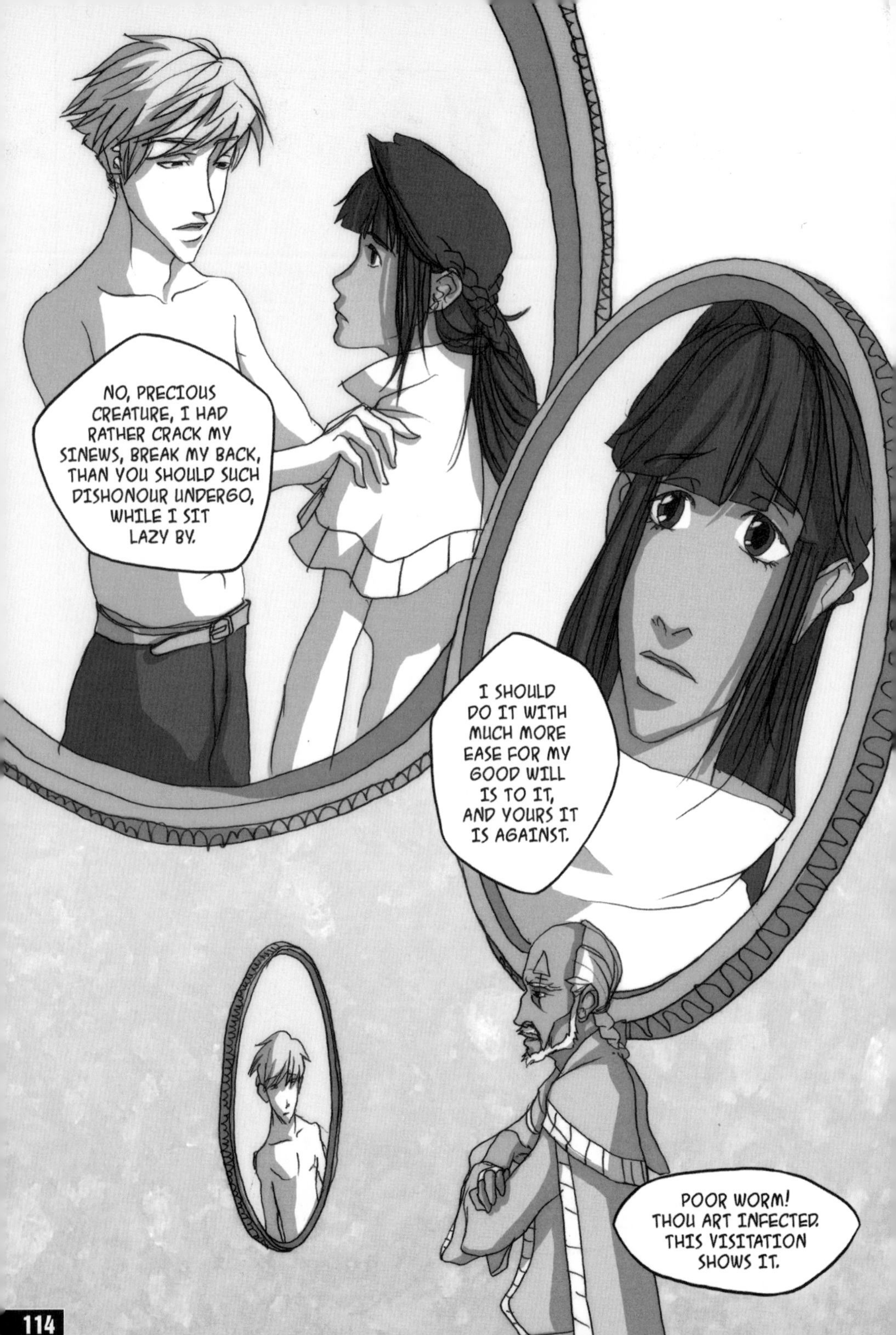
NO, PRECIOUS CREATURE, I HAD RATHER CRACK MY SINEWS, BREAK MY BACK, THAN YOU SHOULD SUCH DISHONOUR UNDERGO, WHILE I SIT LAZY BY.
I SHOULD DO IT WITH MUCH MORE EASE FOR MY GOOD WILL IS TO IT, AND YOURS IT IS AGAINST.
POOR WORM! THOU ART INFECTED. THIS VISITATION SHOWS IT.

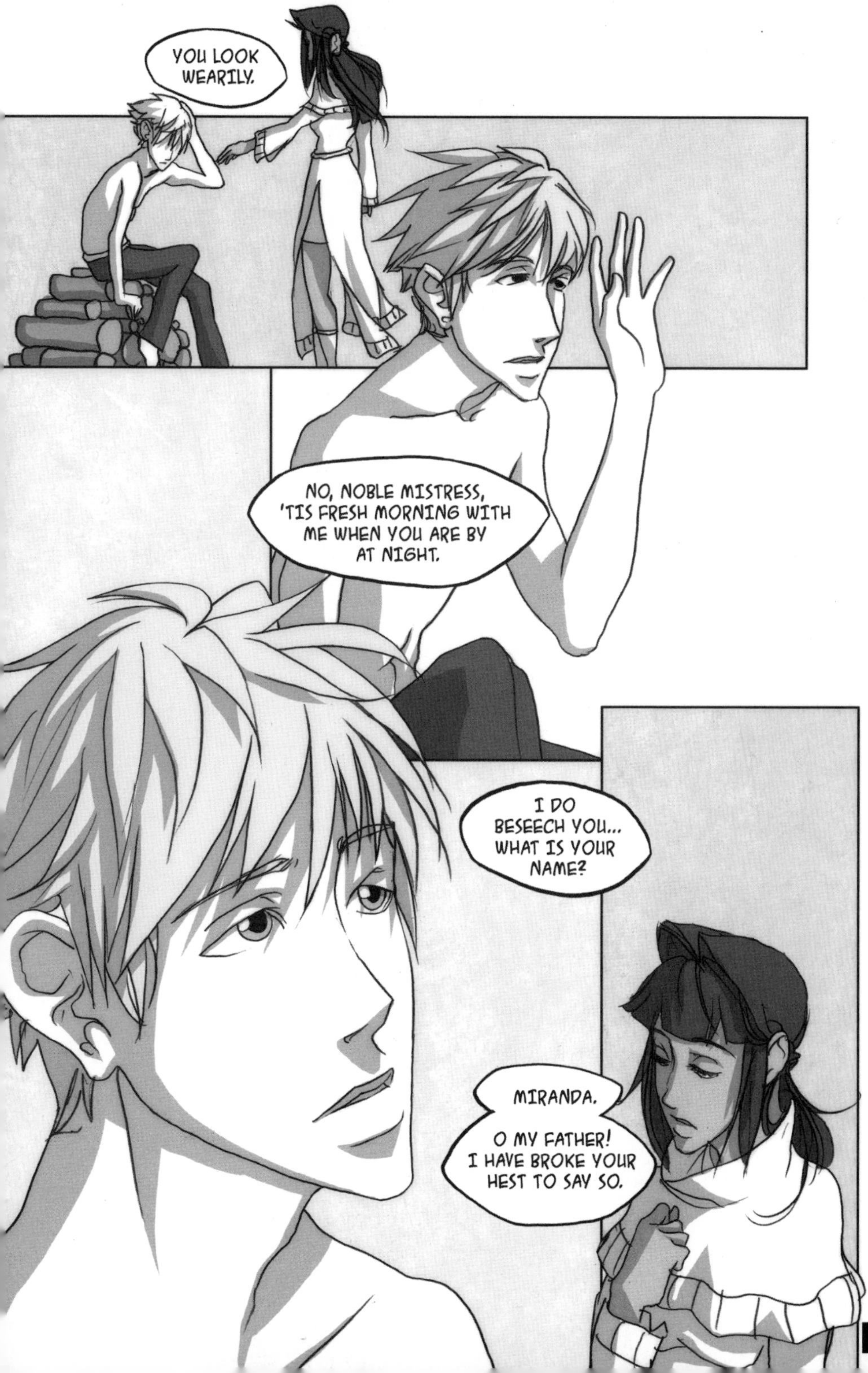
YOU LOOK WEARILY.
NO, NOBLE MISTRESS, 'TIS FRESH MORNING WITH ME WHEN YOU ARE BY AT NIGHT.
I DO BESEECH YOU... WHAT IS YOUR NAME?
MIRANDA.
O MY FATHER! I HAVE BROKE YOUR HEST TO SAY SO.

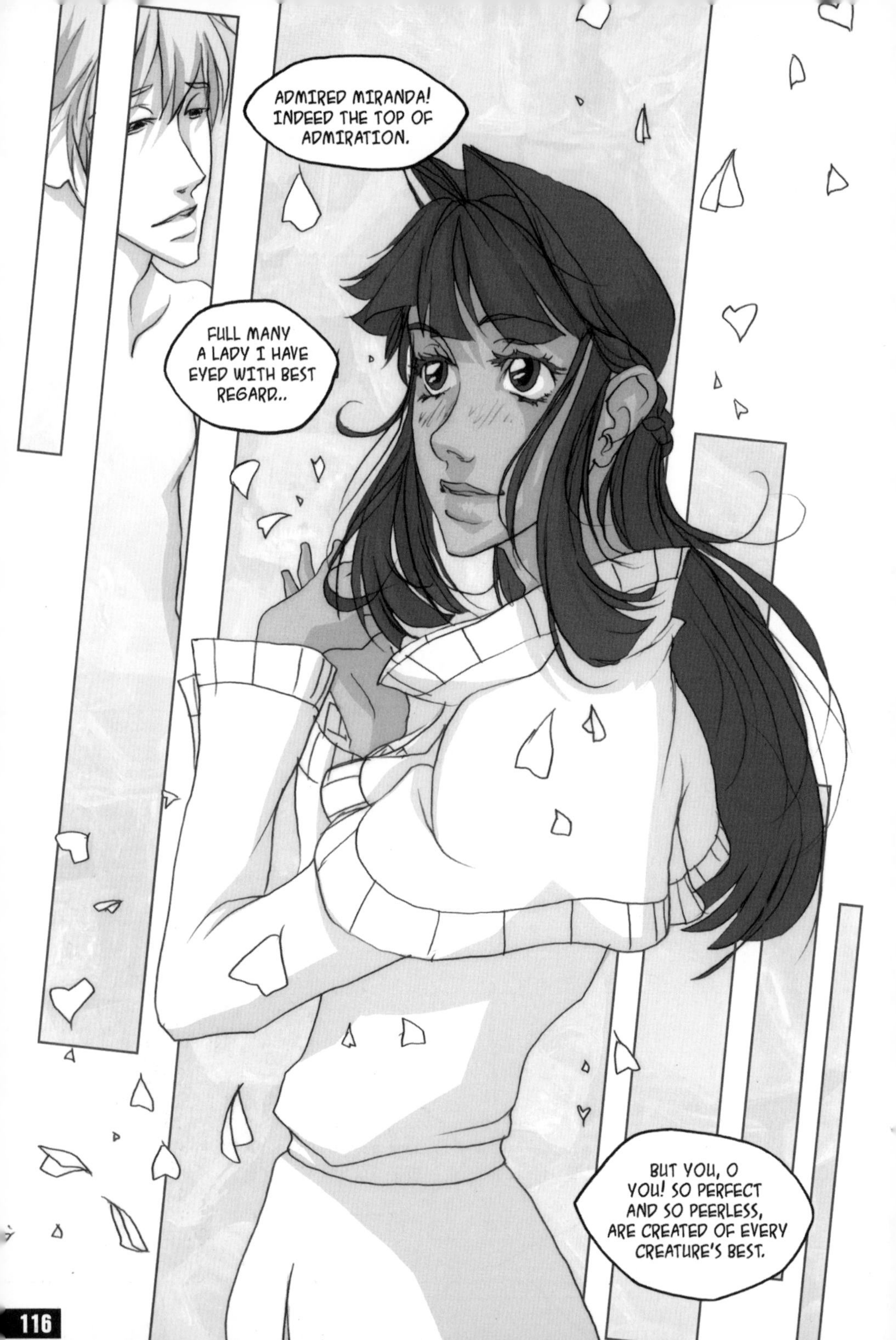
ADMIRED MIRANDA! INDEED THE TOP OF ADMIRATION.
FULL MANY A LADY I HAVE EYED WITH BEST REGARD...
BUT YOU, O YOU! SO PERFECT AND SO PEERLESS, ARE CREATED OF EVERY CREATURE'S BEST.

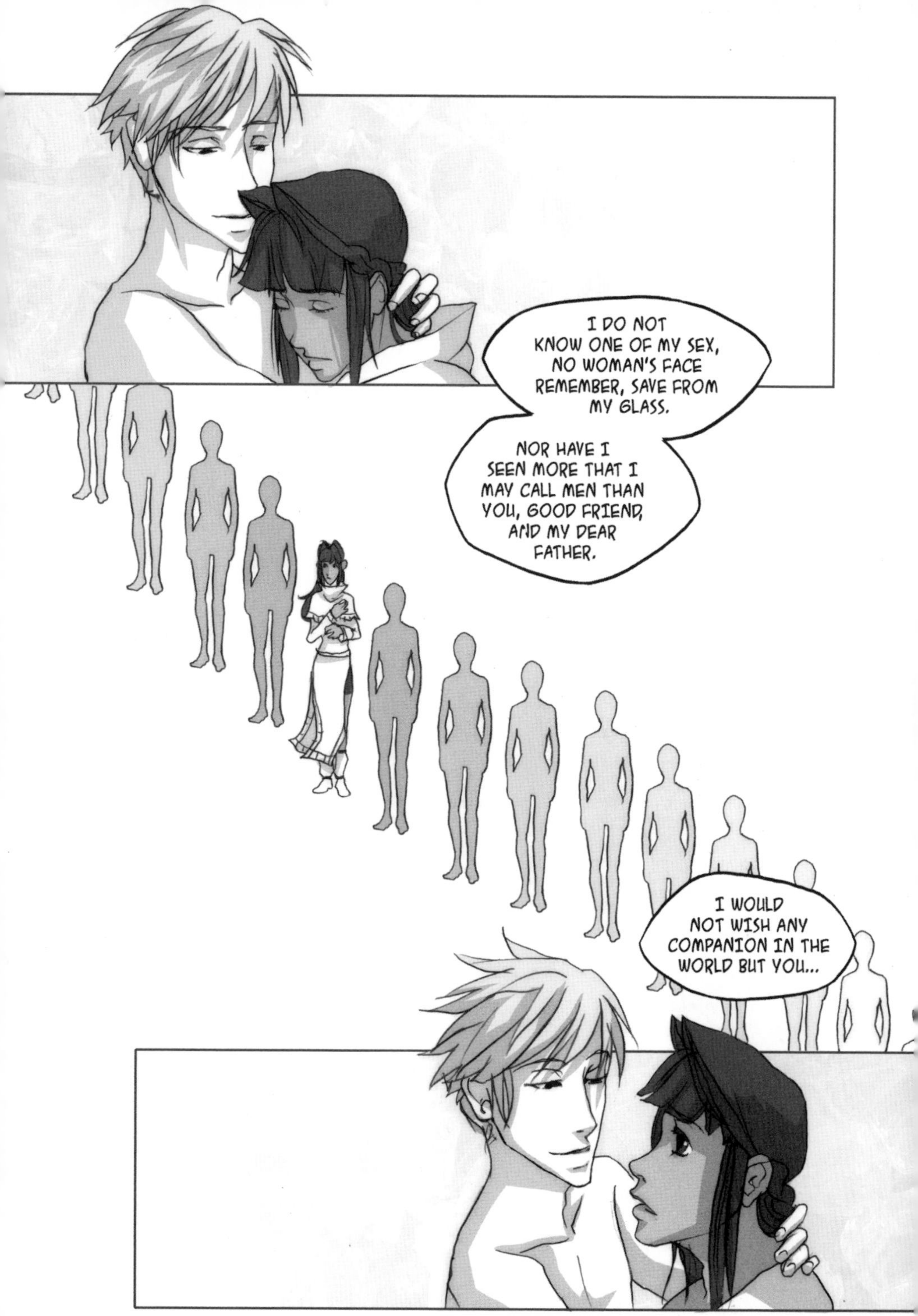
I DO NOT KNOW ONE OF MY SEX, NO WOMAN'S FACE REMEMBER, SAVE FROM MY GLASS.
NOR HAVE I SEEN MORE THAT I MAY CALL MEN THAN YOU, GOOD FRIEND, AND MY DEAR FATHER.
I WOULD NOT WISH ANY COMPANION IN THE WORLD BUT YOU...

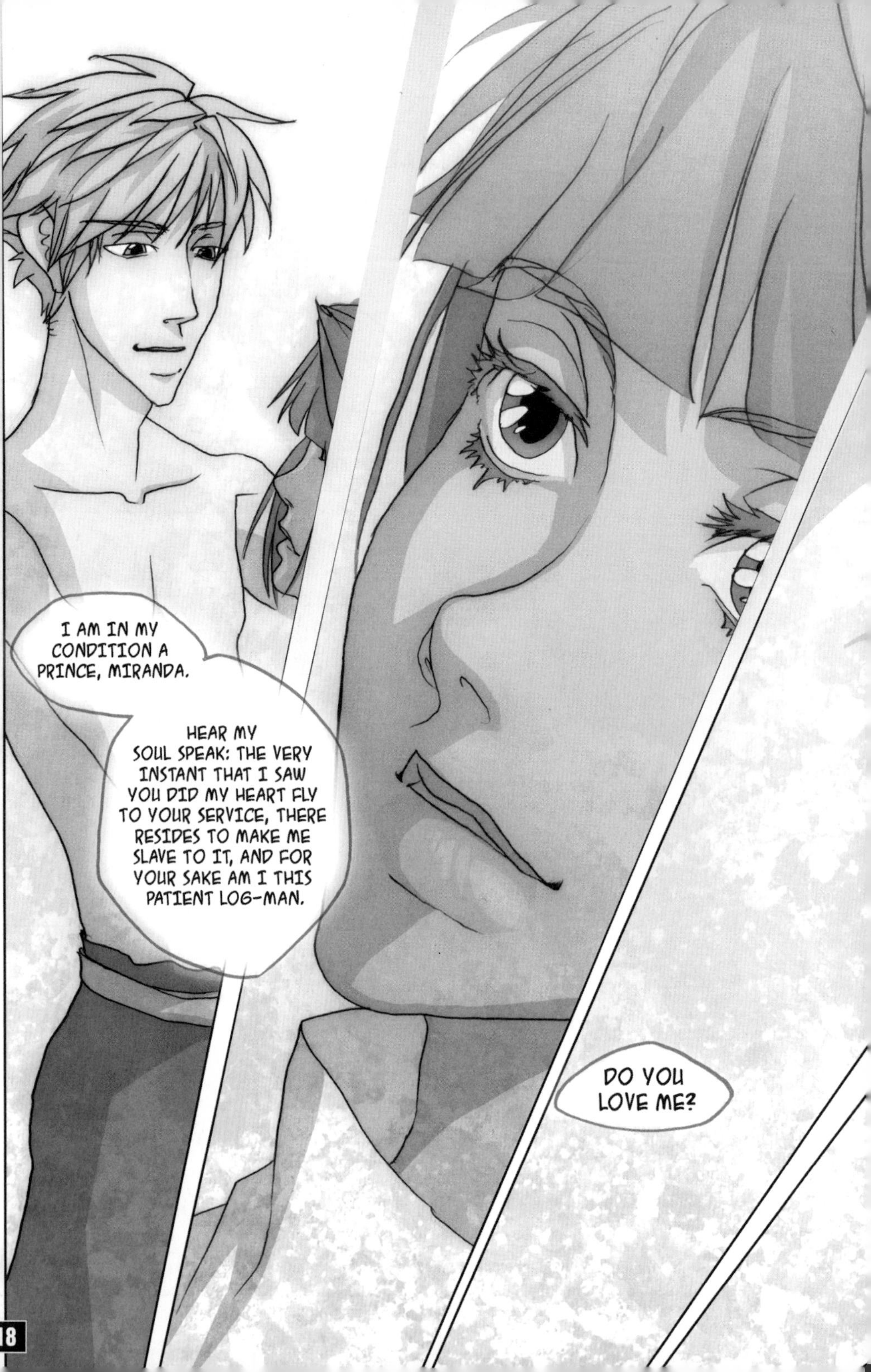
I AM IN MY CONDITION A PRINCE, MIRANDA.
HEAR MY SOUL SPEAK: THE VERY INSTANT THAT I SAW YOU DID MY HEART FLY TO YOUR SERVICE, THERE RESIDES TO MAKE ME SLAVE TO IT, AND FOR YOUR SAKE AM I THIS PATIENT LOG-MAN.
DO YOU LOVE ME?

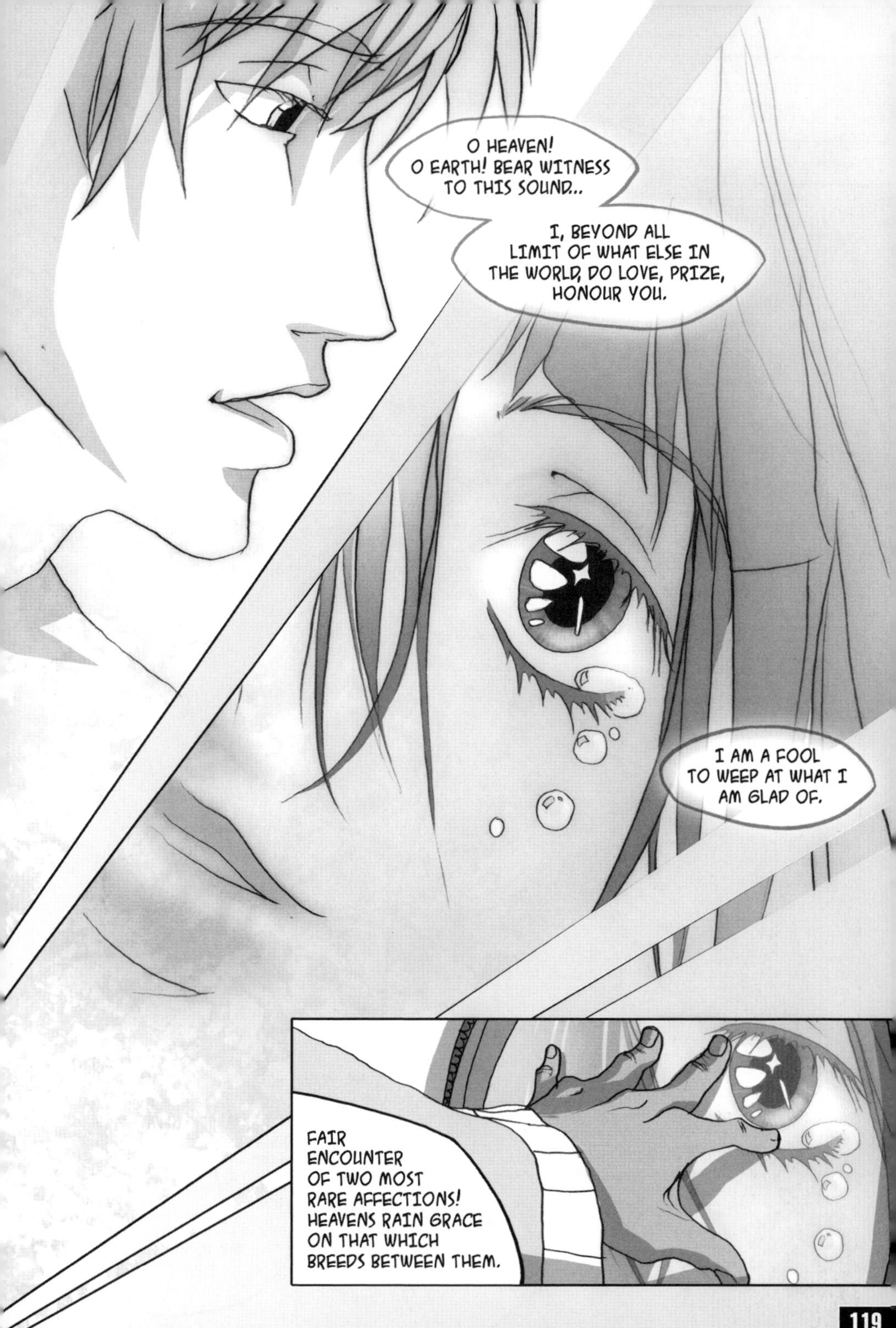
O HEAVEN! O EARTH! BEAR WITNESS TO THIS SOUND...
I, BEYOND ALL LIMIT OF WHAT ELSE IN THE WORLD, DO LOVE, PRIZE, HONOUR YOU.
I AM A FOOL TO WEEP AT WHAT I AM GLAD OF.
FAIR ENCOUNTER OF TWO MOST RARE AFFECTIONS! HEAVENS RAIN GRACE ON THAT WHICH BREEDS BETWEEN THEM.

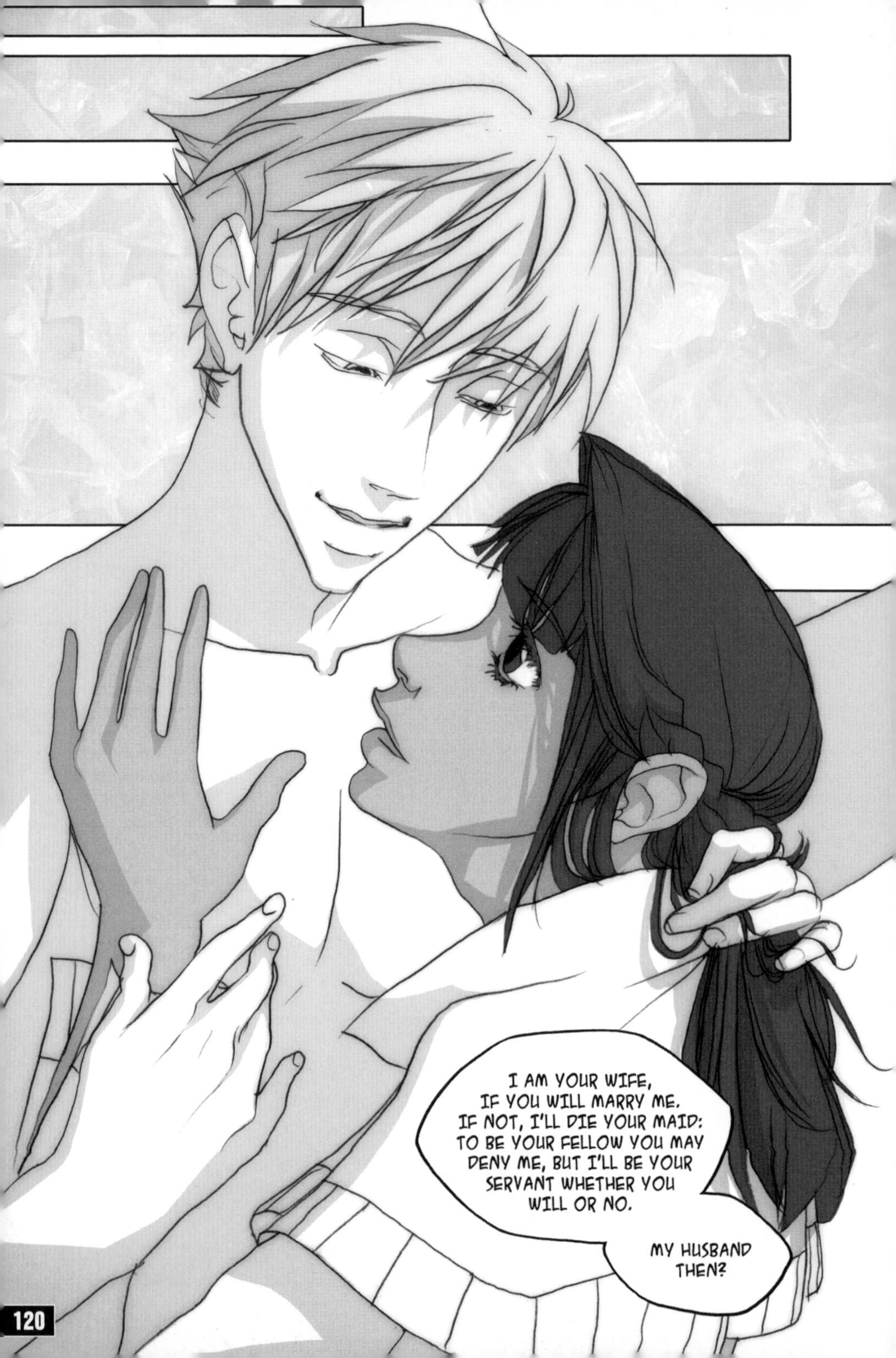
I AM YOUR WIFE, IF YOU WILL MARRY ME. IF NOT, I'LL DIE YOUR MAID: TO BE YOUR FELLOW YOU MAY DENY ME, BUT I'LL BE YOUR SERVANT WHETHER YOU WILL OR NO.
MY HUSBAND THEN?

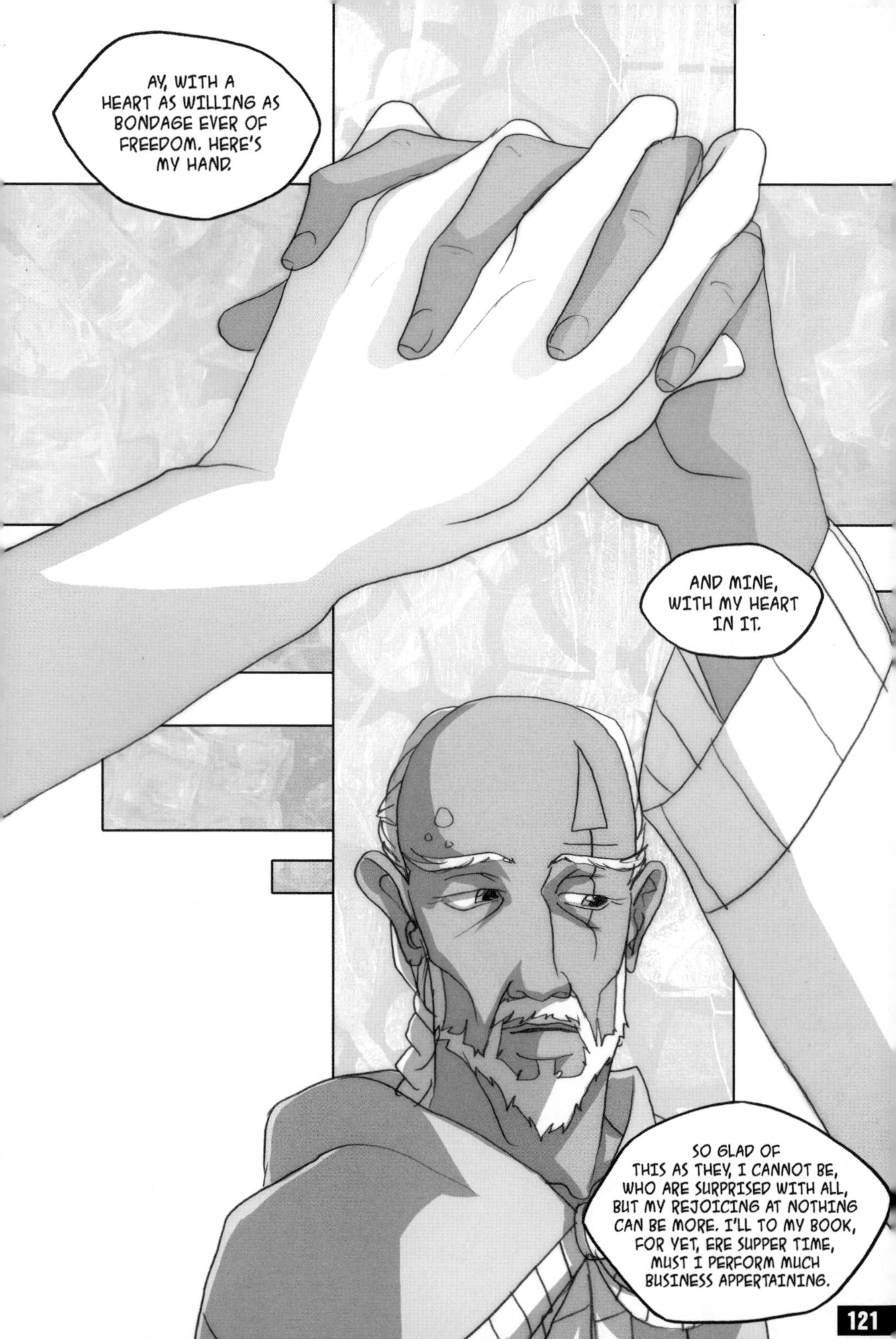
AY, WITH A HEART AS WILLING AS BONDAGE EVER OF FREEDOM. HERE'S MY HAND.
AND MINE, WITH MY HEART IN IT.
SO GLAD OF THIS AS THEY, I CANNOT BE, WHO ARE SURPRISED WITH ALL, BUT MY REJOICING AT NOTHING CAN BE MORE. I'LL TO MY BOOK, FOR YET, ERE SUPPER TIME, MUST I PERFORM MUCH BUSINESS APPERTAINING.

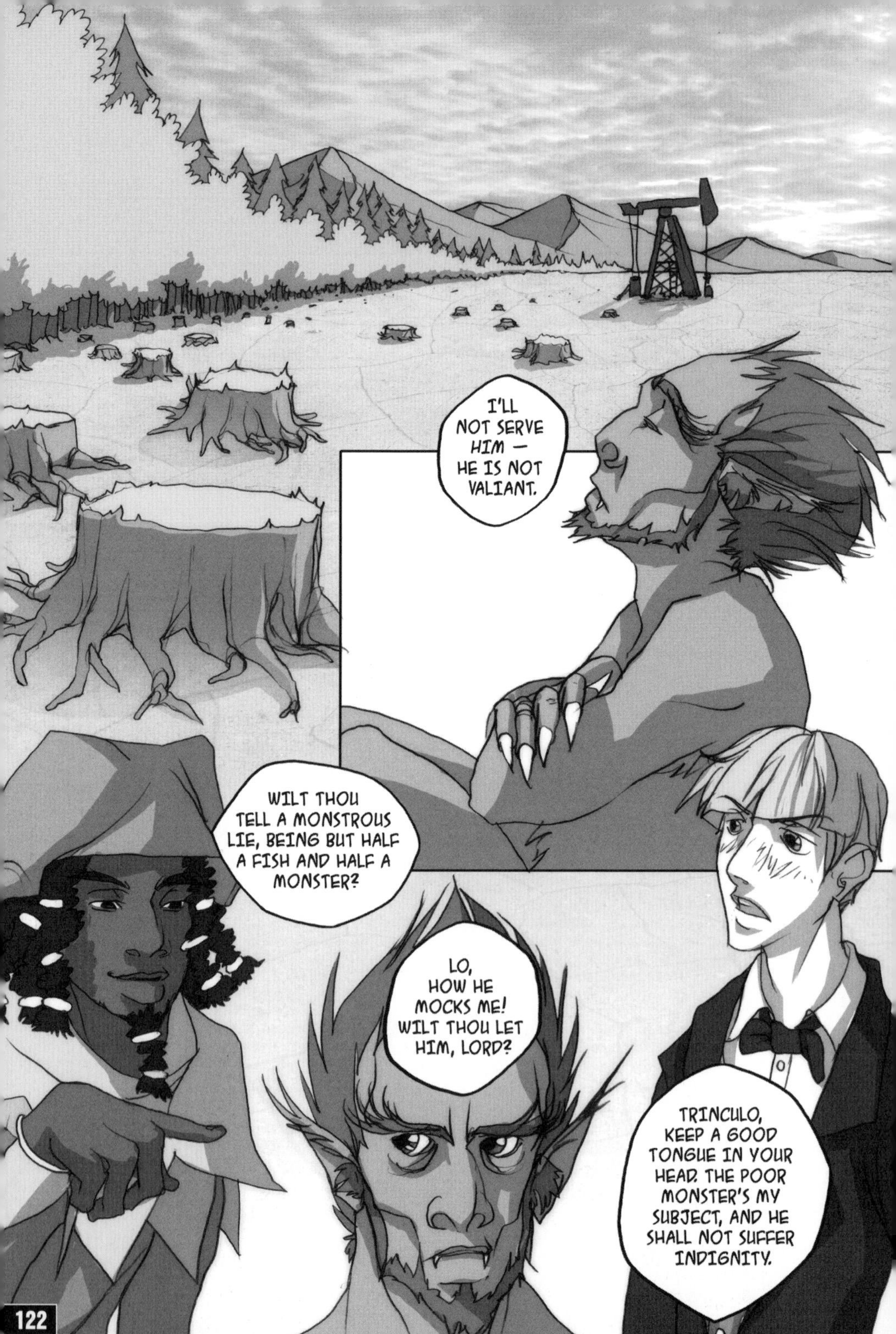

I'LL NOT SERVE HIM — HE IS NOT VALIANT.
WILT THOU TELL A MONSTROUS LIE, BEING BUT HALF A FISH AND HALF A MONSTER?
LO, HOW HE MOCKS ME! WILT THOU LET HIM, LORD?
TRINCULO, KEEP A GOOD TONGUE IN YOUR HEAD. THE POOR MONSTER'S MY SUBJECT, AND HE SHALL NOT SUFFER INDIGNITY.

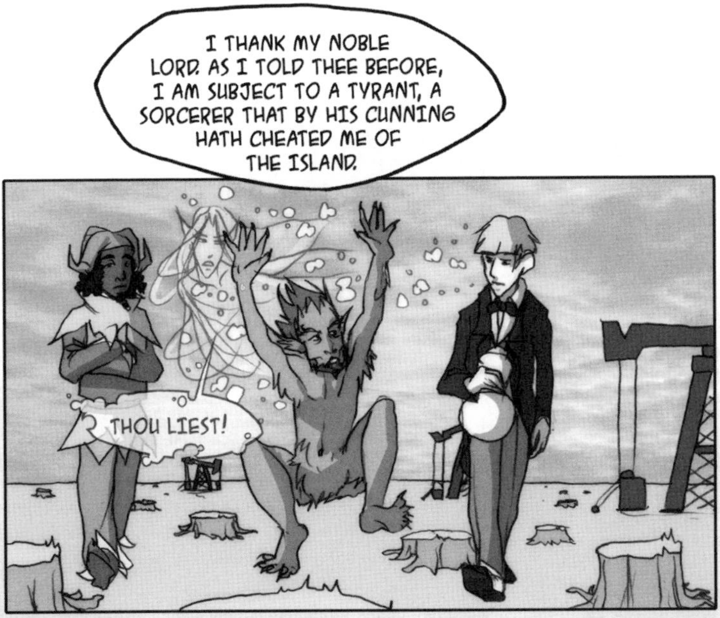
I THANK MY NOBLE LORD. AS I TOLD THEE BEFORE, I AM SUBJECT TO A TYRANT, A SORCERER THAT BY HIS CUNNING HATH CHEATED ME OF THE ISLAND.
THOU LIEST!

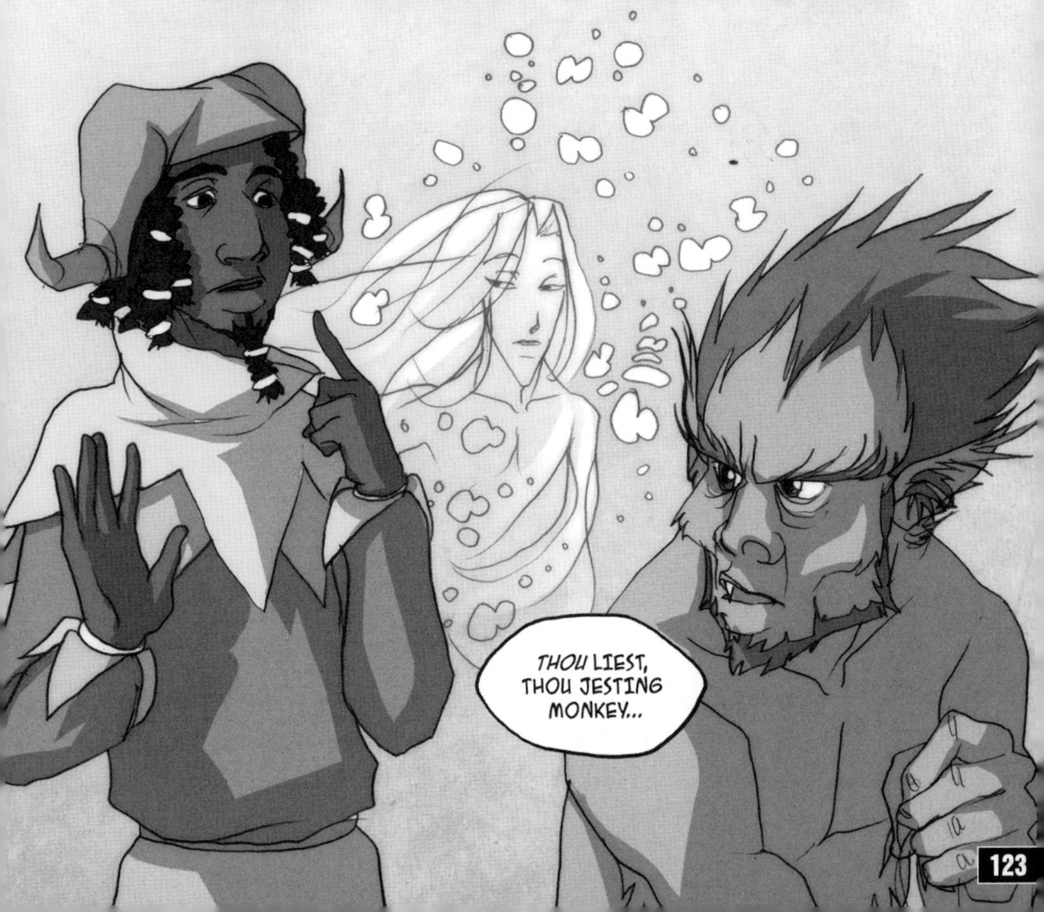
THOU LIEST, THOU JESTING MONKEY...

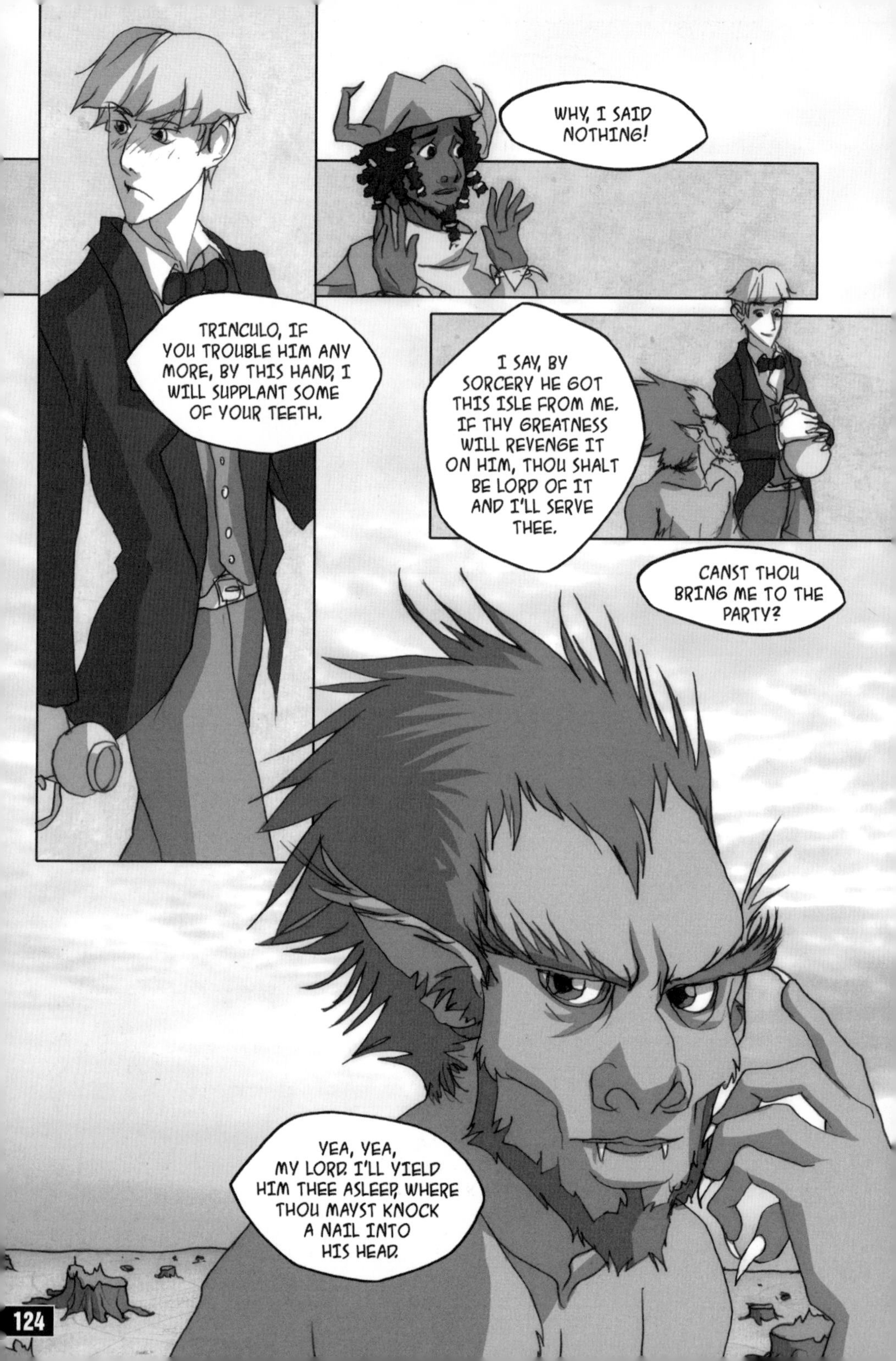
TRINCULO, IF YOU TROUBLE HIM ANY MORE, BY THIS HAND, I WILL SUPPLANT SOME OF YOUR TEETH.
WHY, I SAID NOTHING!
I SAY, BY SORCERY HE GOT THIS ISLE FROM ME. IF THY GREATNESS WILL REVENGE IT ON HIM, THOU SHALT BE LORD OF IT AND I'LL SERVE THEE.
CANST THOU BRING ME TO THE PARTY?
YEA, YEA, MY LORD. I'LL YIELD HIM THEE ASLEEP, WHERE THOU MAYST KNOCK A NAIL INTO HIS HEAD.

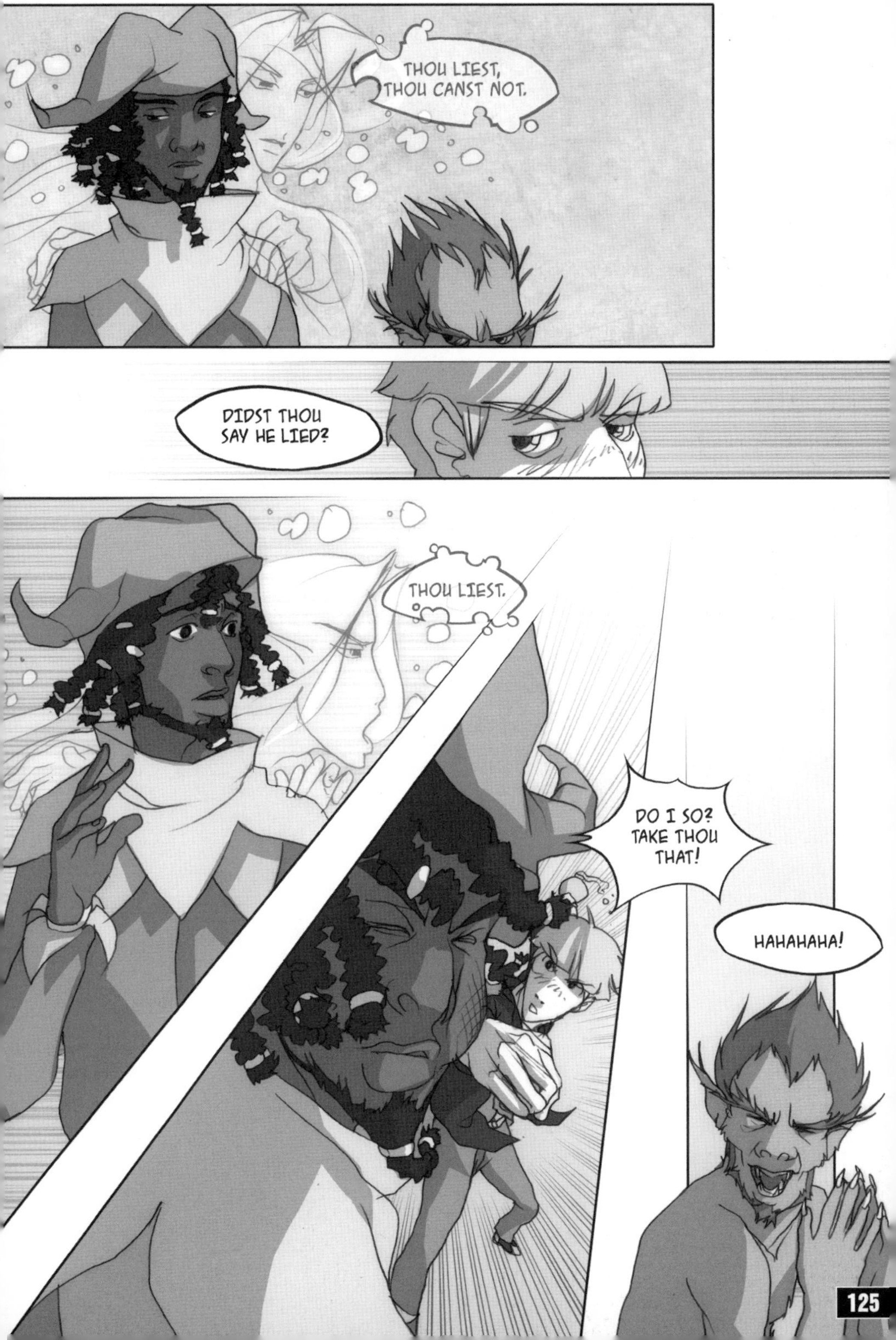
THOU LIEST, THOU CANST NOT.
DIDST THOU SAY HE LIED?
THOU LIEST.
DO I SO? TAKE THOU THAT!
HAHAHAHA!

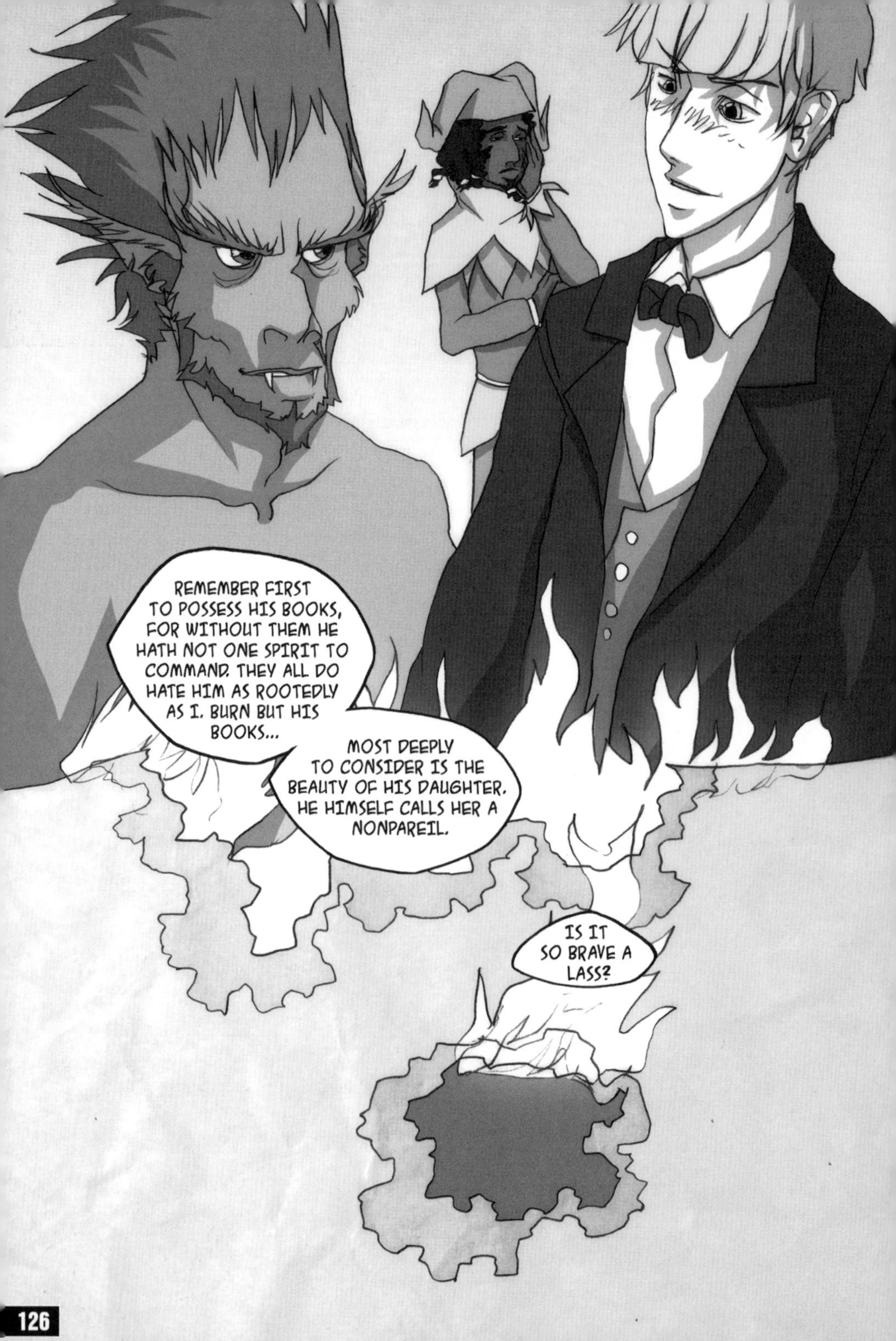
REMEMBER FIRST TO POSSESS HIS BOOKS, FOR WITHOUT THEM HE HATH NOT ONE SPIRIT TO COMMAND. THEY ALL DO HATE HIM AS ROOTEDLY AS I. BURN BUT HIS BOOKS...
MOST DEEPLY TO CONSIDER IS THE BEAUTY OF HIS DAUGHTER. HE HIMSELF CALLS HER A NONPAREIL.
IS IT SO BRAVE A LASS?

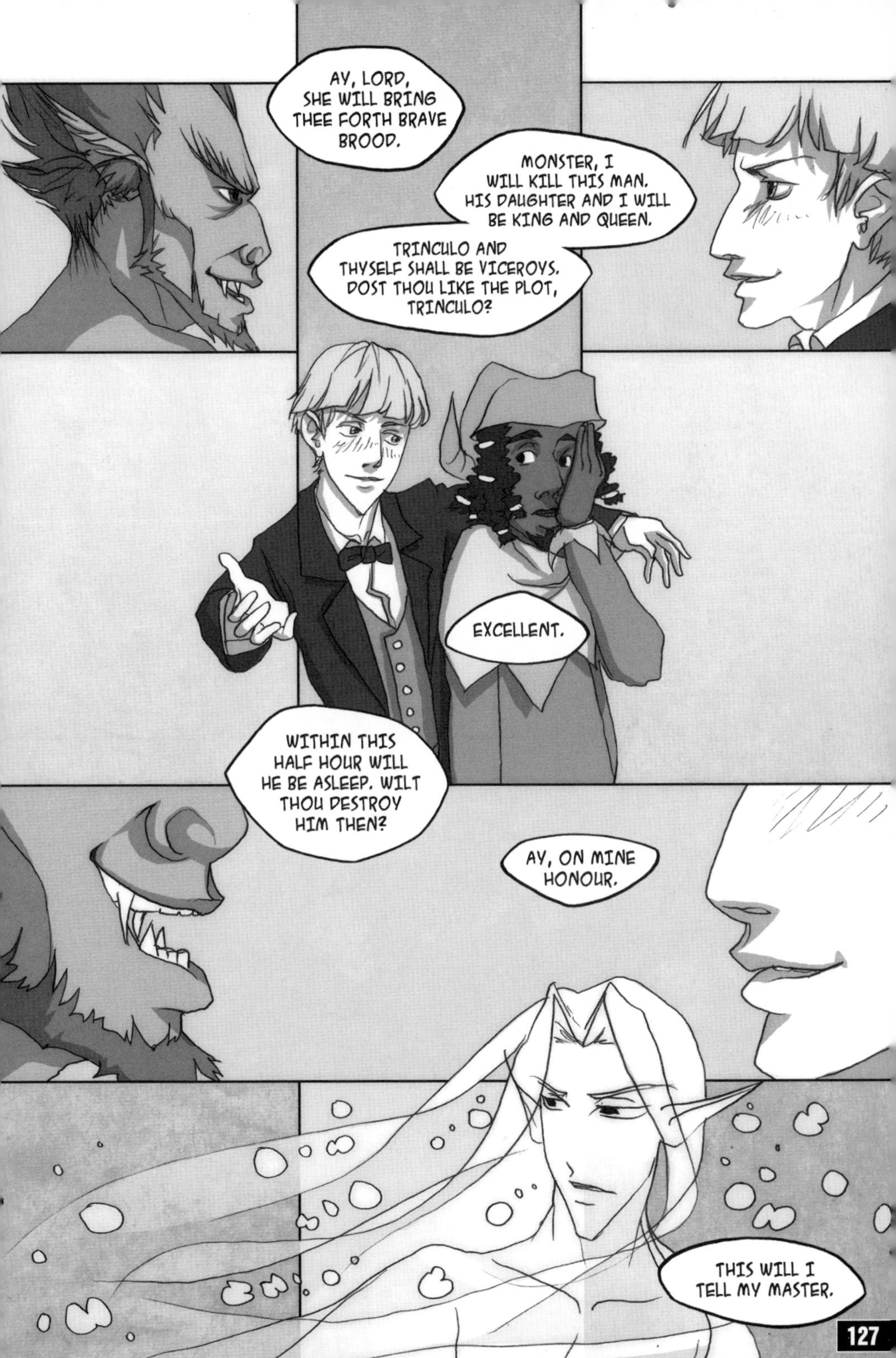
AY, LORD, SHE WILL BRING THEE FORTH BRAVE BROOD.
MONSTER, I WILL KILL THIS MAN. HIS DAUGHTER AND I WILL BE KING AND QUEEN.
TRINCULO AND THYSELF SHALL BE VICEROYS. DOST THOU LIKE THE PLOT, TRINCULO?
EXCELLENT.
WITHIN THIS HALF HOUR WILL HE BE ASLEEP. WILT THOU DESTROY HIM THEN?
AY, ON MINE HONOUR.
THIS WILL I TELL MY MASTER.

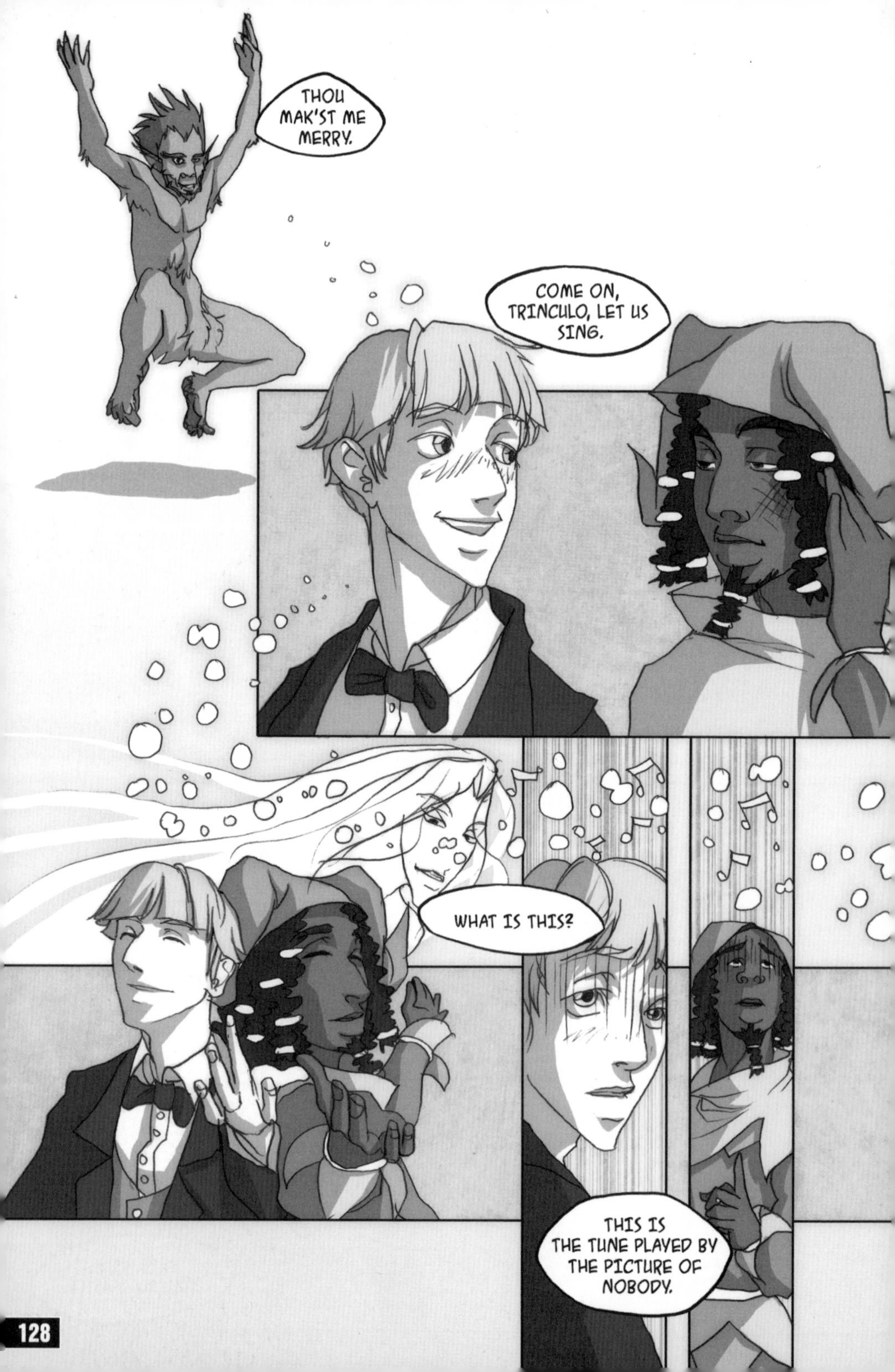
THOU MAK'ST ME MERRY.
COME ON, TRINCULO, LET US SING.
WHAT IS THIS?
THIS IS THE TUNE PLAYED BY THE PICTURE OF NOBODY.

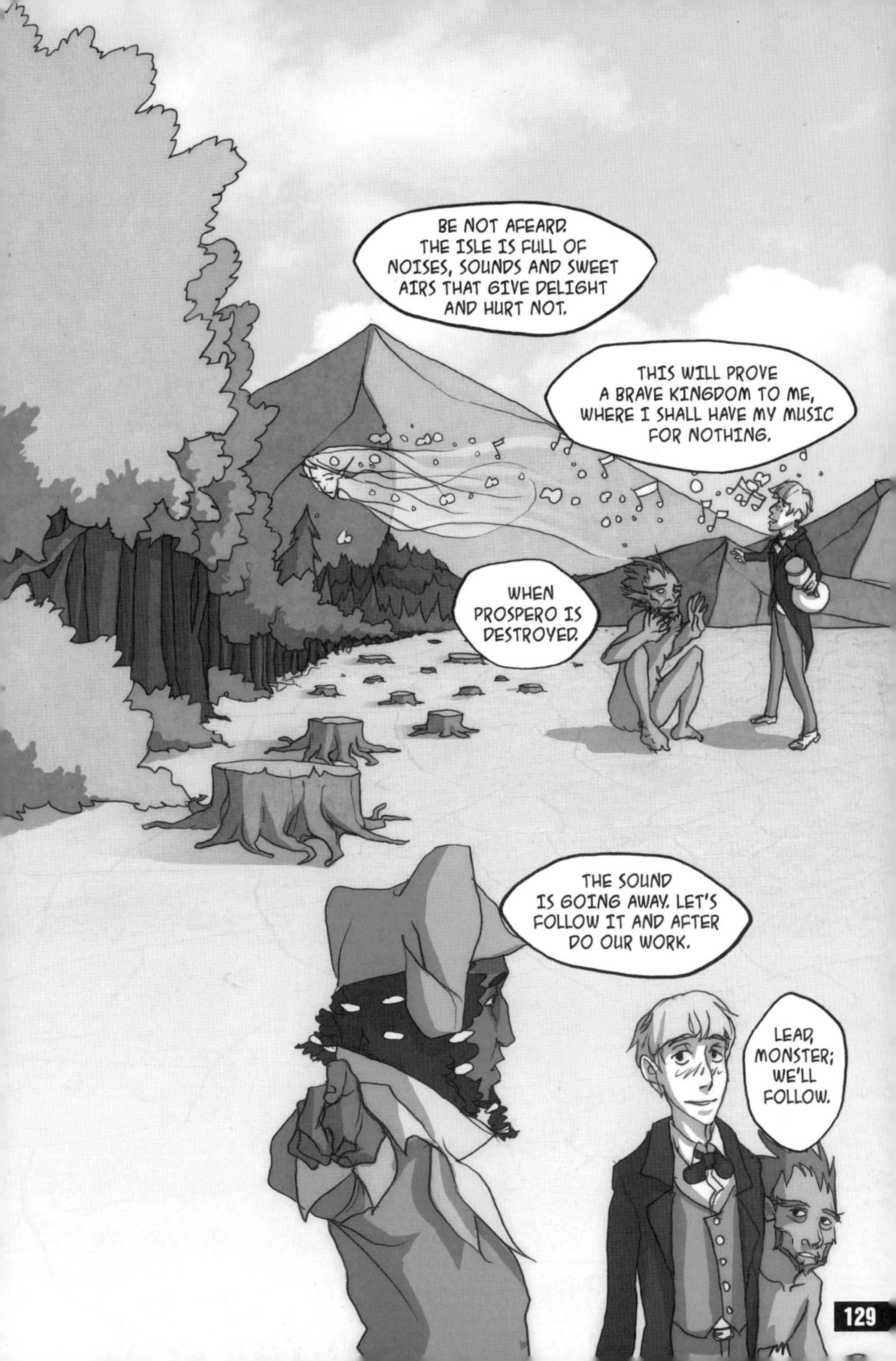
BE NOT AFEARD. THE ISLE IS FULL OF NOISES, SOUNDS AND SWEET AIRS THAT GIVE DELIGHT AND HURT NOT.
THIS WILL PROVE A BRAVE KINGDOM TO ME, WHERE I SHALL HAVE MY MUSIC FOR NOTHING.
WHEN PROSPERO IS DESTROYED.
THE SOUND IS GOING AWAY. LET'S FOLLOW IT AND AFTER DO OUR WORK.
LEAD, MONSTER; WE'LL FOLLOW.

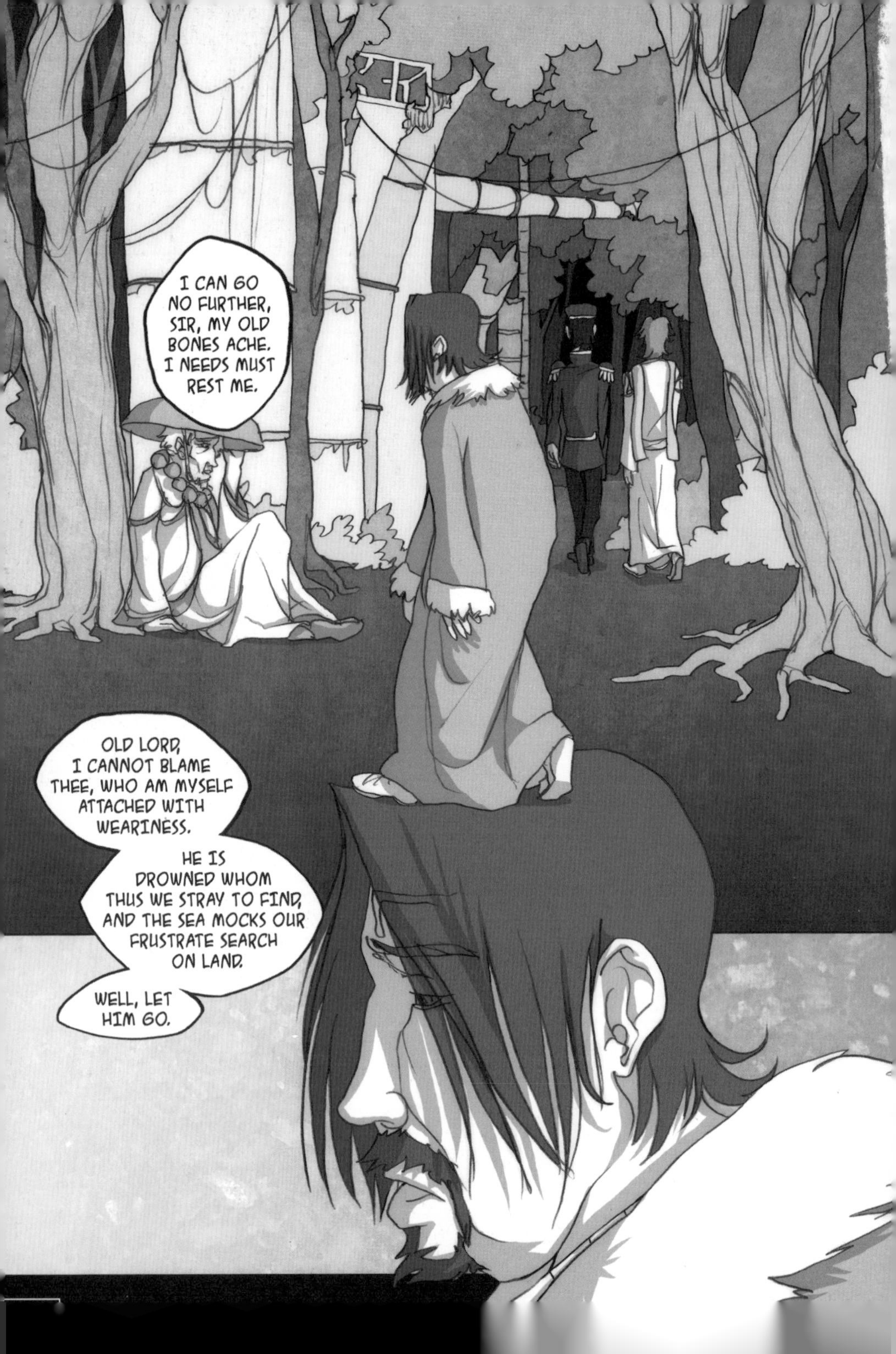
I CAN GO NO FURTHER, SIR, MY OLD BONES ACHE. I NEEDS MUST REST ME.
OLD LORD, I CANNOT BLAME THEE, WHO AM MYSELF ATTACHED WITH WEARINESS.
HE IS DROWNED WHOM THUS WE STRAY TO FIND, AND THE SEA MOCKS OUR FRUSTRATE SEARCH ON LAND.
WELL, LET HIM GO.

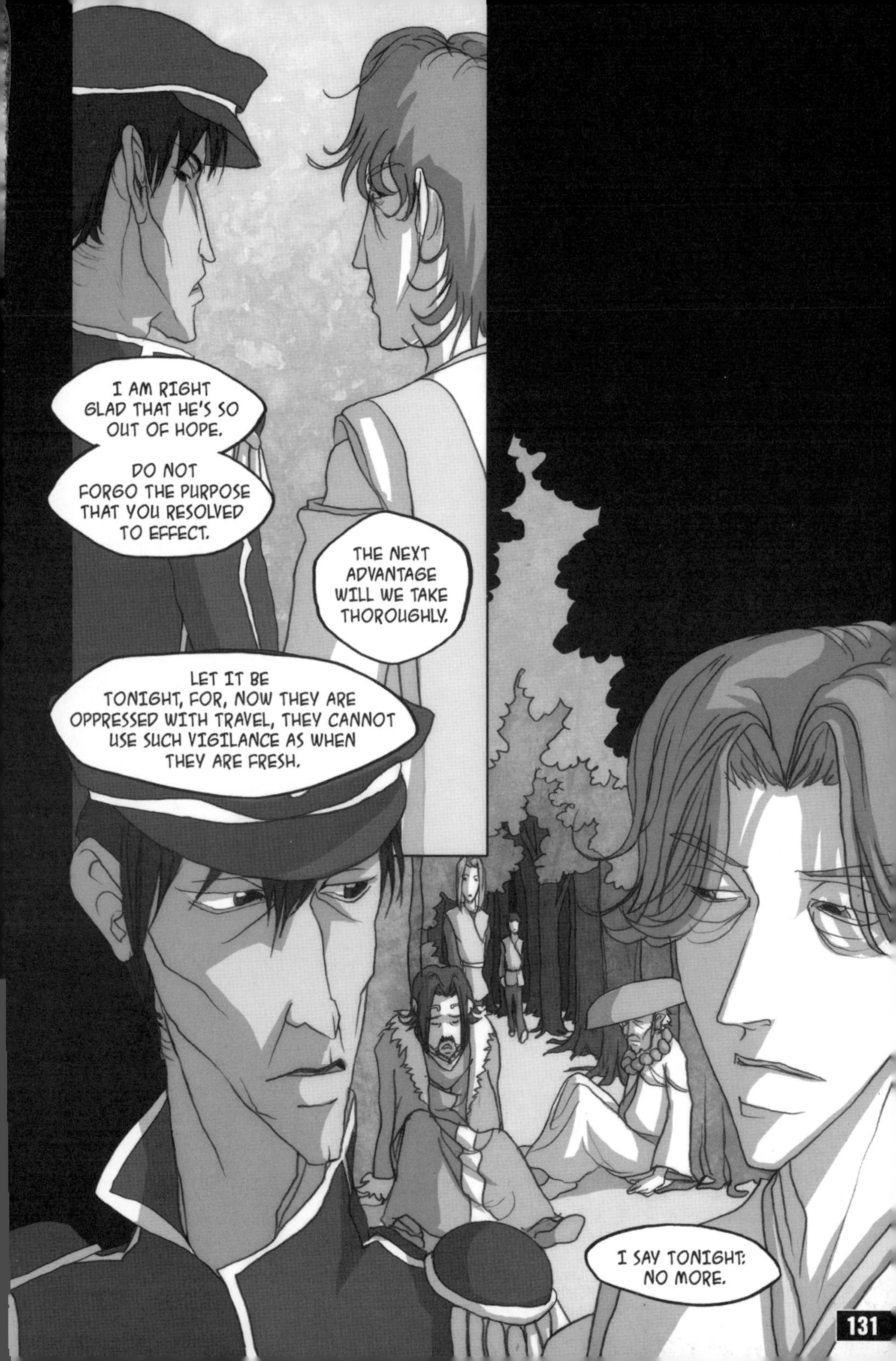
I AM RIGHT GLAD THAT HE'S SO OUT OF HOPE.
DO NOT FORGO THE PURPOSE THAT YOU RESOLVED TO EFFECT.
THE NEXT ADVANTAGE WILL WE TAKE THOROUGHLY.
LET IT BE TONIGHT, FOR, NOW THEY ARE OPPRESSED WITH TRAVEL, THEY CANNOT USE SUCH VIGILANCE AS WHEN THEY ARE FRESH.
I SAY TONIGHT: NO MORE.

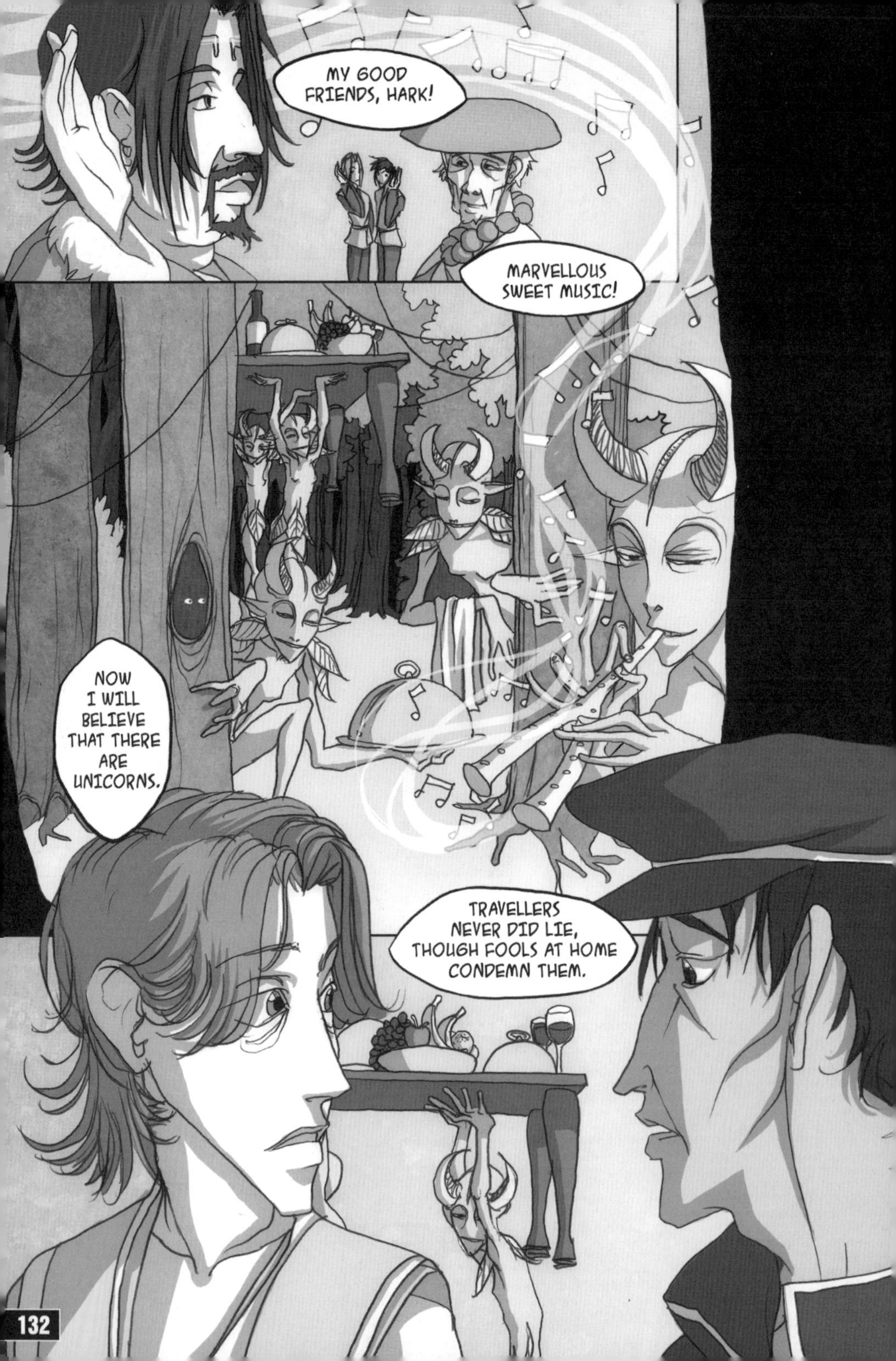
MY GOOD FRIENDS, HARK!
MARVELLOUS SWEET MUSIC!
NOW I WILL BELIEVE THAT THERE ARE UNICORNS.
TRAVELLERS NEVER DID LIE, THOUGH FOOLS AT HOME CONDEMN THEM.

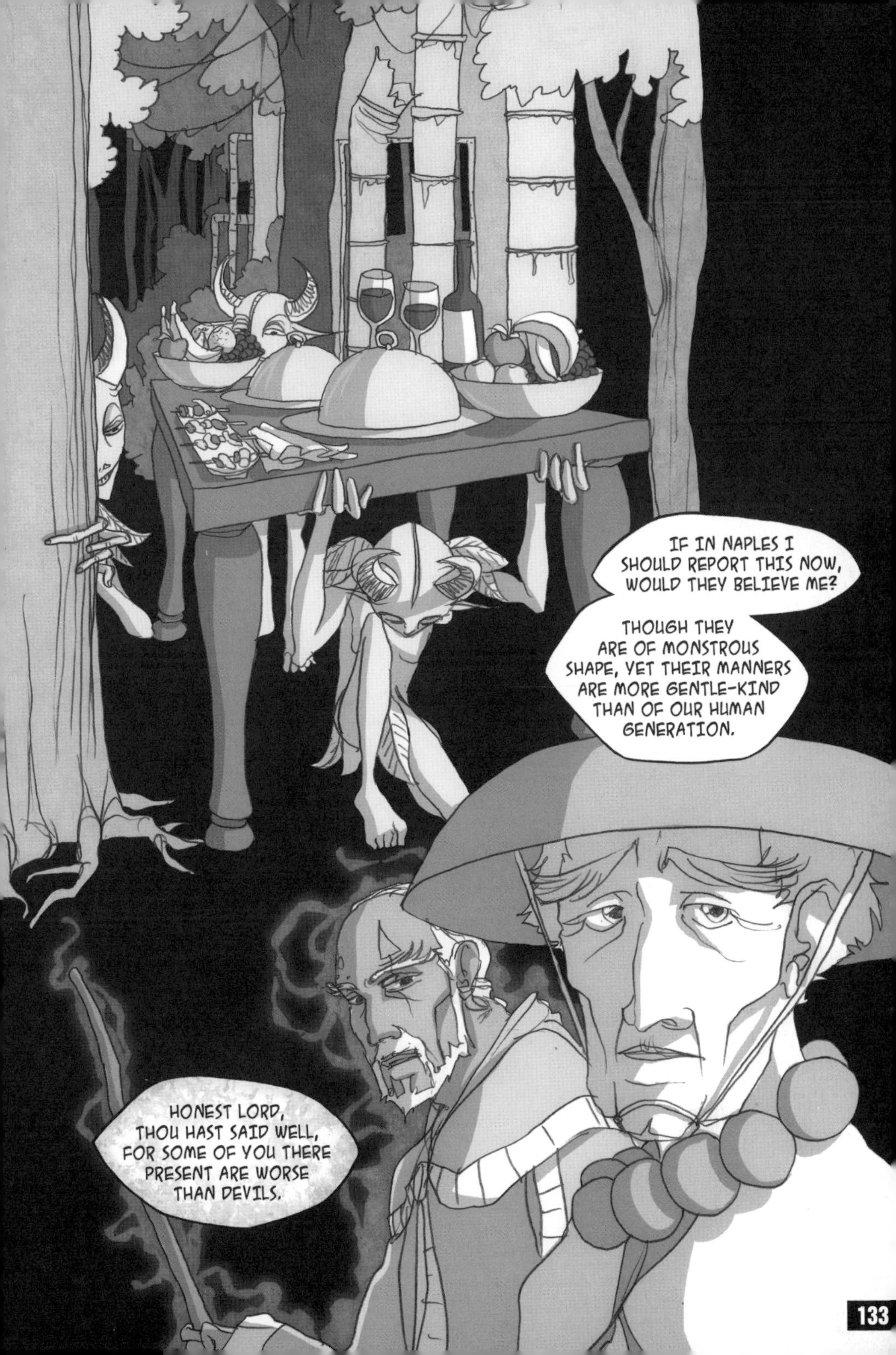
IF IN NAPLES I SHOULD REPORT THIS NOW, WOULD THEY BELIEVE ME?
THOUGH THEY ARE OF MONSTROUS SHAPE, YET THEIR MANNERS ARE MORE GENTLE-KIND THAN OF OUR HUMAN GENERATION.
HONEST LORD, THOU HAST SAID WELL, FOR SOME OF YOU THERE PRESENT ARE WORSE THAN DEVILS.

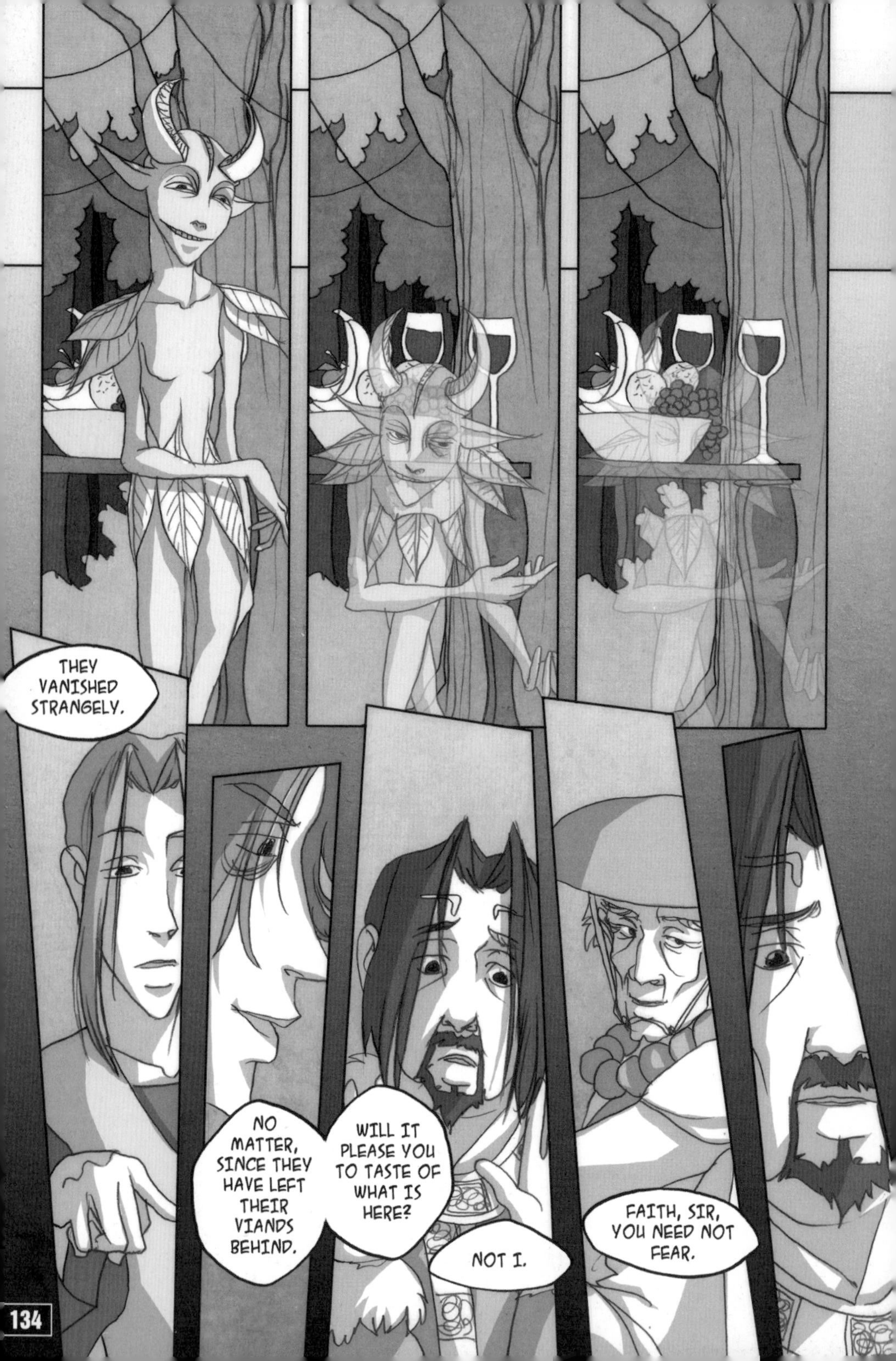
THEY VANISHED STRANGELY.
NO MATTER, SINCE THEY HAVE LEFT THEIR VIANDS BEHIND.
WILL IT PLEASE YOU TO TASTE OF WHAT IS HERE?
NOT I.
FAITH, SIR, YOU NEED NOT FEAR.

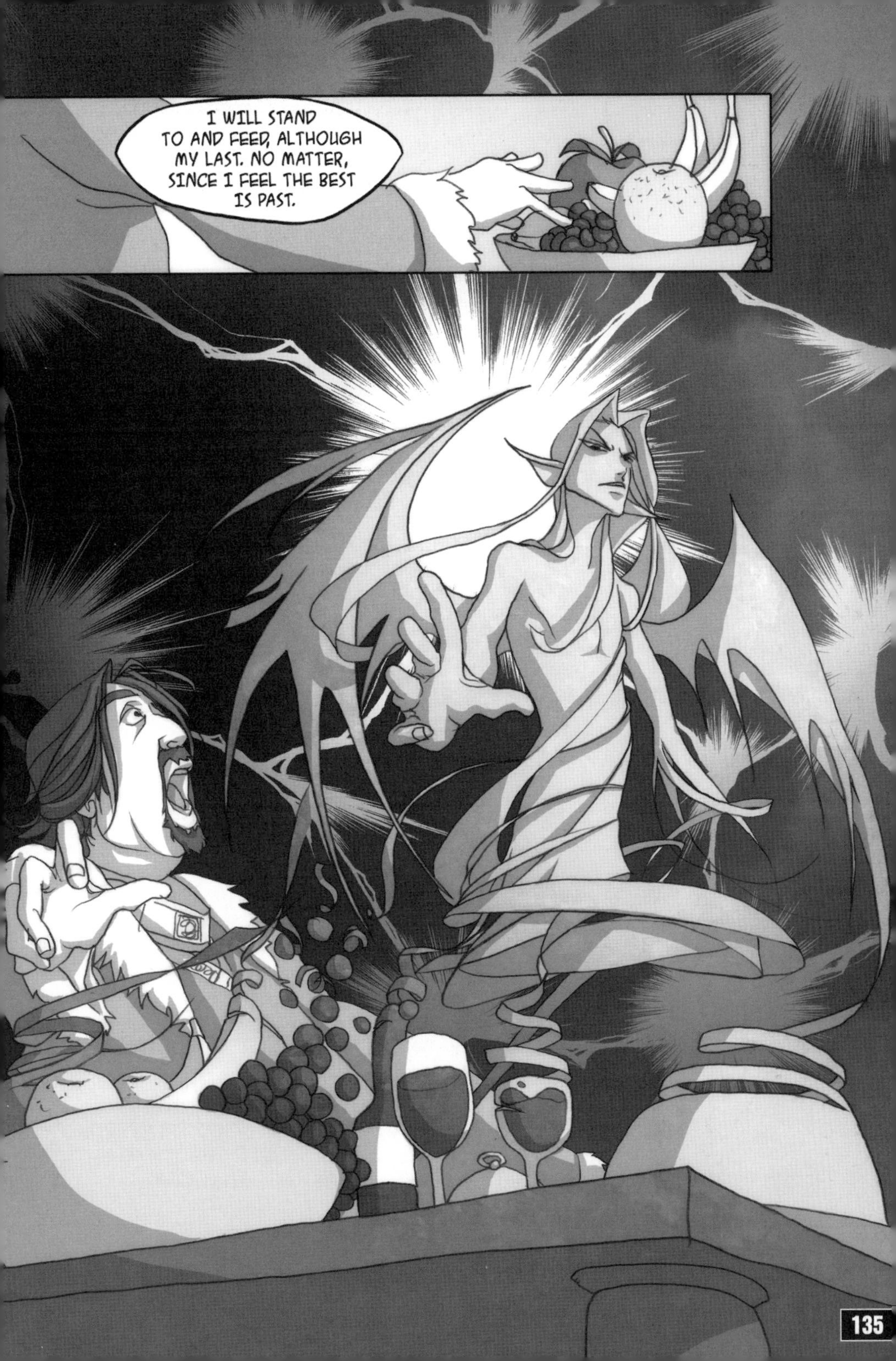
I WILL STAND TO AND FEED, ALTHOUGH MY LAST. NO MATTER, SINCE I FEEL THE BEST IS PAST.

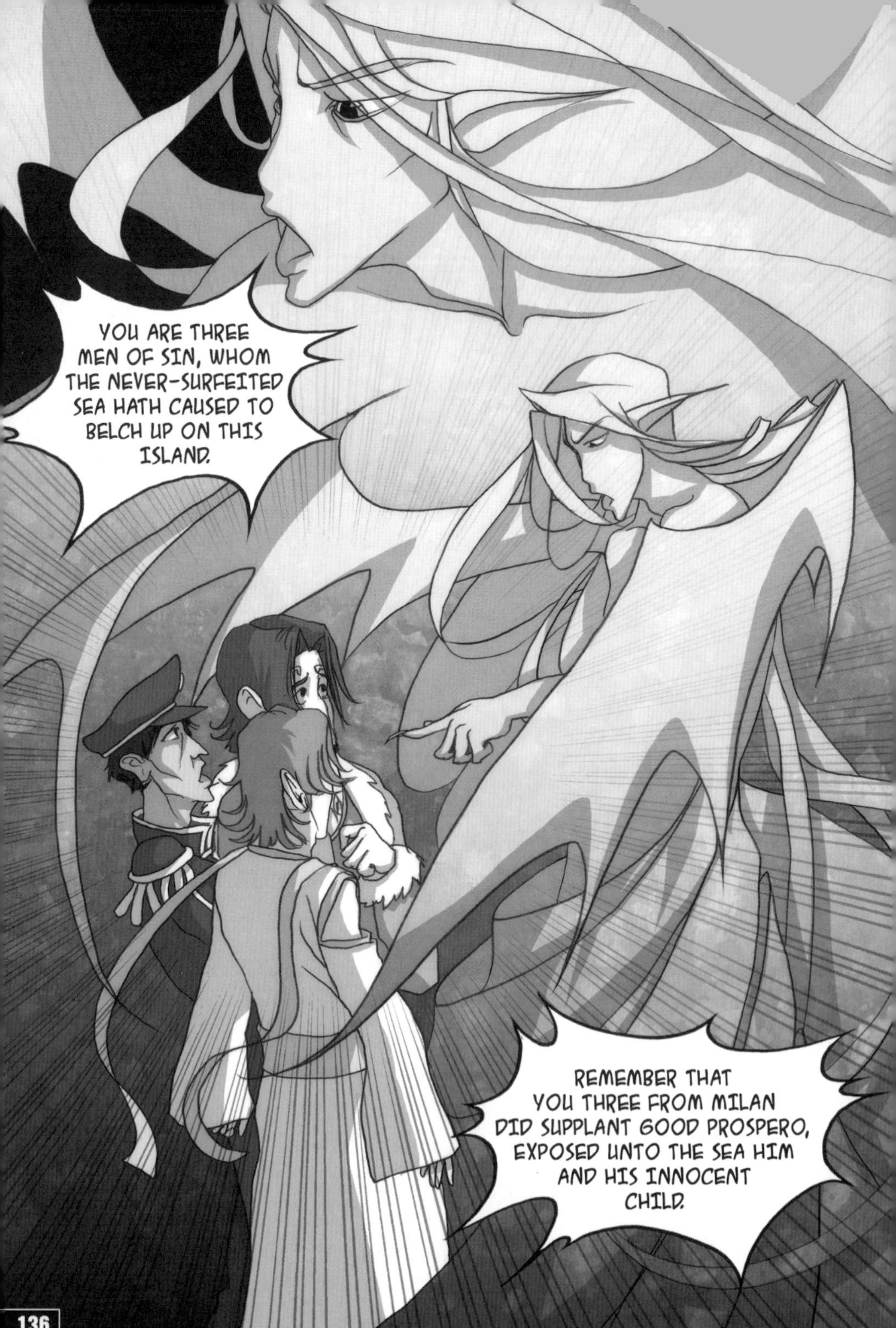
YOU ARE THREE MEN OF SIN, WHOM THE NEVER-SURFEITED SEA HATH CAUSED TO BELCH UP ON THIS ISLAND.
REMEMBER THAT YOU THREE FROM MILAN DID SUPPLANT GOOD PROSPERO, EXPOSED UNTO THE SEA HIM AND HIS INNOCENT CHILD.

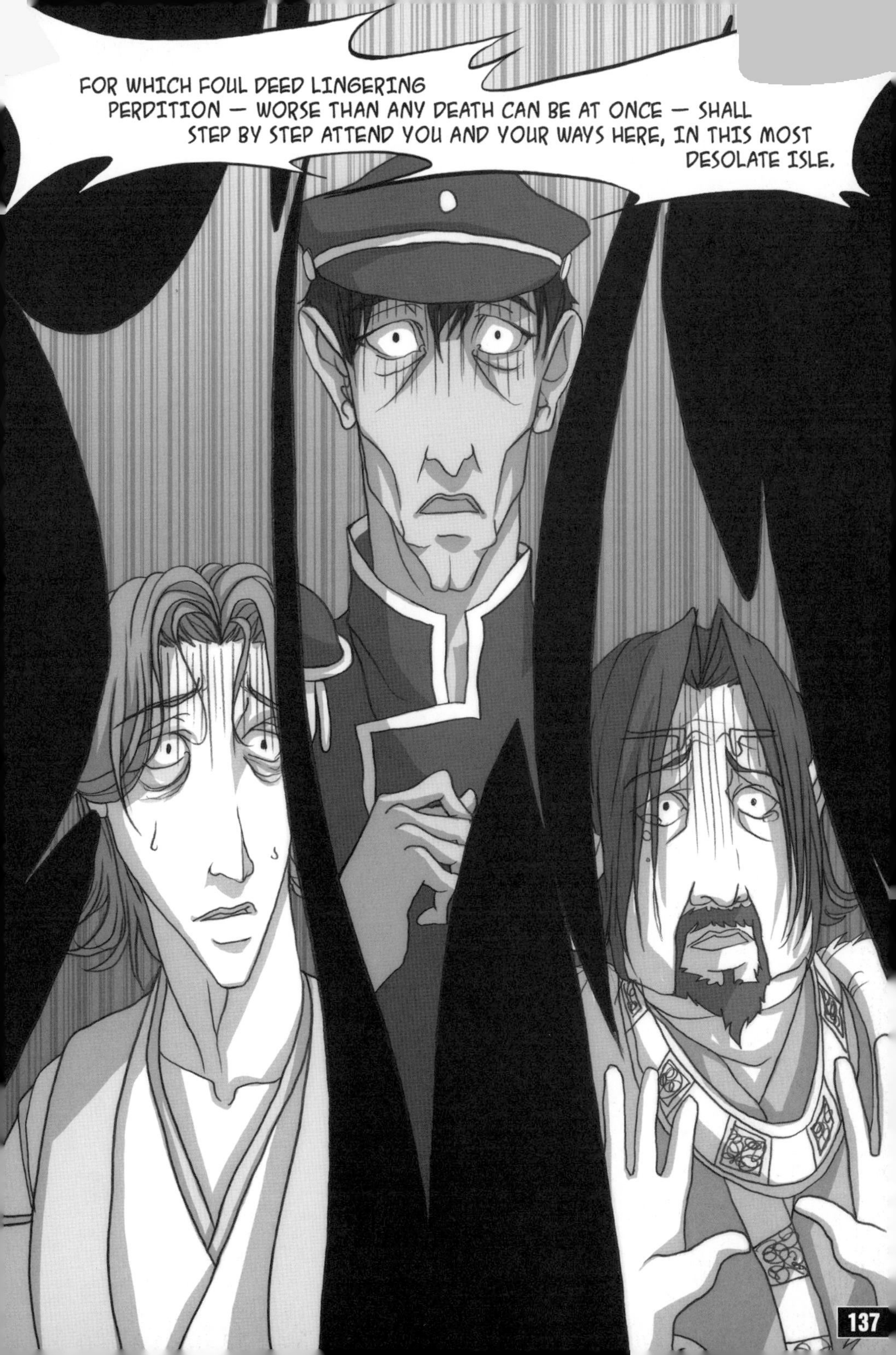
FOR WHICH FOUL DEED LINGERING PERDITION — WORSE THAN ANY DEATH CAN BE AT ONCE — SHALL STEP BY STEP ATTEND YOU AND YOUR WAYS HERE, IN THIS MOST DESOLATE ISLE.

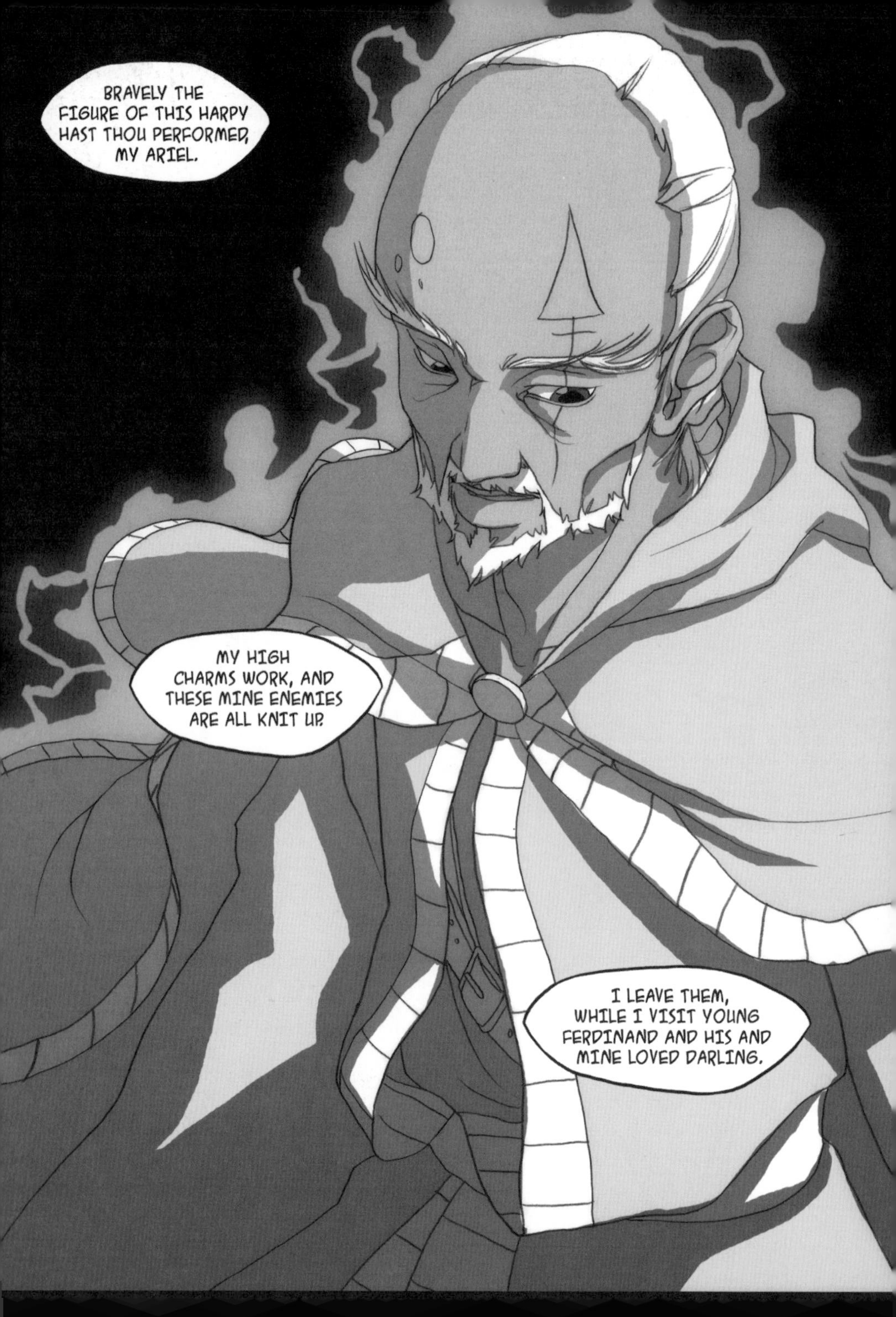
BRAVELY THE FIGURE OF THIS HARPY HAST THOU PERFORMED, MY ARIEL.
MY HIGH CHARMS WORK, AND THESE MINE ENEMIES ARE ALL KNIT UP.
I LEAVE THEM, WHILE I VISIT YOUNG FERDINAND AND HIS AND MINE LOVED DARLING.

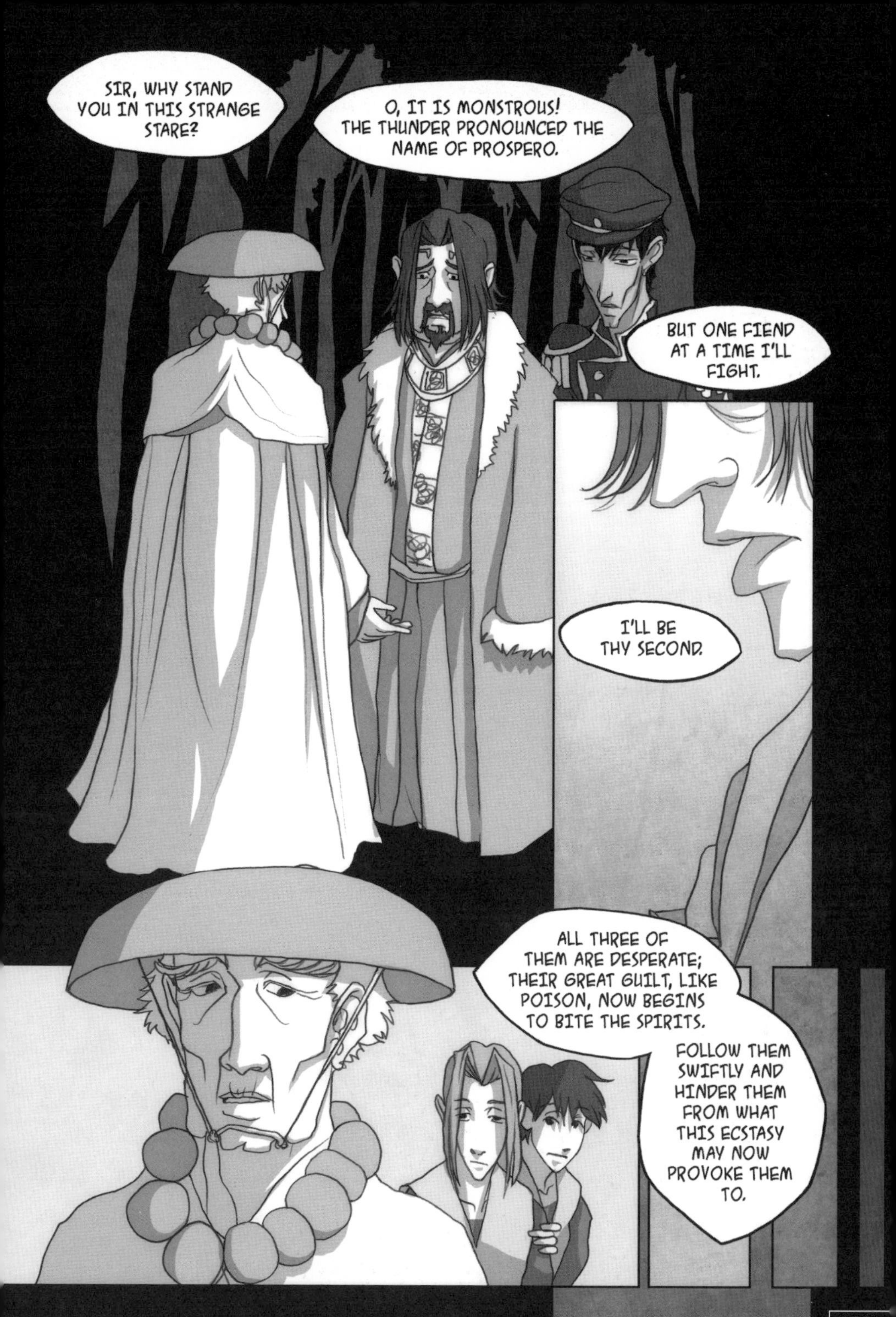
SIR, WHY STAND YOU IN THIS STRANGE STARE?
O, IT IS MONSTROUS! THE THUNDER PRONOUNCED THE NAME OF PROSPERO.
BUT ONE FIEND AT A TIME I'LL FIGHT.
I'LL BE THY SECOND.
ALL THREE OF THEM ARE DESPERATE; THEIR GREAT GUILT, LIKE POISON, NOW BEGINS TO BITE THE SPIRITS.
FOLLOW THEM SWIFTLY AND HINDER THEM FROM WHAT THIS ECSTASY MAY NOW PROVOKE THEM TO.

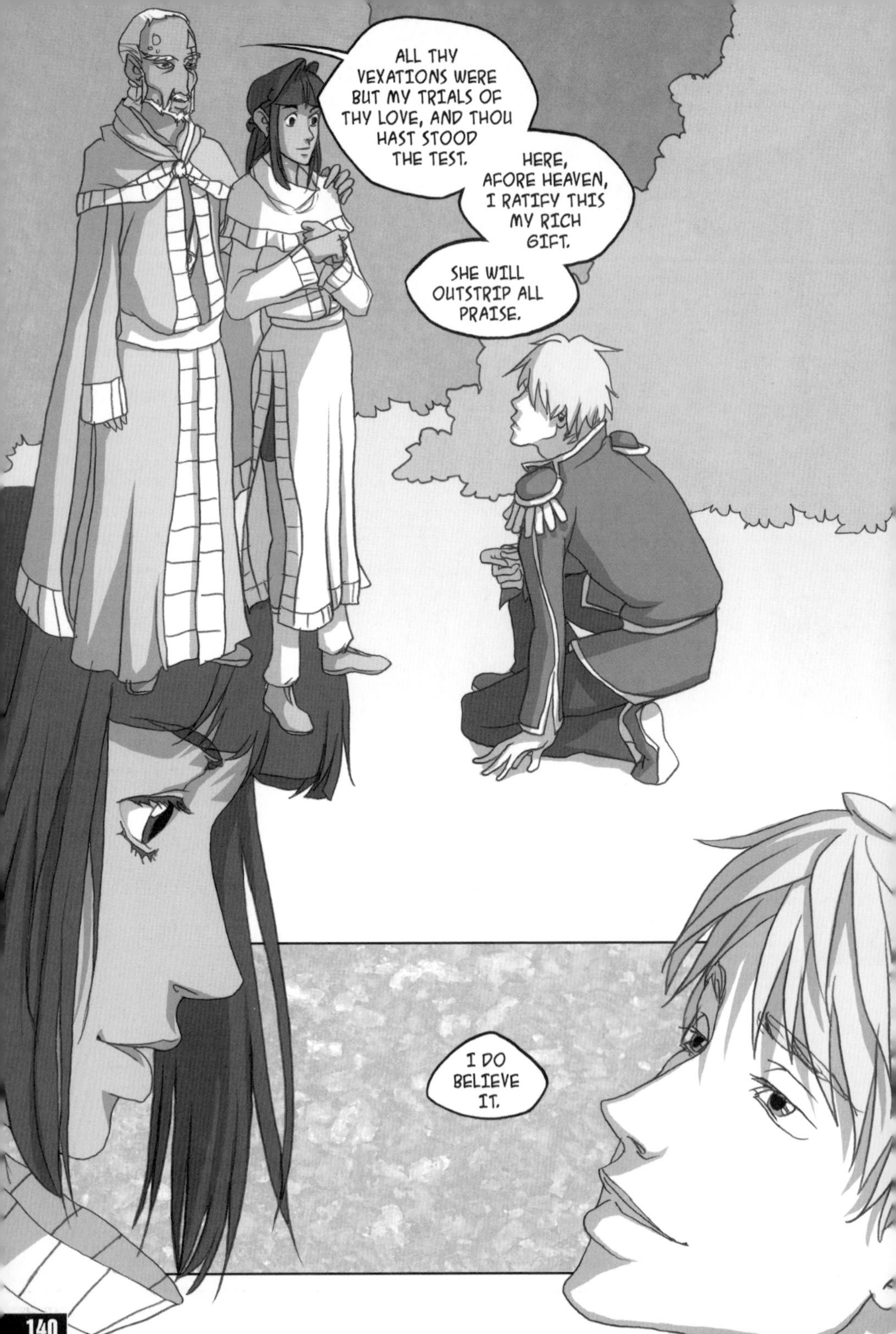
ALL THY VEXATIONS WERE BUT MY TRIALS OF THY LOVE, AND THOU HAST STOOD THE TEST.
HERE, AFORE HEAVEN, I RATIFY THIS MY RICH GIFT.
SHE WILL OUTSTRIP ALL PRAISE.
I DO BELIEVE IT.

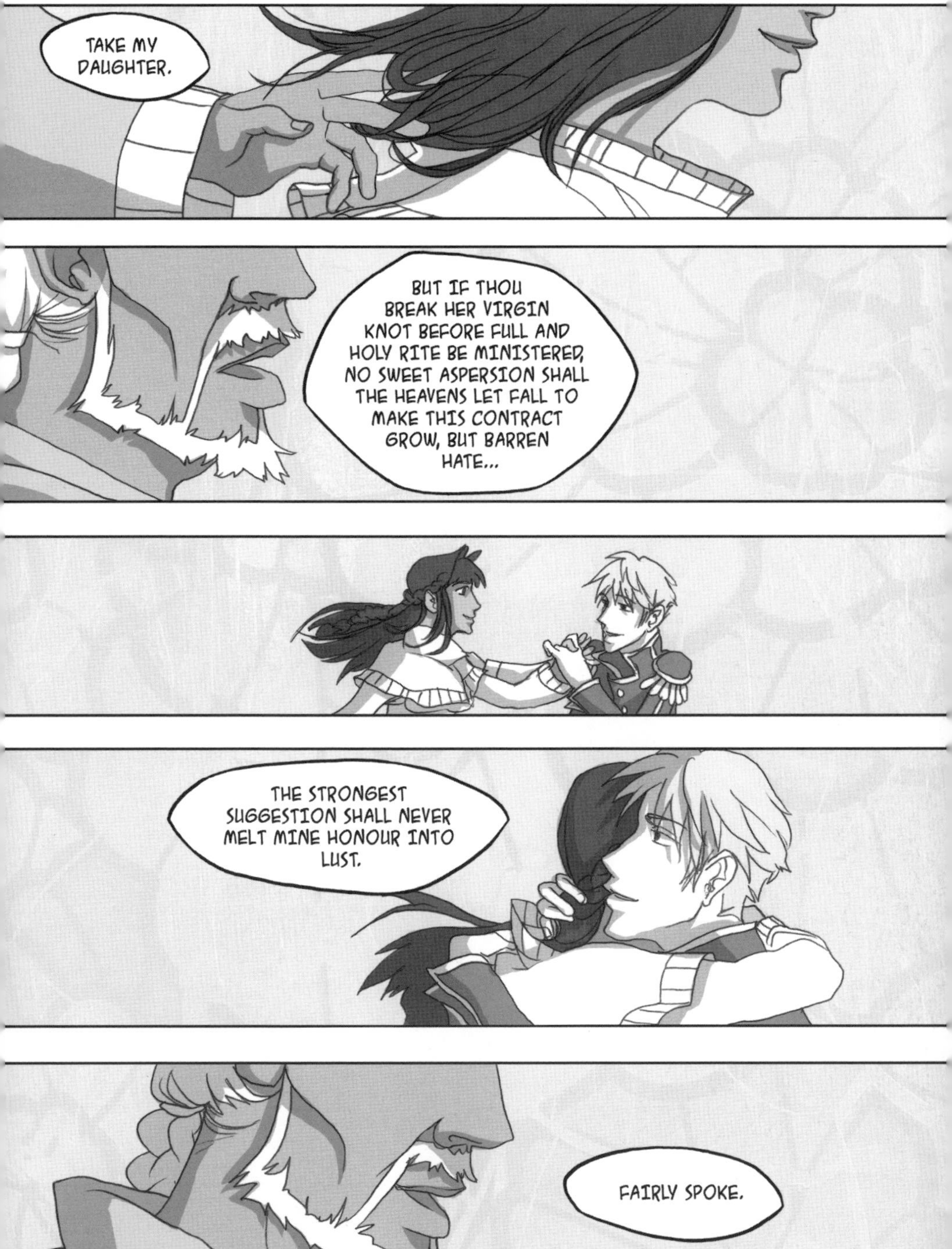
TAKE MY DAUGHTER.
BUT IF THOU BREAK HER VIRGIN KNOT BEFORE FULL AND HOLY RITE BE MINISTERED, NO SWEET ASPERSION SHALL THE HEAVENS LET FALL TO MAKE THIS CONTRACT GROW, BUT BARREN HATE...
THE STRONGEST SUGGESTION SHALL NEVER MELT MINE HONOUR INTO LUST.
FAIRLY SPOKE.

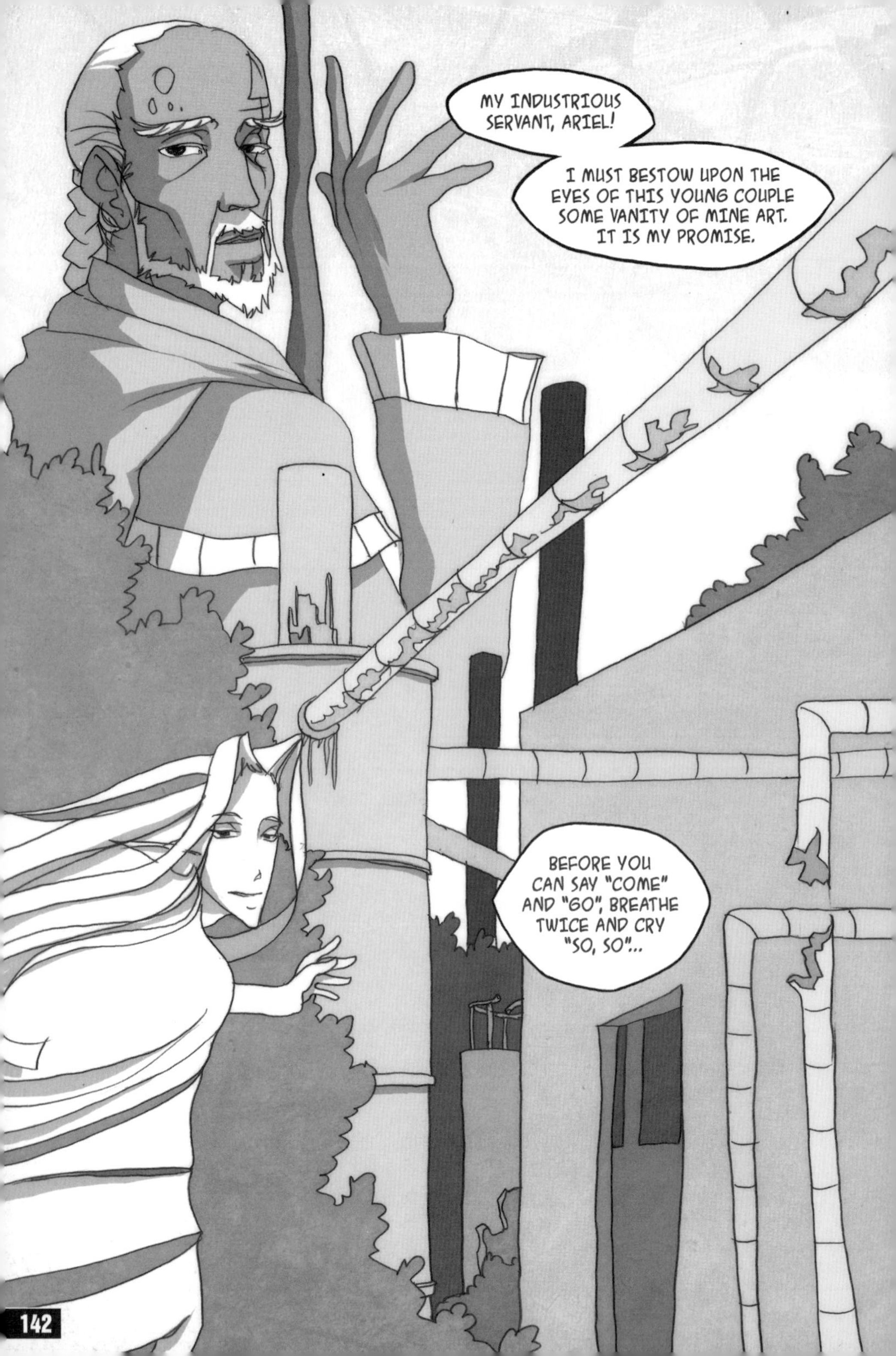
MY INDUSTRIOUS SERVANT, ARIEL!
I MUST BESTOW UPON THE EYES OF THIS YOUNG COUPLE SOME VANITY OF MINE ART. IT IS MY PROMISE.
BEFORE YOU CAN SAY "COME" AND "GO", BREATHE TWICE AND CRY "SO, SO"...

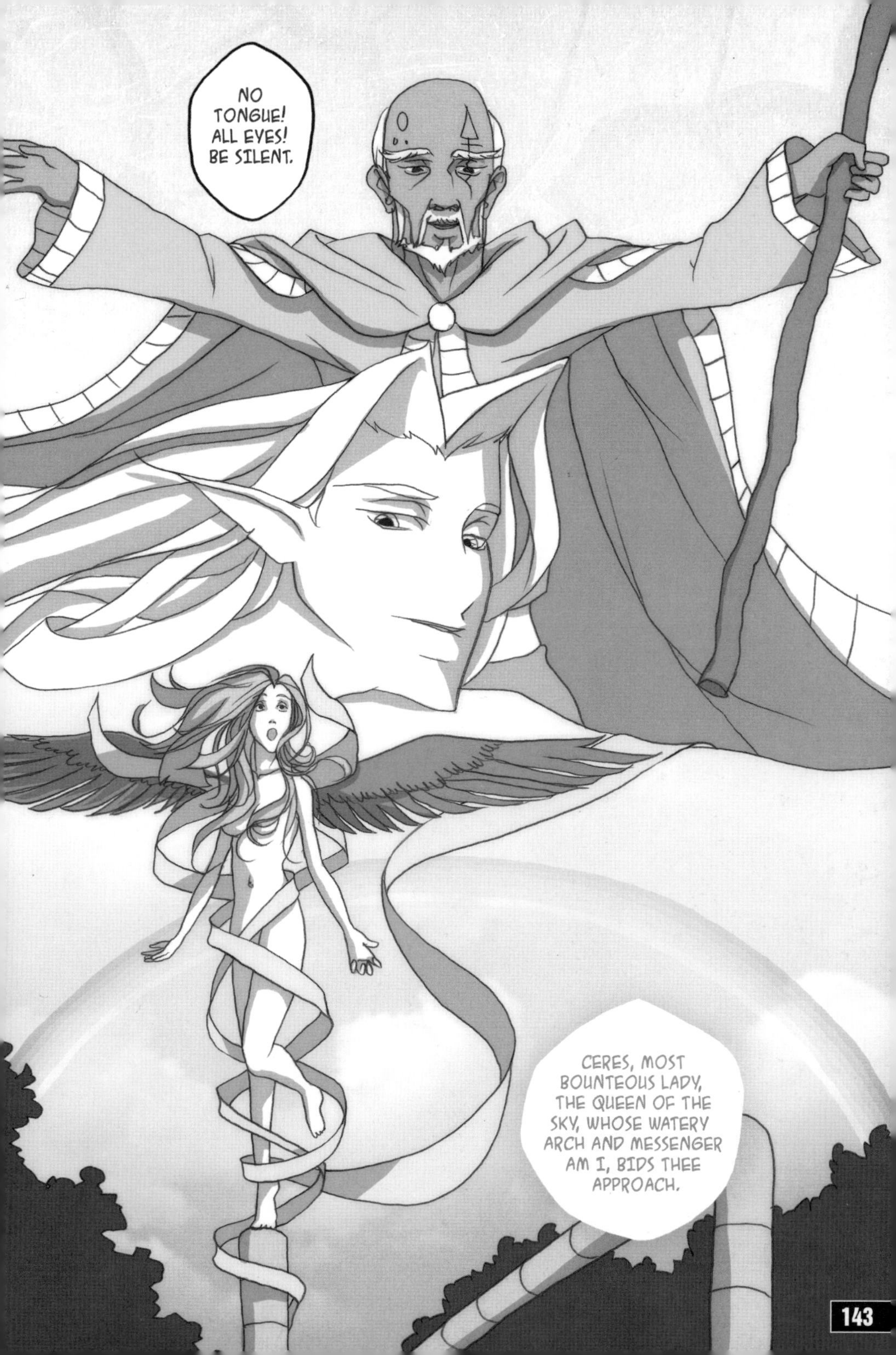
NO TONGUE! ALL EYES! BE SILENT.
CERES, MOST BOUNTEOUS LADY, THE QUEEN OF THE SKY, WHOSE WATERY ARCH AND MESSENGER AM I, BIDS THEE APPROACH.

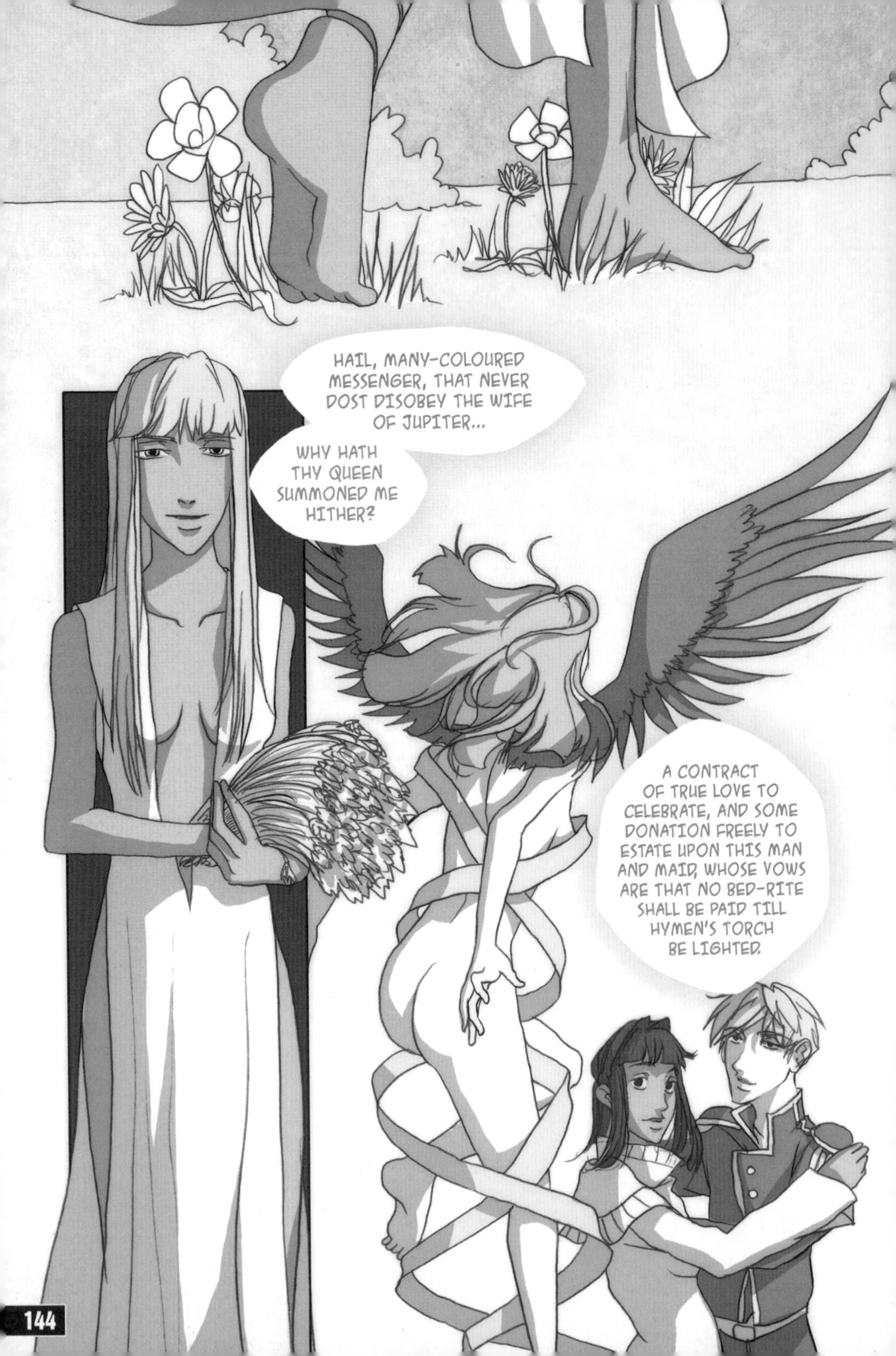
HAIL, MANY-COLOURED MESSENGER, THAT NEVER DOST DISOBEY THE WIFE OF JUPITER...
WHY HATH THY QUEEN SUMMONED ME HITHER?
A CONTRACT OF TRUE LOVE TO CELEBRATE, AND SOME DONATION FREELY TO ESTATE UPON THIS MAN AND MAID, WHOSE VOWS ARE THAT NO BED-RITE SHALL BE PAID TILL HYMEN'S TORCH BE LIGHTED.

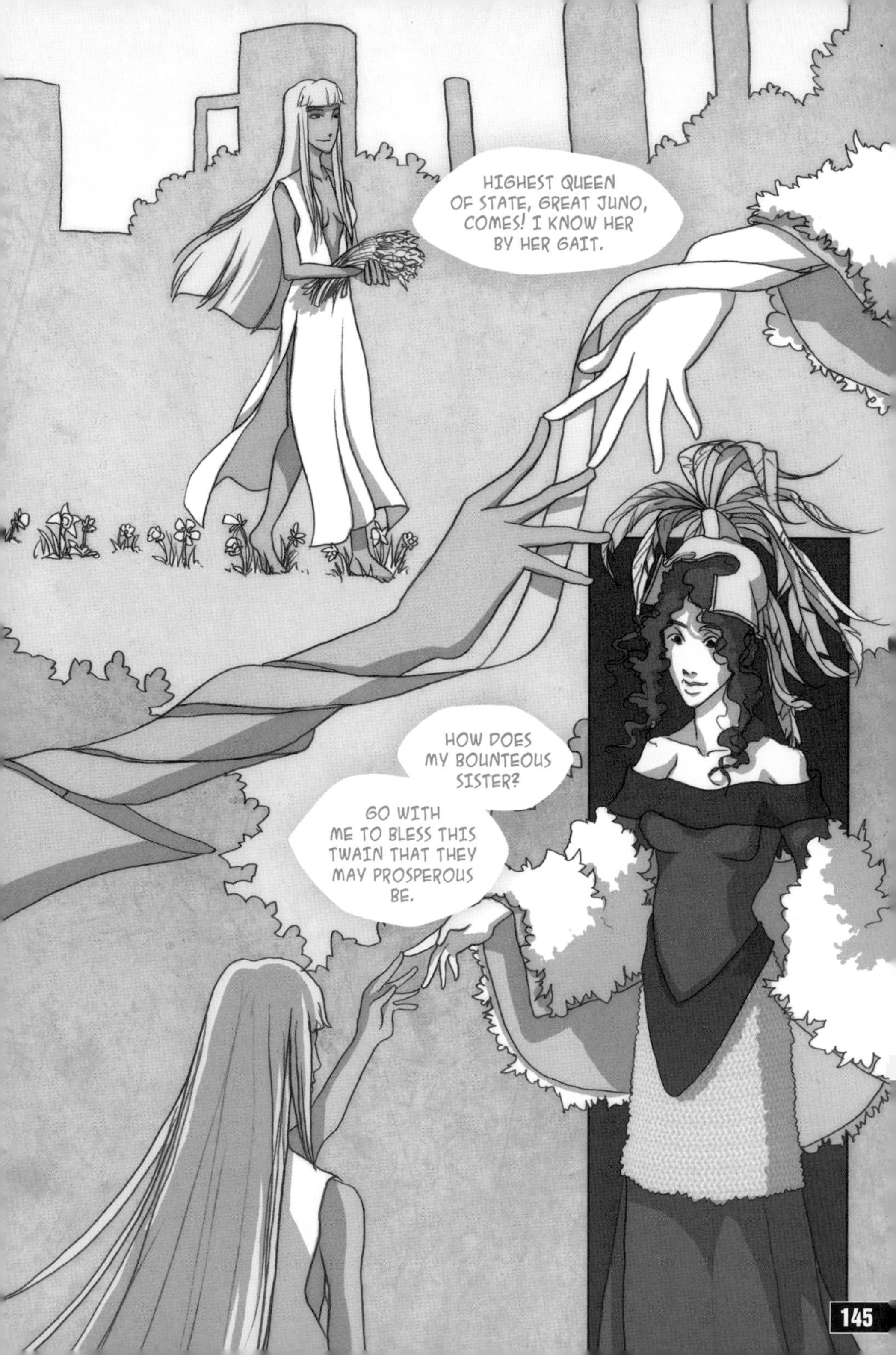
HIGHEST QUEEN OF STATE, GREAT JUNO, COMES! I KNOW HER BY HER GAIT.
HOW DOES MY BOUNTEOUS SISTER?
GO WITH ME TO BLESS THIS TWAIN THAT THEY MAY PROSPEROUS BE.

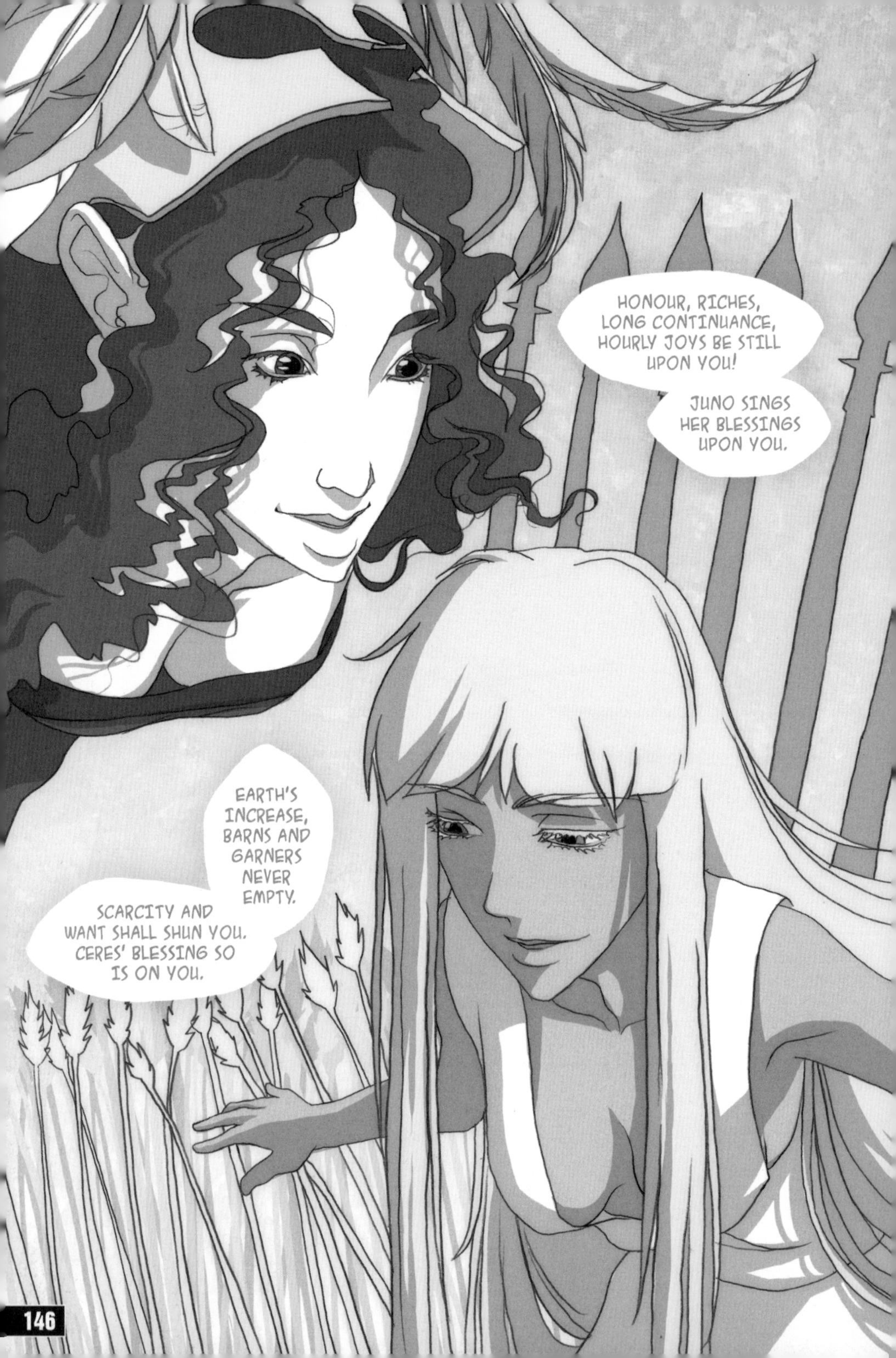
HONOUR, RICHES, LONG CONTINUANCE, HOURLY JOYS BE STILL UPON YOU!
JUNO SINGS HER BLESSINGS UPON YOU.
EARTH'S INCREASE, BARNS AND GARNERS NEVER EMPTY.
SCARCITY AND WANT SHALL SHUN YOU. CERES' BLESSING SO IS ON YOU.

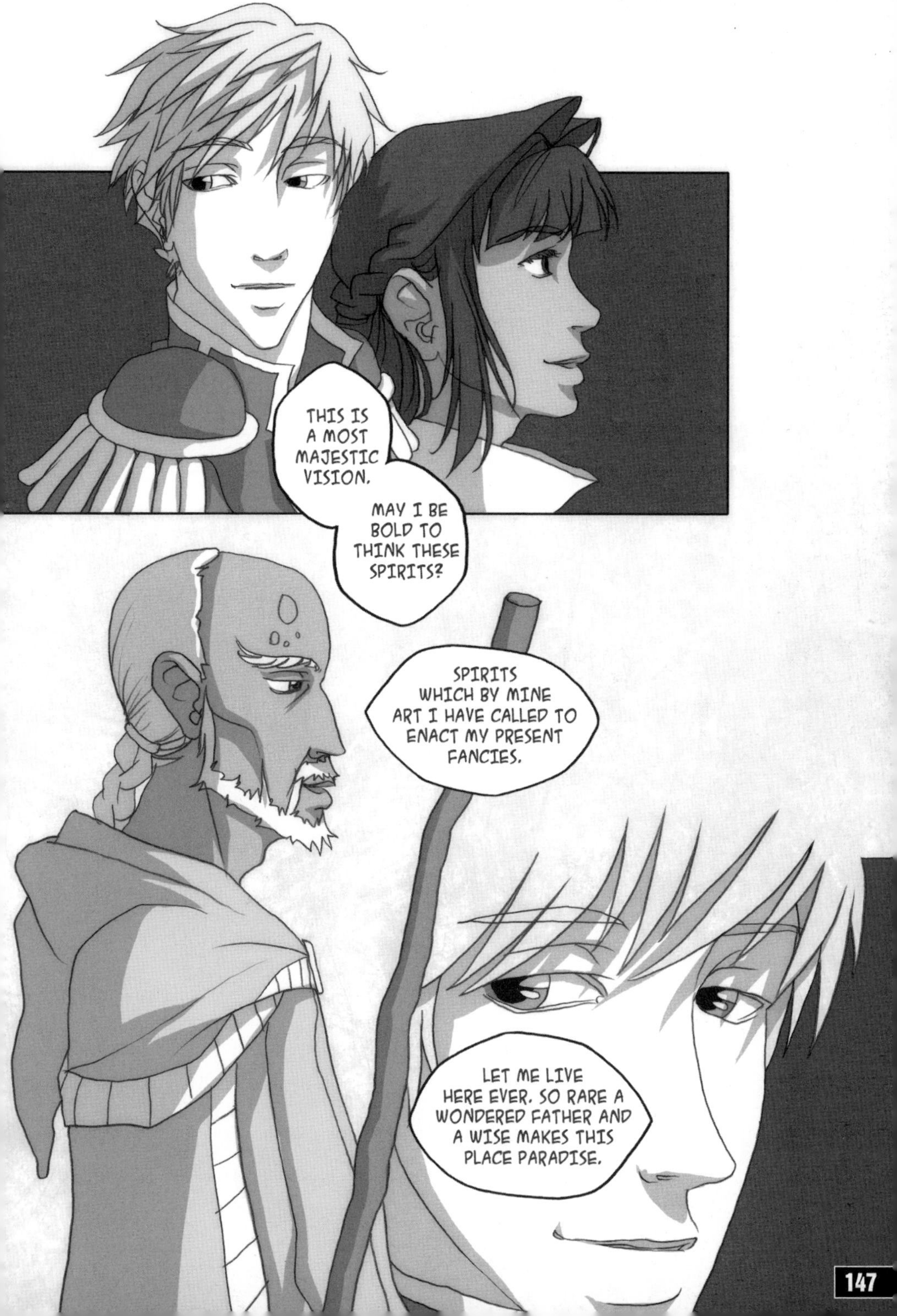
THIS IS A MOST MAJESTIC VISION.
MAY I BE BOLD TO THINK THESE SPIRITS?
SPIRITS WHICH BY MINE ART I HAVE CALLED TO ENACT MY PRESENT FANCIES.
LET ME LIVE HERE EVER. SO RARE A WONDERED FATHER AND A WISE MAKES THIS PLACE PARADISE.

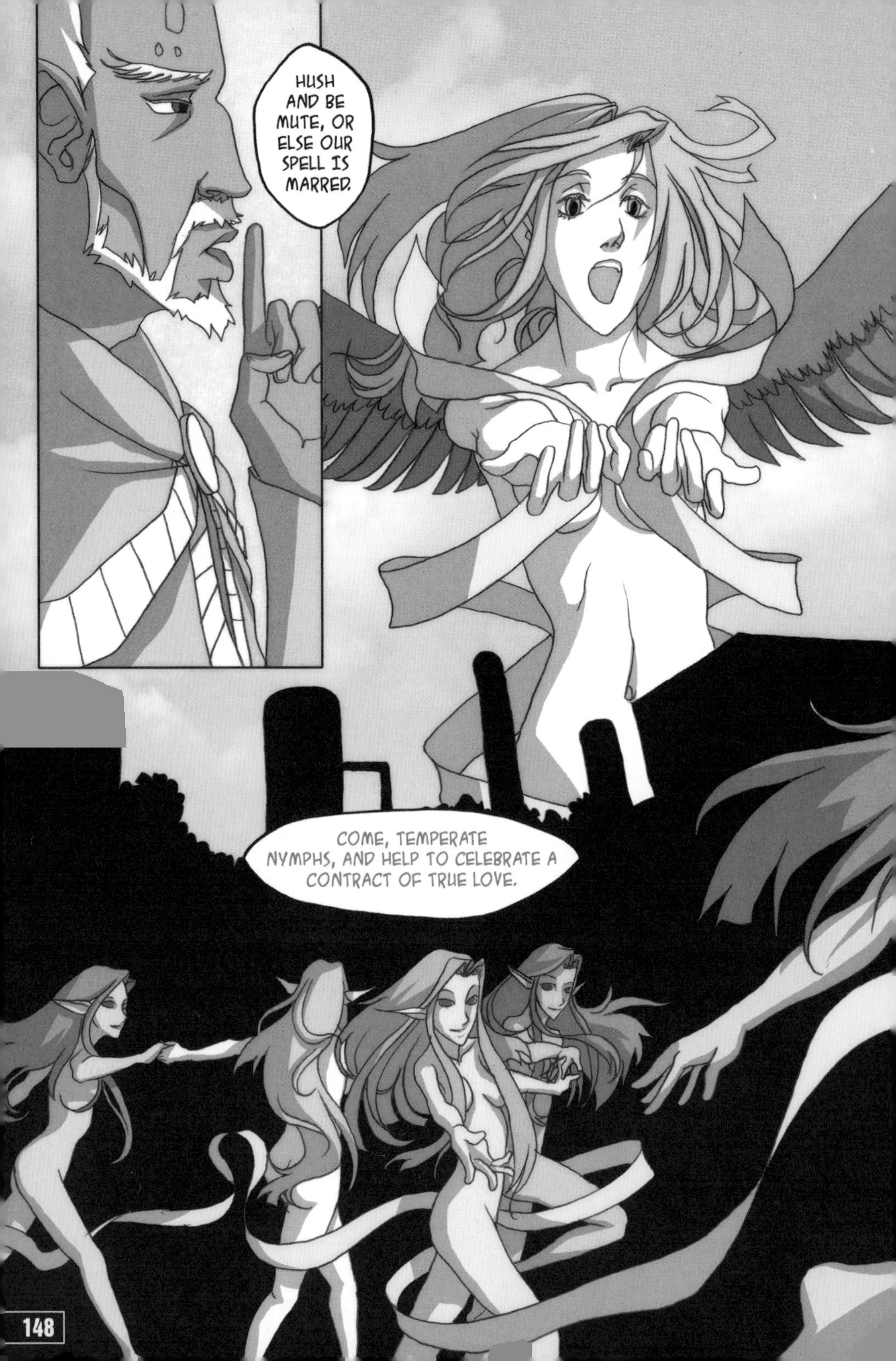
HUSH AND BE MUTE, OR ELSE OUR SPELL IS MARRED.
COME, TEMPERATE NYMPHS, AND HELP TO CELEBRATE A CONTRACT OF TRUE LOVE.

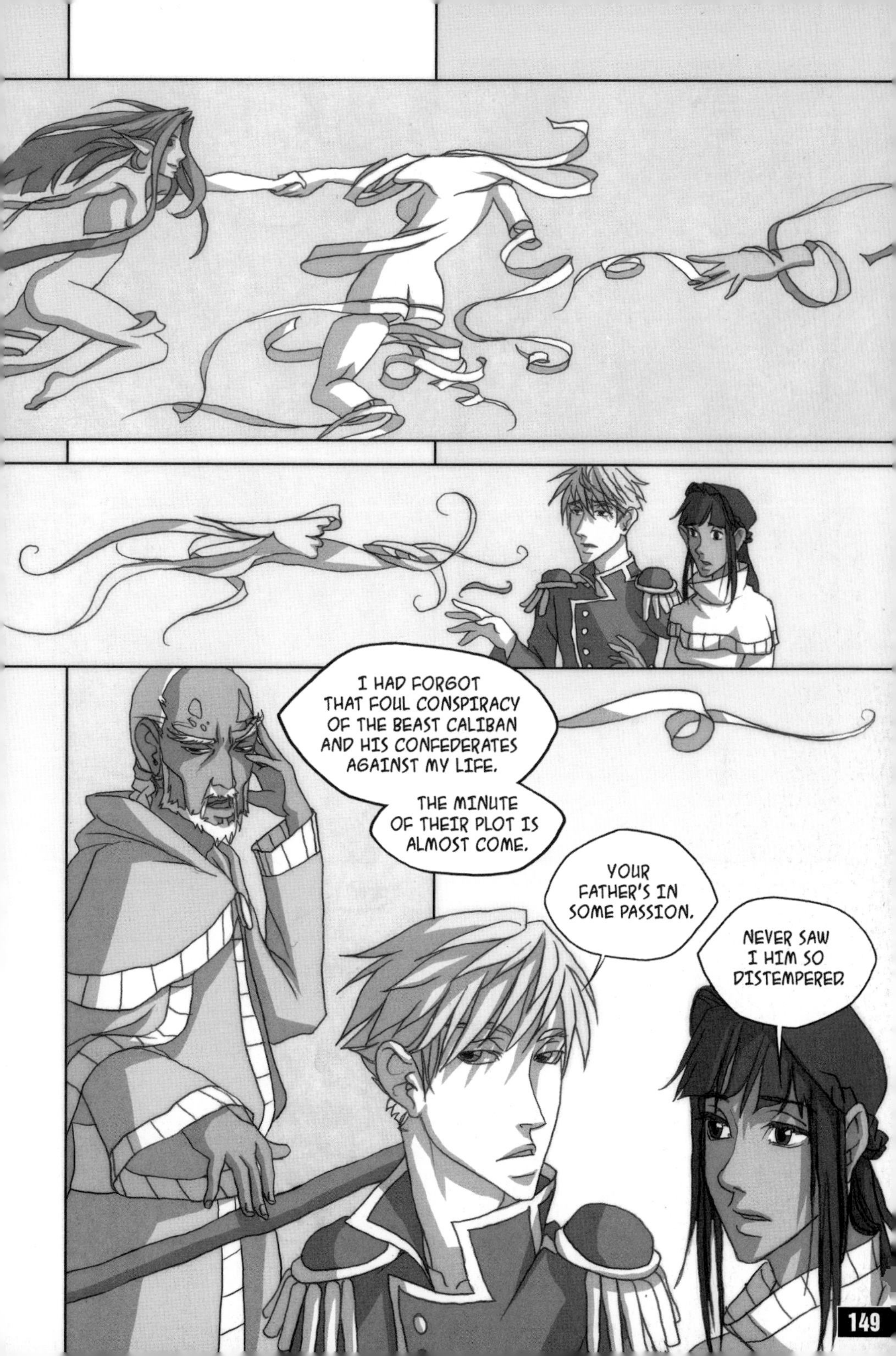

I HAD FORGOT THAT FOUL CONSPIRACY OF THE BEAST CALIBAN AND HIS CONFEDERATES AGAINST MY LIFE.
THE MINUTE OF THEIR PLOT IS ALMOST COME.
YOUR FATHER'S IN SOME PASSION.
NEVER SAW I HIM SO DISTEMPERED.

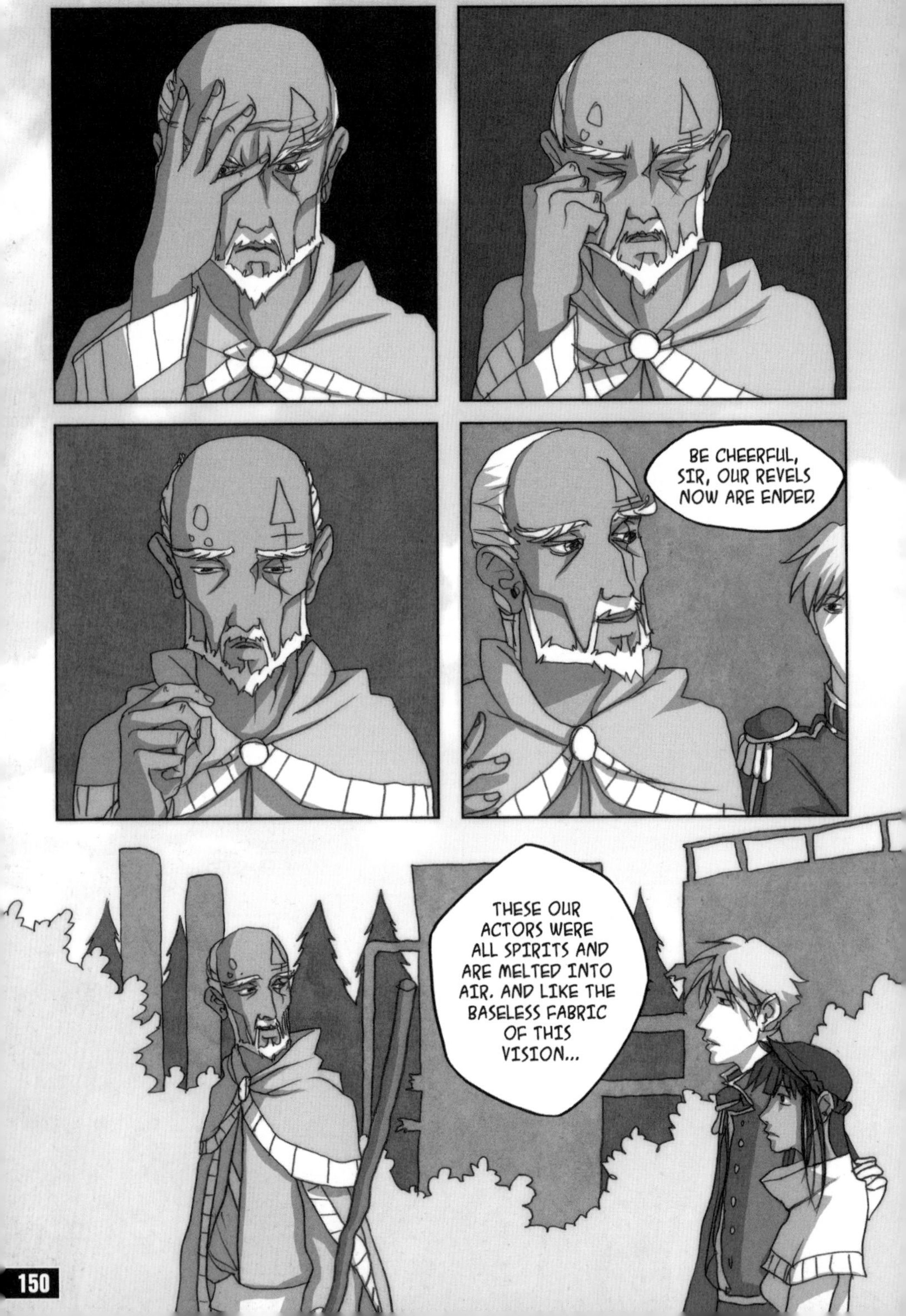
BE CHEERFUL, SIR, OUR REVELS NOW ARE ENDED.
THESE OUR ACTORS WERE ALL SPIRITS AND ARE MELTED INTO AIR. AND LIKE THE BASELESS FABRIC OF THIS VISION...

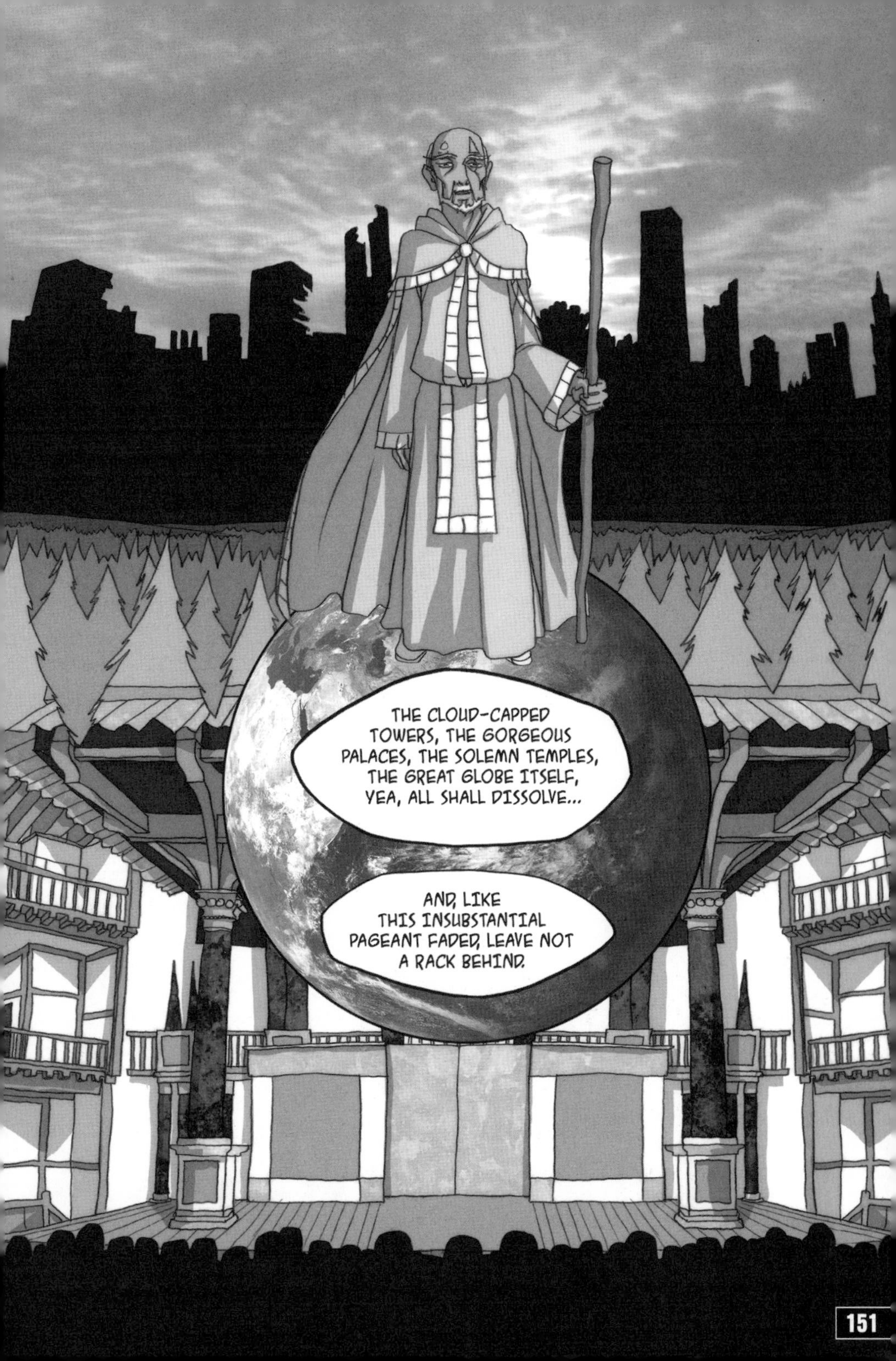
THE CLOUD-CAPPED TOWERS, THE GORGEOUS PALACES, THE SOLEMN TEMPLES, THE GREAT GLOBE ITSELF, YEA, ALL SHALL DISSOLVE...
AND, LIKE THIS INSUBSTANTIAL PAGEANT FADED, LEAVE NOT A RACK BEHIND.

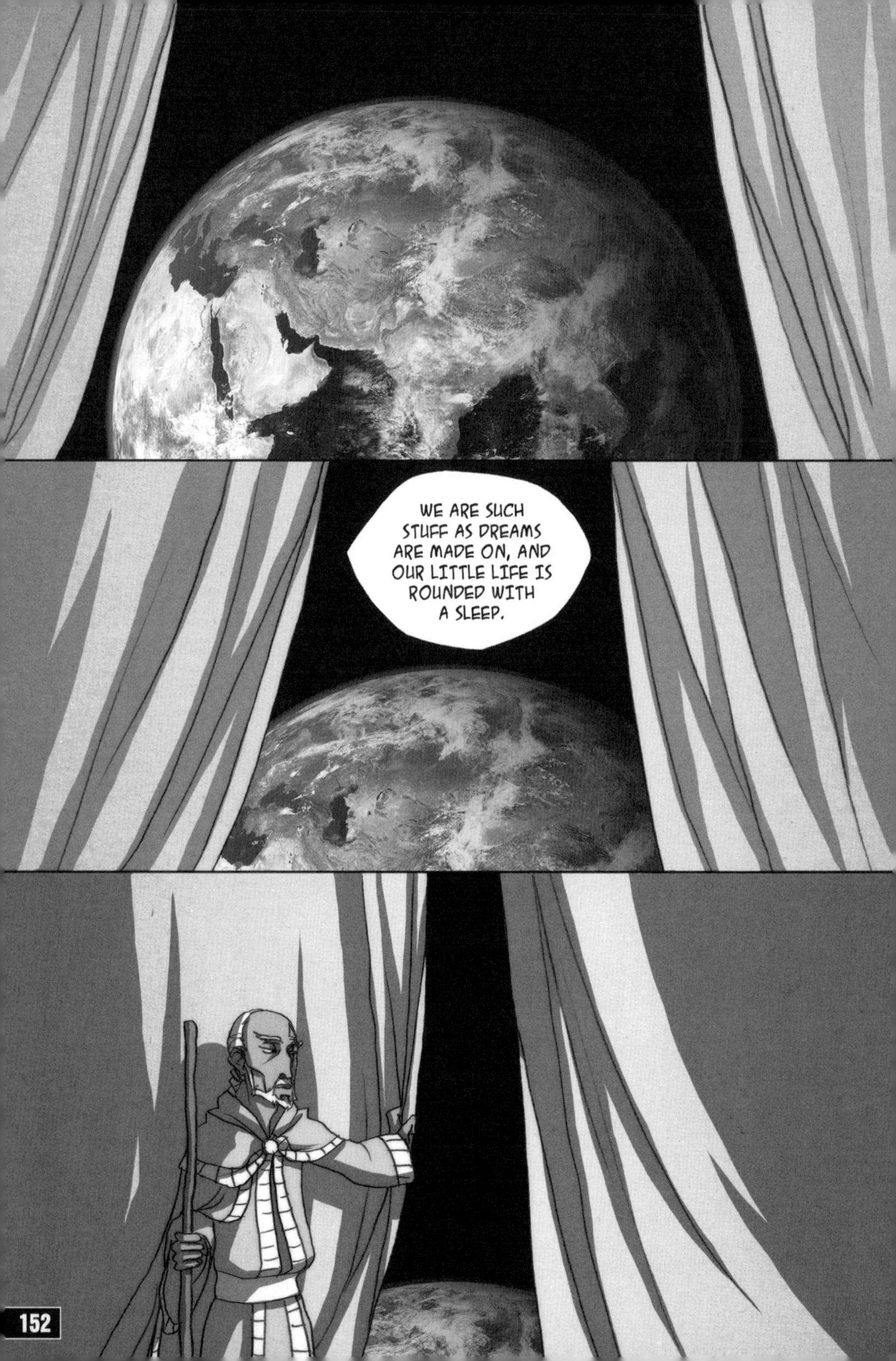
WE ARE SUCH STUFF AS DREAMS ARE MADE ON, AND OUR LITTLE LIFE IS ROUNDED WITH A SLEEP.

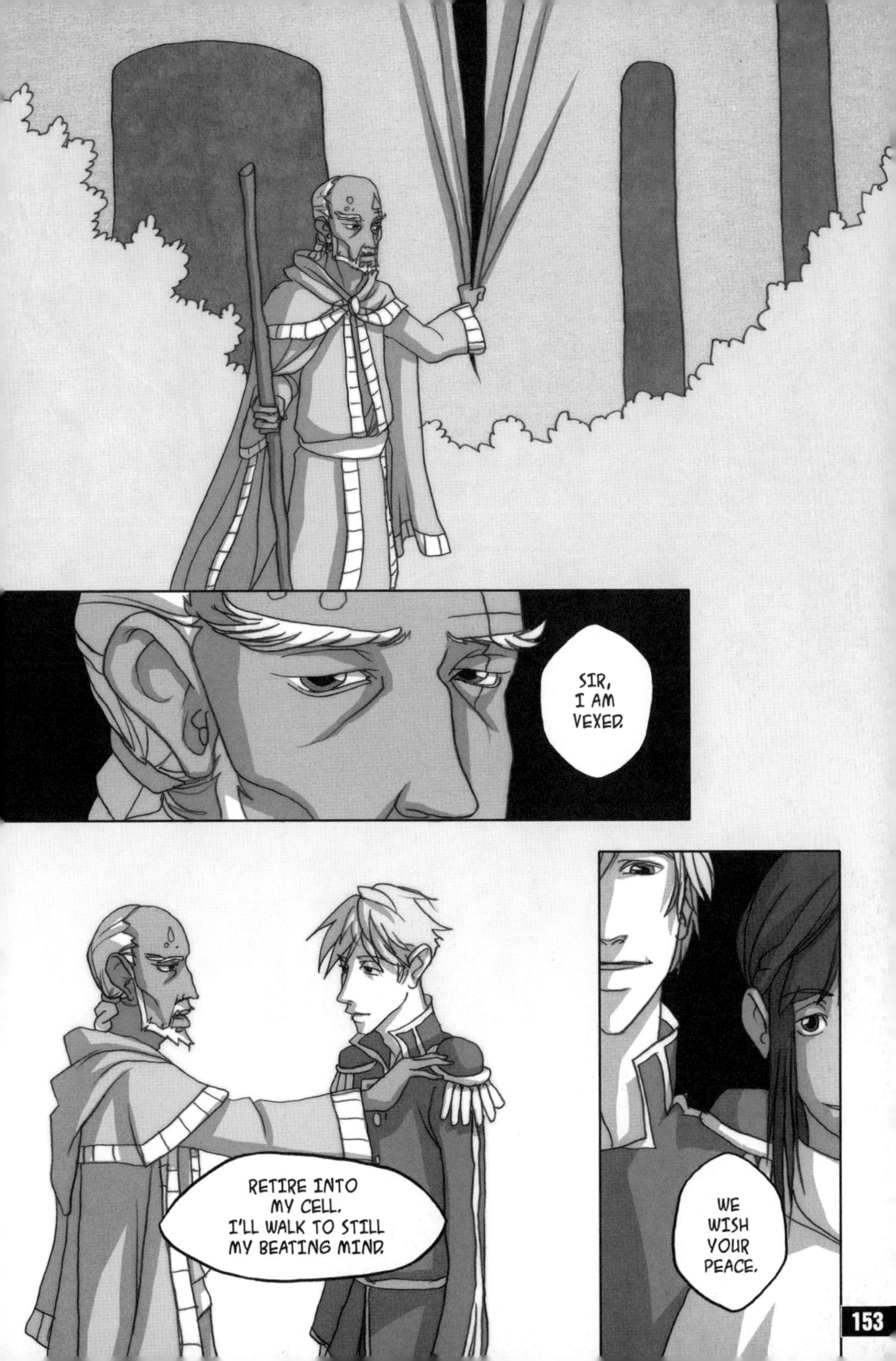
SIR, I AM VEXED.
RETIRE INTO MY CELL. I'LL WALK TO STILL MY BEATING MIND.
WE WISH YOUR PEACE.

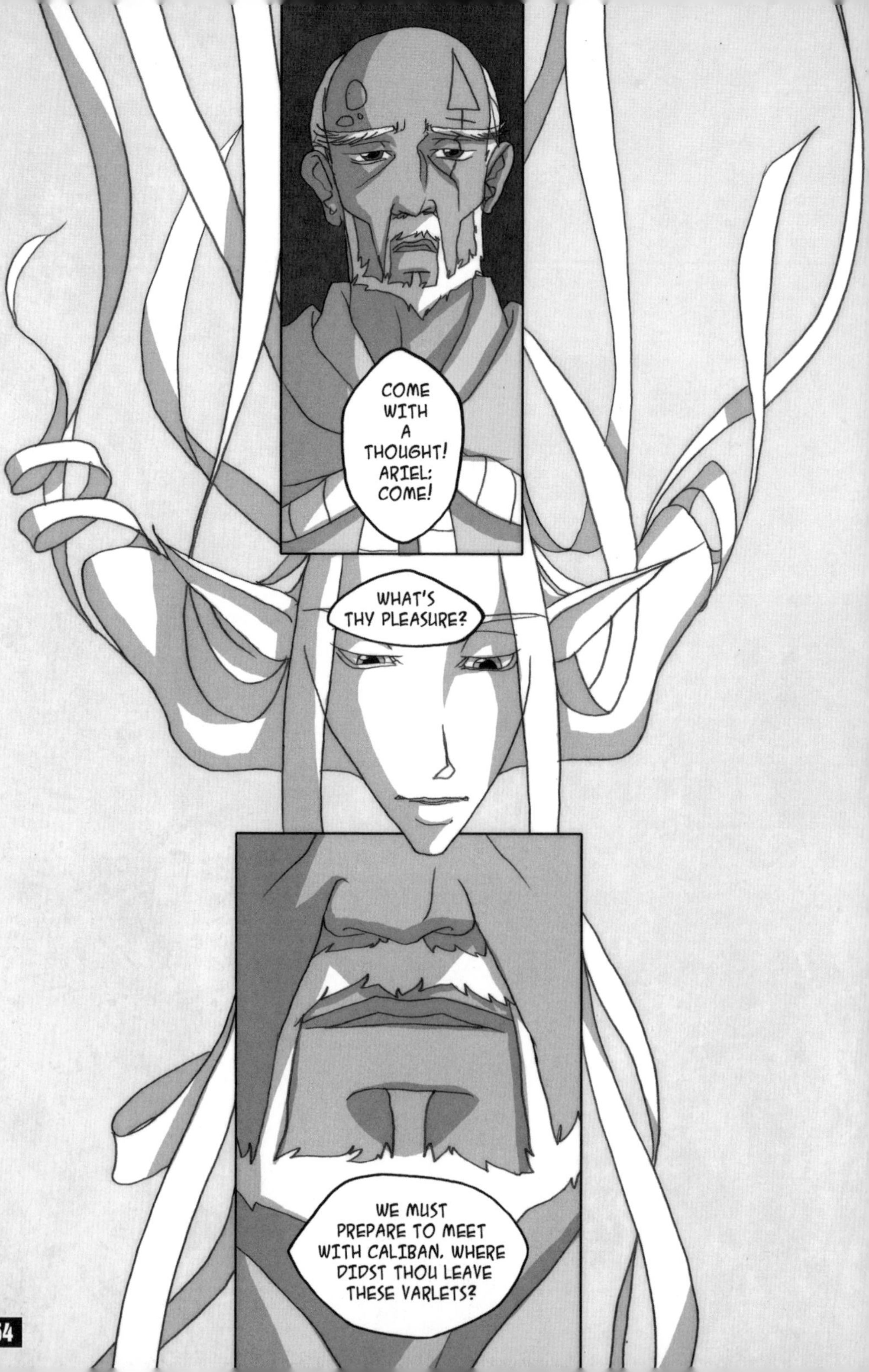
COME WITH A THOUGHT! ARIEL: COME!
WHAT'S THY PLEASURE?
WE MUST PREPARE TO MEET WITH CALIBAN. WHERE DIDST THOU LEAVE THESE VARLETS?

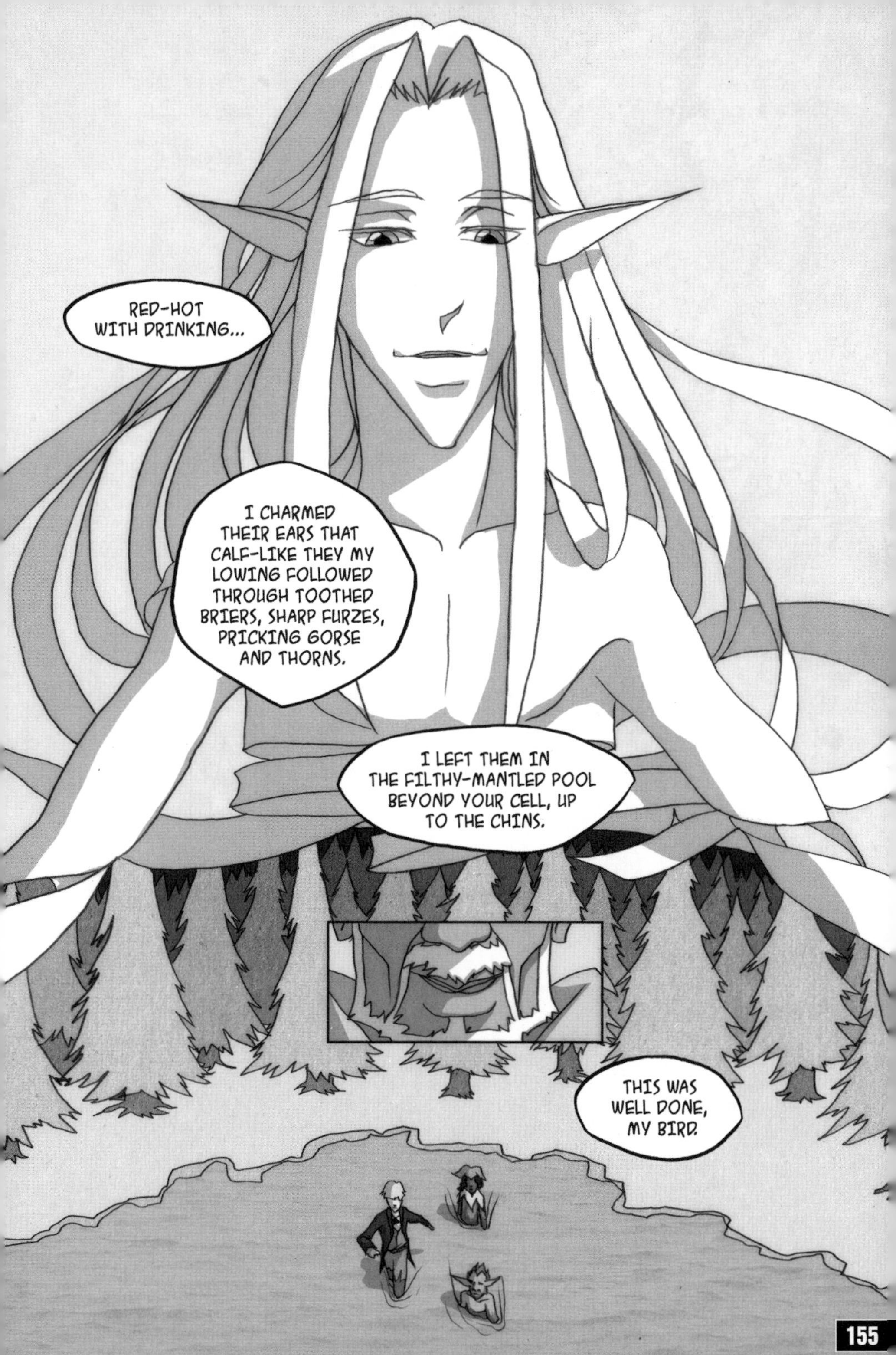
RED-HOT WITH DRINKING...
I CHARMED THEIR EARS THAT CALF-LIKE THEY MY LOWING FOLLOWED THROUGH TOOTHED BRIERS, SHARP FURZES, PRICKING GORSE AND THORNS.
I LEFT THEM IN THE FILTHY-MANTLED POOL BEYOND YOUR CELL, UP TO THE CHINS.
THIS WAS WELL DONE, MY BIRD.

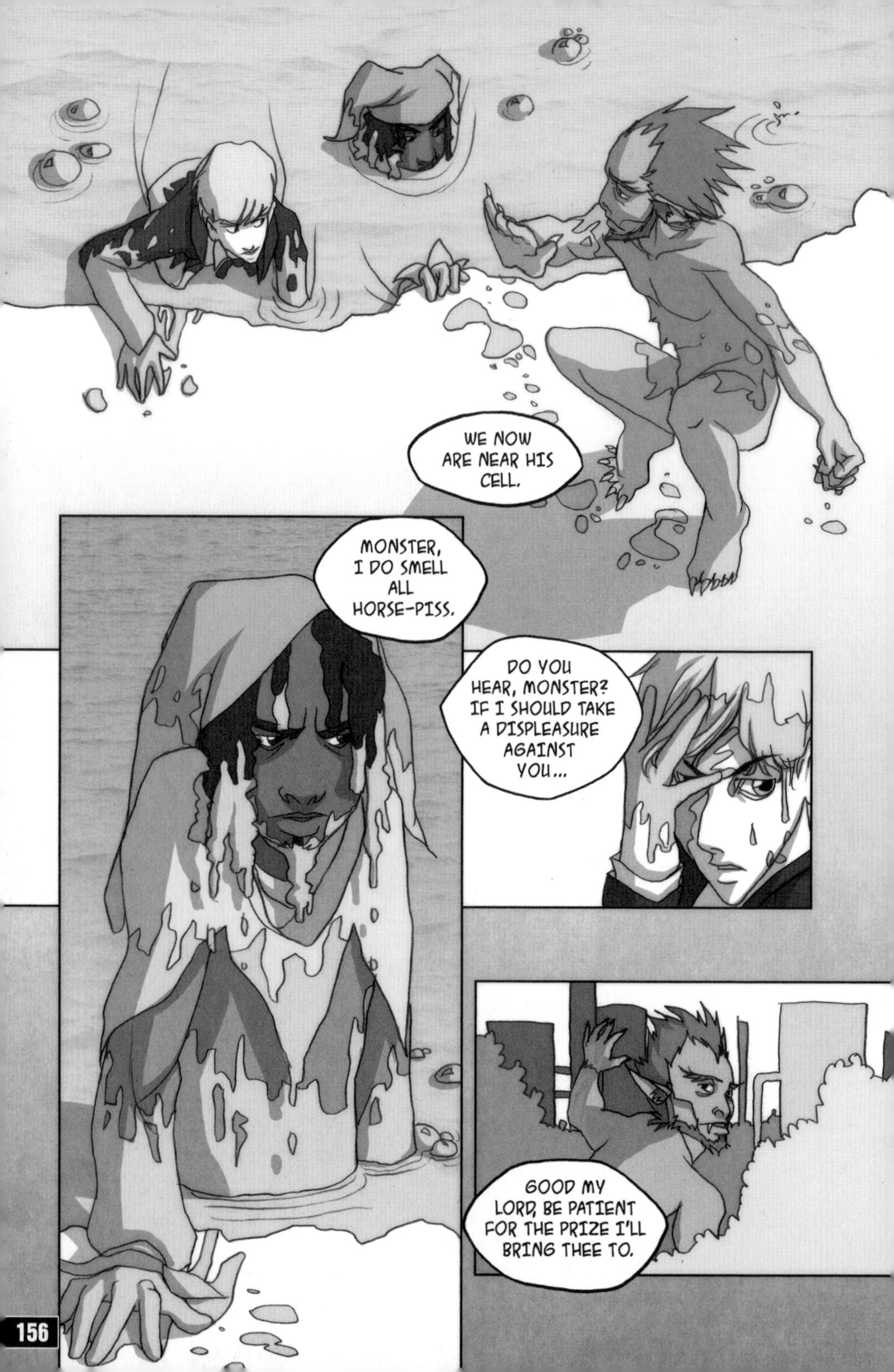
WE NOW ARE NEAR HIS CELL.
MONSTER, I DO SMELL ALL HORSE-PISS.
DO YOU HEAR, MONSTER? IF I SHOULD TAKE A DISPLEASURE AGAINST YOU...
GOOD MY LORD, BE PATIENT FOR THE PRIZE I'LL BRING THEE TO.

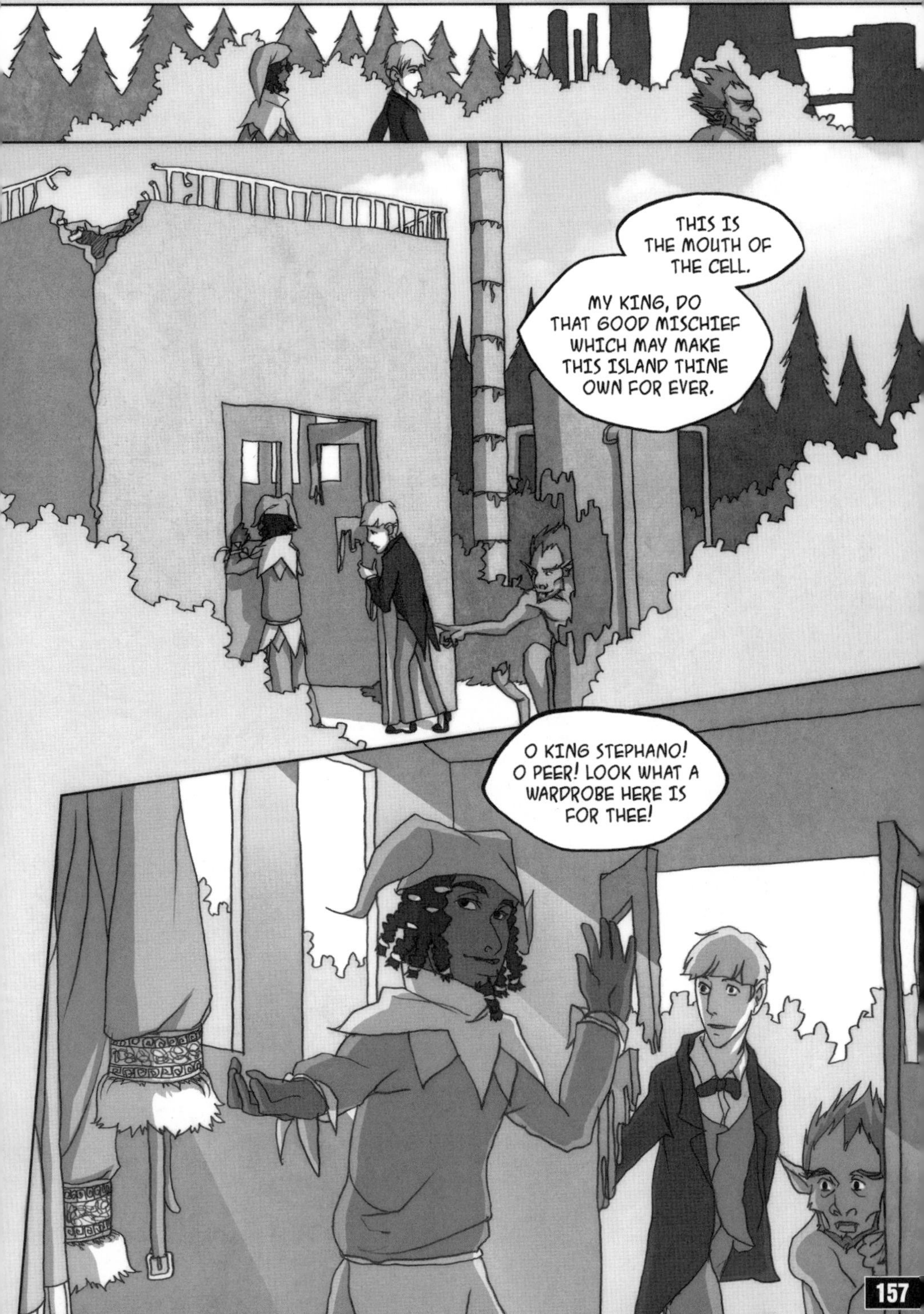
THIS IS THE MOUTH OF THE CELL.
MY KING, DO THAT GOOD MISCHIEF WHICH MAY MAKE THIS ISLAND THINE OWN FOR EVER.
O KING STEPHANO! O PEER! LOOK WHAT A WARDROBE HERE IS FOR THEE!

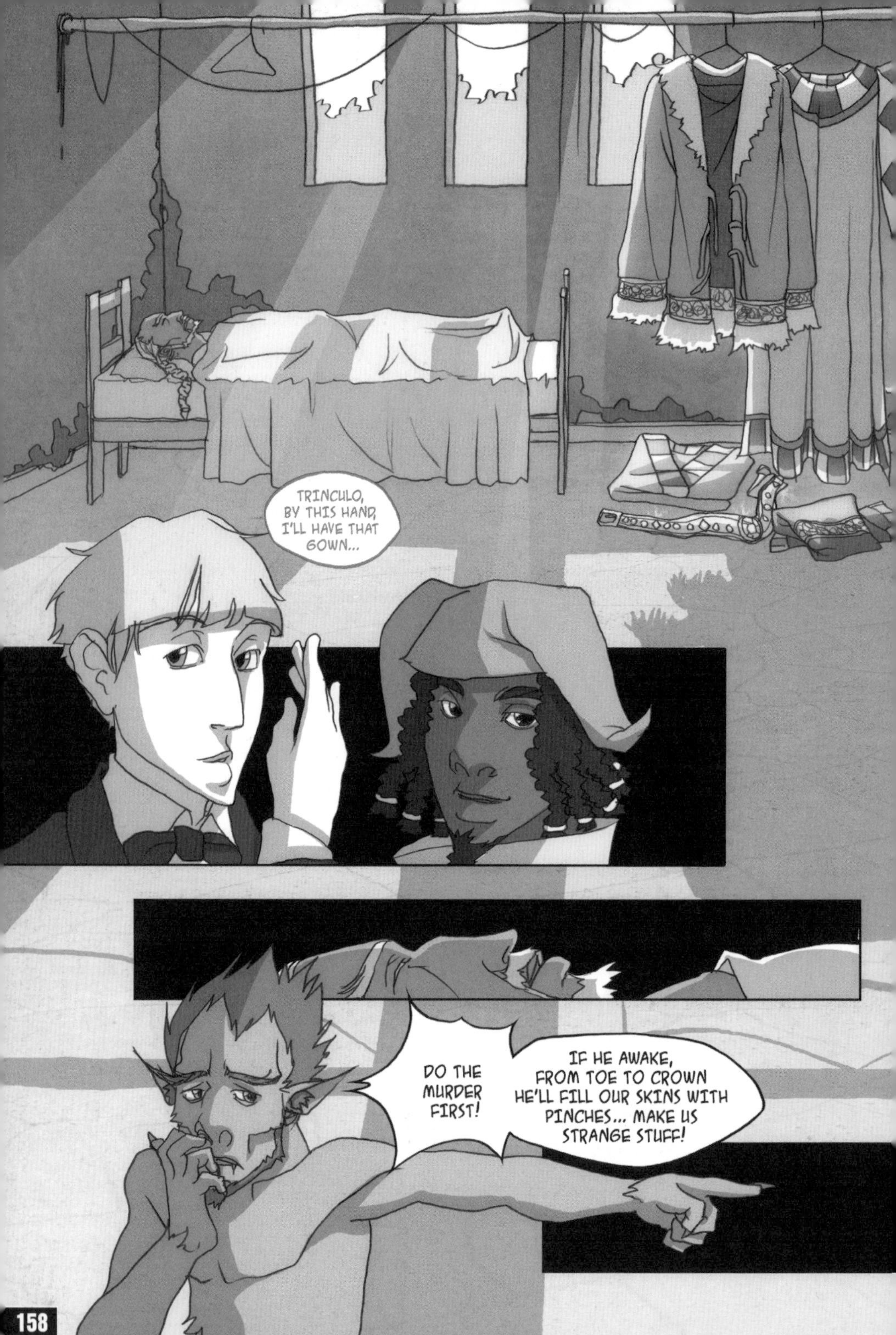
TRINCULO, BY THIS HAND, I'LL HAVE THAT GOWN...
DO THE MURDER FIRST!
IF HE AWAKE, FROM TOE TO CROWN HE'LL FILL OUR SKINS WITH PINCHES... MAKE US STRANGE STUFF!

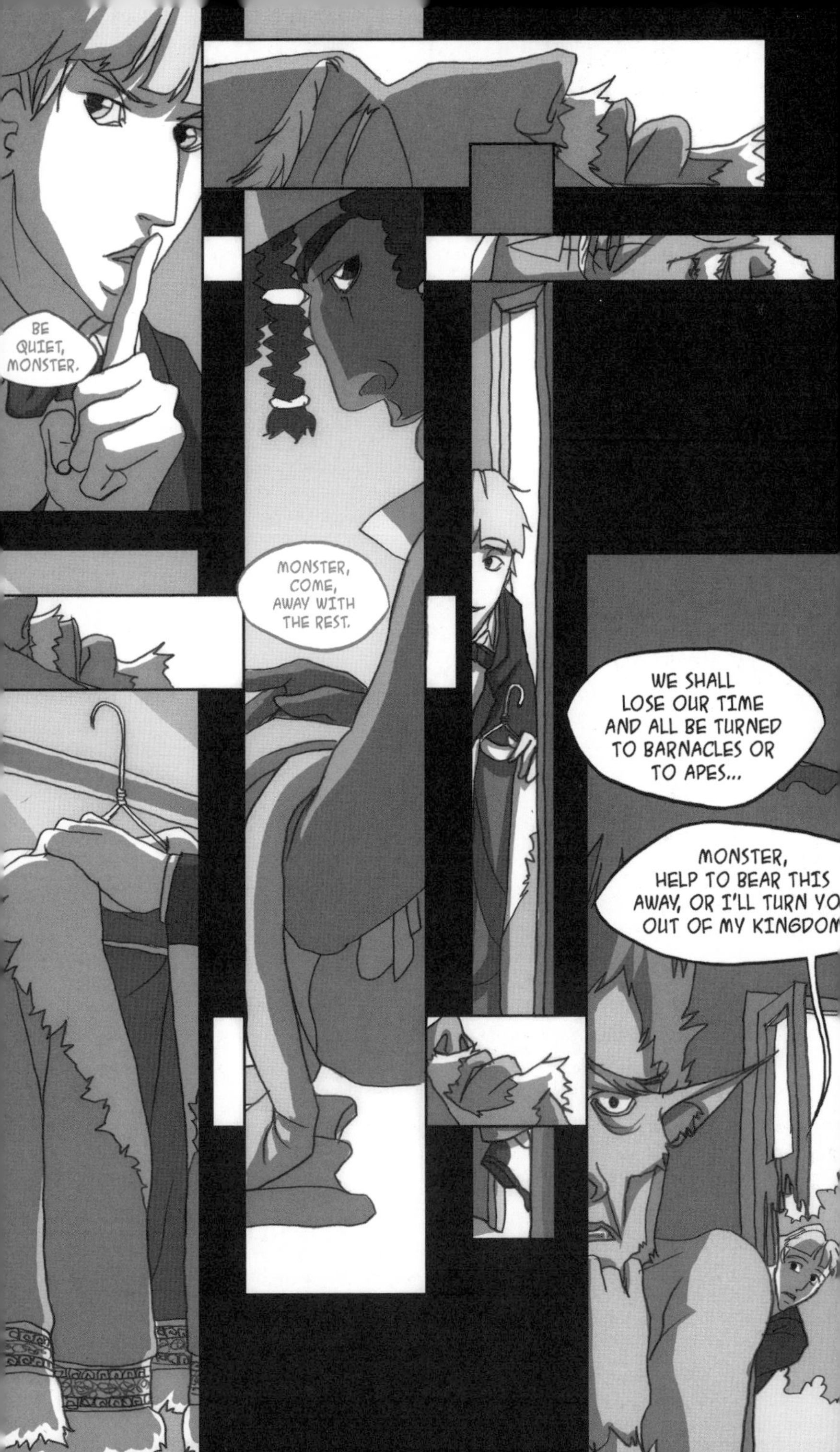
BE QUIET, MONSTER.
MONSTER, COME, AWAY WITH THE REST.
WE SHALL LOSE OUR TIME AND ALL BE TURNED TO BARNACLES OR TO APES...
MONSTER, HELP TO BEAR THIS AWAY, OR I'LL TURN YO OUT OF MY KINGDOM

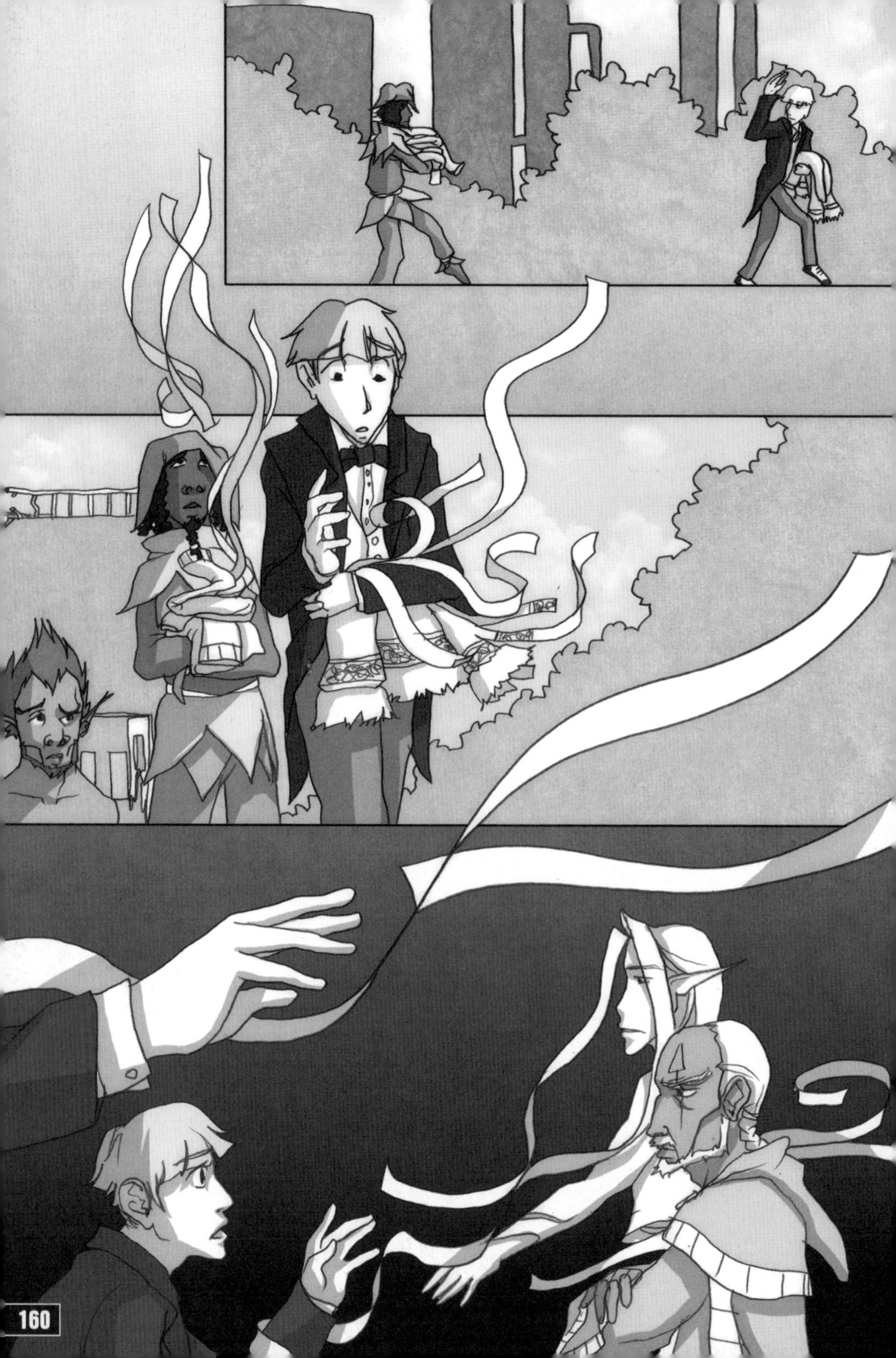

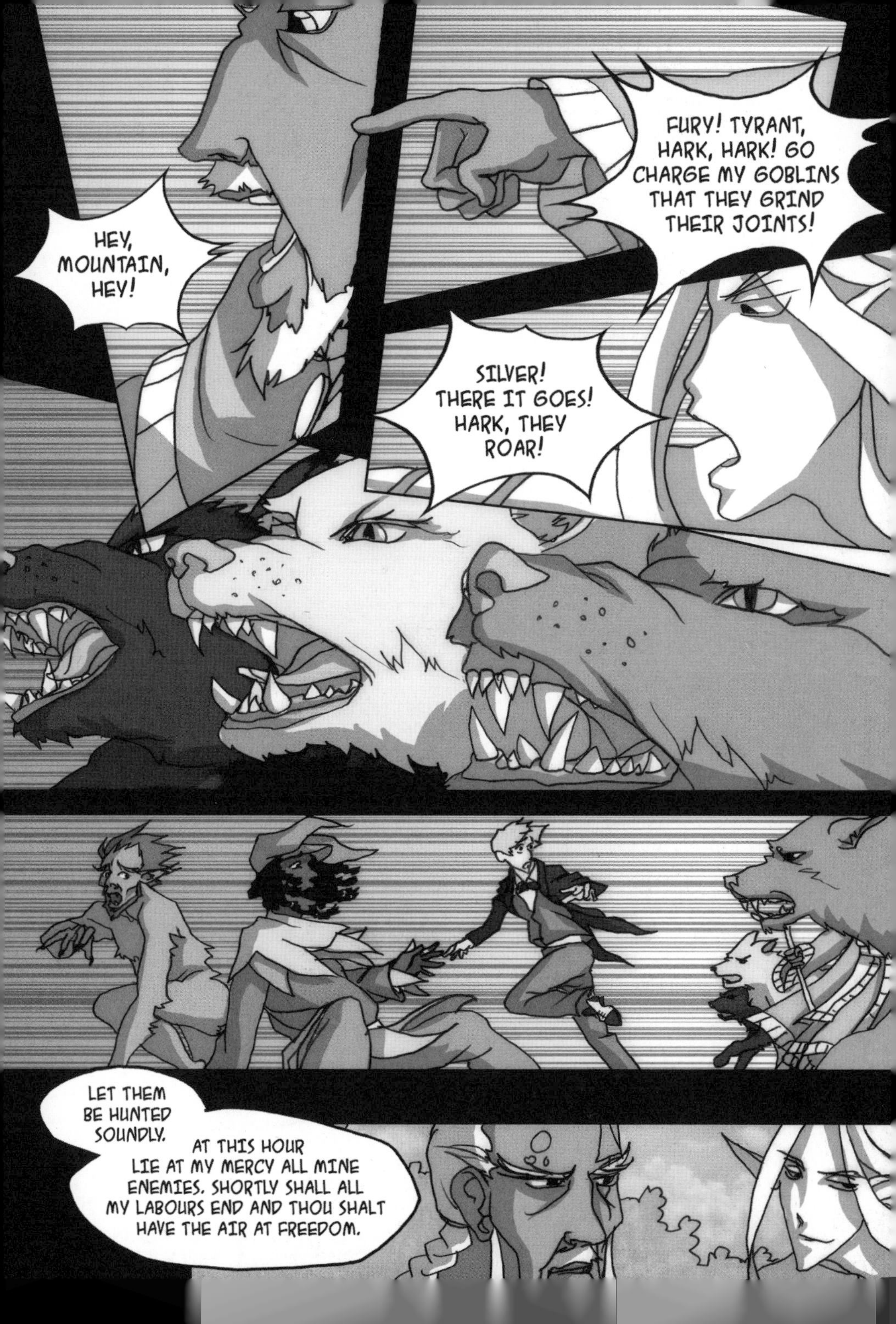
HEY, MOUNTAIN, HEY!
FURY! TYRANT, HARK, HARK! GO CHARGE MY GOBLINS THAT THEY GRIND THEIR JOINTS!
SILVER! THERE IT GOES! HARK, THEY ROAR!
LET THEM BE HUNTED SOUNDLY.
AT THIS HOUR LIE AT MY MERCY ALL MINE ENEMIES. SHORTLY SHALL ALL MY LABOURS END AND THOU SHALT HAVE THE AIR AT FREEDOM.

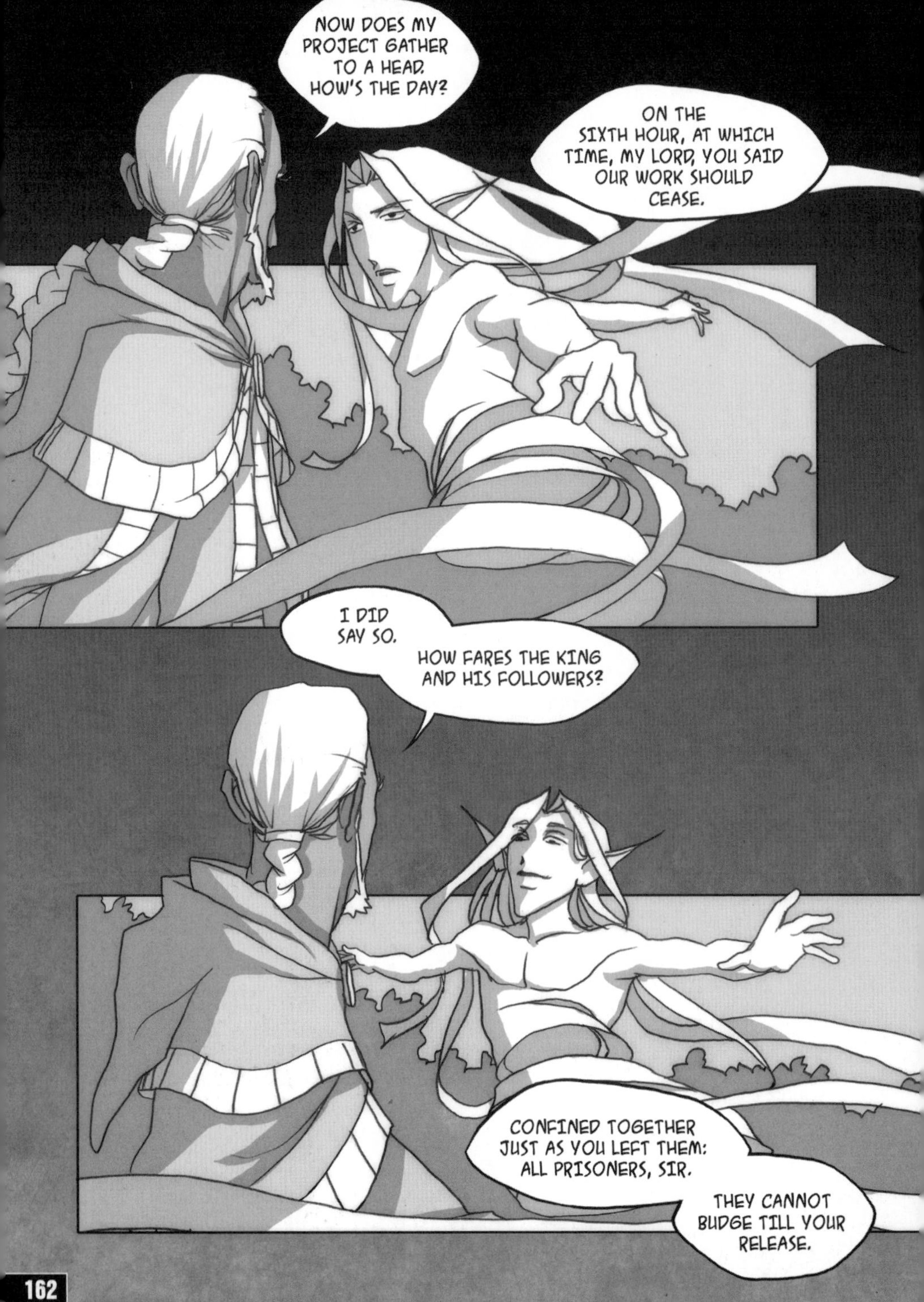
NOW DOES MY PROJECT GATHER TO A HEAD. HOW'S THE DAY?
ON THE SIXTH HOUR, AT WHICH TIME, MY LORD, YOU SAID OUR WORK SHOULD CEASE.
I DID SAY SO.
HOW FARES THE KING AND HIS FOLLOWERS?
CONFINED TOGETHER JUST AS YOU LEFT THEM: ALL PRISONERS, SIR.
THEY CANNOT BUDGE TILL YOUR RELEASE.

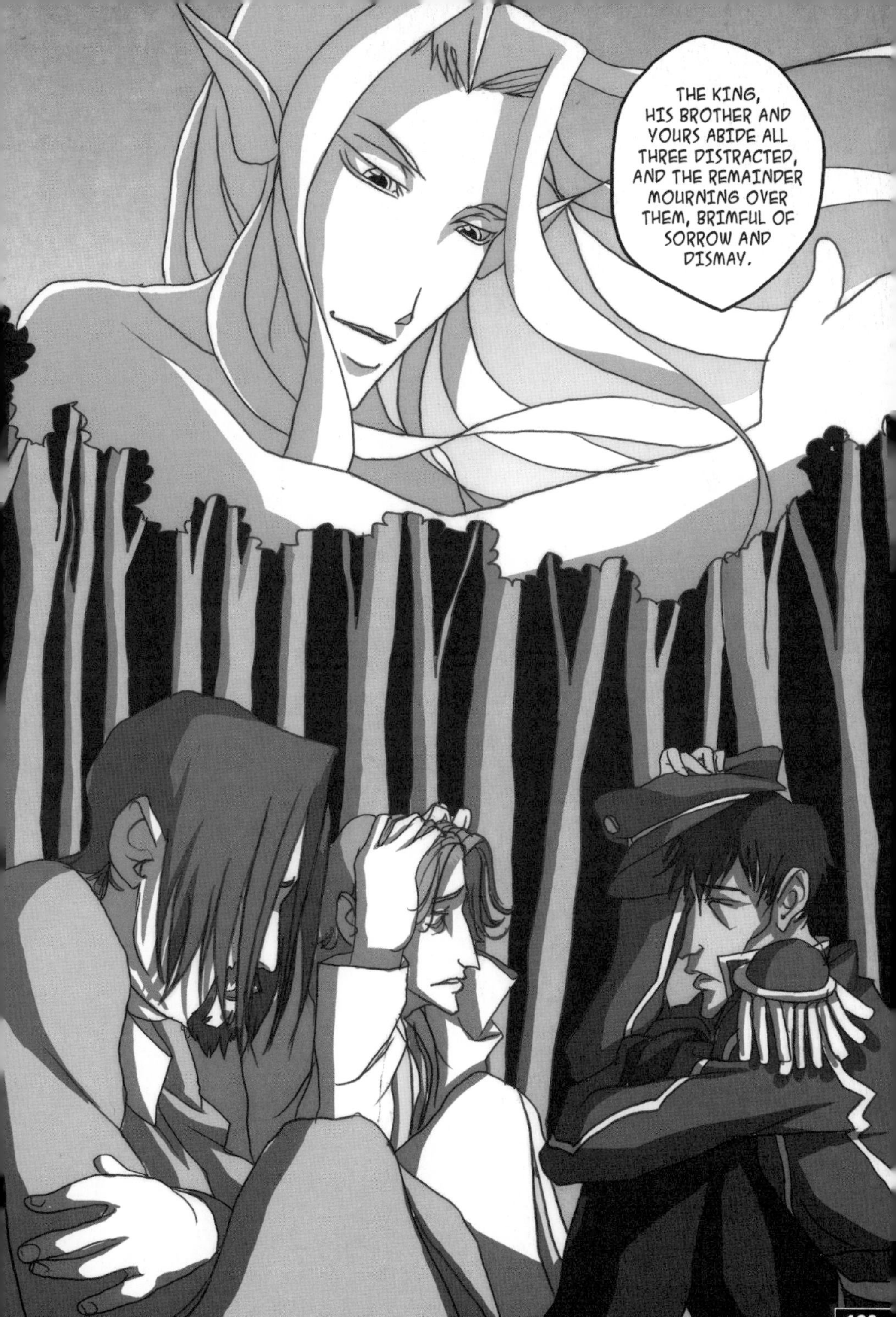
THE KING, HIS BROTHER AND YOURS ABIDE ALL THREE DISTRACTED, AND THE REMAINDER MOURNING OVER THEM, BRIMFUL OF SORROW AND DISMAY.

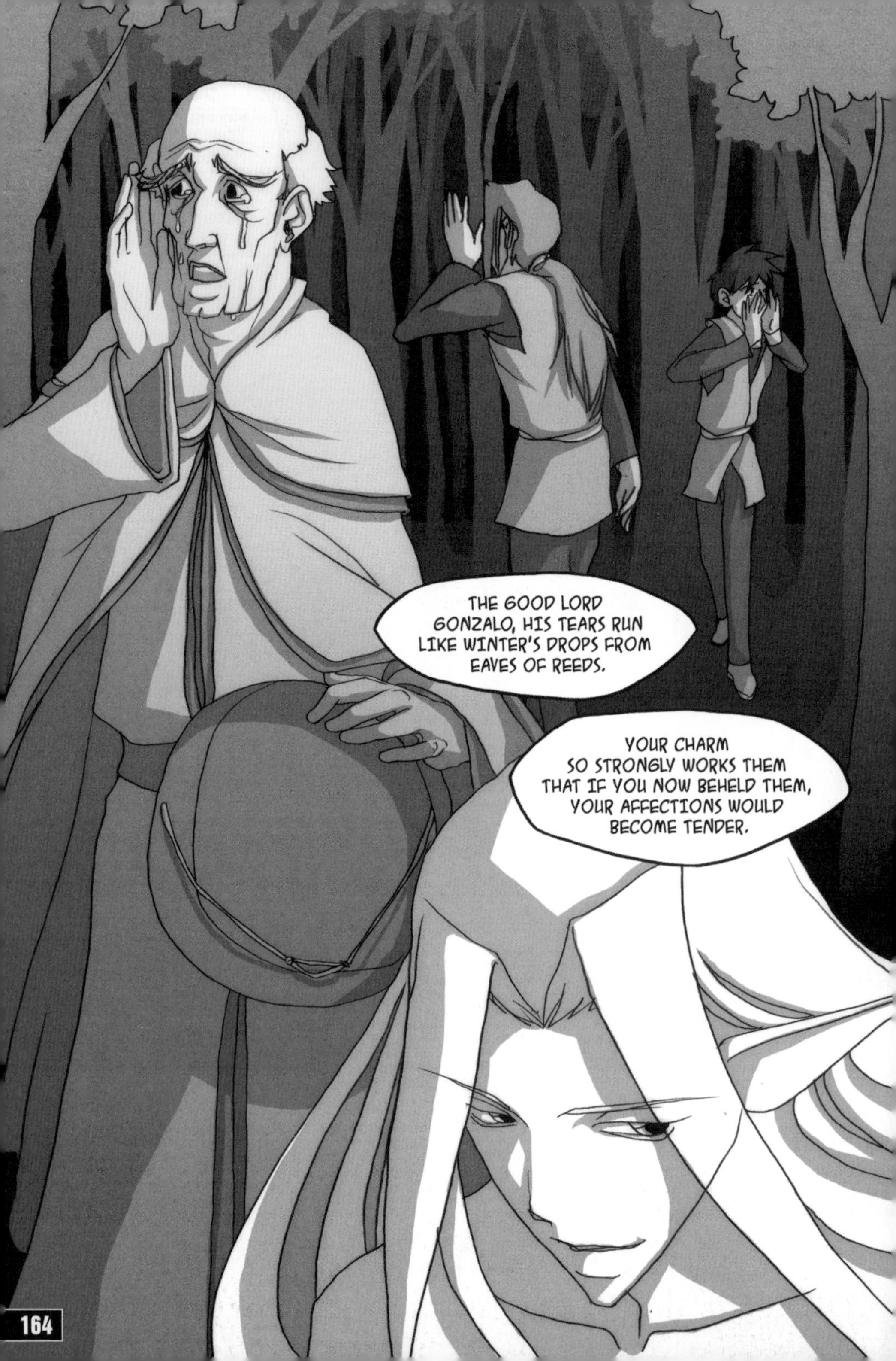
THE GOOD LORD GONZALO, HIS TEARS RUN LIKE WINTER'S DROPS FROM EAVES OF REEDS.
YOUR CHARM SO STRONGLY WORKS THEM THAT IF YOU NOW BEHELD THEM, YOUR AFFECTIONS WOULD BECOME TENDER.

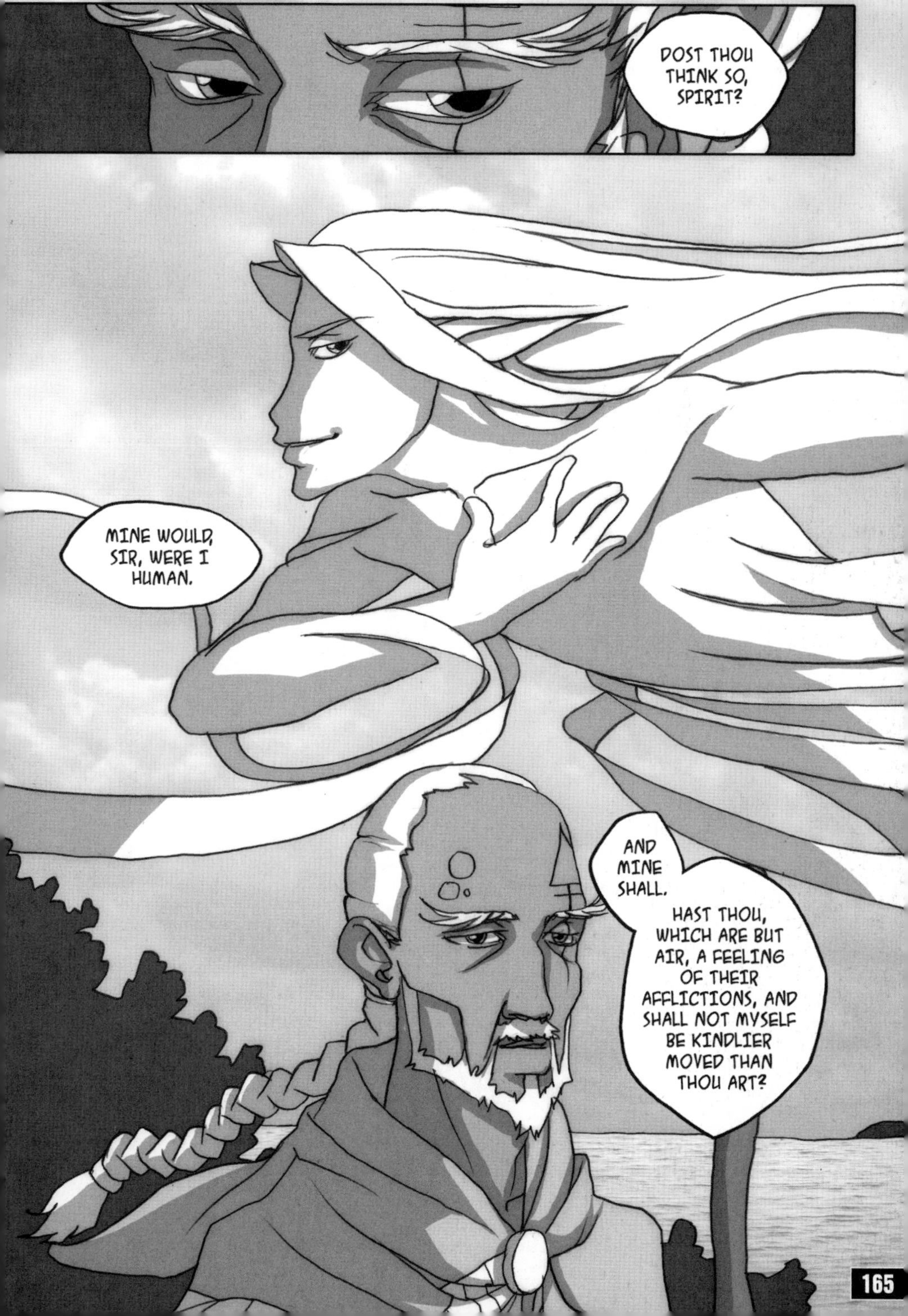
DOST THOU THINK SO, SPIRIT?
MINE WOULD, SIR, WERE I HUMAN.
AND MINE SHALL.
HAST THOU, WHICH ARE BUT AIR, A FEELING OF THEIR AFFLICTIONS, AND SHALL NOT MYSELF BE KINDLIER MOVED THAN THOU ART?

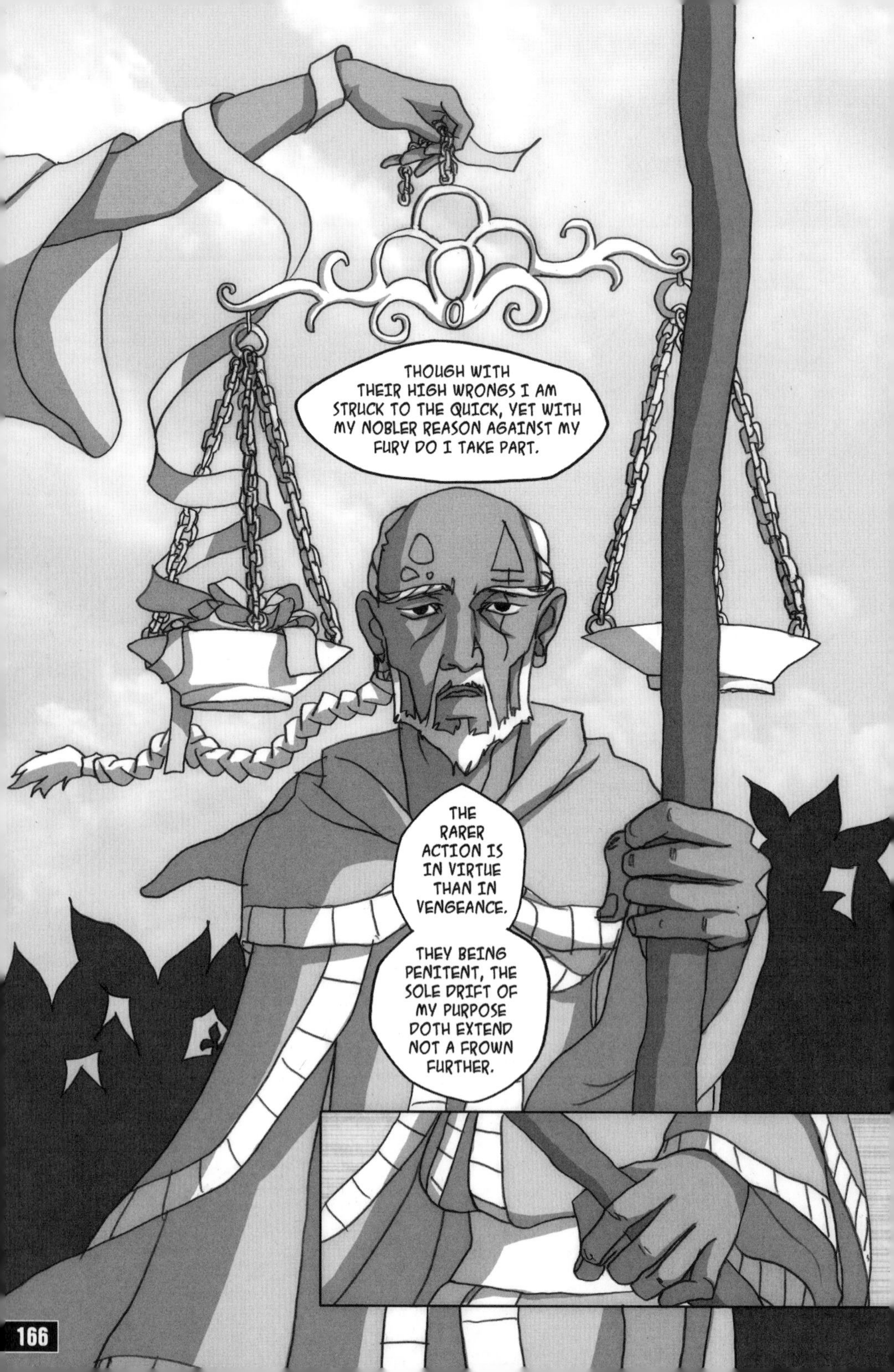
THOUGH WITH THEIR HIGH WRONGS I AM STRUCK TO THE QUICK, YET WITH MY NOBLER REASON AGAINST MY FURY DO I TAKE PART.
THE RARER ACTION IS IN VIRTUE THAN IN VENGEANCE.
THEY BEING PENITENT, THE SOLE DRIFT OF MY PURPOSE DOTH EXTEND NOT A FROWN FURTHER.

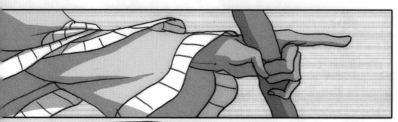

GO RELEASE THEM, ARIEL.
MY CHARMS I'LL BREAK,
THEIR SENSES I'LL RESTORE,
AND THEY SHALL BE THEMSELVES.

I'LL FETCH
THEM, SIR.

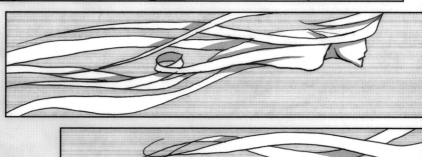

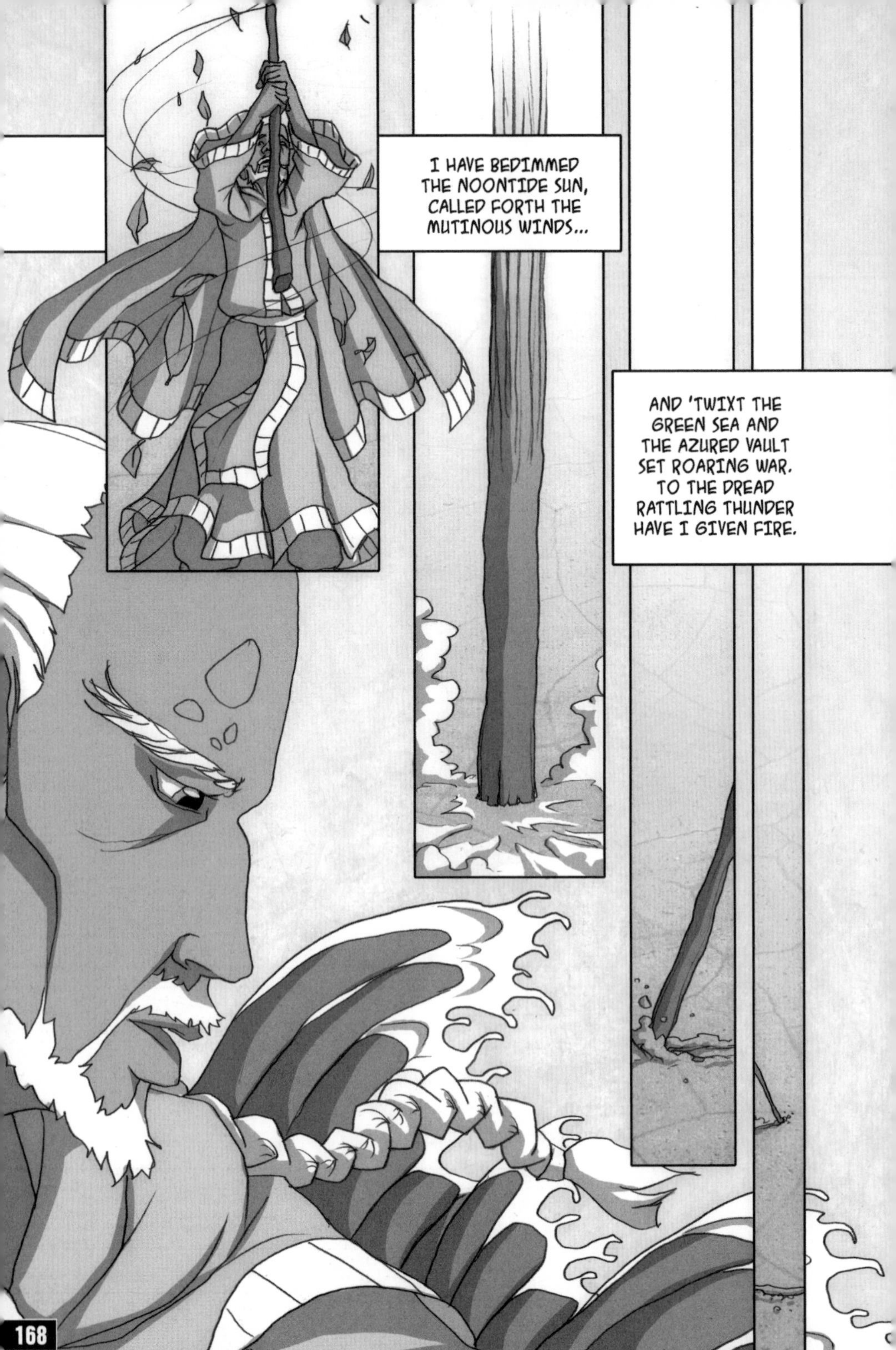
I HAVE BEDIMMED THE NOONTIDE SUN, CALLED FORTH THE MUTINOUS WINDS...
AND 'TWIXT THE GREEN SEA AND THE AZURED VAULT SET ROARING WAR. TO THE DREAD RATTLING THUNDER HAVE I GIVEN FIRE.

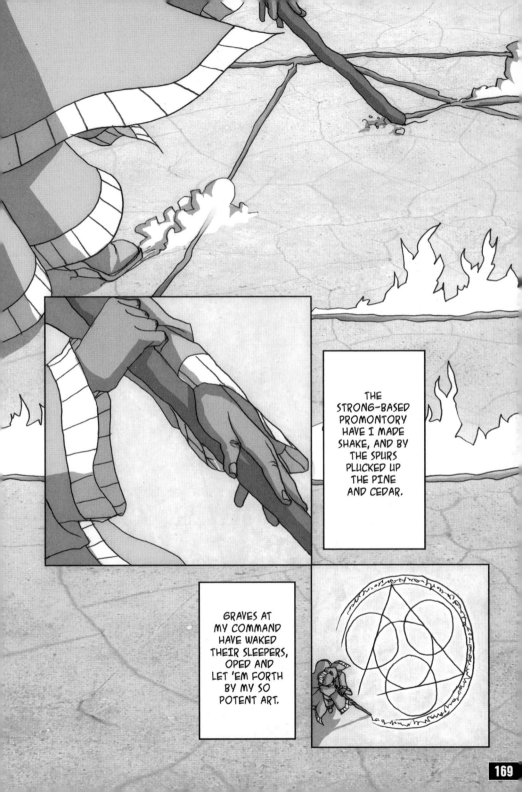

THE STRONG-BASED PROMONTORY HAVE I MADE SHAKE, AND BY THE SPURS PLUCKED UP THE PINE AND CEDAR.

GRAVES AT MY COMMAND HAVE WAKED THEIR SLEEPERS, OPED AND LET 'EM FORTH BY MY SO POTENT ART.

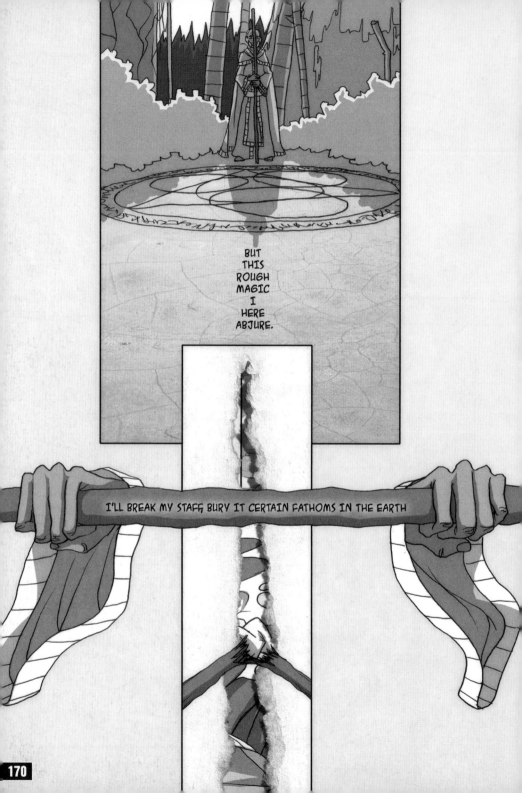

BUT
THIS
ROUGH
MAGIC
I
HERE
ABJURE.

I'LL BREAK MY STAFF BURY IT CERTAIN FATHOMS IN THE EARTH

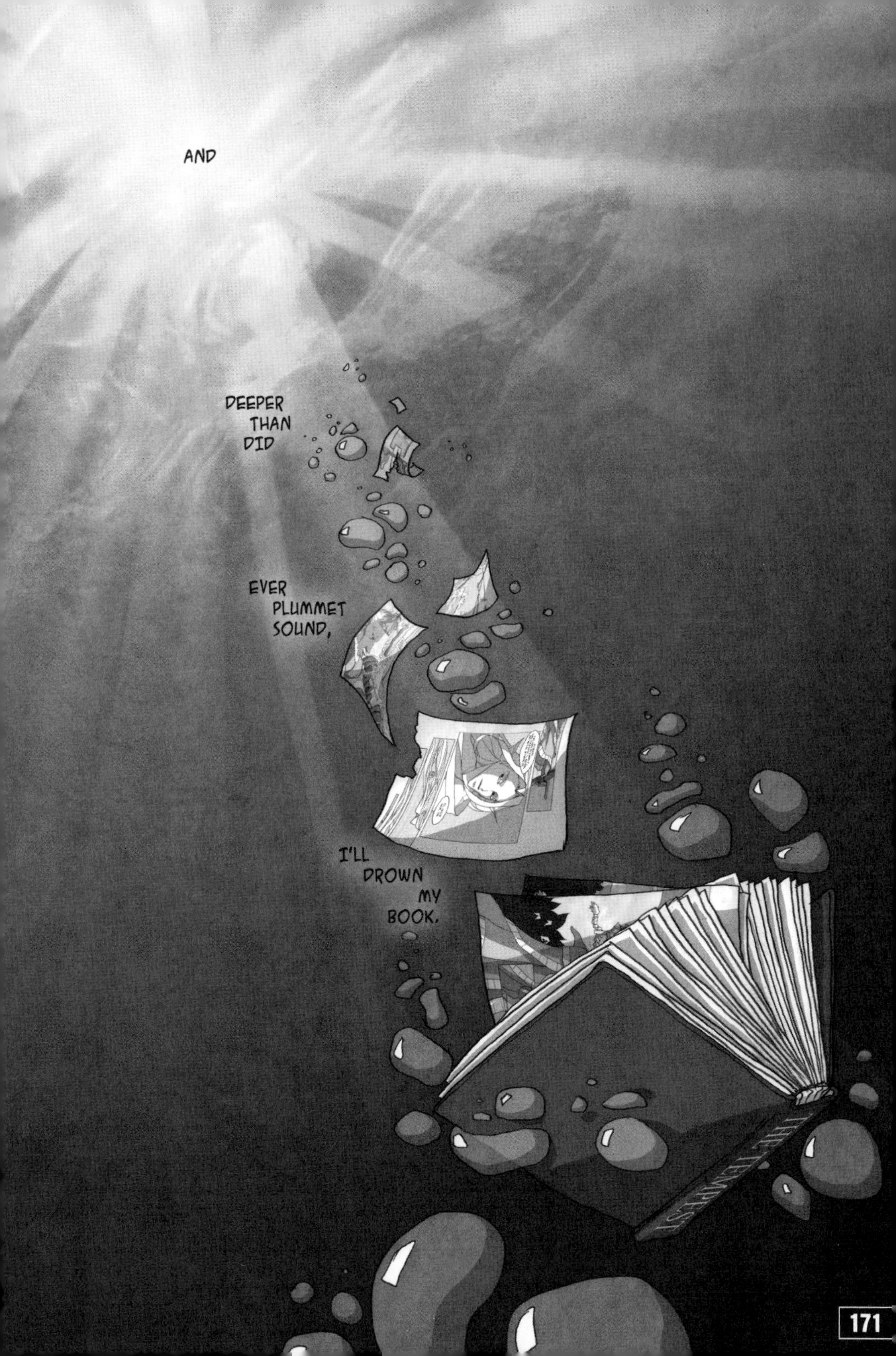
AND
DEEPER THAN DID
EVER PLUMMET SOUND,
I'LL DROWN MY BOOK.
THE TEMPEST

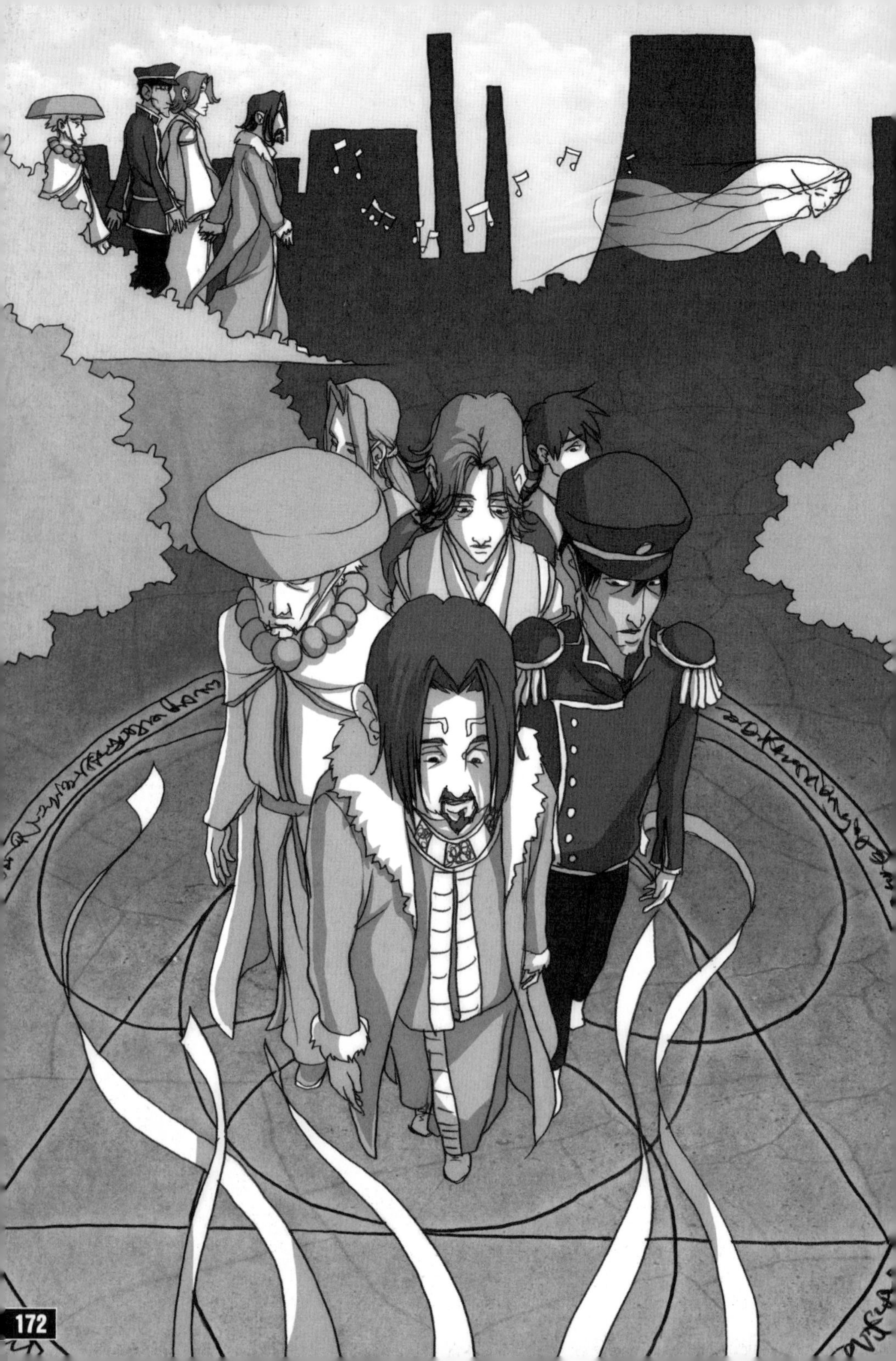

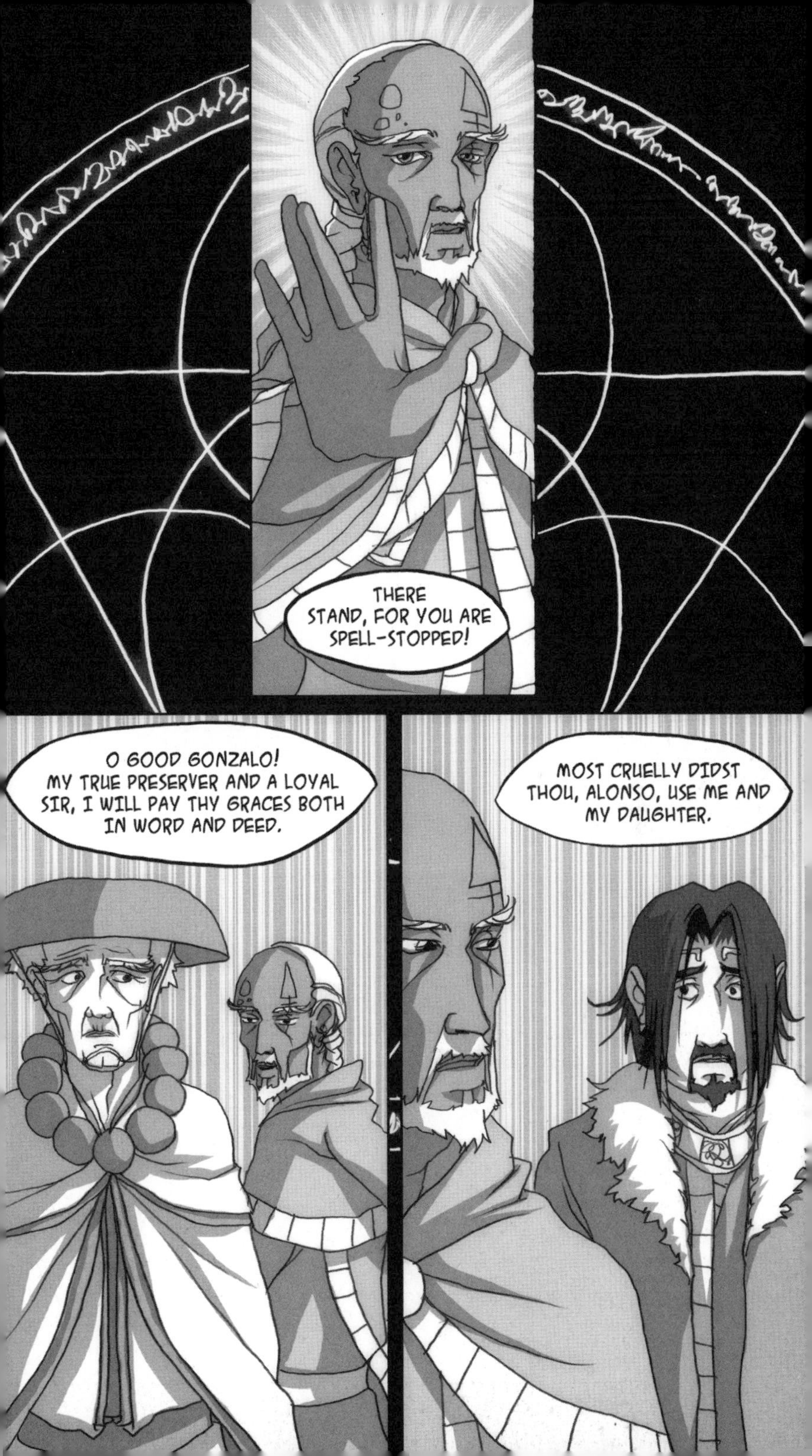
THERE STAND, FOR YOU ARE SPELL-STOPPED!
O GOOD GONZALO! MY TRUE PRESERVER AND A LOYAL SIR, I WILL PAY THY GRACES BOTH IN WORD AND DEED.
MOST CRUELLY DIDST THOU, ALONSO, USE ME AND MY DAUGHTER.

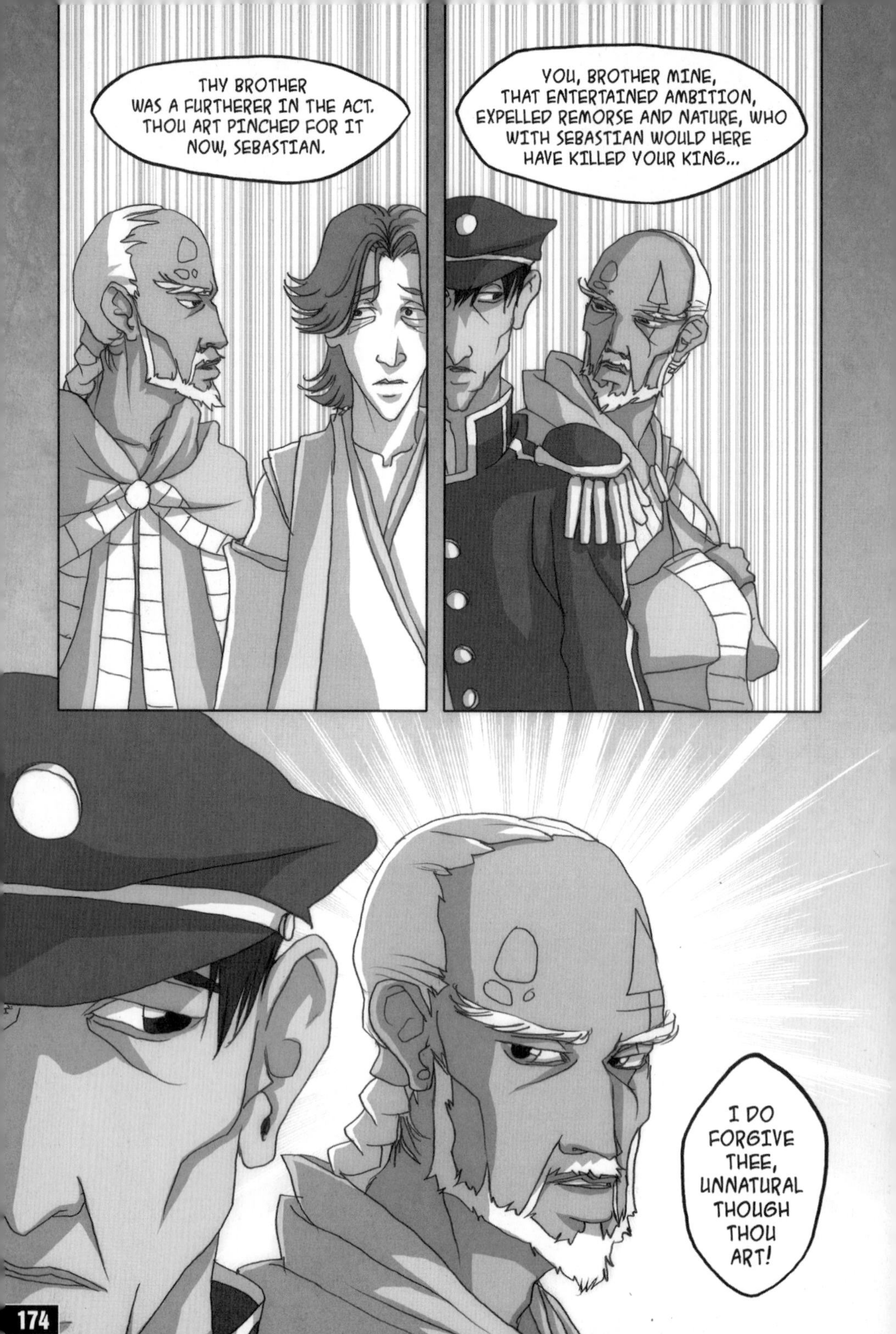
THY BROTHER WAS A FURTHERER IN THE ACT. THOU ART PINCHED FOR IT NOW, SEBASTIAN.
YOU, BROTHER MINE, THAT ENTERTAINED AMBITION, EXPELLED REMORSE AND NATURE, WHO WITH SEBASTIAN WOULD HERE HAVE KILLED YOUR KING...
I DO FORGIVE THEE, UNNATURAL THOUGH THOU ART!

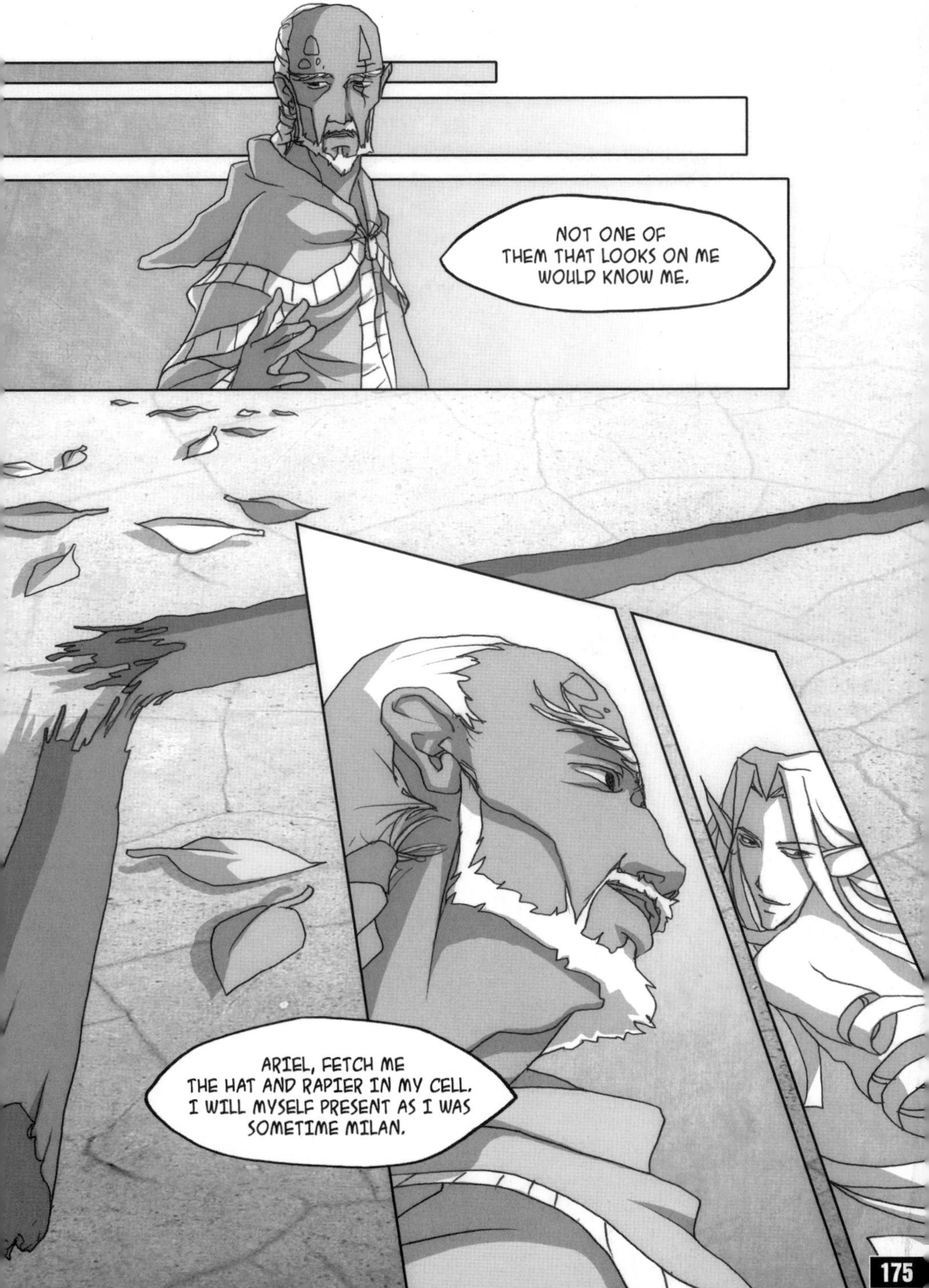
NOT ONE OF THEM THAT LOOKS ON ME WOULD KNOW ME.
ARIEL, FETCH ME THE HAT AND RAPIER IN MY CELL. I WILL MYSELF PRESENT AS I WAS SOMETIME MILAN.

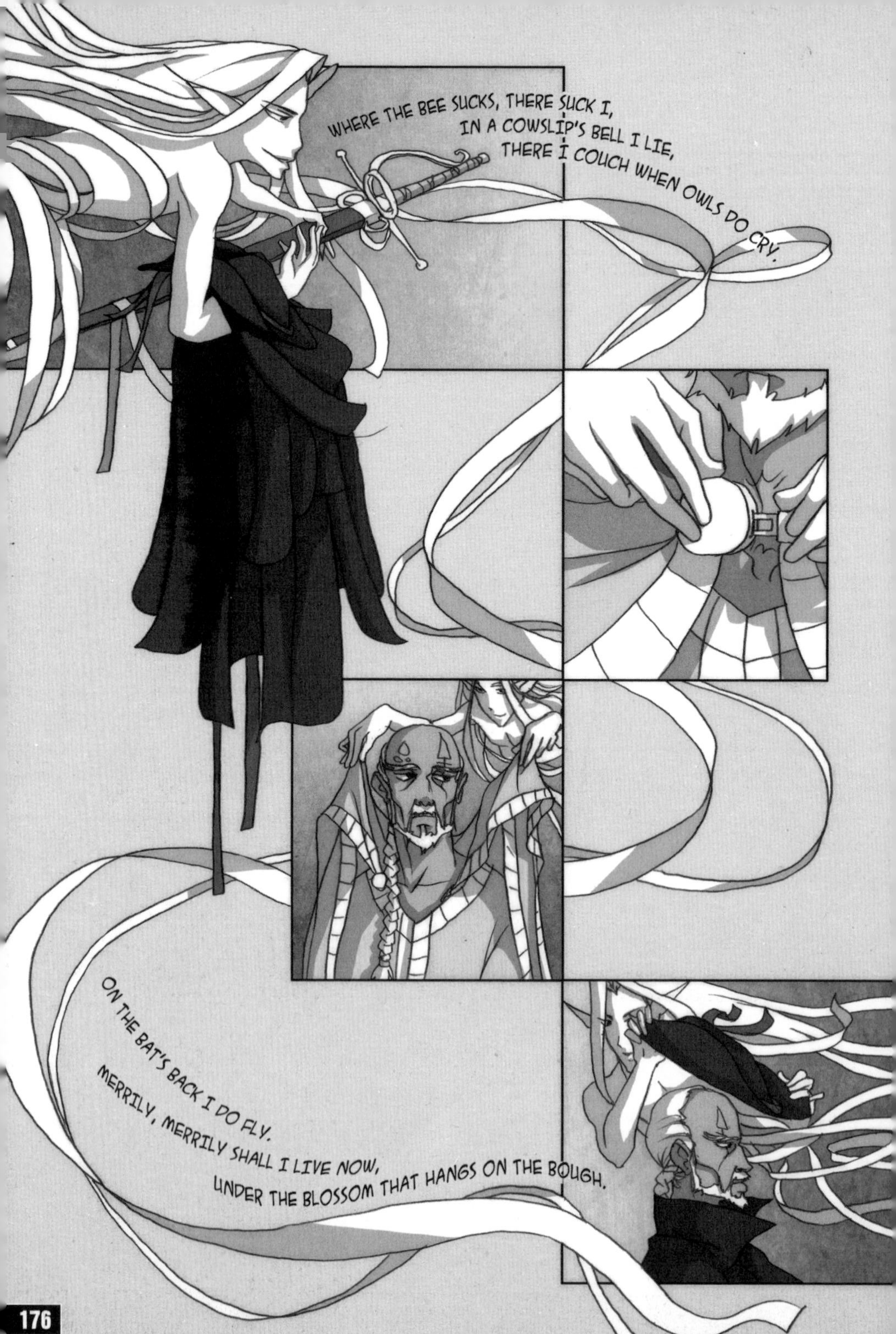
WHERE THE BEE SUCKS, THERE SUCK I,
IN A COWSLIP'S BELL I LIE,
THERE I COUCH WHEN OWLS DO CRY.
ON THE BAT'S BACK I DO FLY.
MERRILY, MERRILY SHALL I LIVE NOW,
UNDER THE BLOSSOM THAT HANGS ON THE BOUGH.

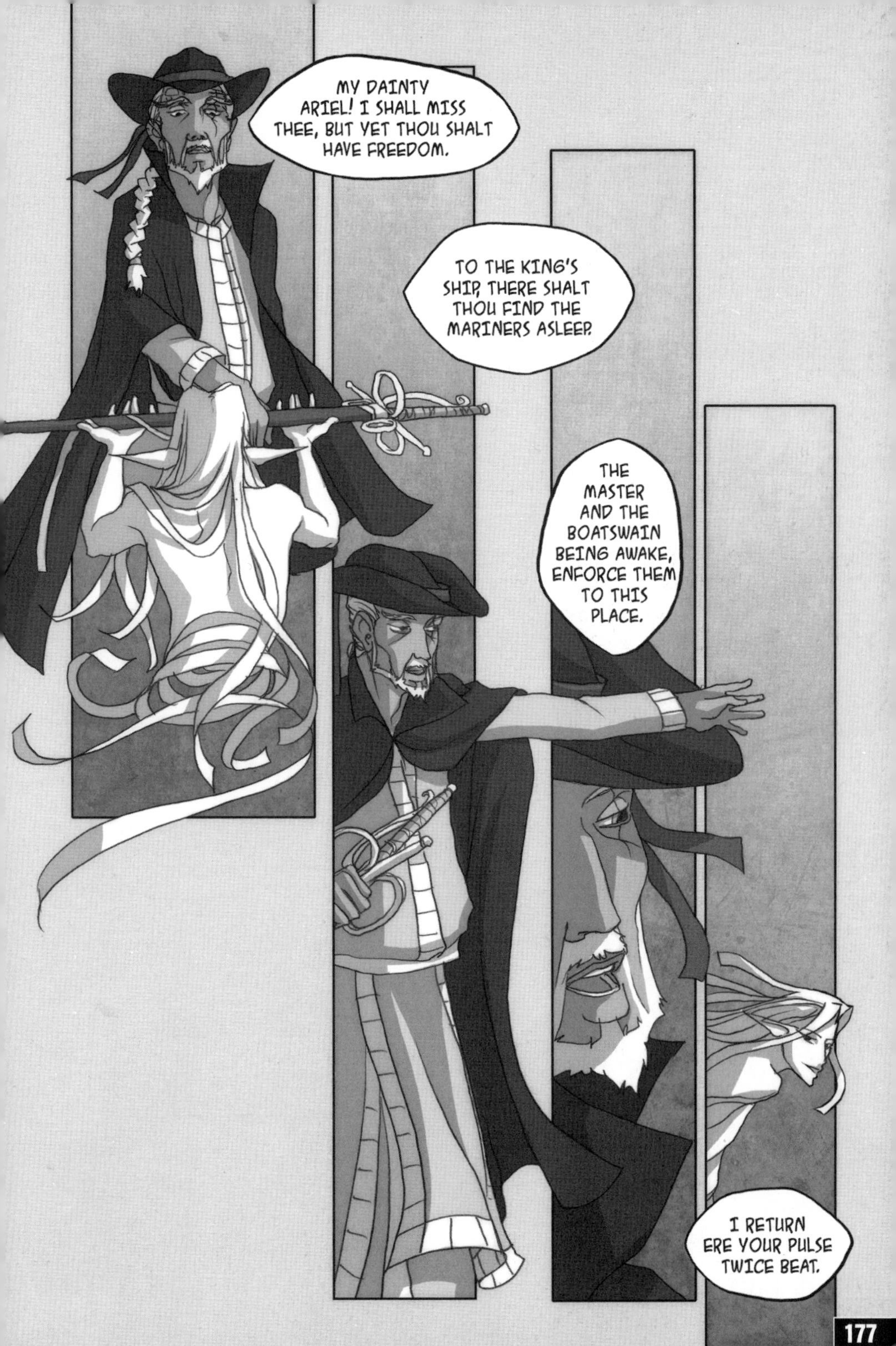
MY DAINTY ARIEL! I SHALL MISS THEE, BUT YET THOU SHALT HAVE FREEDOM.
TO THE KING'S SHIP, THERE SHALT THOU FIND THE MARINERS ASLEEP.
THE MASTER AND THE BOATSWAIN BEING AWAKE, ENFORCE THEM TO THIS PLACE.
I RETURN ERE YOUR PULSE TWICE BEAT.

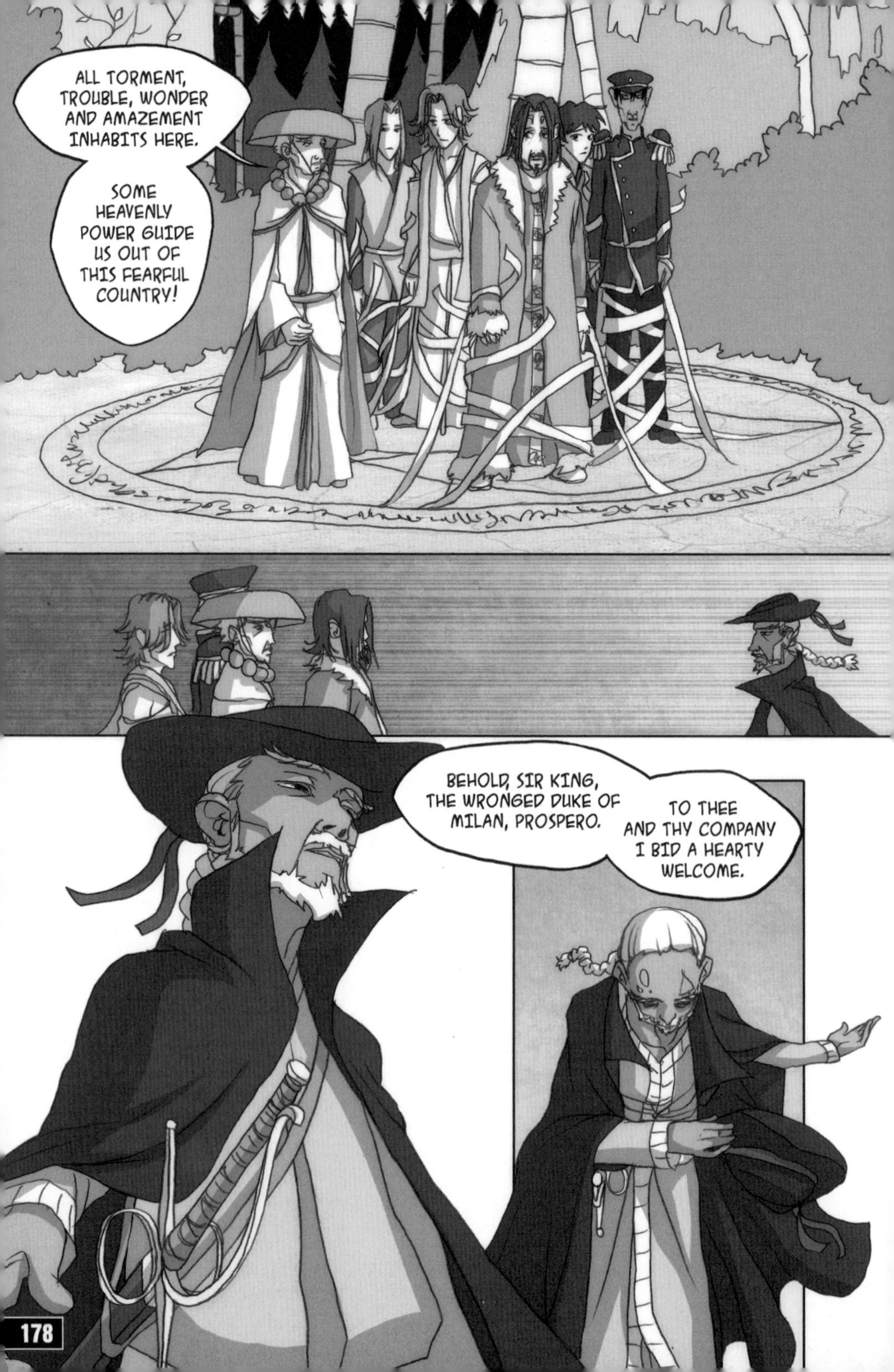
ALL TORMENT, TROUBLE, WONDER AND AMAZEMENT INHABITS HERE.
SOME HEAVENLY POWER GUIDE US OUT OF THIS FEARFUL COUNTRY!
BEHOLD, SIR KING, THE WRONGED DUKE OF MILAN, PROSPERO.
TO THEE AND THY COMPANY I BID A HEARTY WELCOME.

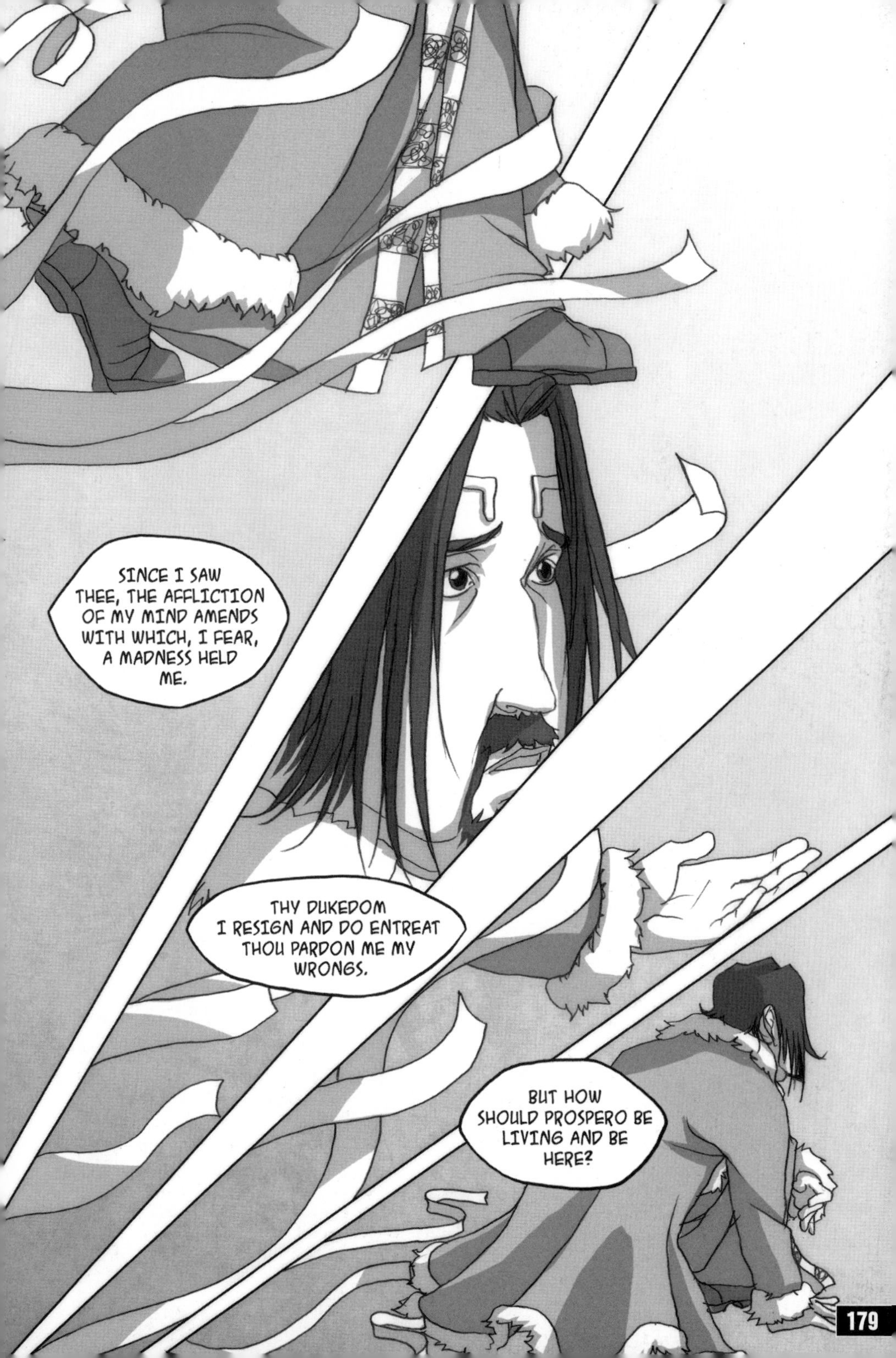
SINCE I SAW THEE, THE AFFLICTION OF MY MIND AMENDS WITH WHICH, I FEAR, A MADNESS HELD ME.
THY DUKEDOM I RESIGN AND DO ENTREAT THOU PARDON ME MY WRONGS.
BUT HOW SHOULD PROSPERO BE LIVING AND BE HERE?

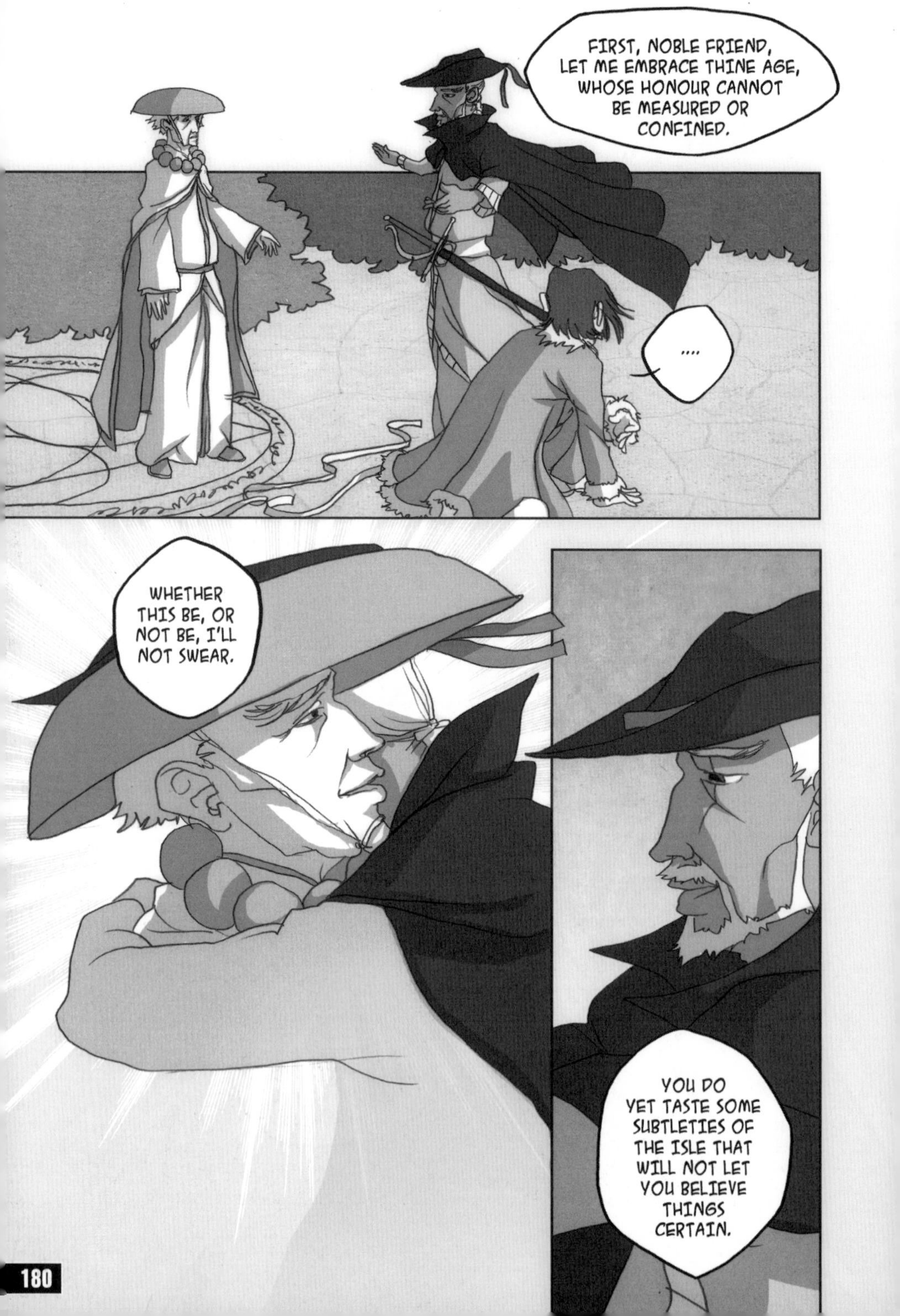
FIRST, NOBLE FRIEND, LET ME EMBRACE THINE AGE, WHOSE HONOUR CANNOT BE MEASURED OR CONFINED.
....
WHETHER THIS BE, OR NOT BE, I'LL NOT SWEAR.
YOU DO YET TASTE SOME SUBTLETIES OF THE ISLE THAT WILL NOT LET YOU BELIEVE THINGS CERTAIN.

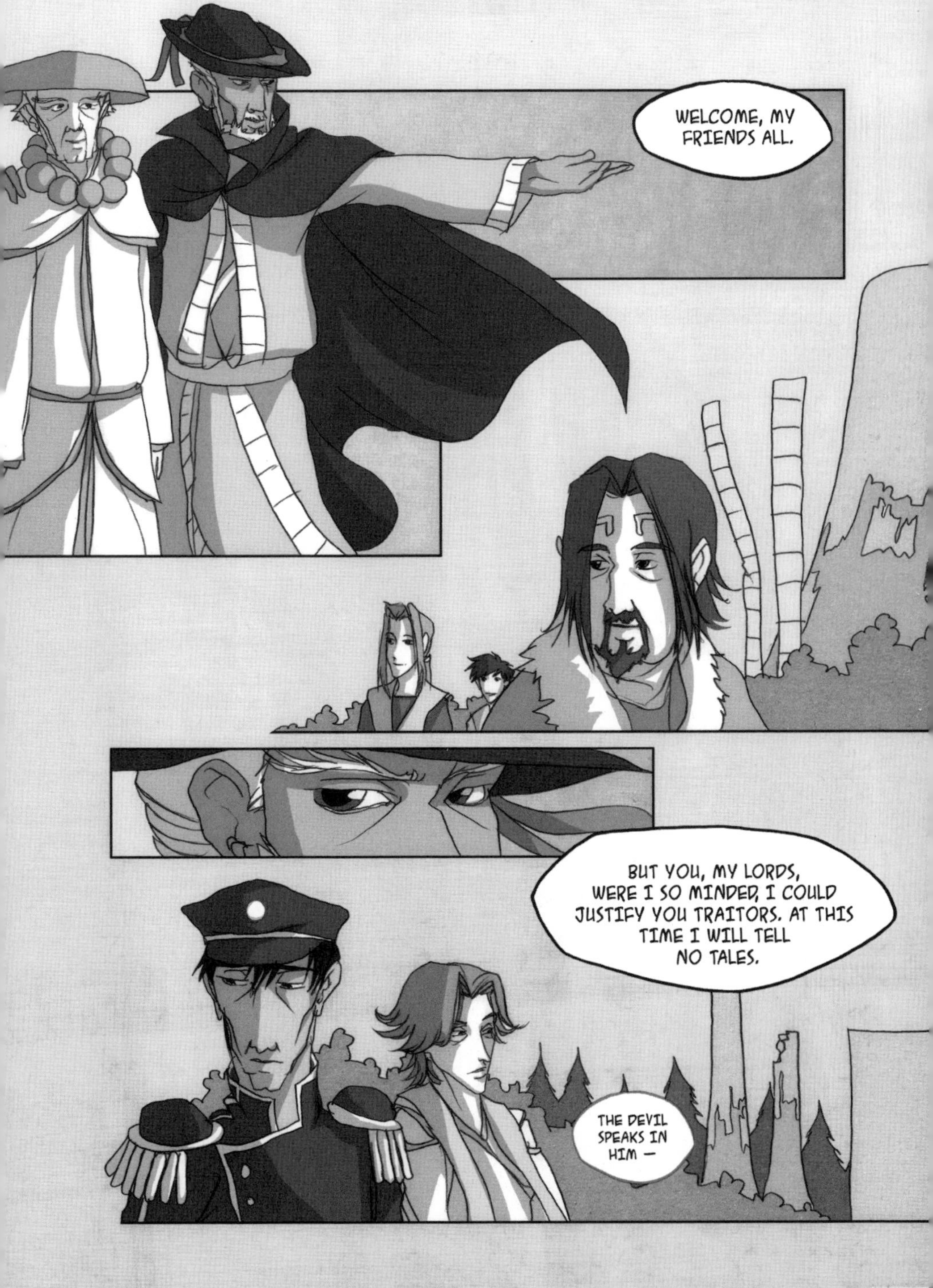
WELCOME, MY FRIENDS ALL.
BUT YOU, MY LORDS, WERE I SO MINDED, I COULD JUSTIFY YOU TRAITORS. AT THIS TIME I WILL TELL NO TALES.
THE DEVIL SPEAKS IN HIM —

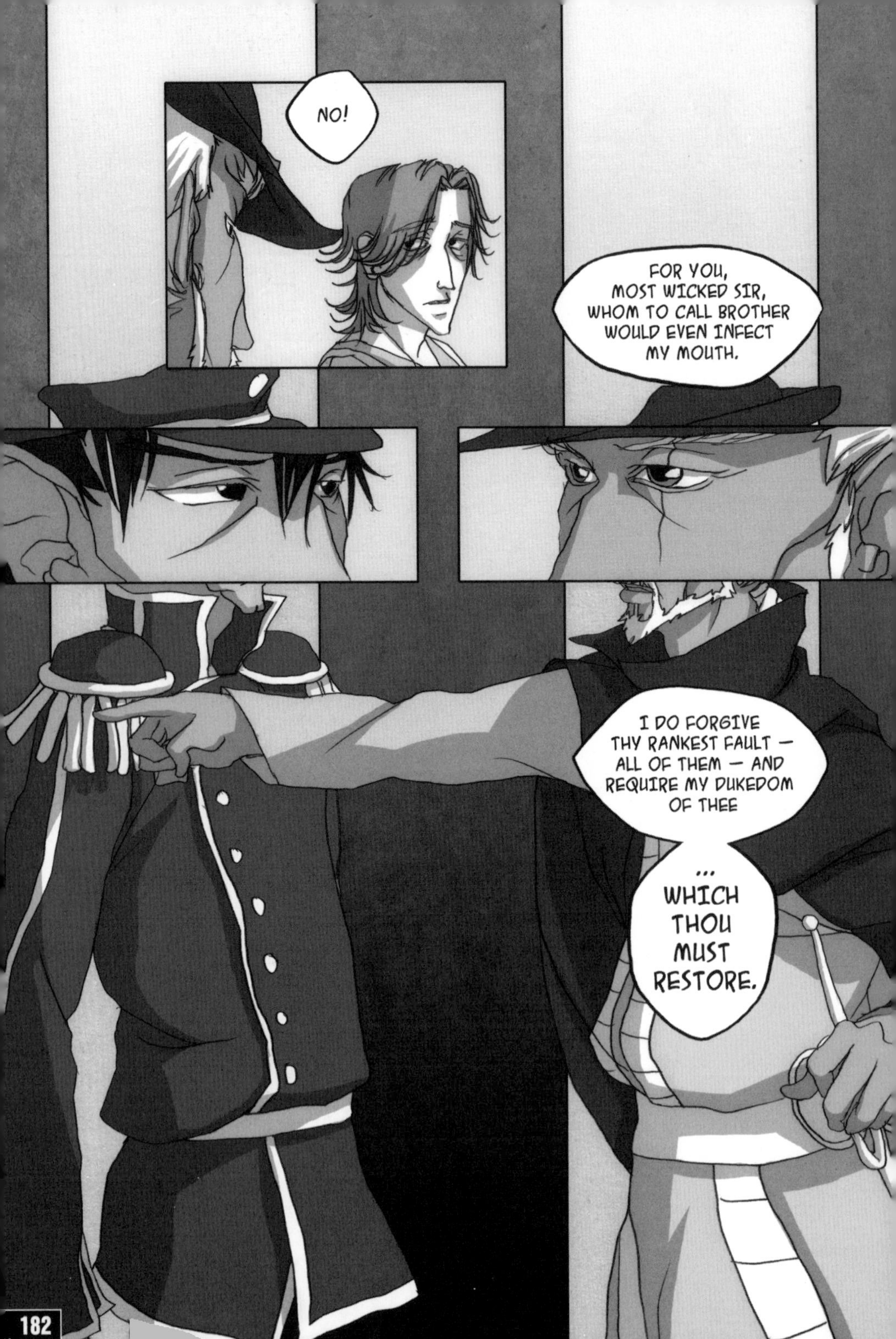
NO!
FOR YOU, MOST WICKED SIR, WHOM TO CALL BROTHER WOULD EVEN INFECT MY MOUTH.
I DO FORGIVE THY RANKEST FAULT — ALL OF THEM — AND REQUIRE MY DUKEDOM OF THEE
... WHICH THOU MUST RESTORE.

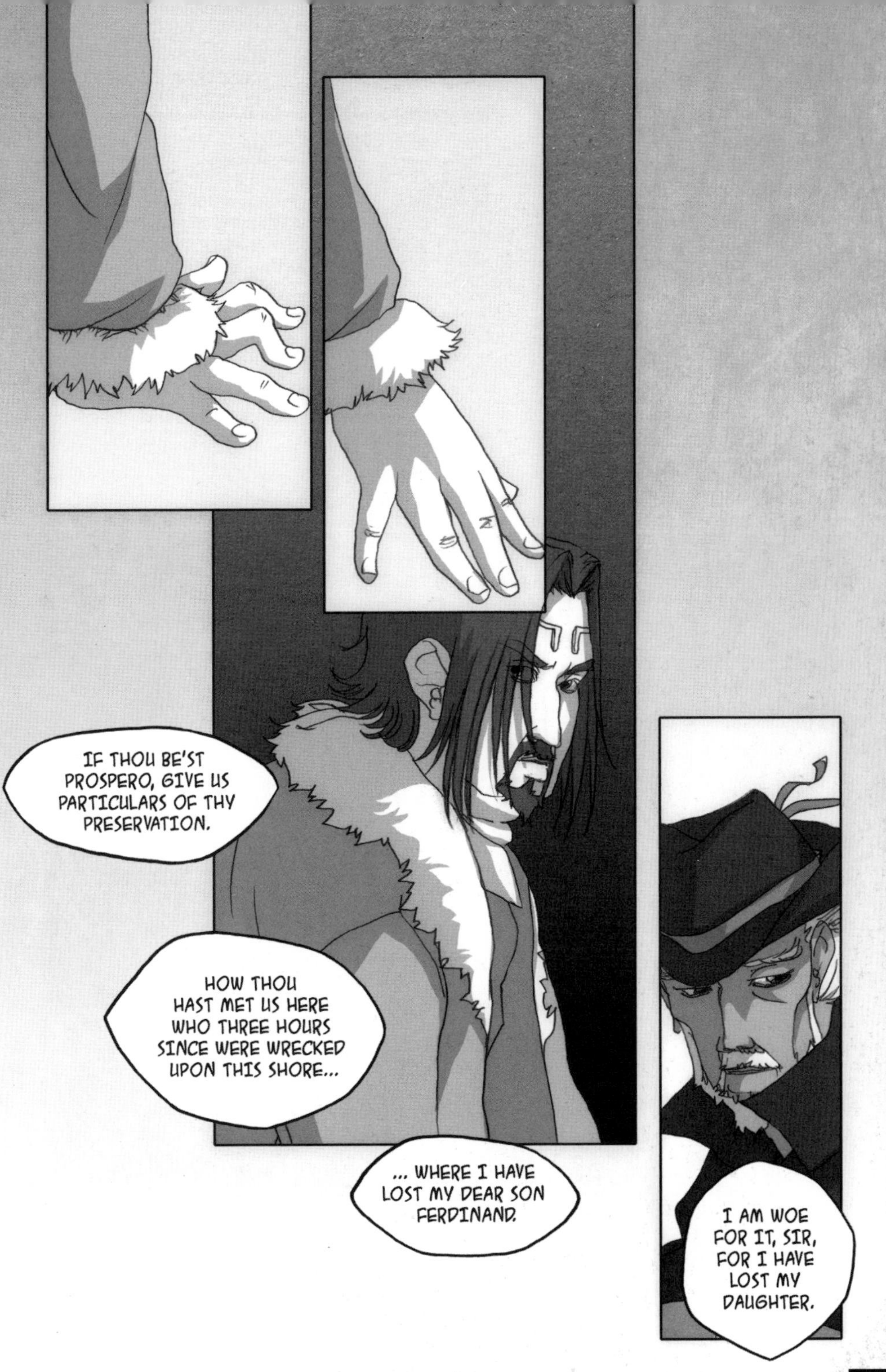
IF THOU BE'ST PROSPERO, GIVE US PARTICULARS OF THY PRESERVATION.
HOW THOU HAST MET US HERE WHO THREE HOURS SINCE WERE WRECKED UPON THIS SHORE...
... WHERE I HAVE LOST MY DEAR SON FERDINAND.
I AM WOE FOR IT, SIR, FOR I HAVE LOST MY DAUGHTER.

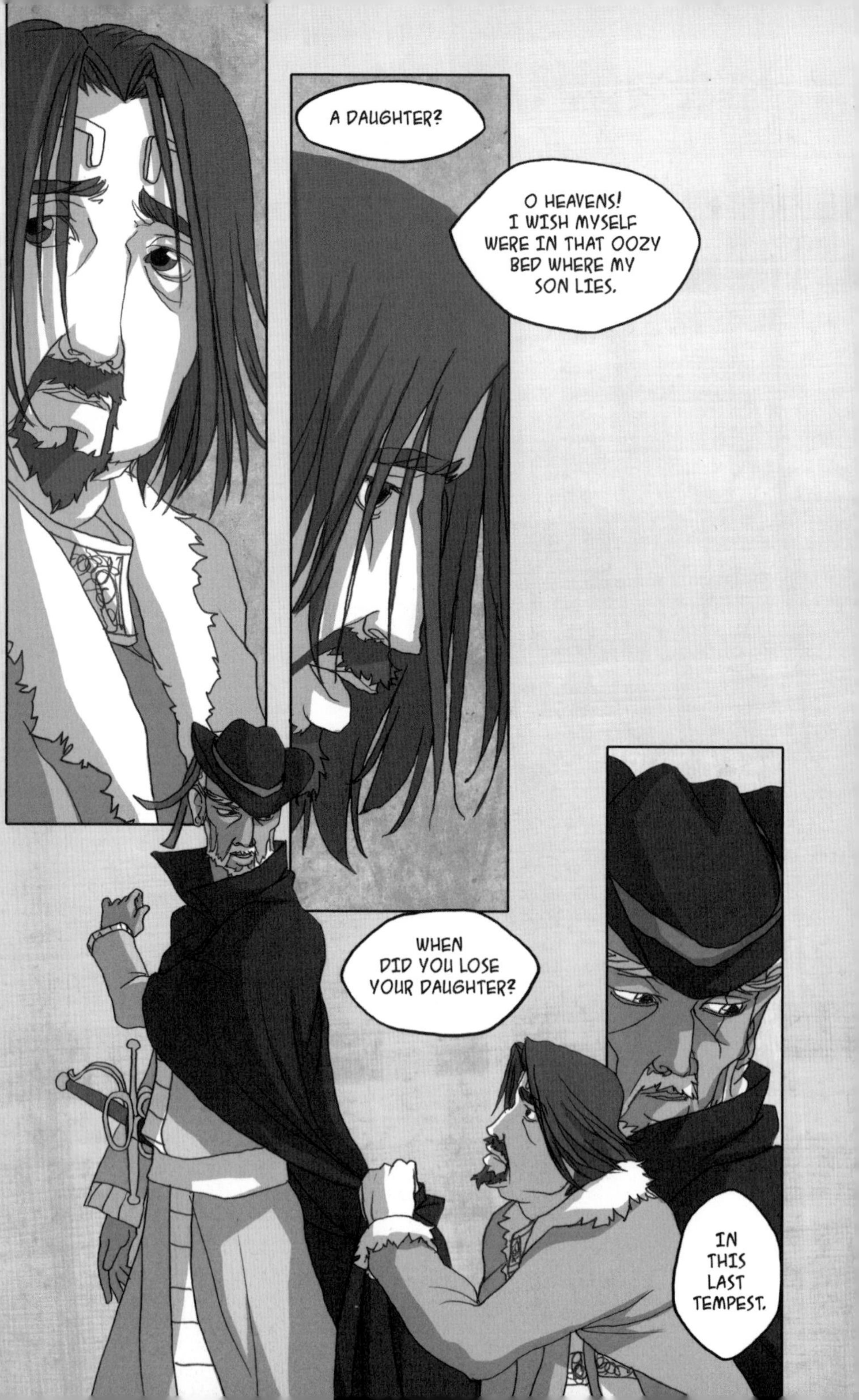
A DAUGHTER?
O HEAVENS! I WISH MYSELF WERE IN THAT OOZY BED WHERE MY SON LIES.
WHEN DID YOU LOSE YOUR DAUGHTER?
IN THIS LAST TEMPEST.

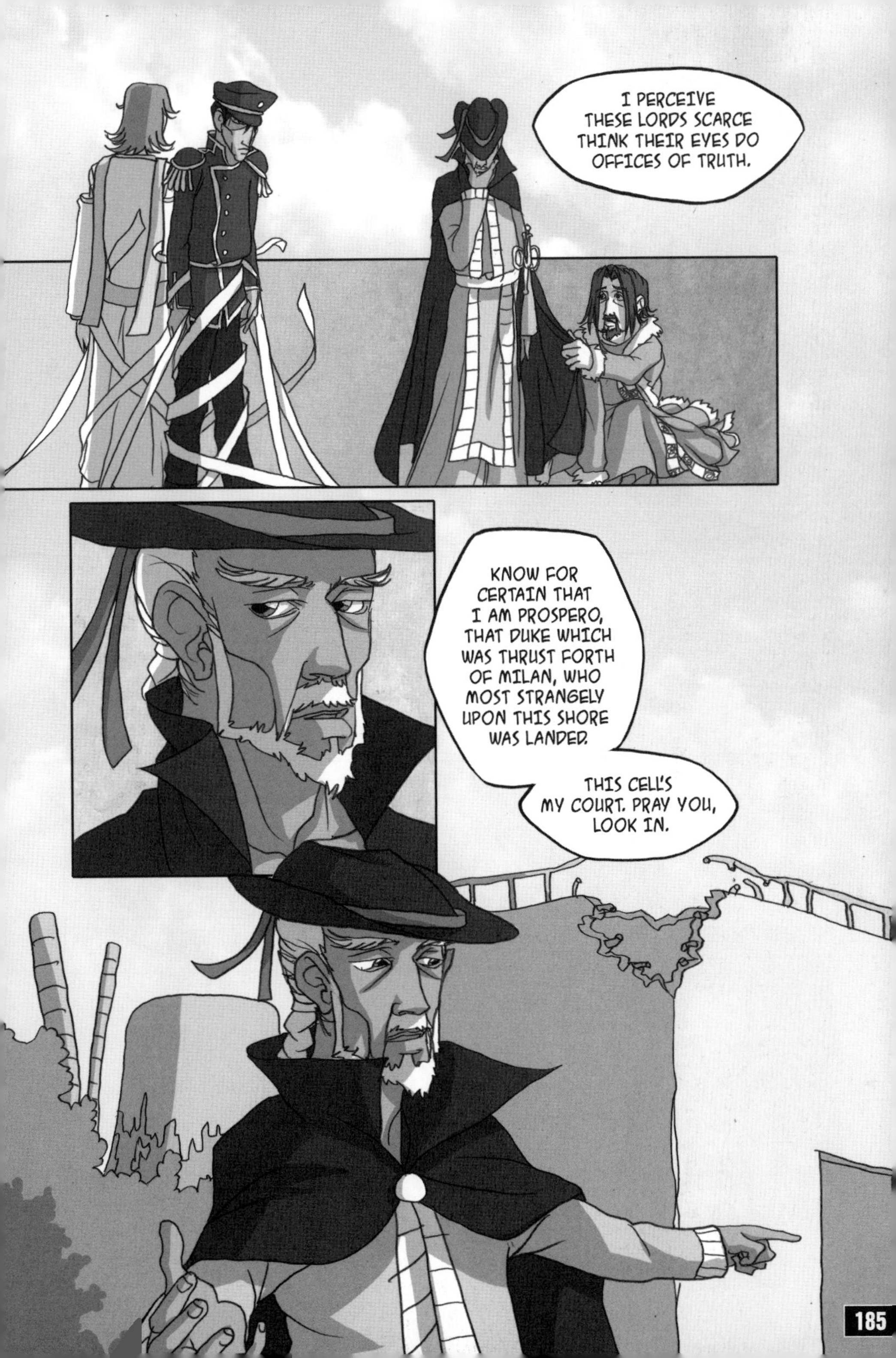
I PERCEIVE THESE LORDS SCARCE THINK THEIR EYES DO OFFICES OF TRUTH.
KNOW FOR CERTAIN THAT I AM PROSPERO, THAT DUKE WHICH WAS THRUST FORTH OF MILAN, WHO MOST STRANGELY UPON THIS SHORE WAS LANDED.
THIS CELL'S MY COURT. PRAY YOU, LOOK IN.

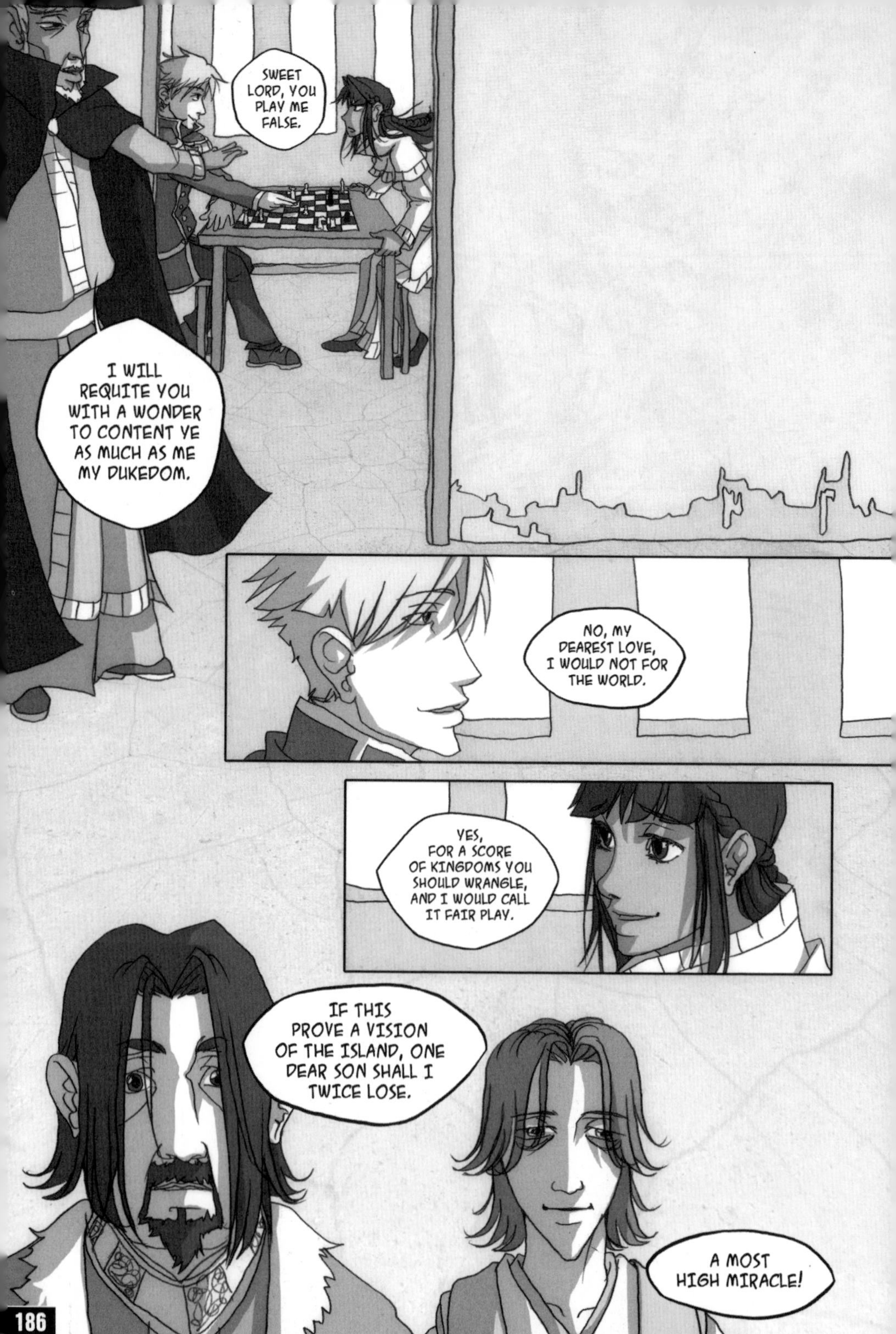
SWEET LORD, YOU PLAY ME FALSE.
I WILL REQUITE YOU WITH A WONDER TO CONTENT YE AS MUCH AS ME MY DUKEDOM.
NO, MY DEAREST LOVE, I WOULD NOT FOR THE WORLD.
YES, FOR A SCORE OF KINGDOMS YOU SHOULD WRANGLE, AND I WOULD CALL IT FAIR PLAY.
IF THIS PROVE A VISION OF THE ISLAND, ONE DEAR SON SHALL I TWICE LOSE.
A MOST HIGH MIRACLE!

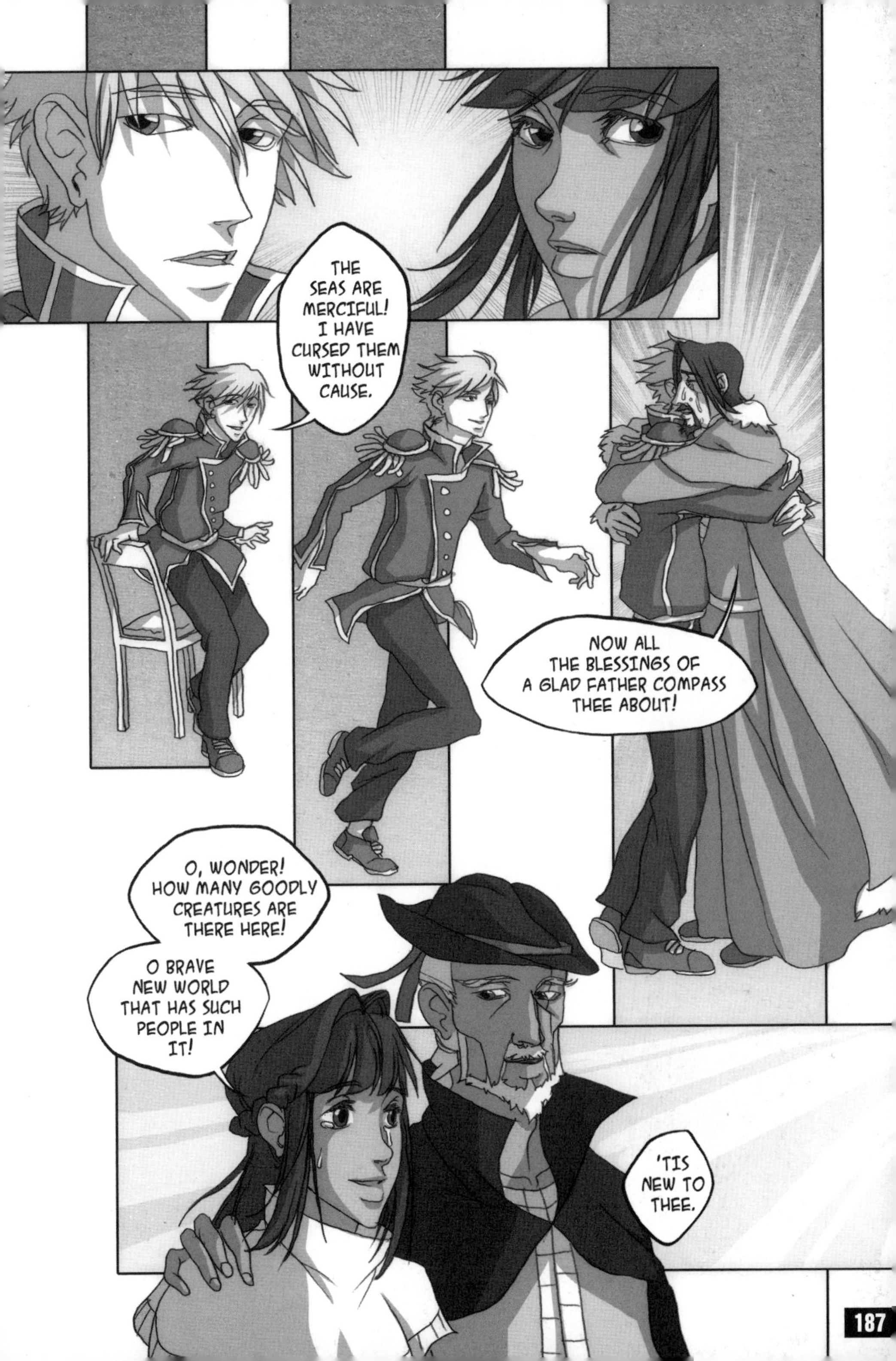
THE SEAS ARE MERCIFUL! I HAVE CURSED THEM WITHOUT CAUSE.
NOW ALL THE BLESSINGS OF A GLAD FATHER COMPASS THEE ABOUT!
O, WONDER! HOW MANY GOODLY CREATURES ARE THERE HERE!
O BRAVE NEW WORLD THAT HAS SUCH PEOPLE IN IT!
'TIS NEW TO THEE.

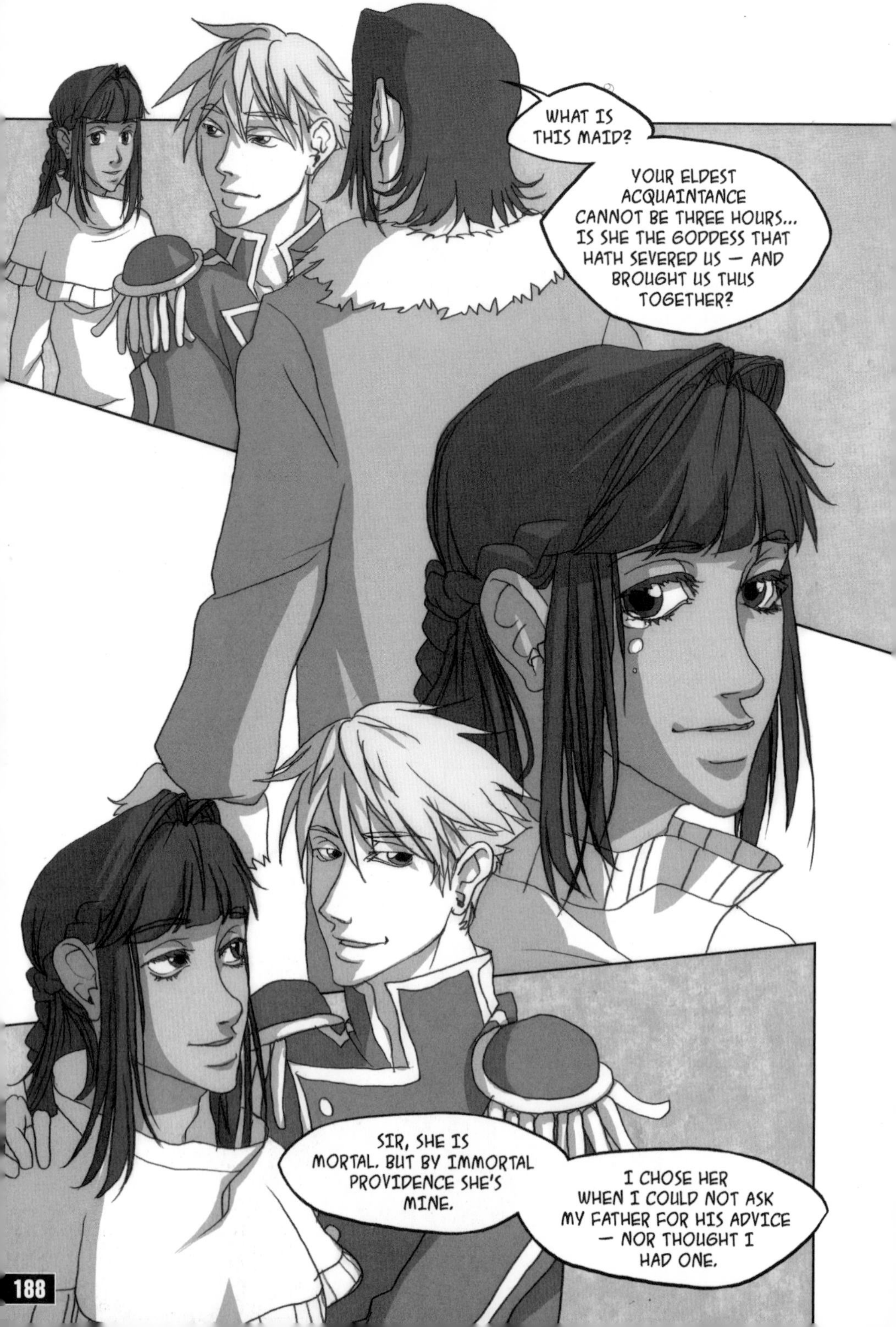
WHAT IS THIS MAID?
YOUR ELDEST ACQUAINTANCE CANNOT BE THREE HOURS... IS SHE THE GODDESS THAT HATH SEVERED US — AND BROUGHT US THUS TOGETHER?
SIR, SHE IS MORTAL. BUT BY IMMORTAL PROVIDENCE SHE'S MINE.
I CHOSE HER WHEN I COULD NOT ASK MY FATHER FOR HIS ADVICE — NOR THOUGHT I HAD ONE.

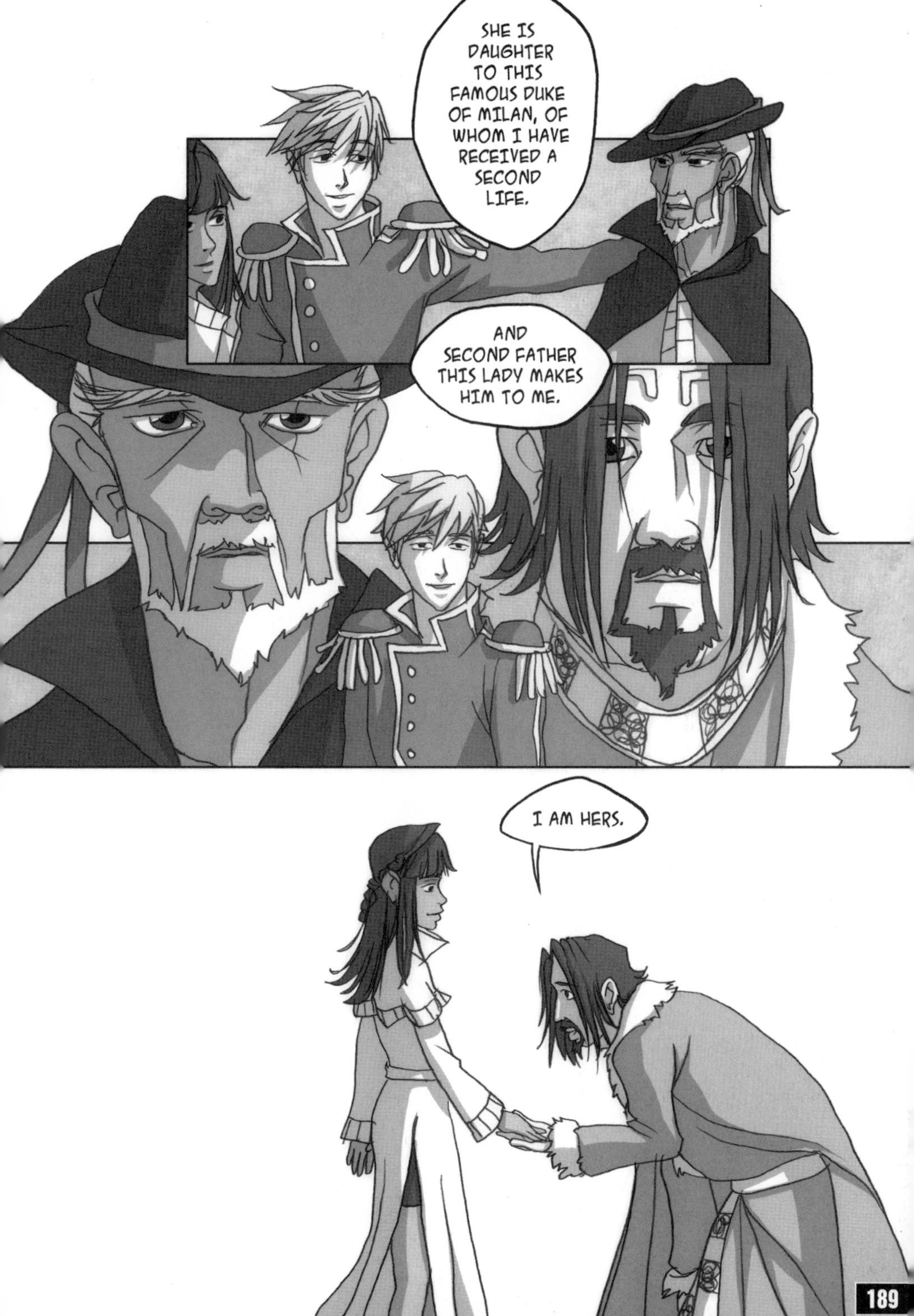
SHE IS DAUGHTER TO THIS FAMOUS DUKE OF MILAN, OF WHOM I HAVE RECEIVED A SECOND LIFE.
AND SECOND FATHER THIS LADY MAKES HIM TO ME.
I AM HERS.

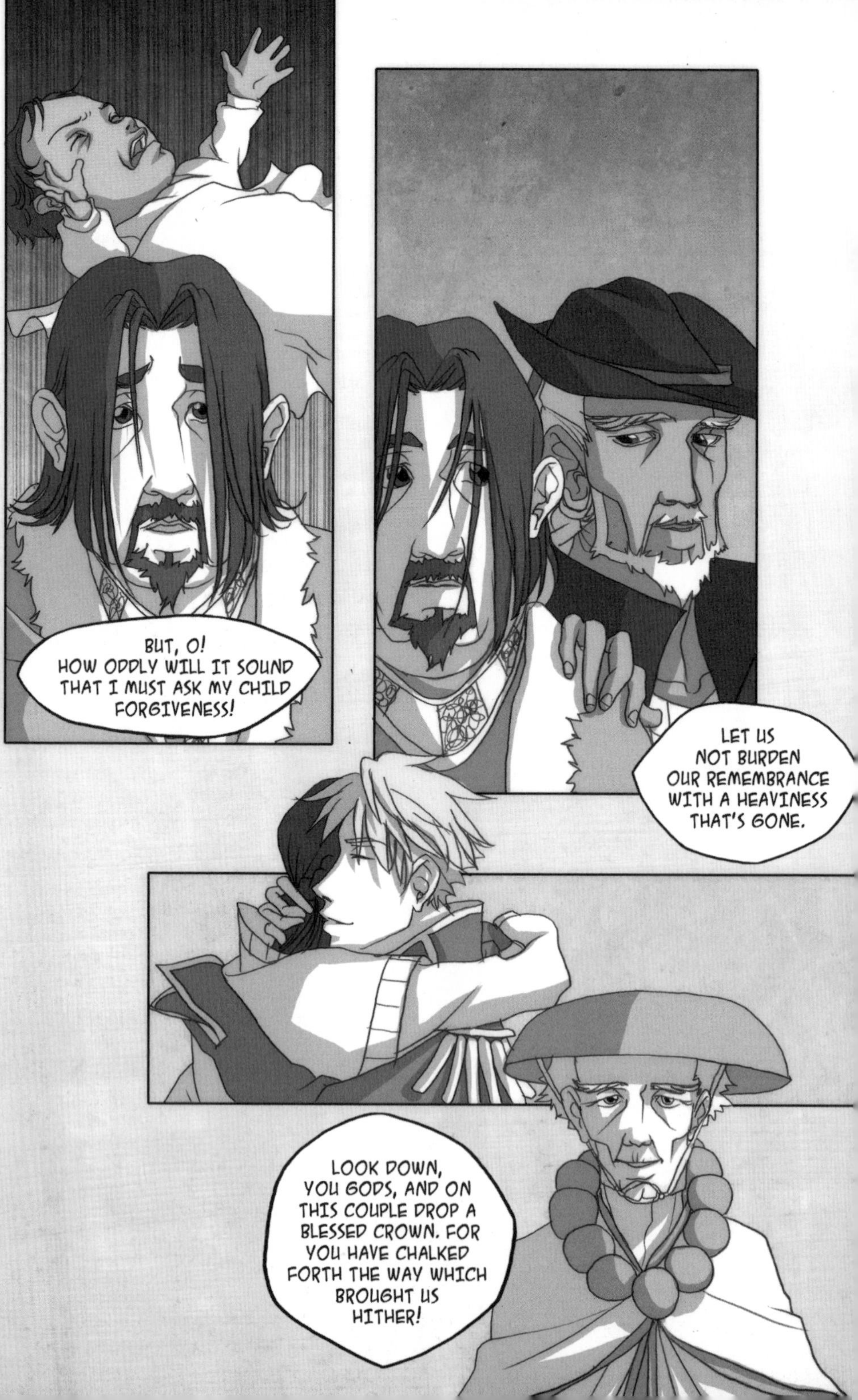
BUT, O! HOW ODDLY WILL IT SOUND THAT I MUST ASK MY CHILD FORGIVENESS!
LET US NOT BURDEN OUR REMEMBRANCE WITH A HEAVINESS THAT'S GONE.
LOOK DOWN, YOU GODS, AND ON THIS COUPLE DROP A BLESSED CROWN. FOR YOU HAVE CHALKED FORTH THE WAY WHICH BROUGHT US HITHER!

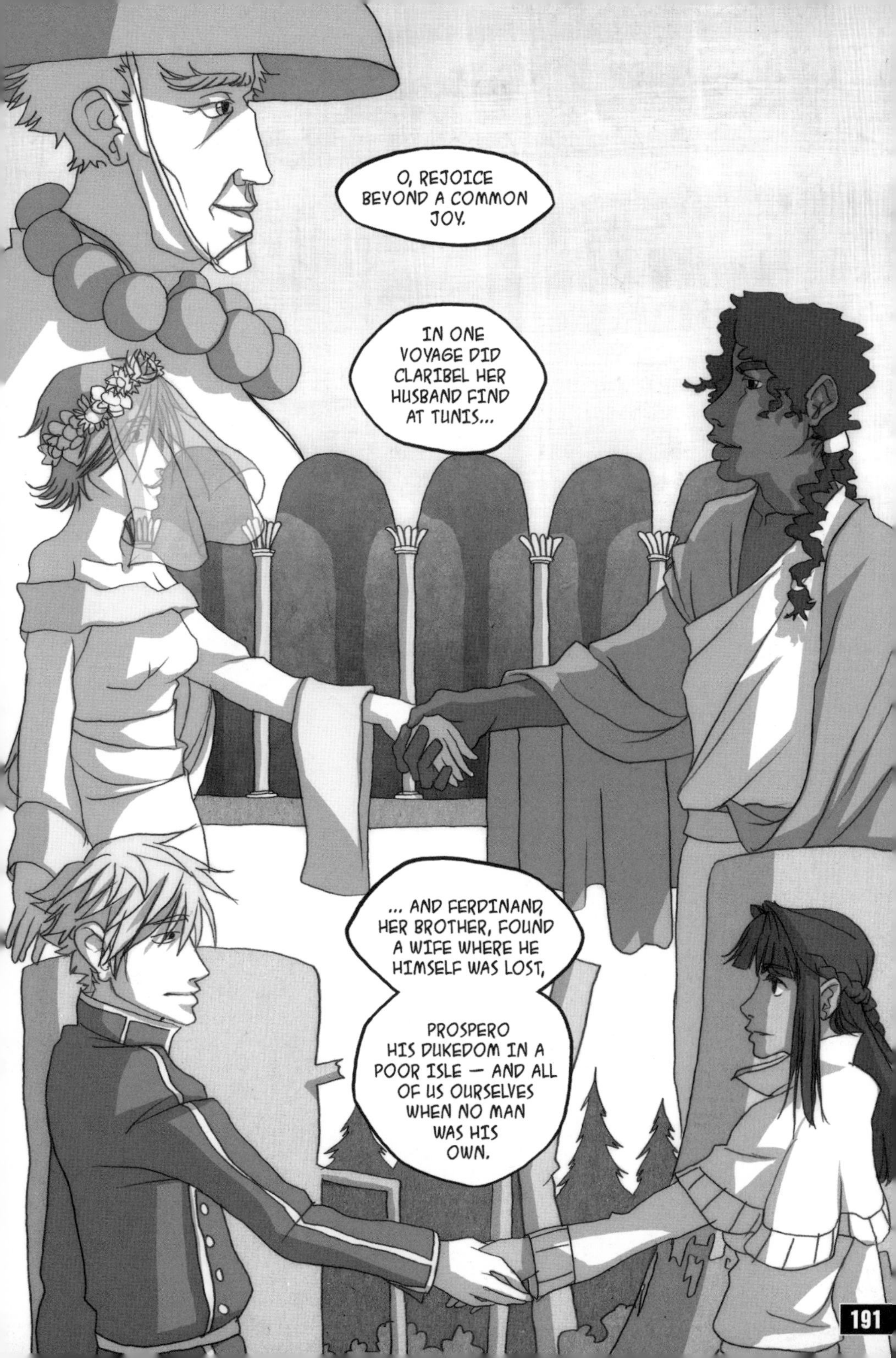
O, REJOICE BEYOND A COMMON JOY.
IN ONE VOYAGE DID CLARIBEL HER HUSBAND FIND AT TUNIS...
... AND FERDINAND, HER BROTHER, FOUND A WIFE WHERE HE HIMSELF WAS LOST,
PROSPERO HIS DUKEDOM IN A POOR ISLE — AND ALL OF US OURSELVES WHEN NO MAN WAS HIS OWN.

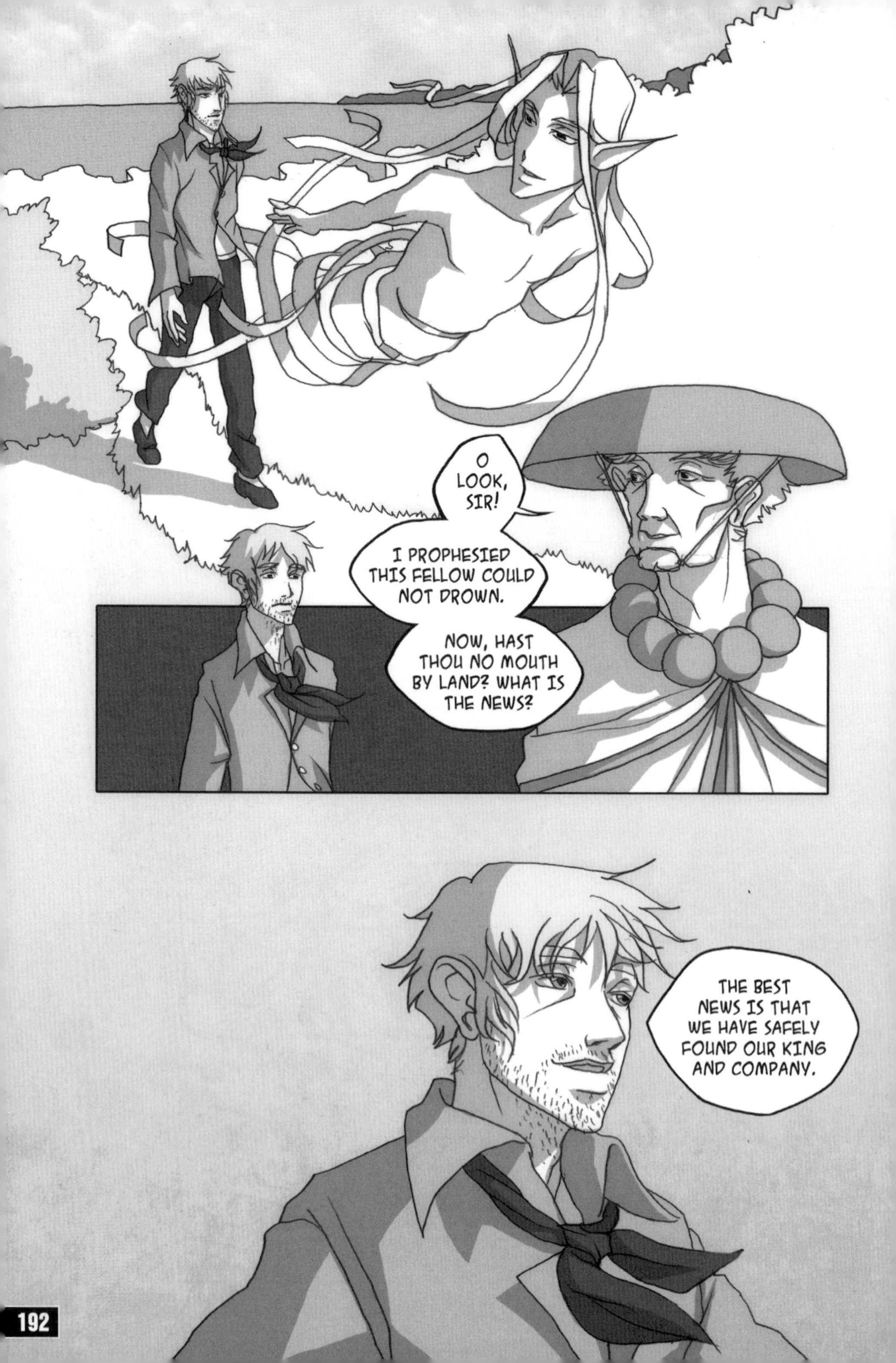
O LOOK, SIR!
I PROPHESIED THIS FELLOW COULD NOT DROWN.
NOW, HAST THOU NO MOUTH BY LAND? WHAT IS THE NEWS?
THE BEST NEWS IS THAT WE HAVE SAFELY FOUND OUR KING AND COMPANY.

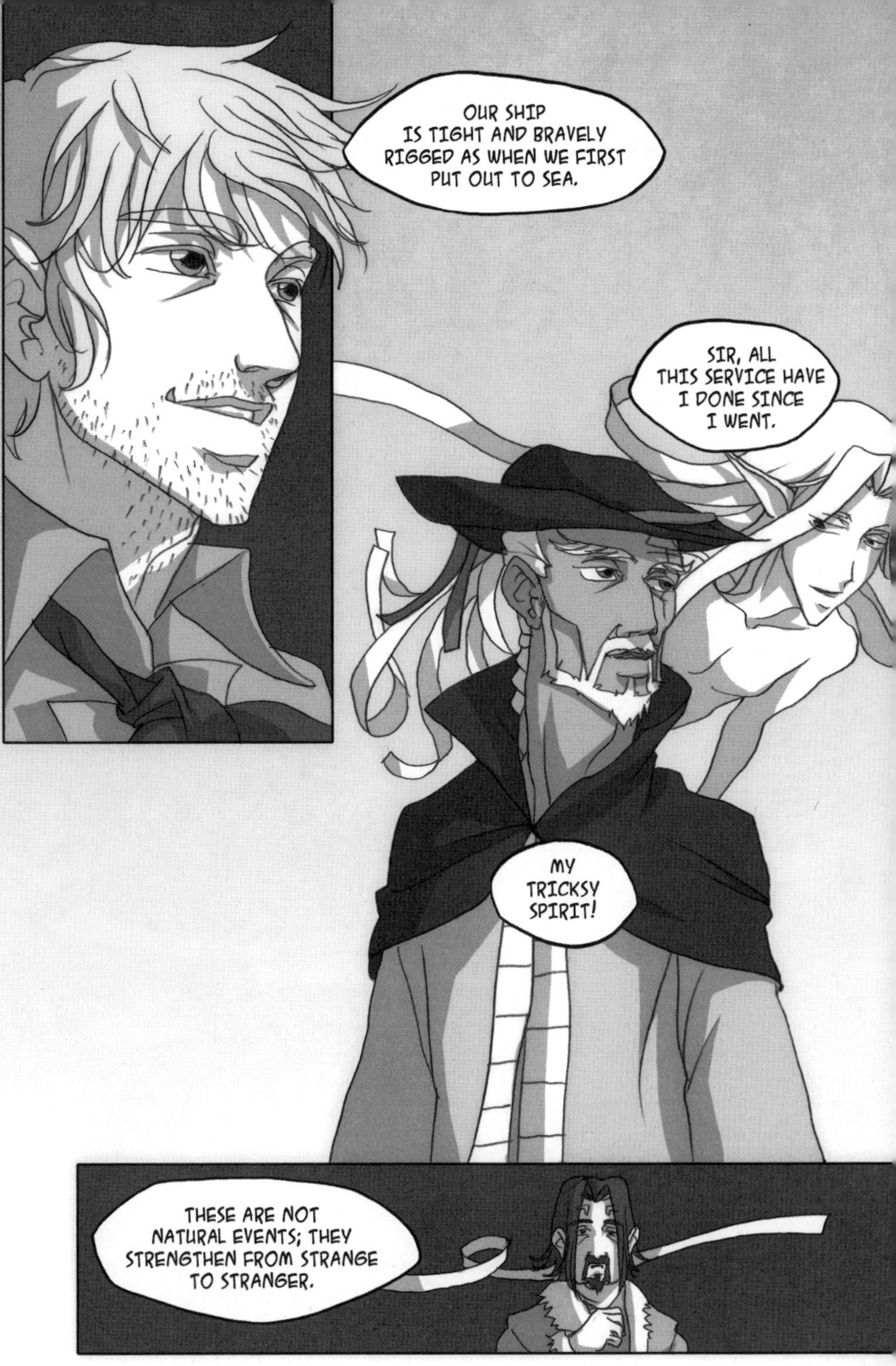
OUR SHIP IS TIGHT AND BRAVELY RIGGED AS WHEN WE FIRST PUT OUT TO SEA.
SIR, ALL THIS SERVICE HAVE I DONE SINCE I WENT.
MY TRICKSY SPIRIT!
THESE ARE NOT NATURAL EVENTS; THEY STRENGTHEN FROM STRANGE TO STRANGER.

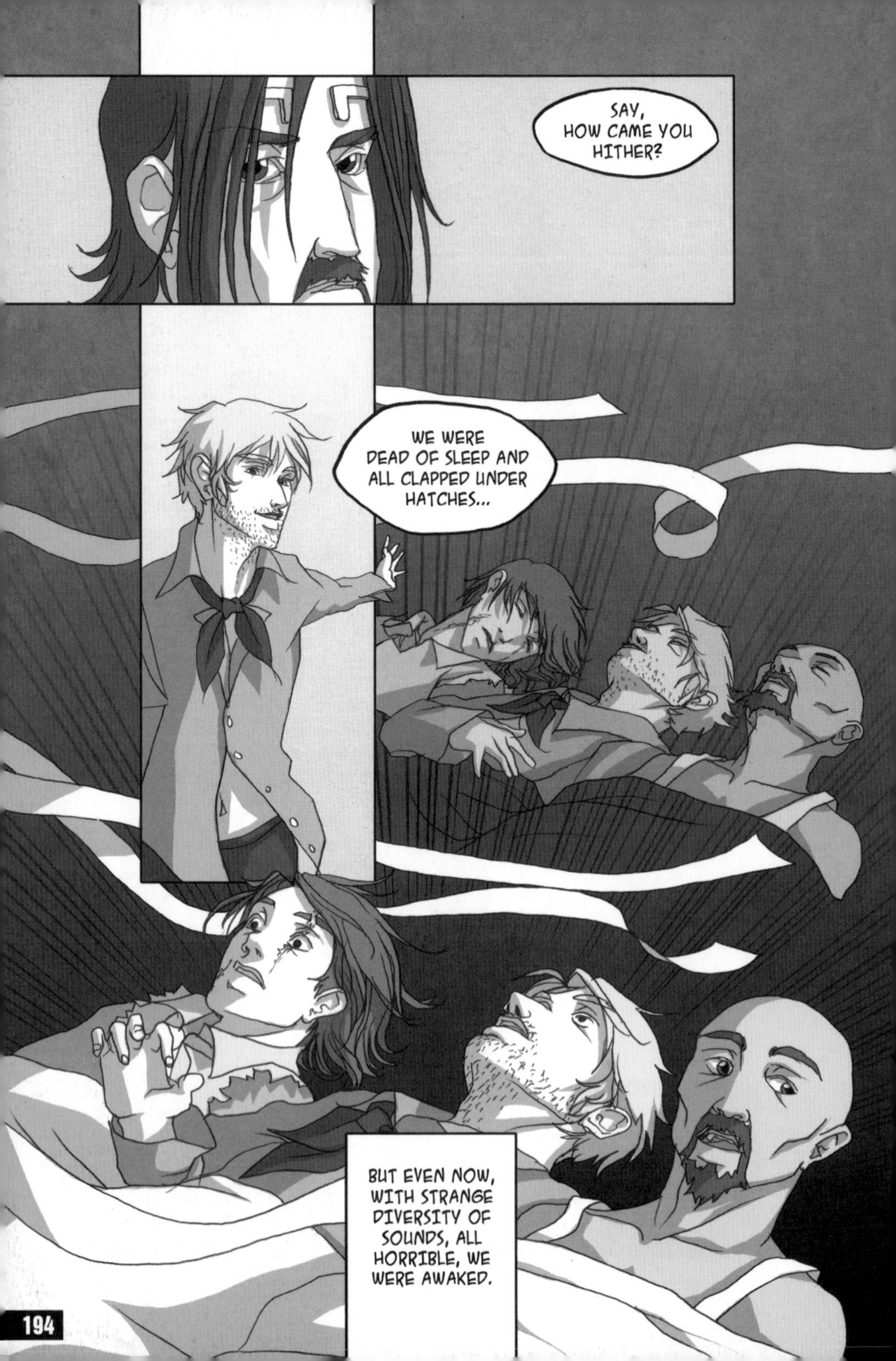
SAY, HOW CAME YOU HITHER?
WE WERE DEAD OF SLEEP AND ALL CLAPPED UNDER HATCHES...
BUT EVEN NOW, WITH STRANGE DIVERSITY OF SOUNDS, ALL HORRIBLE, WE WERE AWAKED.

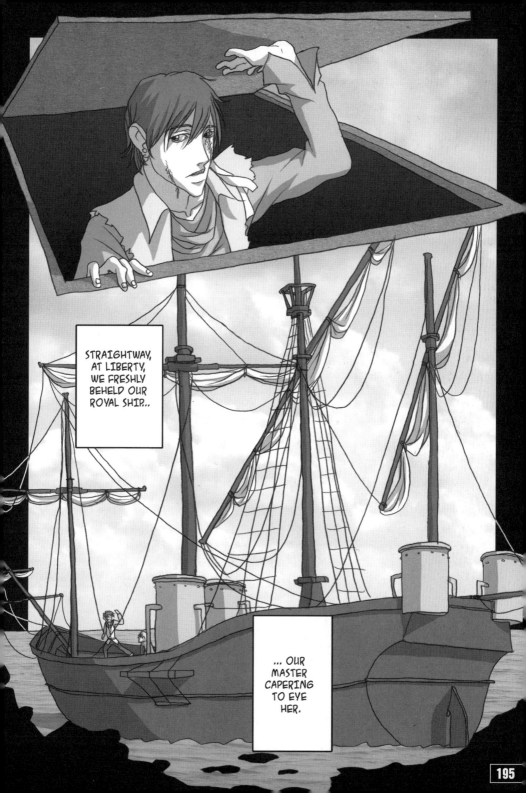

STRAIGHTWAY, AT LIBERTY, WE FRESHLY BEHELD OUR ROYAL SHIP...

... OUR MASTER CAPERING TO EYE HER.

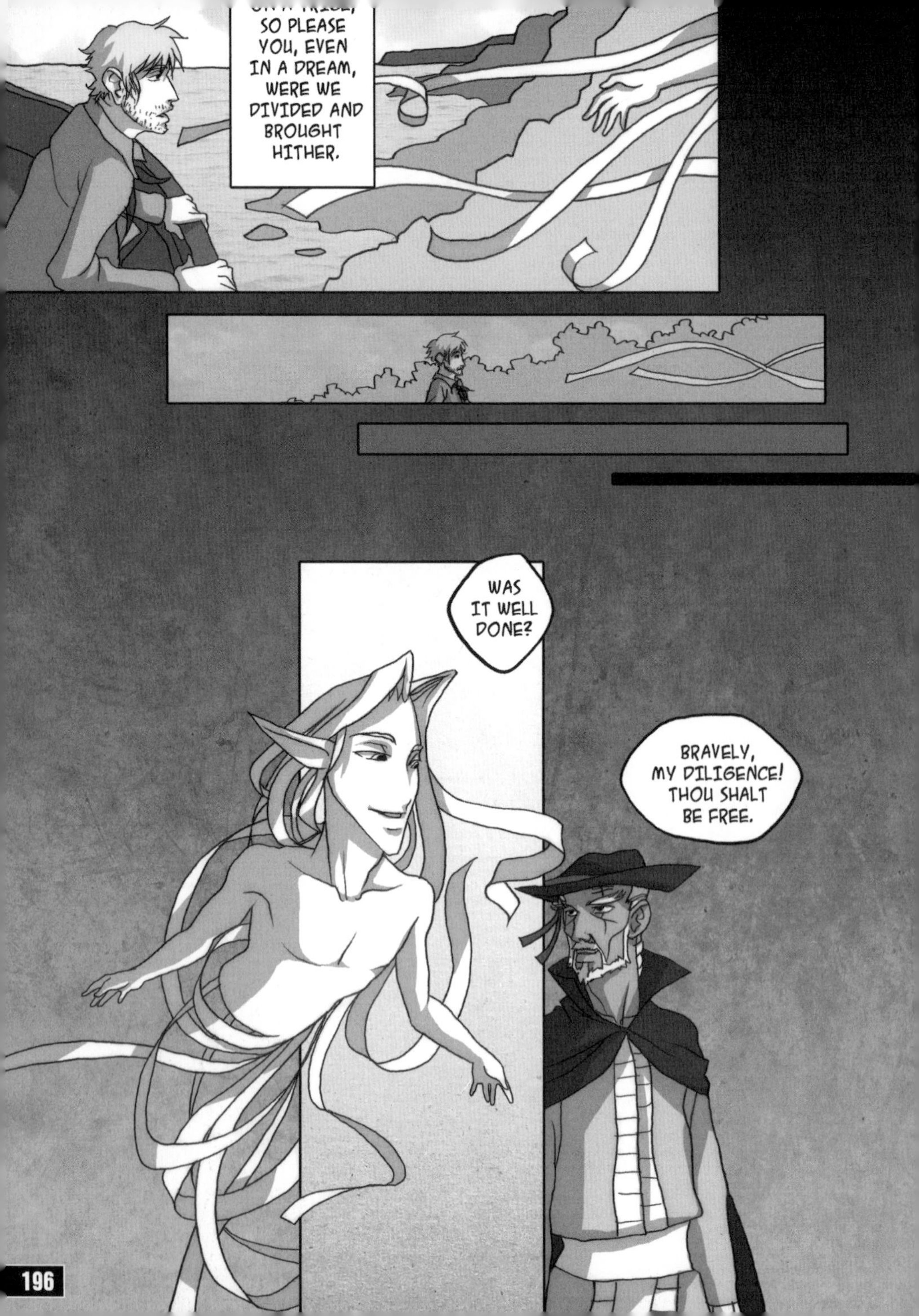
SO PLEASE YOU, EVEN IN A DREAM, WERE WE DIVIDED AND BROUGHT HITHER.
WAS IT WELL DONE?
BRAVELY, MY DILIGENCE! THOU SHALT BE FREE.

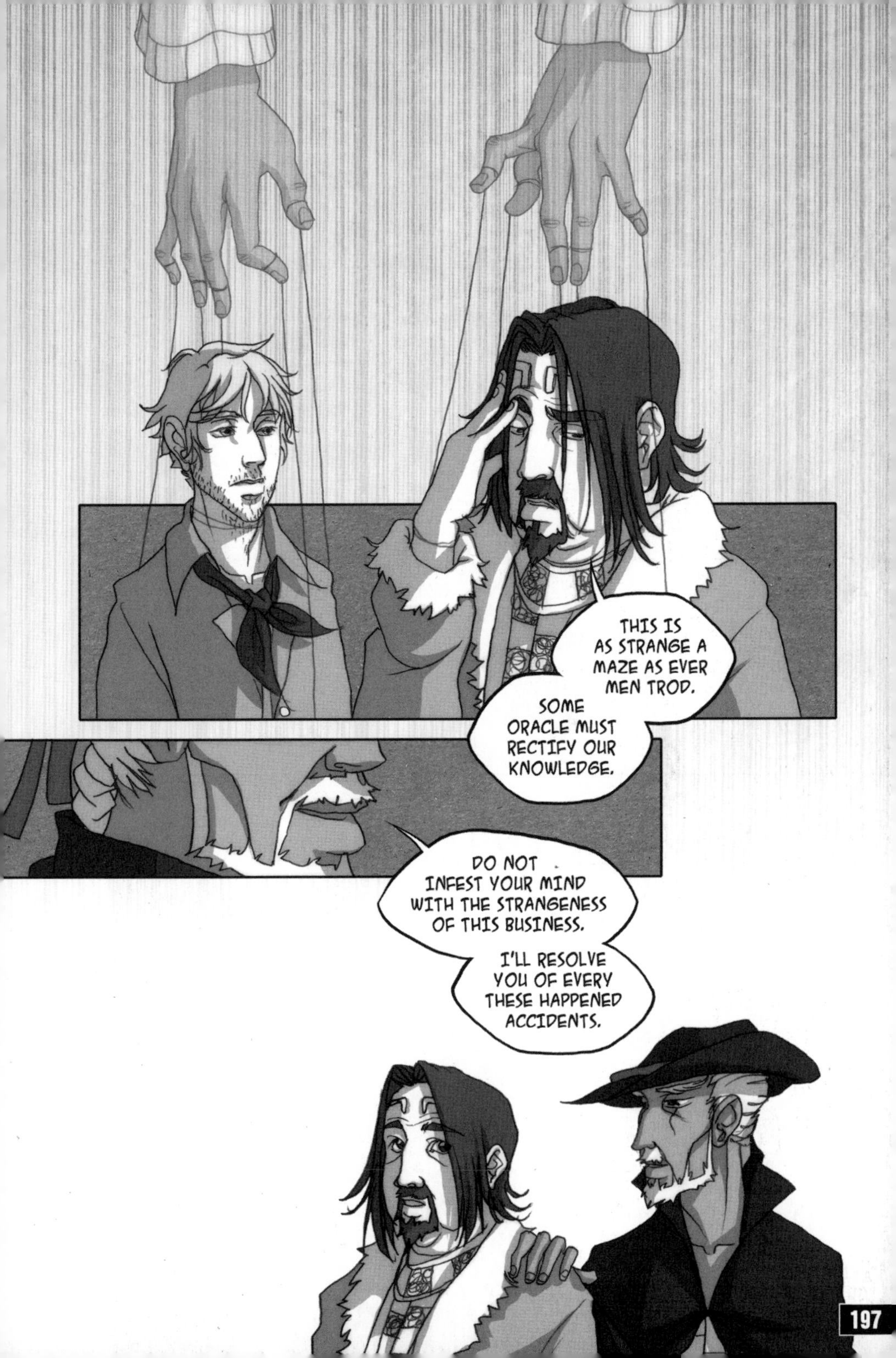
THIS IS AS STRANGE A MAZE AS EVER MEN TROD.
SOME ORACLE MUST RECTIFY OUR KNOWLEDGE.
DO NOT INFEST YOUR MIND WITH THE STRANGENESS OF THIS BUSINESS.
I'LL RESOLVE YOU OF EVERY THESE HAPPENED ACCIDENTS.

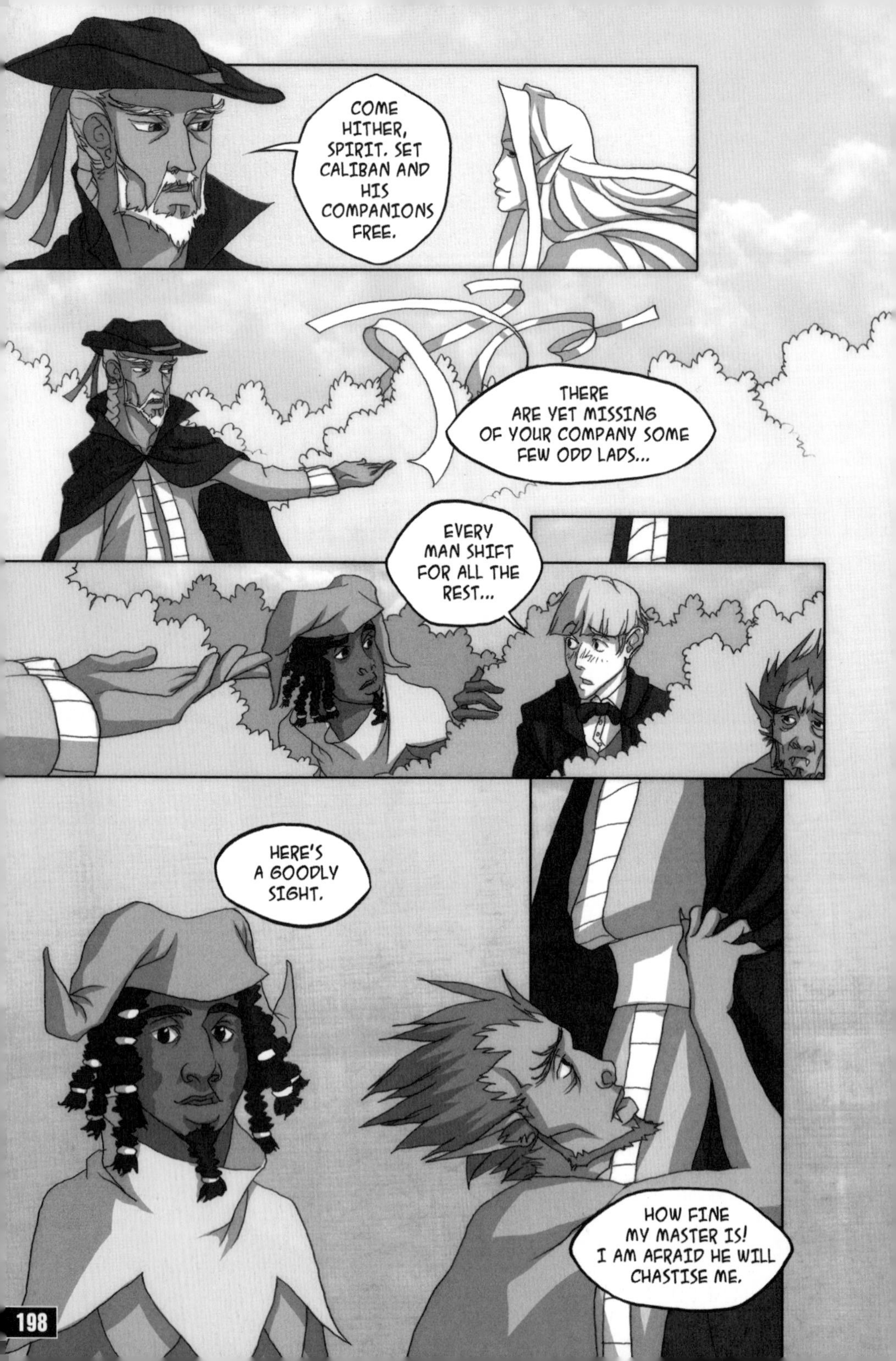
COME HITHER, SPIRIT. SET CALIBAN AND HIS COMPANIONS FREE.
THERE ARE YET MISSING OF YOUR COMPANY SOME FEW ODD LADS...
EVERY MAN SHIFT FOR ALL THE REST...
HERE'S A GOODLY SIGHT.
HOW FINE MY MASTER IS! I AM AFRAID HE WILL CHASTISE ME.

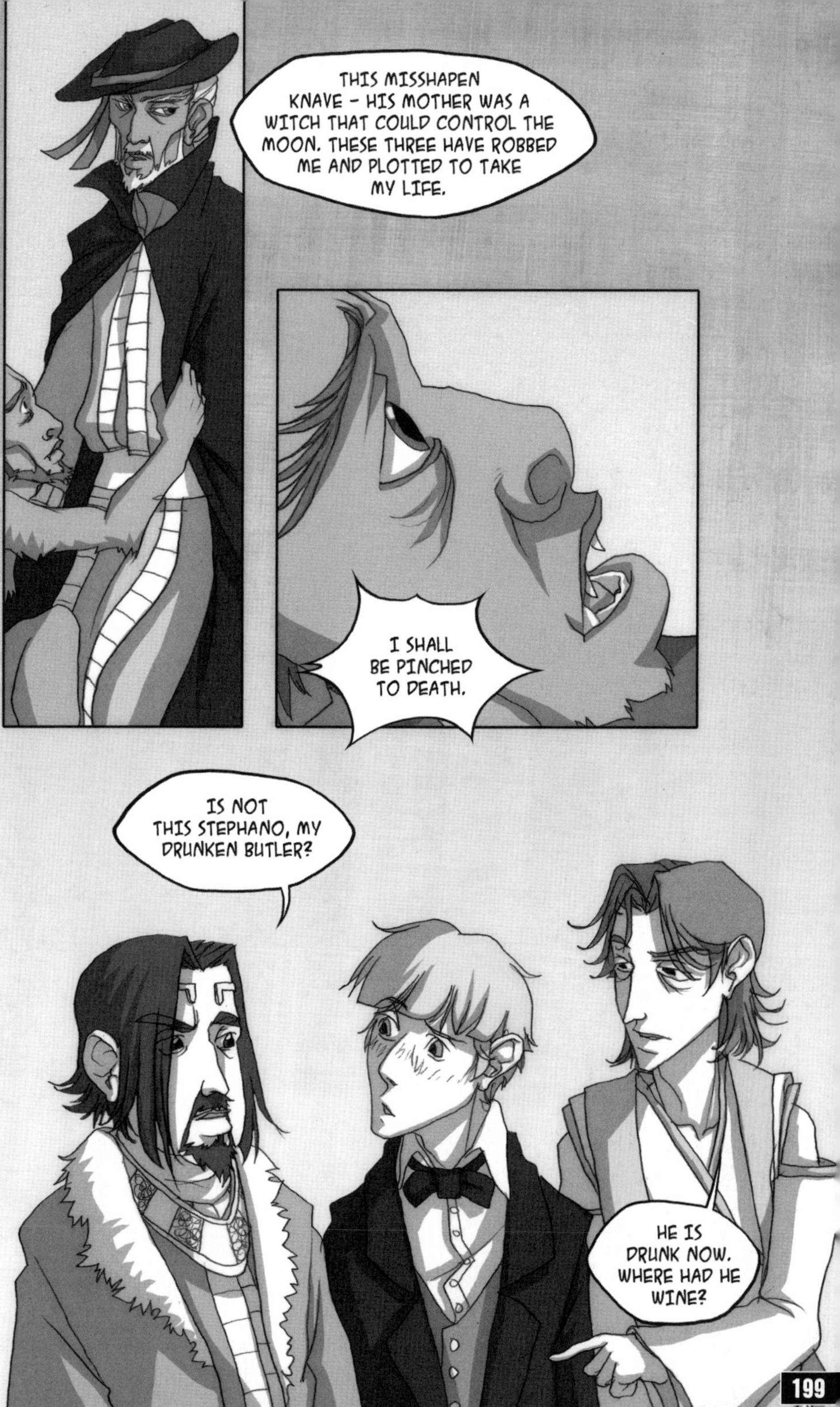
THIS MISSHAPEN KNAVE – HIS MOTHER WAS A WITCH THAT COULD CONTROL THE MOON. THESE THREE HAVE ROBBED ME AND PLOTTED TO TAKE MY LIFE.
I SHALL BE PINCHED TO DEATH.
IS NOT THIS STEPHANO, MY DRUNKEN BUTLER?
HE IS DRUNK NOW. WHERE HAD HE WINE?

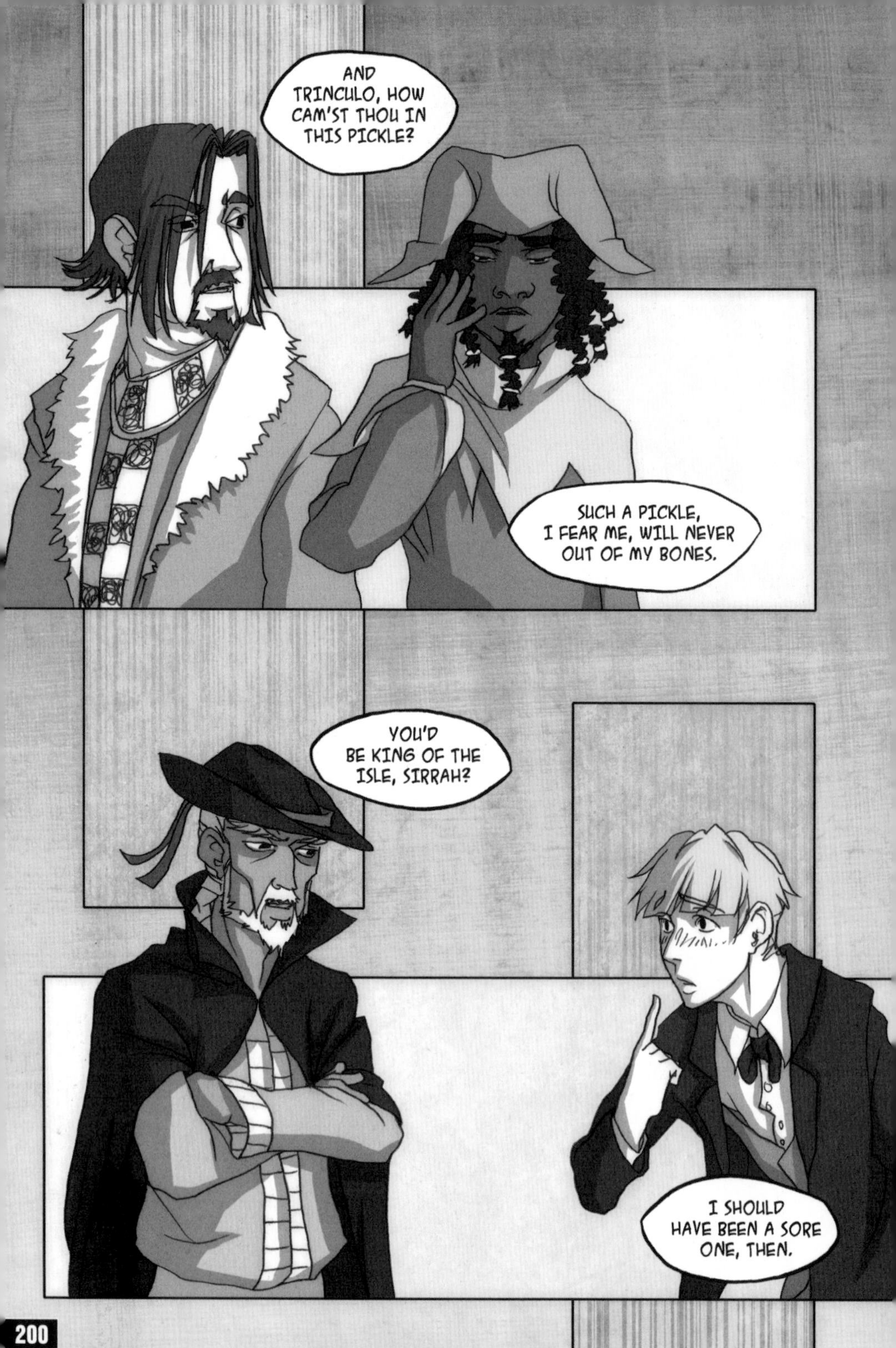
AND TRINCULO, HOW CAM'ST THOU IN THIS PICKLE?
SUCH A PICKLE, I FEAR ME, WILL NEVER OUT OF MY BONES.
YOU'D BE KING OF THE ISLE, SIRRAH?
I SHOULD HAVE BEEN A SORE ONE, THEN.

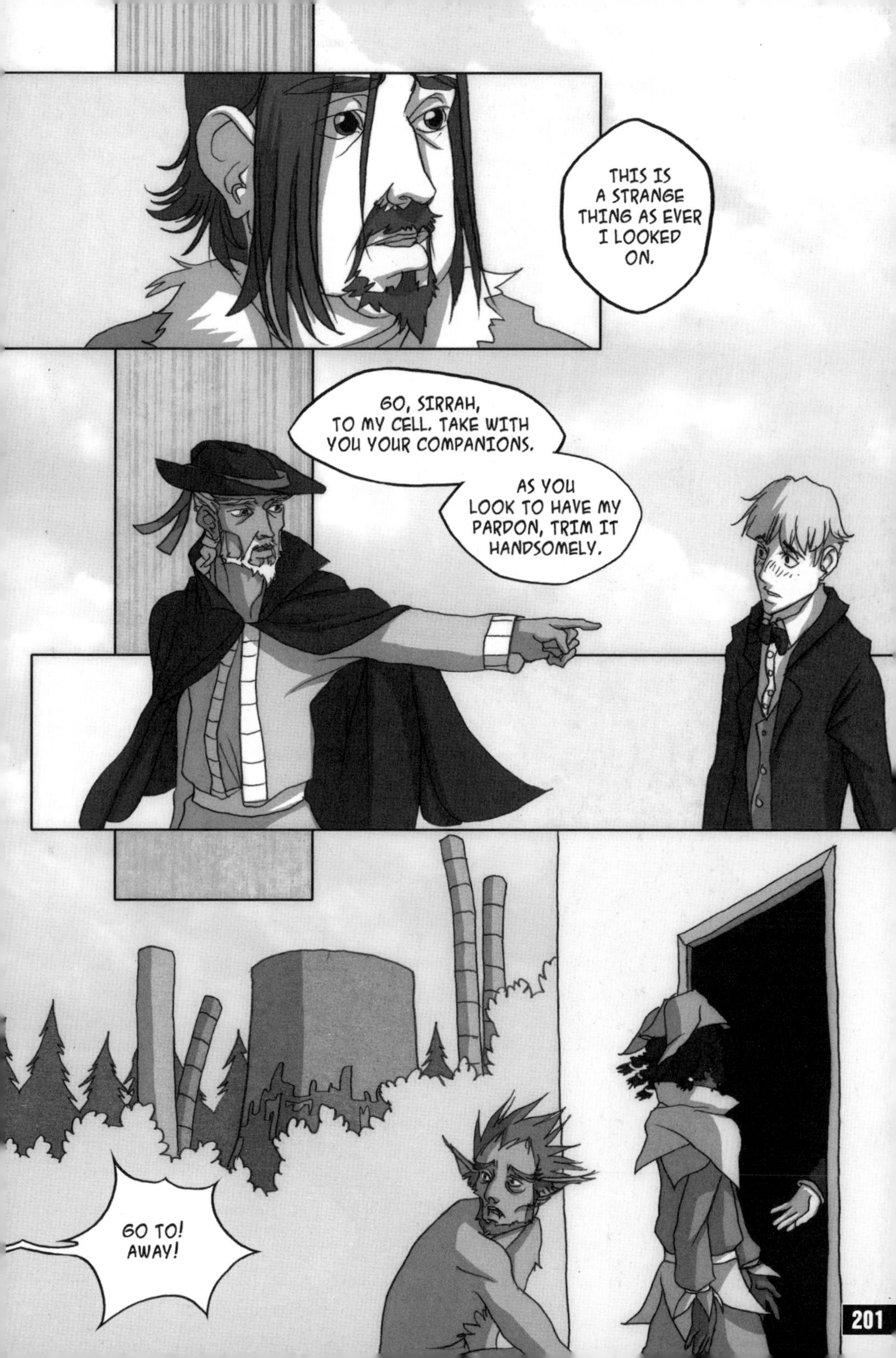
THIS IS A STRANGE THING AS EVER I LOOKED ON.
GO, SIRRAH, TO MY CELL. TAKE WITH YOU YOUR COMPANIONS.
AS YOU LOOK TO HAVE MY PARDON, TRIM IT HANDSOMELY.
GO TO! AWAY!

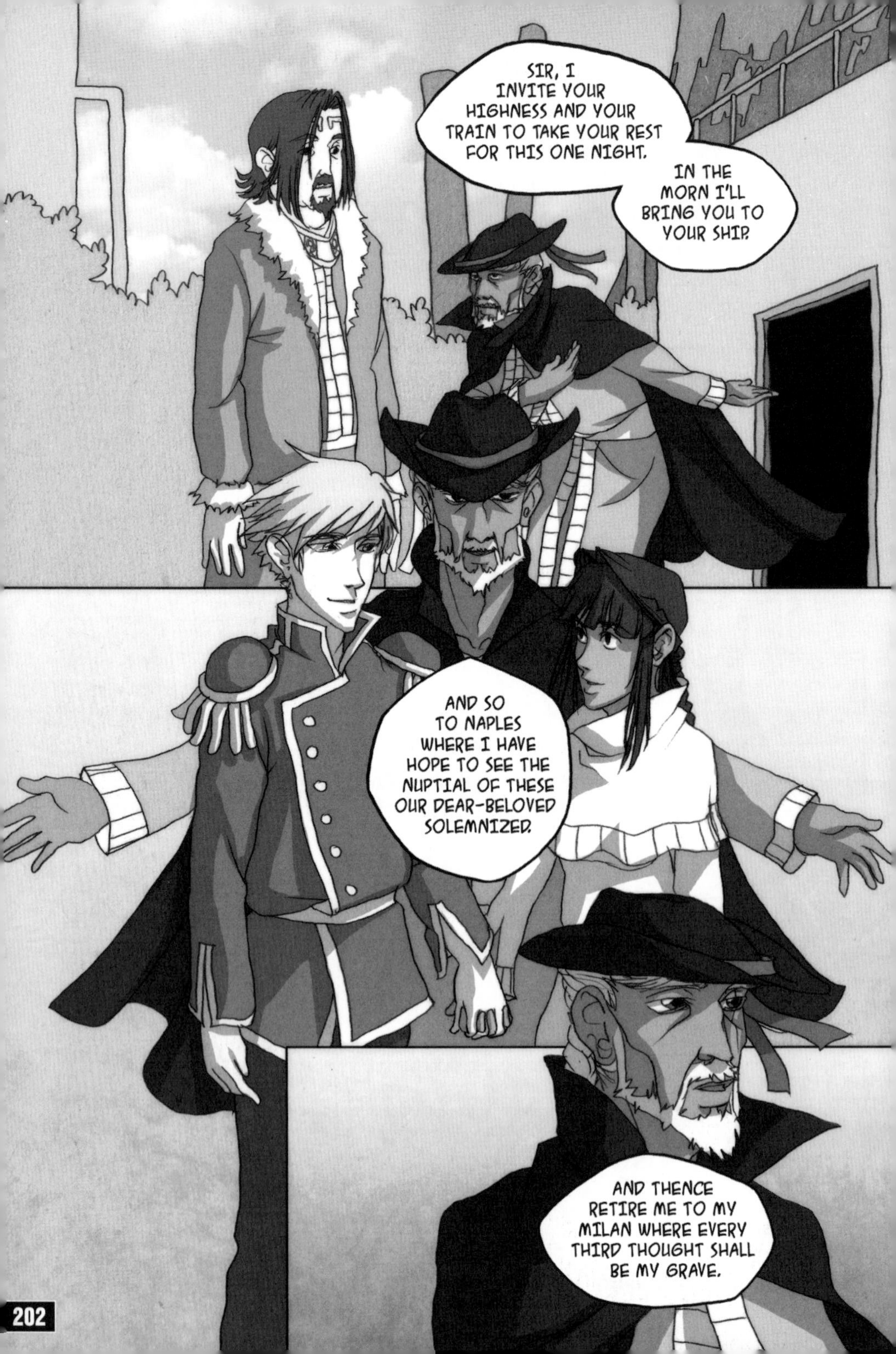
SIR, I INVITE YOUR HIGHNESS AND YOUR TRAIN TO TAKE YOUR REST FOR THIS ONE NIGHT.
IN THE MORN I'LL BRING YOU TO YOUR SHIP.
AND SO TO NAPLES WHERE I HAVE HOPE TO SEE THE NUPTIAL OF THESE OUR DEAR-BELOVED SOLEMNIZED.
AND THENCE RETIRE ME TO MY MILAN WHERE EVERY THIRD THOUGHT SHALL BE MY GRAVE.

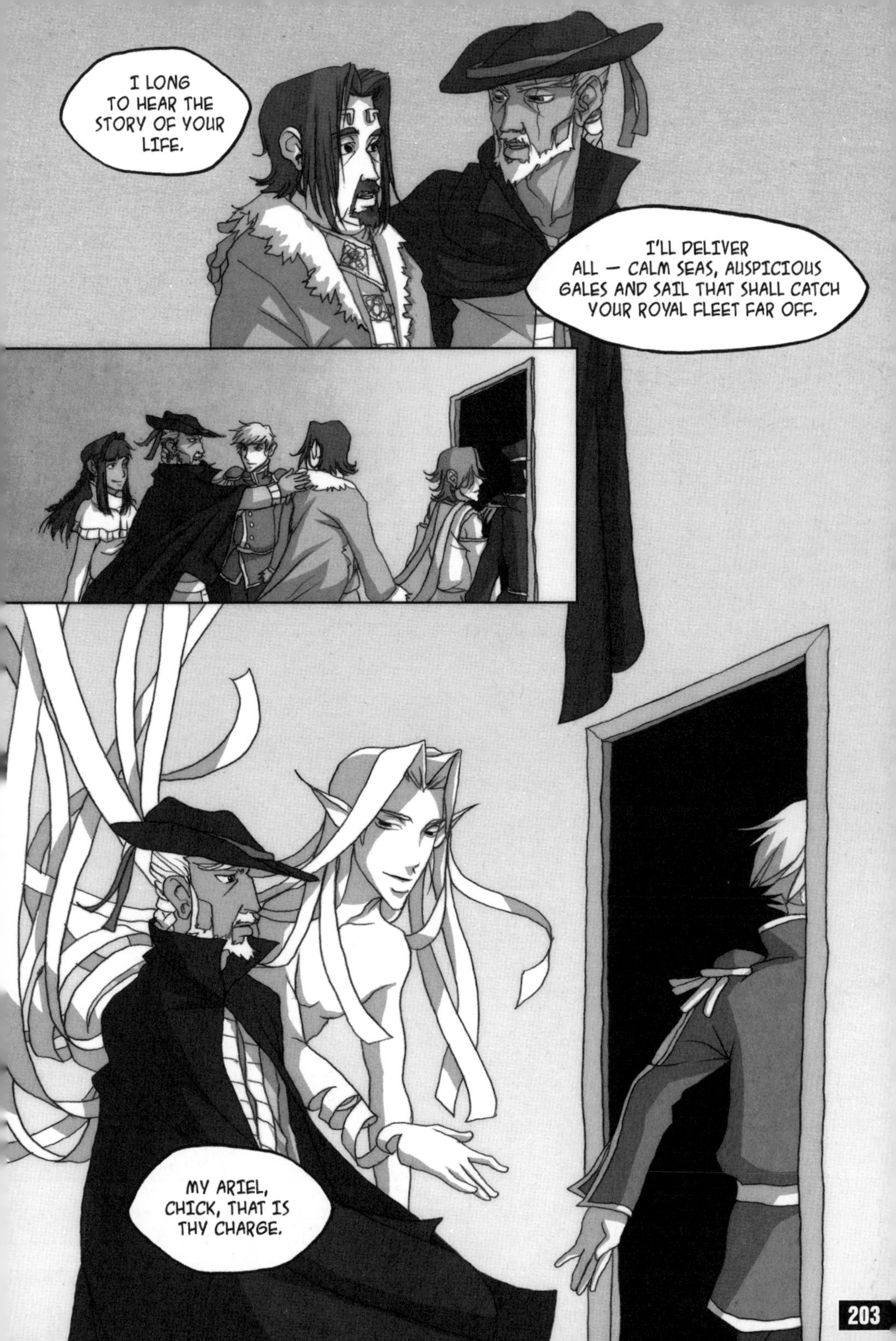
I LONG TO HEAR THE STORY OF YOUR LIFE.
I'LL DELIVER ALL — CALM SEAS, AUSPICIOUS GALES AND SAIL THAT SHALL CATCH YOUR ROYAL FLEET FAR OFF.
MY ARIEL, CHICK, THAT IS THY CHARGE.

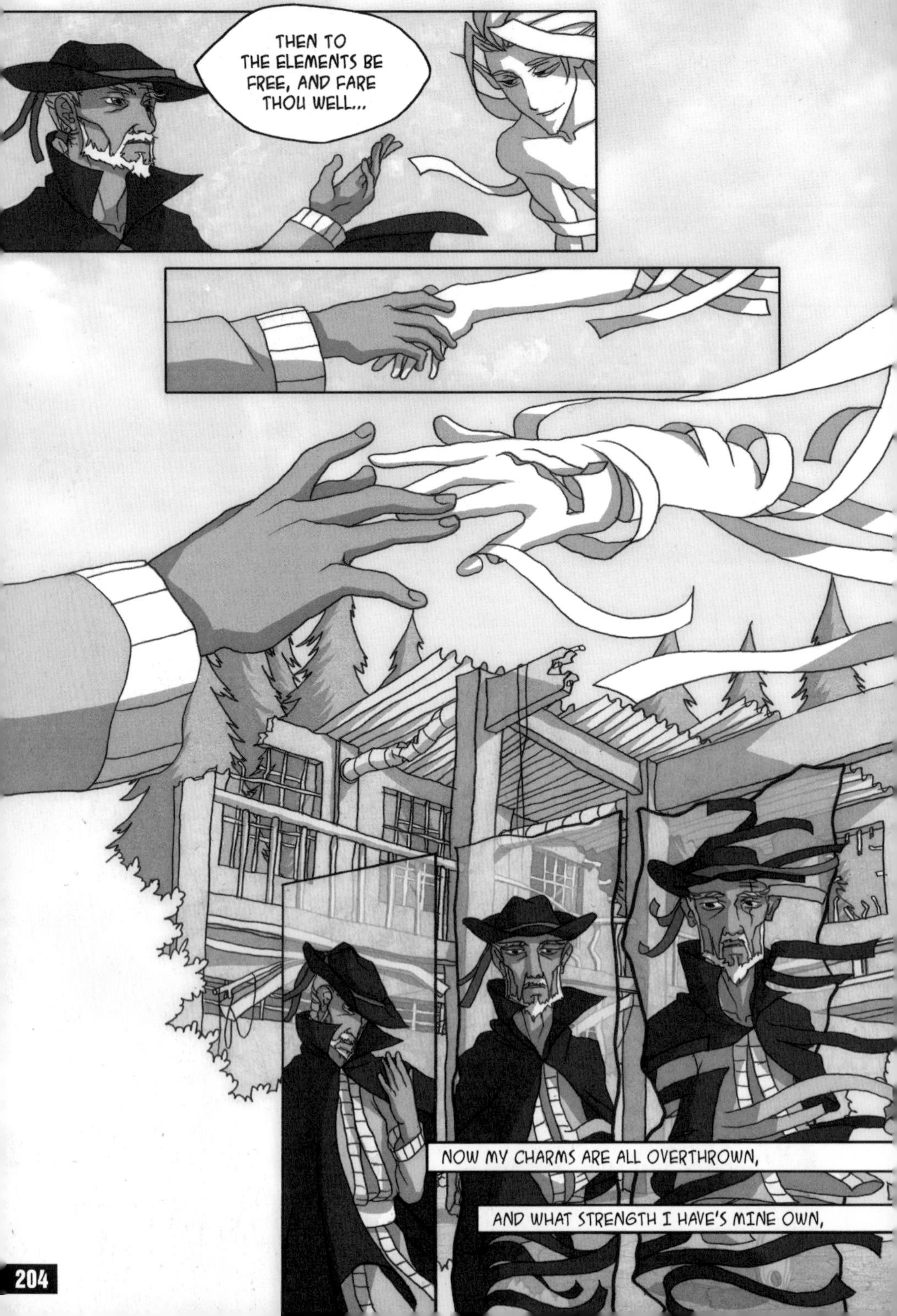
THEN TO THE ELEMENTS BE FREE, AND FARE THOU WELL...
NOW MY CHARMS ARE ALL OVERTHROWN,
AND WHAT STRENGTH I HAVE'S MINE OWN,

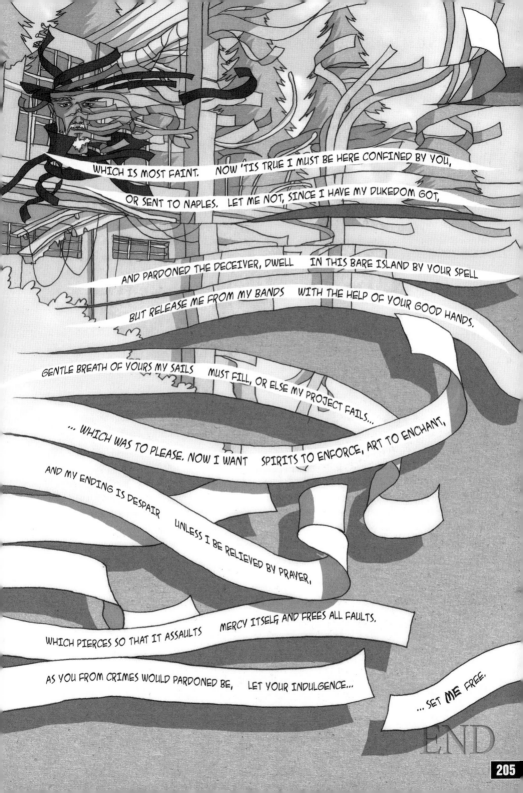

WHICH IS MOST FAINT. NOW 'TIS TRUE I MUST BE HERE CONFINED BY YOU,

OR SENT TO NAPLES. LET ME NOT, SINCE I HAVE MY DUKEDOM GOT,

AND PARDONED THE DECEIVER, DWELL IN THIS BARE ISLAND BY YOUR SPELL

BUT RELEASE ME FROM MY BANDS WITH THE HELP OF YOUR GOOD HANDS.

GENTLE BREATH OF YOURS MY SAILS MUST FILL, OR ELSE MY PROJECT FAILS...

... WHICH WAS TO PLEASE. NOW I WANT SPIRITS TO ENFORCE, ART TO ENCHANT,

AND MY ENDING IS DESPAIR UNLESS I BE RELIEVED BY PRAYER,

WHICH PIERCES SO THAT IT ASSAULTS MERCY ITSELF AND FREES ALL FAULTS.

AS YOU FROM CRIMES WOULD PARDONED BE, LET YOUR INDULGENCE...

... SET ME FREE.

END

PLOT SUMMARY OF THE TEMPEST

This is the story of Prospero, the rightful Duke of Milan, who has been deposed by his treacherous brother Antonio. He conspired with Alonso, the King of Naples, to cast Prospero and his infant daughter Miranda adrift at sea. Both are presumed dead. In fact, however, Alonso's virtuous adviser Gonzalo had stocked their boat with supplies, enabling them to survive until washed ashore on a distant unknown island, where they have now been marooned for twelve years.

A powerful magician, and now lord of the island, Prospero is served by two native inhabitants: the spirit Ariel and the beast Caliban. Prospero has freed Ariel from the curse of endless imprisonment imposed by the witch Sycorax, now dead. Caliban is Sycorax's own grudging and malignant son.

With Ariel's help, Prospero now seizes the chance for revenge, conjuring up a great storm to wreck a ship, carrying his enemies, on to the shores of his island. On the ship are King Alonso, his son Ferdinand and brother Sebastian. Among the others aboard are kindly Gonzalo, Prospero's own brother Antonio, as well as other noblemen and servants. All of them are travelling back to Naples from the wedding in Africa of Alonso's daughter Claribel. Ariel puts the crew to sleep, leaving the castaways safely stranded – but at the mercy of Prospero's plans, which unfold over the next few hours.

The villainous Antonio now seeks to usurp the throne of Naples by persuading Sebastian to murder his brother, King Alonso – now distraught at what he believes to be the drowning of his son Ferdinand. Elsewhere, Alonso's servants, the drunken butler Stephano and the foolish Trinculo, encounter Caliban, who similarly persuades them to assassinate Prospero and take command of his island. Both these conspiracies, however, are closely monitored by Prospero, and each is frustrated by Ariel's enchantments, which lead them all astray.

Meanwhile, Ferdinand has been captured, alive and well, by Prospero, who pretends to enslave him – though his true aim is to test Ferdinand's character in the hope of supplying a worthy partner for his precious daughter Miranda. Prospero's plan works – the couple immediately fall in love – but how severely should he now punish those who have denied him his dukedom? In the end, love and forgiveness triumph over any wish for revenge, and all are reconciled as if awoken from a bad dream. Prospero will return to Milan, once more as its Duke, renounce magic, and at last set Ariel free in payment for his services. The island is Caliban's once more.

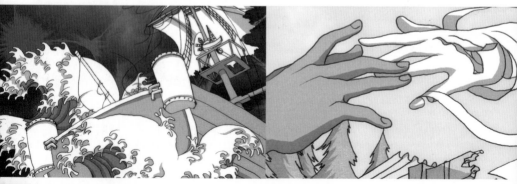

A BRIEF LIFE OF WILLIAM SHAKESPEARE

Shakespeare's birthday is traditionally said to be the 23rd of April – St George's Day, patron saint of England. A good start for England's greatest writer. But that date and even his name are uncertain. He signed his own name in different ways. "Shakespeare" is now the accepted one out of dozens of different versions.

He was born at Stratford-upon-Avon in 1564, and baptized on 26th April. His mother, Mary Arden, was the daughter of a prosperous farmer. His father, John Shakespeare, a glove-maker, was a respected civic figure – and probably also a Catholic. In 1570, just as Will began school, his father was accused of illegal dealings. The family fell into debt and disrepute.

Will attended a local school for eight years. He did not go to university. The next ten years are a blank filled by suppositions. Was he briefly a Latin teacher, a soldier, a sea-faring explorer? Was he prosecuted and whipped for poaching deer?

We do know that in 1582 he married Anne Hathaway, eight years his senior, and three months pregnant. Two more children – twins – were born three years later but, by around 1590, Will had left Stratford to pursue a theatre career in London. Shakespeare's apprenticeship began as an actor and "pen for hire".

He learned his craft the hard way. He soon won fame as a playwright with often-staged popular hits.

He and his colleagues formed a stage company, the Lord Chamberlain's Men, which built the famous Globe Theatre. It opened in 1599 but was destroyed by fire in 1613 during a performance of *Henry VIII* which used gunpowder special effects. It was rebuilt in brick the following year.

Shakespeare was a financially successful writer who invested his money wisely in property. In 1597, he bought an enormous house in Stratford, and in 1608 became a shareholder in London's Blackfriars Theatre. He also redeemed the family's honour by acquiring a personal coat of arms.

Shakespeare wrote over 40 works, including poems, "lost" plays and collaborations, in a career spanning nearly 25 years. He retired to Stratford in 1613, where he died on 23rd April 1616, aged 52, apparently of a fever after a "merry meeting" of drinks with friends. Shakespeare did in fact die on St George's Day! He was buried "full 17 foot deep" in Holy Trinity Church, Stratford, and left an epitaph cursing anyone who dared disturb his bones.

There have been preposterous theories disputing Shakespeare's authorship. Some claim that Sir Francis Bacon (1561–1626), philosopher and Lord Chancellor, was the real author of Shakespeare's plays. Others propose Edward de Vere, Earl of Oxford (1550–1604), or, even more weirdly, Queen Elizabeth I. The implication is that the "real" Shakespeare had to be a university graduate or an aristocrat. Nothing less would do for the world's greatest writer.

Shakespeare is mysteriously hidden behind his work. His life will not tell us what inspired his genius.